Magic Aegis

Rhobin Lee Courtright

A Wings ePress, Inc.
Fantasy Romance Novel

Wings ePress, Inc.

Edited by: Leslie Hodges
Copy Edited by: Elizabeth Struble
Senior Editor: Elizabeth Struble
Executive Editor: Lorraine Stephens
Cover Artist: Rhobin Courtright

All rights reserved

Wings ePress Books
http://www.wings-press.com

Published In the United States Of America

Wings ePress Inc.
3000 N. Rock Road
Newton, KS 67114

What They Are Saying About

Magic Aegis

A Cinderella is found and claimed by a man who will grow to be an unforgettable hero. Mayhem, intrigue, and murder invade the royal court. Enemies from without and within threaten the land. Can the spells from she who lived in the past be fulfilled?

From start to finish, Rhobin Courtright holds the reader spellbound in a web of suspense that doesn't stop until the story's end. This isn't a book for the timid or tame. It is a roller coaster read with captivating characters entrapped in a thrill filled plot, which is set in a world of mystical mystery and spine tingling suspense.

Lois Wencil
A Mistress Gets A Master
Wings ePress, Inc.

Dedication

To Mark,
whose critical comments always help,
and to Bill,
whose encouragement always reassures.
§

One

The teaching master cleared his throat, drawing Vesper from her wistful study of the adjudicator's son. The master's dissatisfied gaze fell equally on all of his students, and they instinctively straightened in their seats. The stifling room smelled of old ashes and sweat-soaked wool, making everyone drowsy and inattentive. Then he looked at her.

Vesper returned the master's derisive glance with equanimity. Norost's mayor, his employer, insisted upon her inclusion in the classroom, but that didn't mean the master treated her as a student. Instead, he relegated her to what he thought her natural position, to wait quietly and serve when requested. Vesper waited with serene expectation.

Noting the teaching master's distraction drew the other students' attention to where she sat at the side of the classroom, Vesper briefly lowered her glance to the floor. Only once had the master ever directed a question at her, hoping, she supposed, to humiliate her. Upon her polite, correct answer, he never repeated his mistake of addressing her. Since then, her presence always seemed to irritate him, but she guessed his uncertainty in how to remove her from his class hindered any action.

He cleared his throat again. Wiping his fingers on the cloth of his surcoat, the master frowned at his students and turned the page. "We have been studying the rich narrative legacy of Kaereya. Many stories, along with many of our customs such as Handfasting, derive from those years following the Cataclysmic Century. This fable comes from a time when the belief in magic still existed, a time when people needed a sense of security and order." He inhaled deeply.

"Long, long ago, after a lengthy war, peace fell over Kaereya. A wearied king surveyed his land and found the country and the people as exhausted as his royal treasury. Anguished by the staggering losses, the king came to abhor the destruction, cruelty, and devastation the war had inflicted on his land and people. Never again, he vowed, would this happen. There had to be a way to protect Kaereya. He asked the bishop who offered prayer. He asked the aristos, who counseled vigilance. The Royal Guards advised him to maintain a strong army; the queen, a wise leadership. Disappointed, the king sank into a deep gloom. At last, he asked the last sorceress of Kaereya to create a magic shield for Kaereya, one to defend the land from any future invasion. 'It is impossible,' the witch claimed."

The teaching master's nose crinkled in distaste, whether from the smell or his students, Vesper could not decide. Experience taught her to have plenty of water, a cold pitcher of cider, extra ink, blotting paper, sand, quills, and all the other items the master seemed to need, so he could find no reason to send her on spurious errands. At least today's reading was interesting, but she enjoyed the time even without the instruction. A chance to gaze at Brandt was pleasure enough.

"Why was she the last?" Alvina asked. Vesper's eyes rose from her close regard of the floorboards to flicker to Alvina and back again to the floor. Usually the mayor's daughter displayed little interest in any type of study. A question from Alvina piqued everyone's curiosity.

The master looked up from his page in disgust at the interruption. Vesper smiled as he held his response to polite tones.

"Perhaps because the belief in magic was already waning. It is only a story, Alvina."

"Never been magic," Brandt said.

"Just sleight-of-hand tricksters and fakes. My granny says so," one of the boys agreed with Brandt's pronouncement.

"Very true, your granny is a wise woman." The Master sighed before he continued. "The sorceress thought a long time about how to best achieve the king's request and at last devised a solution. Four guardians with four loyal aristos would focus and enforce a shield spell. She searched for her shield carriers among the aristos, then among the great and not so great of the court and its surroundings, then further into villages and farms until she had combed the entire land."

"What did she search for?" Alvina asked.

"For someone with magic, I expect," the master answered Alvina's question with acerbic dryness and returned to his reading. "It took eleven years. One selected man had at least an inkling of court etiquette, for she chose a servant of the king's livery, a groom, but one with a touch of aristo blood. The other three were of common blood: a farmer, an itinerant musician, and the last, a teaching master." He smiled to the group at his profession's mention.

"Why did she choose only the lowborn?" Alvina interrupted again, and the Master's smile shriveled.

"Stop it, Alvina." One of the boys gave her a cross look. "We shall never finish if you don't shut up. Besides none of us is aristo, so what does it matter?"

"I am the mayor's daughter! And my grandfather's brother is a viscount!"

"Don't make you aristo."

"It is a shared belief that the common man is more innocent and purer of heart. Please, no more interruptions," the master said. He glared at his students before he continued. "At ceremonies held at four new keeps the king had built during the search, the sorceress invested each man with the title of 'Aegis,' or sacred talisman shield. A cloak pin symbolized their elevation, a wind dragon for the province of Easure, a mermaid for the ocean province of Wessure, a sphinx for the desert province of Kennetsure, and a unicorn for the forest province of Vere. The bishop blessed the men, the keeps, and their endeavor, asking the Holy One's guidance and support. As the witch touched each man, she placed a mark on each, so that any seeing it would know their consecration."

"Is that where the symbols for our Provinces come from?"

"Alvina!" Brandt pleaded.

The teaching master continued as though uninterrupted. "At the last ceremony, held in the far south, the witch turned to the new king. 'I have given the land the protection your father desired. Use the Aegises well, and the kingdom will always stand.'

"Later the witch understood her mistake. The new king didn't want protection for the land, but protection for his own royal right. Loyal to a fault, the Aegises served well, but loyal to Kaereya. Their honesty was above reproach in all their dealings with the court, even telling the king when he was wrong, but the aristos sneered at the Aegises. 'Peasants parroting nobles,' they said. The witch often heard the comment with accompanying laughs. Angry with the Aegises' frankness and rustic manners, the king banished them from his court.

"Saddened, the witch left the king and his court to their own devices and to the inner turmoil that would unsettle a future she would never live to see."

The teaching master closed the book and looked at his students. "That is the folktale of the Aegis of Kaereya. By folk it signifies that it originated among the people and was not penned by a great writer. At its inception, it probably gave our war-torn ancestors a sense of protection from imminent harm. It also provides a source for the symbols of each province. Of course, there is no magic, and Kaereya has suffered through many tumultuous wars. If there is any truth to the story, it is that four good men served their country, and only one keep in Easure was completed of four great keeps proposed to protect the borders."

"But Kaereya has never been invaded," Alvina said. At the master's raised brow, she added in defense, "And they say Egan Keep in Kennetsure still stands."

Vesper listened to her friend's defense of the tale and admired Alvina's loveliness. Alvina's new blue day gown enhanced her fairness and emphasized her blue eyes. Vesper's needle talent had embroidered the foresleeves embellishments, discreetly working Alvina's personal number five into the design. She could remember her finger's pleasure in the smooth texture and her eye's enjoyment of the sky blue color as she worked the fabric. She envied Alvina the gown.

In thanks, Alvina gave Vesper the gray gown she now wore. The cloth remained good, and Vesper had repaired the tattered thread work. Alvina's mother, Winifred, insisted all the lace trim be removed, much to Vesper's disappointment. Containing her covetousness, she reminded herself how lucky the housekeeper's foundling was to share in Alvina's education, even if only as a servant to run errands for anyone in the room. Not that she learned much. Under her foster-mother Eudora's tutelage years before, Vesper had studied the topics the teaching master now taught.

"Kaereya is a strong country. And we have had wars despite the folktale," Brandt said. His eyes quickly flickered to Vesper, letting her understand he thought Alvina foolish. Vesper smiled. Alvina's personal number of five, the number of understanding, learning, and truth, did not seem to be helping her today, or maybe, the negative aspects of five were at play.

"They were wars of aggression, though," Alvina said. "Kaereya hasn't been invaded, and we've never had a war here in Vere."

"There were many wars here before the clans settled their land borders. That was a long time ago," the master said.

"Come, Alvina," Brandt complained with a rude huff. "Magic existed because our ancestors believed in magic, not because it was real. There is no magic, not then, not now."

Vesper bit her lip to keep her smile from growing. Brandt hated sitting with the teaching master and would say or do anything to get the class done and over. The room was heavily paneled, dark and somber, and Brandt was much happier outside exercising with his riding master.

Her thinking of him must have caught his attention, for Brandt turned his head and smiled at her, a sweet, secretive smile of appreciation and future promise. Vesper felt the blush creep up her face and quickly lowered her eyes to her lap. Someone laughed.

Vesper did not mind but felt a shiver of anticipation as her mind leaped into a favorite daydream—Brandt stood before her and asked for her hand. The teaching master cleared his throat. The harsh sound dissolved her lovely dream vision of the Handfasting Festival just before she could accept. The magic argument with Alvina had continued without Vesper's notice. She sighed as her fantasy disintegrated.

"Think of the story's allegorical symbolism, not as a historical account, Alvina. It is a warning to all Kaereyans to remember the vulnerability of the land. How we must work to keep it strong." The teaching master placed the book on the table before him. "You've all had enough for today. With Handfasting so close, you've too much else on your minds. You are dismissed until tomorrow when we will study the geography of the plateau on which our Vere Province rests. Come prepared to explain the origins of the upcoming festival." As the students left the room, the boys teased Alvina about magic. Brandt said, "You must be part clansmen to believe in magic." Alvina slapped his arm, but Brandt just laughed. Alvina's mother called out, and Vesper watched the boys escape through the front door.

"Vesper!" Dame Winifred Kellsie, dressed in puce and an abundance of lace, all perfume and pungency as befit the mayor's wife, called. "Did you pick up the master's room before you left?"

"Yes ma'am." Vesper moved to stand before the unnaturally stiff Dame Winifred and bobbed a curtsy, holding her breath against her mistress's strong scent. Dame Winifred stood on the last step of the staircase leading to the family suite above stairs. A quick glance showed her politeness wasted. Her mistress's face, framed in her severe headdress, remained sour-looking. Perhaps if she loosened her stays, she would be more comfortable. And happier.

"Good, then go to Eudora, she has an errand for you."

Vesper gladly retreated. Behind her she heard Dame Winifred call to her daughter, "Alvina," and noted the acid left her mistress's voice. "I have an errand for you also."

Alvina's plaintive, "But, Mama, I have plans!" followed Vesper through the door. She left through the back door of the manse where a short, covered walkway led her to the kitchen. Vesper found Eudora kneading bread. The ruffle on her collar bobbed with her movements against the dark rosy-hued skin of her neck. Her soft doe's eyes rose to Vesper, but she didn't stop her work.

"Mistress Kellsie said you had an errand for me."

Eudora finished shaping the dough loaf and lifted it into a waiting pan. Then she wiped flour from her hands and went to a drawer, removing a few coins. "I need you to walk into town and buy salt. Freda is pickling cabbage, and we have run out." She walked to Vesper and smoothed the muscat brown curls back from Vesper's shoulder. "You look upset, did Dame Winifred say something?"

"No. I'm just tired."

"Did you sleep poorly? Have bad dreams?"

"No. It was the master's reading. It was warm and stuffy, and it made me sleepy."

"Well then, the walk will wake you up. Don't dawdle, we need that salt today."

"Yes Eudora." She took the coins from Eudora, picked up the shopping basket, and left. A short path took her from the courtyard at the back of the manse to the front bricked walk and the lane leading to the town's trading district. Before she reached the front walkway, she heard Alvina hail her.

"Vesper! Vesper, wait." Alvina's voice floated from the grand front entrance to the mayor's manse. Seeing Vesper approach, Alvina turned to stand before one of the expensive glass windows fronting the manse's stone porch. There she straightened her skirt and primped her long blonde hair.

Vesper walked to the steps leading to the double entrance doors, each heavily carved with the symbols of Vere. Dame Winifred had long ago forbidden her to stand on the porch or steps, let alone enter the front portal, but Vesper liked to look. The lintel and posts were carved in themes of local mythology. A quarter moon and stars filled the flat arch above the door, Vere's earth signs. From previous searches, she quickly found the wolves and the owls among the trees on the doors. They represented Vere's totem animals along with the unicorn found hiding in the door's forest. That mystical animal also frequented local signs. The sacred numbers of Vere, four and eight, were also present, but one had to hunt for them: four owls, eight wolves, four or eight oak leaves bunched together on carved branches. Acorns hid among the leaves. Eudora said for some they represented the seeds of magic, and for others belief.

Her contemplation wove into a daydream. She and Brandt rode through the forest, chased by wolves. Brandt yelled for her to keep going as he drew his sword from its sheath with a whispering hiss.

"I'm ready." Alvina shook out folds of a too ornate for town surgown; the silk of her chemise whispered with her motion.

Alvina had flounced down the steps before Vesper blinked back to reality. Drawn from her revel, she sighed.

"I really don't know why she couldn't send you," Alvina said in a waspish tone.

"What do you have to do?" Vesper asked, wondering what important errand neither she nor Eudora could complete for Dame Winifred.

With a shake of her head, Alvina said a rude word never uttered before her mother. "She ordered me, ordered!" Alvina's small soprano reached shrill tones. "I am to give a letter to a mail runner in town."

From the corner of her eye, Vesper saw homely little Alfred mimic Alvina's swaying walk from underneath the overgrown hedge. A rasp of laughter broke from her mouth before she could stop it. Alvina's lips tightened in temper. Alfred threw one of the numerous acorns lying on the ground at Vesper. She sidestepped it.

"Don't laugh at me! I will have to frank him too. I bet he is an old, ugly, smelly, and disgusting low rider," Alvina said, her lips firming with displeasure.

"But Alvina, it's an excuse to enter the trade district. Somewhere Dame Winifred usually doesn't let you go."

A tiny considering smile at strange odds with her otherwise angelic face skirted the corner of Alvina's mouth. "That's true."

While they walked the lane leading to the shopping district, Alvina started a story about one of her friends. She possessed a deadly talent for exposing everyone's errant moments. Often Vesper found this entertaining, but today Alvina mocked Brandt, and Vesper refused to listen. From the yew bushes lining the lane, Alfred made insolent faces at Vesper as he continued to mimic Alvina's exaggerated gait. Orange and red autumn leaves clothed him and jiggled with his steps. A laugh burst from Vesper.

"It really is not that funny," Alvina chided.

"I'm sorry," Vesper replied, not having listened to Alvina. Blinking her eyes made Alfred disappear, proof that he was just imaginary Eudora said. He vanished but not before she saw Alfred's outrage. Alvina looked furious, too, so Vesper turned the topic.

"This will be your first Handfasting. Are you excited?"

"And my last," Alvina said in self-assurance. "No. There is nothing to be excited about except for my new gown. All else is arranged." She shook her lace cuff to fall more attractively over her hand.

"Arranged?" Vesper, her eyes envisioning her own hand emerging from the lace cuff of Alvina's sleeve, turned her regard to Alvina's lip-pursing smile. She knew it would be Vesper's third time.

"Of course. You don't think my father would leave something so important to chance, do you?"

"Mayor Kellsie chose for you? But what if you don't like your father's choice? What if this man is mean, or ignores you?"

"Ignore me? Don't be silly," Alvina said, her brows rising. "I suppose you will stand again this year, and you will not know any better than I, less even. Well, if you are not chosen, you may take a position on my mother's house staff."

Vesper gasped but took no offense; it was just Alvina's way. "Eudora said I must find another position if I am left standing," she stammered at last, "I may not stay at your home. I don't want to be left standing. This is my last chance. Aren't you the least worried?"

Alvina laughed. "My father is much wiser in this than I am, and in the end, it makes very little difference."

"Little difference? How can you say so? Doesn't love count?"

"Knowing someone before or after doesn't promise love. Besides, love is much overrated. It really doesn't last that long, you know. Do you have any expectations?" Alvina said with a sideways glance.

"I'm not sure. Perhaps." She didn't wish to tell Alvina more. "Town is very busy with the influx of people for the festival. I expect looking for the good luck promised in a Norost handfasting."

Alvina gave a spurt of sound. "Good luck to be handfasted in Norost? How stupid can people be?"

"Because the priests teach that the numbers of the universe are strongest in Vere and because Norost is the largest city in Vere. Norost's sacred number four, four, and besides being the feminine number of God, it represents God's four treasures of life, love, law. and learning..."

"Oh stop, Vesper, I know all that, and I've heard it all too often."

"I'm sorry. Anyway, handfasting in Vere is considered very romantic." Vesper did not confide that she did not want to stay in the Kellsie home.

"Romantic, really? And good luck, too, like magic?" Alvina looked taken with the notion.

"I suppose so. It must be. Eudora told me," Vesper said, surprised at Alvina's ignorance.

"And the festival comes from the Cataclysm?"

"Just after, when it became important that every woman bear a child in the Holy One's rites."

The younger girl had more exposure to people outside Norost, to travel, and to society. Vesper knew her knowledge came from study and discussion with Eudora. She yearned for experience. She wanted to start living her life. Everything counted on Brandt, which brought another thought. "How do you know when someone loves you?"

Alvina looked dumbstruck at the question. "You just know!" she said.

"That's no help to me, Alvina. You have all the experience here. You must have a better answer than that."

"Well," Alvina said, her face displaying her deep thought. "If they smile whenever they see you and compliment you about everything, it's an indication. When they want to touch you, kiss you, and do all sorts of silly things for you, you know."

"Alvina you haven't—"

"Of course," Alvina said. "You have to learn how to do it. You don't want that to be the first disappointment love holds. It's not like book learning. You can't read how to do it."

Shocked, Vesper reviewed her own circumstances. Eudora made sure Vesper had no opportunity to kiss any boy. She glanced at Alvina's casual posture. *Too casual, she lied; she must be lying. It wouldn't be the first time.* Alvina liked Vesper to think her the more sophisticated of the two. Vesper knew that Alvina's position in the household and community provided that anyway, but did it provide the opportunity of physical compromise such as Alvina described? Vesper thought not.

"Here we are," Alvina said as they came to the town's tavern, the Sated Beast.

"Pickling vespiary," Vesper said, repeating Eudora's disparagement of the place.

Alvina giggled and summoned a boy over. "Would you inquire inside for a courier bound for Wessure? Here is a coin," she dropped a copper, "for your trouble." Her smile bewitched the boy, but he caught the coin and entered the tavern.

True to Alvina's prediction, a low rider eventually approached them. His tardiness stretched Alvina's temper.

"You the miss asked for me?"

"My mother, the mayor's wife, demands this delivered," Alvina said crisply.

"Demand's a big word, girly," the rough man said, not reaching out to take the package from Alvina's outstretched hand.

"Pardon, sir," Vesper said. "My friend is in a poor temper. The walk here was dusty. She has silver coins for your labors." Vesper smiled and a discerning smile reflected in the man's eyes.

"That's good then," the man said, taking the package while holding his hand out to Alvina. "Poor temper's understandable on such a thirst-inducing day, I'll be glad of the coins."

Alvina looked into his face as she placed one coin in his hand. The hand didn't withdraw. She reluctantly pulled two more coins from her purse. His fist closed on the coins, the man tipped his hat to Vesper and turned away to enter the tavern.

"Rude, disgusting, dog man. Why did you do that?" Alvina said pinching Vesper's arm. "I could have kept two of the coins for my efforts!"

"Alvina, your mother knew how much was needed to deliver the package. Do you think he would take it for less? Be sensible." Vesper refused to rub the soreness away.

"Sensible? That? From someone so stupid!" Her eyes flew around the busy walkway, and she waved. "Go about your own chores now, Vesper," Alvina said loudly. "I'll make my own way home." She turned and walked away to another friend and was soon oblivious of Vesper.

Vesper turned and left for the salters. Before she left the tavern's yard, she noticed a woman from Kennetsure, the southern province, noticeably out of place in the high northern country. The honey-skinned woman's split skirt beneath a calf-length tunic vented front and back to the waist seemed very foreign. Perhaps plain riding clothes in Kennetsure, but very exotic for Norost. It seemed so much more sensible than all the fabric Vesper wore around her legs. The woman caught Vesper's regard and smiled. Vesper returned the smile, then lowered her eyes and hurried to her task.

"Eudora making some scents or putting meat by?" the salter asked. Several town women loitered in conversation outside the shop's entrance, their voices drifting into the premises that smelled of sweet spices, pepper, and salt. They had all greeted Vesper on her way in.

"Pickling cabbage."

He nodded and handed her Eudora's order with a farewell greeting. Vesper left, again asking pardon of the ladies she needed to walk between.

Low whispers often caught Vesper's attention as she passed, and this time, the same refrain floated to her, "a dead sister's child, indeed. The sister's name was shame." Despite her knowledge of the rumors, Vesper blushed painfully and felt her eyes water as she walked away.

~ * ~

Chloe's Story

Chloe sighed as she slowly straightened from leaning over her patient.

"Go, Mistress Chloe. I know how fatiguing this work is. You need to get some fresh air and then rest. I can handle the final bandaging."

"Thank you, Monsignor, but there are others needing help."

"None so serious; all will live with nature's healing. Go."

"You are tired, too."

The edges of his eyes creased with his smile. "We will need your talents later when I am resting."

Slow travel through the war-torn country meant their patients arrived with infected, morbid wounds. Chloe had argued she could be better used closer to the actual battles, but permission had never come.

She nodded and gave the infirmary's senior cleric the short curtsy his position demanded. Chloe felt more comfortable working with him than anyone else. Monsignor Otto was the only one who did not fear her and seemed to appreciate her efforts. Even as she left the ward, the heads of lesser clerics turned from her, some surreptitiously fingering the witch warding sign.

Her experience here in Kaereya's royal city taught Chloe it was best to ignore what would not change, but it made her long for the war to be over so she could leave Cliff City. She wished for her home in Kennetsure.

Her calling and service to the Holy One demanded her presence here, but she missed her home more each day. Easure was very different from hot and sunny Kennetsure. Here, everyone thought her a daughter of the Doane Desert, but she had come from the coast of Zankir, the garden peninsula, and knew it susceptible to attack by Sunderlune's great fleet. She wondered how her home fared.

A short walk took her past the forbidding walls of the Eternal Palace and its great towers. A little further and she reached the city's wall. Her daily walks saved her sanity. Beyond, the grass seas covering the island's promontories waved as water from a brisk offshore wind. Puffs of clouds skittered across the sky. Sometimes, on a clear day, Chloe could see her homeland as a misty strip of purple on the watery horizon. The quiet and solitude outside the bustling city brought her mind peace after the grisly sights found in the hospital's wards.

Reports told of the fighting on the north side of Thousand Island River, told of the deadly battles in the Seer Pass, where the Sunderlune armies had penetrated. Sunderlune held Seer Pass now, along with the low hills around Vere. It was reported the Vere Clans had taken severe losses holding their own lands. Chloe wondered if ripping the Vere Plateau from Kaereya's territory was not Sunderlune's goal.

The wounded poured into the city, and they were not only soldiers. Indeed, the army sent wounded, but the ravages of war injured all who stood in the battle's path. Refugees, mostly women and children, sought healing and shelter. Rape, assault, and mutilation were common ailments treated at the hospital. Some needed Monsignor Otto's ministering words more than flesh healing.

It wasn't only the gore and anguish she encountered in her work. Everyone called her a witch. The stares and the frightened expressions met every day wore her down and eroded her confidence. Those from the monks scared her. Often in turning she caught them making the warding sign. Explaining achieved nothing.

They watched her heal the wounded and saw more than could be accounted for with needle, stitch, and salve. It was true. She 'saw' the wounds, knew how to pull them together with her mind, how to speed the healing. The process was unexplainable. Chloe didn't know how it worked, only knew it did.

Monsignor Otto understood and was grateful for her help. After realizing she noticed the many furtive hand signs, he had placed a hand on her shoulder. "Ignorance causes fright," then, "times will change."

She wondered if change for good or bad, though. The church in the past few years had turned from those with magic gifts. In truth, she could not blame them because for everyone who magic helped, as many were injured in its misuse.

Chloe wrapped her cloak tight around her body to repel the cold spring wind. Standing back from the cliff's edge, she closed her eyes, feeling the sun's weak warmth. Taking a deep breath of the cold air, she let nature's elements enter her being and refresh her soul.

"Help!"

She looked around, not sure if she had heard or imagined the voice.

"Help!" It was a young voice, faint, but shrill in desperation. "Help me! Down here. Please, someone!"

Approaching the cliff's edge on her knees, Chloe used bushes for handholds and cautiously looked over the side. A young boy clung to the cliff. The wind diminished his voice and made it barely audible where she knelt. Even from her perspective, she saw his small body shivered, his eyes were huge and wide, and his dirty fingers clawed at grass tufts growing from the rock face.

"Stupid woman! Don't just stand there! Get me help."

"There is no one else within shouting distance to help. You will have to do with my help as I choose to give it. Hold on just a moment more." Chloe took off her cloak. Underneath, her stained apron still covered her work gown. She took that off and tied both garments into a rope that left the apron straps dangling. She saw the path the boy had followed down the edge.

Her witch gift showed her which rocks would hold her weight, and she thanked the Holy One with each move she took. She crawled down the cliff with great care, hugging the rocks, concentrating only on where to place each hand and each foot. Several times a shoe slipped in loose rock, and she hung, eyes closed, white fingers clenching stone until all sound and motion ceased. When she could get no further, she braced her back against the cliff. "Where are you?"

"Just below you. Hurry up! What's taking you so long?"

"Heights frighten me. I'm lowering you a rope. Put your arms through the shoulder straps and hang on. When I pull, you climb."

He did as she told him, but he was heavier than she had anticipated. She had to lower him twice before she could find a brace to wedge her feet against for leverage. Still, she thought he did little to help. When his head showed over the ledge she stood on, she gave one last heave, then caught his jacket and pulled him up.

"I can make it from here."

"What? No thank you?" Chloe asked his disappearing back end as he crawled over her and ascended the rough path. From glimpses of elegant but torn clothing as he squirmed over her, she judged the boy an aristo. Her month's wages could not buy the braid on his jacket. "I'll follow you up to make sure you make it," she said dryly.

He glanced back at her, his expression disdainful and completely aristo. The cliff's edge projected outward some distance above them.

He looked up, then down at her, and had the grace to look abashed. "Sorry, thank you."

She followed his foot and handholds as they clambered upward. His boots scuffed loose pebbles and dirt down on her head. Occasionally he threw her a look of contempt when a fear-filled gasp tore from her throat, but he said nothing. He fell onto the grass once on top, and Chloe followed suit.

"How did you get down there?" She picked up her cloak and wrapped it around him.

"I was hunting hawk eggs." He suddenly sat up and put a hand into his pocket but pulled only a slick yellow slime from its interior. "Curst luck! They broke."

Chloe looked at the remains of the eggs and felt bad for their loss, then her own as he wiped his hand on her cloak. "You are lucky that you kept your own life. It is a long drop to the shore."

His eyes rolled to her. "I've thanked you already. You won't tell anyone, will you?"

"No. I don't know who to tell anyhow."

He grinned. "True enough," he said and jumped up. "I've got to get back." In an instant, he matched his actions to his words.

"Ungrateful brat," Chloe said to herself, shivering. "He took my cloak and my apron, too." She headed back to the hospital and her room in the adjacent building. At least she would have a humorous entry in her journal for a change.

Two

Dinner was prolonged and hungry for her own meal, Vesper thought it would never end. Dame Winifred picked and complained over the toughness of the meat. It hadn't been prepared properly. Vesper stood by the sideboard to bring items as asked. It was hard to stay alert, easier to tune-out Dame Winifred's whining voice with more pleasant thoughts.

"Vesper! For heaven's sake, this is the second time I've had to ask you to pour wine," Dame Winifred complained.

The sharp voice started Vesper from her daydream. Picking up the pitcher, she quickly moved to Dame Winifred's place. As she poured, she swore the mistress jostled her arm, causing the liquid to spill.

"Hayden Kellsie you simply must do something about this. It is intolerable that we should be so served." Dame Winifred said as she wiped at the spot with exaggerated care.

The mayor looked from Vesper to his wife with resignation. "Vesper, retire to the kitchen and have Eudora send Freda out to finish."

Glad of the respite, Vesper quickly left. The kitchen's warmth soothed the chill felt from the dining room. Its cozy atmosphere brought an unspoken relief. Eudora and Freda were putting the finishing touches on the family's dessert and looked up in unison as she entered. Vesper lowered her eyes. "Hayden has asked for Freda to finish serving," she said not looking up from the floor. Freda huffed and groaned before she left with the desserts. A quick side-glance caught the rebuking glance Freda threw her way.

"What happened?" Eudora asked.

Vesper looked at her foster mother to judge her temper. "I spilled the wine. Some stained Dame Winnifred's sleeve."

Eudora stood calmly cleaning up the worktable. Her strong features seemed neither upset nor harried as the soft brown eyes regarded Vesper. A simple embroidered white cap framed her oval face with its beaked nose and high slashing brows while hiding the black and silver hair braided and coiled beneath it. "Is there a mess to clean up?"

"No, Dame Winifred wiped it up with her napkin."

"Were you careless around the mistress?"

"Yes," Vesper said. It was useless to suggest her arm was nudged. She sighed. "The mistress's talk put me in a trance, by the time I heard her request, she had to repeat it. I hurried, that is all. I am sorry, Eudora."

"Sit and eat your own dinner."

"I'll help you clean up, then we can sit together," Vesper offered, guilt stricken for the lack of a reprimand.

Eudora nodded and placed the plates in the warmer. "Freda eats with us tonight as with the full moon and harvest, Marwyn will be late from the fields. You need to stay focused, Vesper."

"I know. It's hard. They talk of nothing, except maybe meanness. Not like you and I talk about all manner of interesting things in the evening. It was boring and I was thinking of something else."

"You were daydreaming. You should make no judgments, Vesper. Can't you feel the unhappiness in this house? The mistress is deserving of your sympathy."

"Dame Winifred?" Vesper scoffed. "She has everything she wants."

"No, Vesper. Not everything. Some treasures can never be gained without the loss of another."

There was no answer for that, and Vesper mindlessly helped her aunt until Freda finished. Before they sat, each washed her hands in a special basin for that purpose, then Eudora held a pitcher of warm scented water and poured it over their hands. Freda sniffed at Eudora's required mealtime ritual, and Vesper hid her smile as she wiped her hands on a linen towel. Closing her eyes, she smelled her palms and enjoyed the lingering scent of rosemary and lavender. The smell reminded her of Eudora's tales of life in the south. The washing ritual always reminded her of Eudora's stories making her seem less familiar and more exotic. Freda's voice called her wandering attention back to the Kellsie kitchen. Freda placed their plates before them, and after a few simple words of grace, they sat down.

"Do you miss Kennetsure?" Vesper asked.

Stopped mid-chew, Eudora slowly finished her bite before speaking. "Sometimes. Why do you ask?"

"I saw a Kennetsure woman outside the tavern today. She seemed so free, so unrestrained. I thought, as a native of Kennetsure, surely you must miss the south—the sun and the warmth. A place where learning is cherished and where women aren't so constricted." She couldn't help her petulant tone.

"That's what you get filling her head full of all that learning," Freda said. "How is she to ever find a position?"

"I found one," Eudora said. "Vesper, everyone has restrictions. You just don't see those imposed on others, whether from different families, different towns, or different provinces. You must see beyond the obvious and gratifying to the problems, the faults, and the restrictions,. Accept them and you can truly learn to love."

"People or places?" Vesper asked.

"Both."

"You've taught me much of Kennetsure—how to read and study for enjoyment, the pleasure of making beautiful things, about herbs, and making scents and cosmetics. It must be wonderful there," Vesper said sighing. She closed her eyes to envision the prospect. "I think I love it, already."

"Did Alvina walk into town with you?"

Eudora brought her back to Vere with a crash. "Yes." She told Eudora what had happened during the afternoon. "I saw the Justiciar's wife at the door to the salter's shop. Several of the town ladies were talking just outside the shop. She asked if you had made up more of that hand ointment she likes so well."

"Bunch of gossiping old crows," Freda said her cap shaking with her head movement. Wisps of mousy, gray-streaked hair had escaped shortly after this morning's placement and still draped down her neck. "They all need honest employment for their idle hands."

"Crows are the Holy One's messengers," Eudora said without inflection. Looking at Vesper she added, "I have some extra made. Tomorrow you can take some to her."

Hiding her reluctance, Vesper nodded, wondering if Eudora knew what message the Holy One was spreading.

After dinner Freda left, wanting to get home before the night's promised coldness settled. Eudora sat with Vesper near the warmth of the great brick stove. Already Eudora had banked the fire's embers to last the night, so before long, as night's cold entered, they would retire to the room they shared on the backside of the oven. It would stay warm there.

"Is that a handfasting gift you work on?" Eudora asked, her own needle making even stitches in the cloth she worked.

"Yes."

"For Brandt?"

Vesper didn't speak immediately, placing several careful stitches.

"Is it wrong to think so?" she asked at last.

"Has he encouraged you?"

"He has spoken no words," Vesper said with absolute truthfulness. Her eyes flicked toward Eudora then back to the pocket pouch she embroidered. Fantastic animals cavorted amid a forest of trees and flowers.

"Sometimes they don't need saying. It doesn't seem appropriate."

Vesper wondered if she meant wanting Brandt and decided she meant the choice of the gift. "I meant to make foresleeves."

"Why didn't you?"

"I don't know." Vesper sat and escaped into her fantasy world for a moment before resuming her stitches. "This came to mind, and I couldn't let it go."

"The amulet buckle from your mother's trunk would fit well in the pocket."

Vesper chewed on her lip, then looked at Eudora searching for the truth. Graceful and kind, even beautiful in an unusual way, Eudora had cared for Vesper with a patient but stern discipline, and surely love? Every evening she shared her wisdom and learning with Vesper, taught her all sorts of things the teaching master's students would never encounter in his classroom. Eudora was the only mother she had known, but a mother in truth? Her past and her motives were a mystery to Vesper, for Eudora seldom spoke of herself. When Vesper asked, she turned the question or greeted it with silence. Finally, Vesper asked. "My mother's trunk?"

Eudora's hands stilled their even pace. "Have tongues been wagging?" She looked at Vesper. "Yes, I thought so." She let the silence grow tendrils before speaking. "Your mother's trunk. Not mine. Your mother's."

"Your sister?"

"No. You have nothing to be ashamed of Vesper. Tomorrow I will give you the surgown from the trunk. I think she would have liked you to have it. You may change it as you wish. If you can sew Alvina's gown so finely, I'm sure you can do so for yourself."

"Really, Eudora, tomorrow? Really?" Vesper asked her voice rising. "There is not much time, but the gown is lovely, nearly ageless in cut." Vesper hardly heard Eudora's answer as she chattered about how to change the dress.

"Tomorrow. The silvery green will show your eyes well," Eudora encouraged. "You will look most becoming."

~ * ~

When Vesper left for service in the teaching master's classroom, Eudora went to her room of seventeen years. All their possessions, except their clothes, fit into one trunk that also served as a table. Hooks along the wall held their few garments: chemise, tunics, day gowns for three days and one good gown apiece. Removing the lamp, the housekeeper noticed it needed oil and clucked her tongue. The books and other items sitting on top went on the floor next to the lamp.

Briefly she fingered the pocket Vesper had embroidered as she lifted it. It was beautiful, the craftsmanship superb. Too fine for the young man she favored. Eudora frowned. Vesper had reason to hope. Master Brandt freely bestowed his smiles and lingering gazes on Vesper. It disturbed Eudora. They were totally inappropriate for each other, and she personally doubted Master Brandt interested in handfasting an orphan, especially one reputedly a bastard.

Her motion stirred a leaf set on the trunk, setting it swirling on a journey of soft arcs to the floor. She picked it up. Autumn coloring charged the leaf's common beauty with gilded veins traced against a vermilion background. A small gift from Vesper, too pretty to be missed because Eudora was busy within the house. She sat back, kneeling on the floor, and looked out the small window.

A fey child often lost in fantasies with an imagination unbound by reality—that was her Vesper. A childhood filled with 'seeing' all manner of people and creatures no one else could observe, including her imaginary friend Alfred.

She remembered a long-ago incident of five-year-old Vesper talking with Alvina about Alfred within Winifred's hearing. The mistress demanded Vesper to retract her lies which brought a furious denial earning Vesper a hard palm across her cheek. Eudora's lips tightened at the memory. It was the last time Winifred Kellsie dared touch her child. Eudora huffed softly, remembering the tumult. Her poor Vesper, already haunted by nightmares that seemed to conjure what was yet to be, then set upon by a vindictive woman. Eudora had hoped Vesper's imagination was created by her lack of all the toys and objects Alvina possessed in abundance, and prayed it wasn't the mother's curse come upon the daughter. Now she knew.

Eudora shook her head, letting her fingers play over the designs carved into the trunk's top. It was not really hers but of Wessure fashioning as the mermaid decoration attested. A friend had kept it while Eudora had searched for a new, secure place to live and hide. Even then she had waited years before having the trunk sent to her. Her friend reported no one had come looking for it or even inquired about it. She had kept it locked since two years before when she found something missing but certainly not by Vesper's hand. Each month she opened the trunk and hoped the missing item would somehow be there, somehow overlooked in her past searches. As she lifted the lid, the combined scents of lavender, tansy, and wormwood wafted from inside the box's core.

Item by item she removed the contents, shaking out the clothes and cloth only to carefully refold them, forming a pile on the floor. For long moments she held a fine wool baby's blanket, delicately embroidered with mermaids, and then buried her face in the downy weave. It still held a faint hint of rose and talcum. She folded it and placed it with the rest. Near the bottom the elegant fabric of a costly surgown formed a folded mound.

She lifted the dress and shook it out. A wool fabric with threads as fine as spider's web, then shot with silver and silk to form a fern pattern, draped over her hand. The color suggested evening mist, spring rain, and mystery. Just like Vesper's eyes. Perhaps too costly even in its age for a servant's child to wear? *No.* Eudora's lips firmed. *Not this once.* Such a subtle fabric was seldom seen and by the residents of Norost never at all. It would be safe. It was enough Vesper would know.

On her last reach into the trunk she withdrew the amulet. A tarnished, but cleverly designed buckle filled her palm. The sun, the moon and stars decorated its surface. She turned it over to read the rune inscriptions on the back. Why was this not taken with the other item? Did the thief not recognize the value? She looked inside the empty trunk. The missing item remained missing. She closed her eyes and brought the amulet to her heart with a brief prayer. Certainly, if evil was the purpose of the theft, it would have occurred by now. *Vesper was safe. Please, Holy One, let her be safe.*

Three

From the window embrasure of his tower room, Wilhelm Norbert, Earl of Rikon, observed the river-lake extending around him. The view filled his long-tamed heart with the strong urge to escape, a desire for the freedom of his youth fired his frame, but he would not go. Far to the southwest a gray mist matching his mood obscured the horizon. It would close in on the river within a few candle-marks, bringing its damp chill to the rooms and curtain the window's magnificent view. His eyes dropped to follow the ancient stonework below the window to where the smooth cut blocks blended into the granite cliffs and then fell in a dizzying slope to the river far below.

Everyone called it '*Thou River.*' His vantage point gave credence to its real name, Thousand Island River, for land dotted the watery view. Many of the islands lay as marshy specks, barely breaking the river's surface. Some few, like Hawk Island, jutted like giant granite brows, worn to rounded surprise by ages of weather. Others, like the Tiny Steps between Hawk Island and Anatole, rose-like jagged spikes with a web-work of bridges between them. He imagined it remained much as it had eight hundred years ago after the completion of the first fortress. His own selection and tenure in this apartment didn't seem long, but it had been twenty years. During those years how many of the realm's problems had he contemplated from this exact position? He couldn't remember how many.

Now he wrestled with another. The aristos would find nothing within the realm wrong. He would, however, not give what he believed to be a deceptive report on the realm's wellbeing. That was his dilemma, and it needed solving in only twenty-one days.

The double holiday of Handfasting, the day of commitment, followed by Gifting Day, approached. After, only the sixteen holy days of mystery and faith celebrating the holy number of seven remained before culminating in the triad holiday of the Holy One's Last Day, First Day, and Second Day. Last Day culminated the year with the entire court spending the night at the cathedral in religious ceremony. This time, he would pray to avoid the looming negative aspects of one, damnation, nothingness, and the darkness of the abyss. Last Day's prayers were followed by the Feast of Duality at the start of First Day.

On Second Day, the traditional day of beginnings, court convened. His report on the realm had to be given before King Frederick's Aristo Session. He ran a hand over his barren scalp in frustration.

The overcrowding of Cliff City was part of the problem. During the last century habitation within the city had burgeoned. The growth stretched the limited land resources until palace, city, and island seemed nearly one as evident on the palace's northern side where new buildings now obliterated the ancient fortress's imposing stone walls, a result of the court's endless quest for more room. Windows facing north in the new palace looked out on applied grandeur where over-planned gardens, ornate architecture and sculptures, colorful kites, banners, and the endless changing fashion of the people walking the palace grounds.

As the King's Marshal, Norbert understood the problem all too well. Neither palace nor city could expand further without demolition of the existing structure. The once spacious island groaned in a tight corset. Overcrowding of any population always brought the unpleasant side effects of conflict and crime. Something the king and aristos didn't want to hear.

The clatter of horse hooves in the narrow courtyard three stories below his rooms disturbed his musings. Several young men, mere boys to him, rode in through the archway. They dismounted, slapped their sweaty horses and each other in comradery. They threw their horse's reins to grooms. Steam rose from the sweat-frothed animals as the grooms led them away with accompanying clopping-hoof sounds.

Laughing, the boys teased one of their fellows, tossing his hat from one to another. From the red hair, Norbert recognized the youth as Duke Constantine's son Tate. Shouts from the boys' play expelled great puffs of visible vapor. The weather had changed, bringing the first cold spell of the season.

Identification of the rowdy group was easy. King Frederick's youngest son, Warrick, dressed in his usual blinding colors, this time red and yellow, led the caper. The last child of Frederick's first queen, Warrick, the king's favorite, remained the wildest of the royal get, proving the negative nature of his personal number two. Norbert found the young man negligent in duty and possessed of an oversized appetite for life's pleasures.

In this, his fair looks and innate charm helped Warrick achieve his goals as much, if not more, than his title. A laughing indifference to every punishment devised for him and a rare ability to manipulate others often created both family and court dilemmas. He wondered if Warrick would ever embrace the positive side of his number, commitment.

The group's return also raised suspicions about the boys' recent whereabouts. Like much most of Frederick's palace, the throne room was in the midst of renovation. The master builder had come to him earlier in the morning to tell him that a lead box found inside the crumbling throne was missing. Since only the granite base was to be kept, he reassured the man that a national relic had not been stolen or mislaid. There was no record of anything like the box in any historical record, but Norbert had a hunch about the disappearance. Warrick and his friends had been shooed out of the work area the previous evening. The incident with the box was not worth taking to the king.

Warrick's nonchalance about handfasting the girl selected had already caused diplomatic problems. Pia, his foreign fiancée, sat sullen and angry in her rooms, dismissed from the boy's mind. A sign of the times. Norbert inhaled and exhaled a long, deep breath. Warrick disliked him. An unfortunate but inescapable reality, it made his intervention or alleviation of the problem impossible.

The king refused to reprimand Warrick's behavior, even though the problems he created plagued Norbert. What need? Warrick had an elder brother, boring in his royal dedication, and the aging King Frederick enjoyed the stories of wayward Warrick's escapades.

Turning from the view, Norbert returned to his desk and the papers scattered there. The king and courts' anticipation of the approaching two days of holiday made any business needing the king's undistracted attention difficult. Sometimes Norbert felt any holiday was one too many in a year.

The realm seemed in as merry a frolic as the diversion below his window displayed. Except under the festivity, destruction and death prevailed. A pattern discernable in the past few years suddenly intensified. Over a hundred fatal 'accidents' and another seventy-five unsolved murders had occurred in the last year alone. An urgency shadowed his report about this unprecedented occurrence in Kaereya.

Many of the accidental deaths involved aristos. That alone aroused suspicion. Norbert paused, picking up one report. That number now included the wife and heir of his good friend Raymond Aurelias, Duke of Lambere. Raymond's titles and wealth provided little solace for his unlucky married life—a first wife dead by her own hand, taking a newborn son with her, and now the death of a second wife and son in a carriage accident. It seemed nothing more than a cruel whim of fate, even though Raymond's son had possessed as reckless a streak as Warrick. He laid down the report, detaching himself as much as possible, from his friend's tragedy.

Among the unsolved murders of ordinary folk, the number of victims bearing unusual birthmarks, often called witches' marks, seemed significant, but how? The marks differed in size and shape and always occurred on either hand or wrist. It made no sense and aroused a deep worry. He knew the superstitious peasantry still believed in magic and ritual, but no word of public hysteria or fright of witches had come to him.

There were other problems. Criminal activity had reached epidemic proportions within the cities. In the countryside, bands of outlaws roamed vandalizing homes, terrorizing the inhabitants, destroying crops and property, and stealing anything of value. Yet the aristos refused to provide added protection for the areas. Royal Guards patrolled, and they caught many of the outlaw bands, but more cropped up just as fast. He would face the aristos' blatant disbelief and disregard of this issue when he proposed a new tax levy at King's Council Session on Second Day.

Leaving his lofty room in the southwest tower, Norbert made his way through often-renovated corridors, myriad winding marble staircases and colonnades, and the gilt and portrait-lined alcoves of the Eternal Palace. Each successive refurbishment had left its embellished mark on the decor. Depictions of the eternal numbers and the four symbols of Kaereya dominated relief sculptures, gilded moldings, murals, and tapestry motifs and patterns.

The last set of staircases appeared commonplace in contrast but took him to the subterranean tunnels that allowed quick access from either the palace or the ancient fortress flanking it to one another. Remnants of an earlier building beneath the elegant rooms and corridors above, the dark tunnels smelled of mildew, dampness, urine, and decay. Only pages, craftsmen, general laborers, servants, and a few court officers like himself, used them, and those mostly boys and men. Many sought quick relief. Women seldom used the tunnels because of the smell and the vermin that frequently roamed there despite the cats, dogs, and traps.

In the northeastern corner of the old fortress stood the circular tower in which the court's resident genealogist and herald lived. Puffing up the five flights of narrow stairs, Norbert knocked on the thick wooden door. This ancient section of the fortress lacked the amenities of the newer wings of the palace or even those of his own lodgings and office.

A young boy struggled to open the heavy door and Norbert reached out a hand to shove the weight back. The sandy-haired youngster did not recognize him. A heavy dappling of freckles and a turned-up nose gave him an impertinent look. Norbert snorted. His usual undecorated gray clothing seldom inspired respect in the resplendent court and now not even his continence brought it.

"I am the King's Marshal, Earl of Rikon, Wilhelm Norbert. I wish to speak with the Court Heraldist on matters of business."

The door opened as wide as the boy's eyes, and Norbert entered. The rooms smelled of an odd combination of old paper, ink, paint, and solvent mixed with wood smoke. Logs burning in t.he fireplace added little warmth. Several apprentices sat at tables working on drawings, beautiful in obscure detail and bright colors gleaming with gilt. Work stopped with the scribes' attention centered on Norbert as he followed the boy. The youngster was a slight twig who whipped through the tables with snake-like ease.

Even as the boy swung wide the door to the heraldist's inner sanctum, Norbert saw Master Godfry's eyes flicker with a squint of recognition, but he then looked down at his table. Differing from Norbert in every way, Master Godfry sat yellow-gray and portly, his bland, rounded features appearing dull-witted. Norbert knew otherwise. The man's ink-stained hands held a magnifying lens to inspect the work before him. He continued to leaf through an immense pile of unbound manuscript pages on his tilt-topped desk even as Norbert stood within the small antechamber.

"The King's Marshal," the youngster said in a brassy-shrill child's voice. He grinned at Norbert and trotted out, closing the door behind him.

"How may I help the Earl of Rikon?" the heraldist asked, laying down the lens and the page.

"My regards to you, Master Godfry, I bring you a problem of mine. Here is a list of Aristo names. I need to know if there is any common factor among them."

"Always blunt and down to business, Norbert?" Taking the list, Master Godfrey read the names. "Ah, yes, I recognize some of the names. Dead, are they not?" At Norbert's nod, "You investigate then; about time." With ponderous care he left his stool and searched the books on the shelves behind him. Pulling several down, he returned to his stool.

Snorting softly at the dismissive behavior, Norbert looked around, found a stool, and sat. He would not let Master Godfrey annoy him. He wanted answers. A candle-mark elapsed before Master Godfrey, save grunts and mutters as he leafed through parchments, gave any more awareness of Norbert's presence, or spoke to him in any manner. Norbert rose and nosed about the room inspecting some of the pages scattered on tables. Aristo Agino was having his new grandson's name added to his family tree. Several merchants were having royal emblems designed for their business.

A draft blew out a candle and shifted several of the parchments on the table. Lighting the candle, Norbert noted Aristo Yonger sought to have the Easure dragon added to his crest. *That ought to raise eyebrows.* Just because he claimed land once belonging to a reputed aegis didn't mean anyone would allow him to usurp the magic symbol. It was too ingrained in the symbolic icons of all of Easure.

Master Godfrey cleared his throat, drawing Norbert's attention. "Earl Rikon, it all has to do with magic, but there is a problem."

"What?" Norbert heard his own incredulity.

"Some of my family histories are missing. Perhaps only mislaid, I will need to check with my staff."

~ * ~

Tired from a long wild ride on the Rock Coast, and an even longer sedate ride through Cliff City to the Eternal Palace, Ottillie entered her father's rooms. Mist droplets drizzled from her oiled-wool cloak in the too-warm room. He stood shadowed and framed by the window, his back to the last of the day's bright light, which had finally broken through the overcast sky. The respect given the king's marshal usually filtered down to his daughter but not the tribulations. She guessed a worrisome problem oppressed him.

"I don't know why they still call it Hawk Island," she said. "The buildings have overrun every nook and cranny. No hawk could perch anywhere. Hello, father." She threw off her wet, generously full riding cape. Droplets rained to the wood floor as the fabric fell over a carved ebony chair. Chaffing her hands to bring back warmth to her cold fingers, Ottillie's glance returned to her father. She extended her hands to the crackling flames in the fireplace.

"I've seen them nesting on the cliffs below my window."

At his distracted tone, Ottillie looked at her father. Bright red wisps of her hair, dislodged by her ride, divided her view into segments. She pushed them aside. "Only because no human can nest there. Is something wrong? You sound very gloomy."

He walked around his desk, and as he left the bright window, his thin face with its curved nose became clear. He picked up her discarded cloak and hung it on a wall hook before handing her a handkerchief. While Ottillie wiped her damp face, he poked the fire into renewed vigor.

"I'll never understand why you've never handfasted," he said looking at her.

"Oh no, is it that again!" Even as her alto voice boomed through the room Ottillie softened it. "No, Father, I'm too old to stand one more time, don't even think it. And don't blame yourself. It's not my illegitimacy. Don't you see? I'm taller even than you, and no slim miss into the bargain? Besides, I've come to terms with it," she gave him a wicked grin, "and even enjoy my freedom." Then she added offhand, "And you give me everything I wish already."

She laughed at his harrumph of displeasure. He would give her anything she wanted and gave her much she did not, probably because he could not give her what he wanted most—her legitimacy. Her mother broke the handfast early despite her pregnancy, and it was her family that refused to recognize their daughter's child. More importantly, her father shared his thoughts and pleasures, his worries, and his problems with her. That trust always brought her pleasure, but to save him from hurt and anger, she did not always reciprocate.

She briefly wondered if her father knew how many of the aristos who shunned her at handfasting approached her later with less honorable proposals. Her eyes flickered to her father's clear hazel gaze, and she guessed maybe, but probably better ignored.

An old item of court gossip about the fall from grace of a young noble and his dismissal from court crossed her mind. The aristo's downfall came from his own politically unwise actions, but the expulsion had pleased her because of her umbrage with the young man. A bolt of revelation stunned her. Only one person could have brought it about. She blinked and pursed her lips in contradictory feelings, one of love for her father, the other, anger at her lack of privacy. She thought he had not known.

"Don't blame your mother either. She couldn't help how her family felt."

She looked at him. It was an old story. A sigh escaped her. "You have been pensive."

"I worry about you and about the future."

"What's happened to put you in this mood?" she asked, kissing his cheek and turning to flop wearily into a leather chair before the fireplace in one smooth motion. Her southern-style brown and ocher trews kept her modesty and exposed her lack of it. Her father frowned.

"You are not a southern hoyden."

"Father, there is nothing that will ever make me acceptable to most of the aristos at court. Accept it. I have." She shrugged with a smug smile. "So I am free to do as I please. This style pleases me, the trews makes riding easier, and is far more comfortable than a traditional riding gown."

"Will you wear a gown to Second Day?"

Ottillie grinned. "Yes, if it pleases you. An index finger twirled a red lock around itself in a comforting ritual. "Is your speech ready?"

"No." He pushed a report across the desk to her. "What do you make of this?"

Her eyes quickly scanned the pages. "Who would do this? To what purpose? Nobody believes those old legends." The sheets held the names of deceased aristos whose bloodlines supposedly traced back to mythical and magical beginnings.

"Someone does. Someone has researched aristo lines very thoroughly. Every family with a hint of magic in their background is slowly disappearing. Master Godfrey noticed it some time ago."

"And he didn't come to you?" She sighed. "Perhaps not. Not many listen to the old myth monger. Systematically or coincidentally?"

"What do you think?"

"Coincidence happens, but perhaps not this frequently."

"My thoughts exactly."

"Raymond's wife is on this list." She looked at her father with watery eyes. The duke's second wife had been a close friend. "Does this mean it wasn't an accident?"

"I don't know. The report raises ugly suspicions, and legend hints even the royal family bears the taint of magic."

"So do I if one believed Mother about her family." She rubbed the small birthmark on the back of her hand. Her mother had called it proof, but her father had laughed at the concept. When his serious eyes caught her frequent motion without his usual dismissing laugh, she stopped. "You'd think people had become wiser with the passing ages. I guess not." She looked at the list searching through the names. "Can I help?"

"No, I want you safe."

Ottillie made a rude noise. "Nowhere is safe. You should have Corbin question the library's clerics. Research of this scope takes time." She noted the doubt in his face. "I can take care of myself, Father. Did Master Godfrey give you any insights?"

Her father started laughing, a subtle derisive sound. "Yes. He suggested I contact an old man living in Egan Tower. Said he might be of help."

"The Aegis?" Ottillie asked, sitting straight, her eyes widening. "One still lives?"

"The title hasn't been recognized in a hundred years. What do you know about it?"

"I spend a lot of time reading. Would you like me to research it for you?" she asked, suppressing her eager arguments. The library at Egan was reputed to be the finest in all of Kaereya, but distance made it the most difficult to enter.

Her father's face filled with humor, his eyebrows lowering as he suppressed laughter. "You needn't sound so eager. Delving in dusty books at the Queen's University isn't a holiday."

"It is for me."

"You're a believer?"

"Not necessarily. More of an investigator." She raised her brows and smiled, "And the fact is—Egan exists."

~ * ~

Chloe's Story

An infirmary aide pulled on Chloe's sleeve and whispered. "Monsignor Otto asks you to come to his antechamber immediately."

Chloe thanked the woman, smiled at her patient, and slowly finished bandaging his wound. The wound was clean and the edges mending. She nodded to her assistant and indicated she would return.

It was a short walk to the room off the main hall. Her steps slowed as she saw courtiers idling in the hall along the way. A monk, carrying a tray of used ale tankards, descended the steps. Chloe looked down at herself and removed her apron. She ran fingers through her hair to push it into place. Upstairs Royal Guardsmen stationed at Monsignor Otto's door opened it for her. Inside, a middle-aged man with russet hair and clear-blue eyes turned to her. He wore an elaborate and heavily decorated coat over an embroidered tunic and held a jeweled cap.

"Here she is, this is Chloe. She has a rare gift of healing, Your Majesty, a rare gift," Monsignor Otto said as she entered. *King Ewald.* Chloe fell into a deep curtsy. "Your Majesty." Fine shoes stepped into her floor view.

"We believe thanks are owed you, Mistress Chloe." His hand lifted her chin, then spread before her to take her hand. He helped her rise. "Our son has belatedly told his tutor, and then us, of events in the past sennight. We believe this is your cloak?"

A page, unseen before, stepped forward with her cloak. Another cleric stood nearby. If indeed, this was King Ewald, then this was Bishop Thidrek, the King's Bishop. One glance told Chloe he had no pleasure in this visit. His glower burned through her.

"Yes, Your Majesty."

"We were quite worried when he gave us this." King Ewald's page handed her a bloodied apron.

"I am sorry to have caused you concern, Sire, it is my work apron."

"No, no. We were just glad to find you so quickly and in good health. You did a very brave thing. Boys are notorious for finding adventures. The prince is no exception."

"It was my pleasure to help, Sire."

"Monsignor Otto tells me you are a witch."

Bishop Thidrek protested, "Evil, Sire, evil," making the warding sign with his hand.

Chloe cringed. "I am not evil, Your Majesty."

"No, we don't believe such nonsense. Ignore Bishop Thidrek. He is a fussy old man, aren't you, bishop?" The king's chuckle filled the room again and his eyes lighted on the bishop. Other soft laughs emerged from the courtiers surrounding him. The man frowned but lowered his head in submission. "It is as Monsignor Otto says, a rare gift. We are glad you are here to help our stricken people." He had kept hold of her hand and raised it to brush a kiss across its back. "We came to give you a reward for your service to the crown."

"Please, Sire, no reward is needed. I did not know him to be your son, he could have been anyone's boy."

King Ewald chuckled and looked at Otto. "A pleasant surprise. Our court could take a lesson from this young woman. Usually petitioners are all too eager to tell us of their deserving works. You will take it, for you have earned it." He turned her hand palm upward and took an object from his page and placed it in her hand. The dragon symbol of Easure stared up at her, a golden weight with eyes of emerald and wings of lapis.

"It is beautiful, Your Majesty, I thank you for your generosity." Chloe knew there was no way to decline.

"Thank you, Mistress Chloe, for the prince's life."

He dropped her hand and engaged in goodbyes with Monsignor Otto. Within a thrice he was gone, Chloe lowered in another deep curtsey. She took a deep breath and looked up at her friend and mentor. "I am overcome," she said, rising.

Monsignor Otto looked at her face with a serious expression and said, "Be careful, Chloe."

"I did but help a child from the cliff's side."

"I know, but it has brought you to the attention of the king."

Four

Far to the west of Hawk Island on the banks of the Northern Thou River where it meets the Peace Ocean, Raymond Aurelias, Duke of Lambere, viewed the land stretching out before him. The peninsula of Lambere stretched in vast fertile fields along the west coast. Unicorn Island crowned his property in the west, and the ancient, forested foothills of the Vere Plateau framed it to the north. What he did not own came under his direct governance.

During the days of his bereavement, he had withdrawn from court and returned to his estate. Since, he had spent his time riding, managing his lands, and trying to understand the fate that took away two children, two heirs. No wisdom or acceptance had enlightened him. Returning from a long ride, he gave over his mount to a waiting groom and watched the man lead the horse toward the covered arch leading to a second courtyard and the stables.

He stood in the forecourt regarding his home. Parts of the estate house were nearly as old as the oldest parts of the Eternal Palace, and the house was nearly as jumbled in juxtaposing architectural styles. The tower of the original fortress, square and forbidding, anchored the western side of the entrance building. Once a palisade enclosure, the house wings had grown from the main structure until now only the gated fourth side remained free of building. A second ornate tower, vastly different in character and age, secured the eastern side. To Raymond Aurelias's eyes, no dissimilarity, or incongruity existed. His family had built for the times they lived in and the results were extraordinarily rich and beautiful.

The question looming in his mind never left, especially when regarding his property. *Who would inherit?* He supposed he was not too old to father yet another child, but the thought of a third wife daunted him. This last marriage had been disheartening and unsatisfying.

A servant brought him from his reverie.

"Sir, a message came while you were out. It is in your study."

Aurelias realized his contemplative introspection had upset the staff. Their solicitousness during these last months, urging him to this or that occupation whenever he seemed lost in morose thought, had not escaped him. It had been a sennight now since they had found the need. For many of them, it was the second bereavement they had gone through with him.

He turned to his man. "Is the messenger waiting?"

"No sir. He was paid and left."

Aurelias nodded and started for an entrance as gilded and grand as any at the Eternal Palace. Within the entrance hall male ancestors' visages looked down from lofty perches on walls lined with deep, painted, and gilt moldings. The portraits' elaborate frames continued in a seemingly unending row. The female ancestors carried the second floor's walls. In all these portraits an astute observer, after several moments of study, might notice a family similarity of the chin line and a marked indentation found there, and perhaps a definition of the ear or eye, but not in hair or eye color or general appearance, which varied dramatically.

Certainly, the current titleholder differed in those respects. Neither excessively tall nor thin, short nor stout, the current Duke of Lambere's appearance seemed exceedingly average, almost common. It was something about which Aurelias never worried.

He entered his study and sat in the great chair behind the enormous inlaid desk. On one corner sat the half-day candle, its delineated sides burned down between the fourth and fifth lines. A delivery folder lay centered on the blotter. The envelope inside was addressed to him in a hand he did not recognize.

Flipping it over he stopped. While the missive remained sealed, he was arrested by the fanciful bird signet embedded in the wax. He recognized it. He had buried the seal with its owner eighteen years ago. The moment seemed frozen forever, but at last, he took his knife and slid its edge under the wax. The paper unfolded, but the wax remained intact, gripping the flap. In the lines covering the missive he identified the same unknown hand as addressed the letter, but the signature, though shaky, brought recognition. Later he did not know how many times he reread the message before finally absorbing its meaning. Long afterward, he still sat immobile.

Rousing, he went to the door and shouted. "Have my valet, steward, and Quillon come to me," Aurelias ordered. The man who heard his summons nodded and left. Shortly both the valet and steward stood before him. He gave orders to his valet to pack. To his steward he gave orders for the immediate care of the estate.

~ * ~

Tall and dark with his southern heritage, Quillon quietly entered his duke's office and stood while the duke talked with the others. His wait lasted no longer than a quick upward glance from the duke, who then dismissed the retainers.

"We are leaving at sixth-mark. Ready an escort for the journey. I expect a trip of some fourteen days. From this journey we will travel directly to Court. I must be there by Second Day. Here are written authorizations for lodging and stabling along the way. Send riders out now for accommodations. Take the usual precautions." He looked up. "I want Kissre with us."

"You expect trouble?"

The duke exhaled heavily and looked thoughtful. "No, but outside of yourself she is the most experienced."

"She thinks for herself, and she is newest."

Aurelias paused briefly. "Has she ever refused an order or acted in any way to cause you to doubt her motives?" Aurelias asked his tone one of consternation at Quillon's flat tone.

"No. She would be an asset if you expect trouble, but she is also a mercenary, ready for anyone's hire, and a relative stranger to us. Her looks draw too much attention. These are things to consider."

"We will take her. Watch her, though, if you question her loyalty." Aurelias half-smiled. half-grinned at Quillon. "You are right, though, she looks outlandish and godless. Tell her to wear riding gloves, that tattoo will draw more attention than is necessary or desired."

As a knight of the Zekarac Order and sworn man to his duke, Quillon needed no further explanation, but gave his nod of acceptance and left to carry out the duke's desires.

A while later, from the shadowed doorway of the barn, Quillon watched the new hire, an already trained soldier, as she finished removing her mount's tack in the yard after a hard training session. She ran her hand down the animal's smooth muscles still damp with sweat, murmuring softly as she worked. In the lantern's dim light the wheaten color of her mount's shoulder gleamed in pale cream, nearly matching the lighter strands of his owner's hair. His cooling body emitted air-distorting sheets of heat and horse scent. Huge puffing breaths formed clouds although his sides had long since slowed their billowing rhythm.

The hand on the animal's lead line drew Quillon's attention. A tattoo of a strange, fantastic creature, part bird, part serpent, circled the wrist and ran onto the hand. That, with a small gold band piercing her brow and the hoops in her ears, made her foreignness apparent. The tattoo seemed to make up for her bland attire lacking any decoration.

The horse was also unusual. Sunderlune breeders seldom let their horses go at a price a common soldier could afford. The animal's possession might cause covetous trouble among the rest of the troop.

Quillon watched her check the horse's coolness. Satisfied, she led him to the barn where she groomed him. Finished, she put the horse in his stall and fed him his measure of grain and two armfuls of hay to see him through the night. As she filled his water bucket, Quillon approached behind her. Kissre instinctively moved to sight the intruder without spilling the bucket's contents as she hung it in the stall.

"He is a fine animal," Quillon said as he drew near. Kissre surveyed him, caution and assessment clear in her eyes. She disclosed no bias at his Kennetsure coloring. Her gaze fell to the badge of the Zekarac Order on his otherwise ordinary gray clothing. Suspicious of her, he sensed her own wariness of him, even though she outwardly stated gratitude for her hiring. Female mercenaries were rare in Kaereya. If Quillon had been from anywhere but Kennetsure, she would not have been hired at all. He approached her horse, Bother, with caution, but when the animal stretched his head out and mouthed his jacket with friendly intent, Quillon ran a gentle hand over the front of Bother's long face and down his neck. "He is very young."

"He is three."

"They say these giants don't live long."

"Most battle-trained horses die young."

"A rare treasure for a mercenary."

She reluctantly responded to his inquisitive expression. "Bother was less because of his small size and off-color."

"I watched him today. He goes well. Who else helped in his training?"

"Only me."

His curiosity satisfied, he said, "Aristo Aurelias leaves for the north tomorrow. You will accompany us. As you do not reside with the rest of the riders, I'm telling you to be ready."

His tone was purposely flat and commanding. He had given her private quarters, which segregated her from the rest of the troop in more ways than one.

"What time?"

"Predawn, sixth-mark. We gather in the front courtyard. Prepare for several sennights of travel."

"Yes sir."

"You address me as Quillon, not sir." His eyes left his inspection of Bother and glanced at her. "We ride into a superstitious province. Duke Aurelias asks that you wear gloves to cover the tattoo."

Kissre nodded, showing no offense. Quillon gave a short nod back and with a last gentle swipe at Bother's neck, turned and left. He felt Kissre's attention until he disappeared. Walking away, he heard the stall door close. Before he reached his own quarters, he heard the barn door close and footsteps moving in another direction.

~ * ~

Groomsmen held lanterns when the duke descended the steps to the entrance court. Everything was in order. Unlike many aristos, Aurelias seldom traveled by carriage, preferring to pack light and ride hard. They left with the clatter of hooves echoing on the courtyard paving stones.

Quillon answered his aristo's request for haste, pressing the mounts and riders. Dusk was streaking the darkened sky with pink and gold when they reached the Rikon foothills. They camped there and rose before daybreak and made good time, passing the Cascade Falls by afternoon. Their breaks were brief, more suited to the mounts' recovery than the riders' relief.

Within another half day's ride, they were at the Cascade River ferry. On the other side of the river lay the pine-covered shore of Vere, rising like a green tapestry to the province's high plateau. It already felt and smelled different from the seaside flavor of Lambere. Many travelers waited for the crossing, and Aurelias indicated to Quillon that they should wait their turn. He nodded, knowing the break would give the tired horses benefit of an extended stop, even though at this time of year, dusk approached quicker.

Three ferry crossings later, they led their horses onto the large raft. Kissre led her buckskin past Quillon. As always, he heard her speaking low, indistinguishable foreign words to the well-built stallion. The horse placidly followed his mistress. The animal's good temper was a wonder and helped steady the other horses.

As the other riders filed past, Quillon kept an eye on Kissre. She knew of his regard but ignored it. He knew he would not feel such suspicion of a Kennetsurean woman soldier. There, women were regarded differently. Here in the north, though, women did not work in this capacity. This woman was not Kennetsurean or even a Kaereyan, but from Sunderlune, and was certainly of Cygnese stock. No one trusted the Cygnese, but he decided it was the horse that roused his suspicion more than anything. It was too far beyond the means of most mercenaries.

Kissre played down her femininity, and so far, had caused no trouble between the men, but Quillon discerned what she concealed. Her riding cap covered her hair, but the escaping sun-gilded strands were of honey and harvest-oats colors. Most travelers and local inhabitants inspecting the small troop of riders probably thought a comely young man rode with the troop.

He wondered at the duke's hiring, and then looked at horse and rider again. The stallion would be a good stud animal, a fact Quillon was sure Raymond Aurelias, the practical farmer beneath the title, had noticed. He wondered if his employer knew his hired mercenary a trainer too, and then did not doubt it. Aurelias interviewed every applicant before their hire, and never wasted opportunity.

As the last man boarded, Quillon followed. Each rider stood by his horse's head while the tired animals' signaled unease with the motion of the raft. Last on, he led his own animal and watched the gate side of the raft's fencing lining close. A discernable gliding motion pulled the ferry as it smoothly slid away from the shore.

Midway across the ferry jerked with a vibration felt underfoot. The horses threw up their heads, backed, and sidestepped, their snorts of fear filling the pine and damp smelling dusk air. Their riders worked to control their mounts serving slaps and rough profanities.

Looking at the far shore Quillon saw the shadow of a man strike a second time at the corded ropes guiding the ferry's progress across the current, making the flat barge tremble. Someone shouted, and heads turned. "On the far shore, they cut the cable!" Even then, a third strike hit the guide rope.

"Start unloading now, swim with your horses," Quillon yelled above the sudden tumult. It would be a dangerous swim in the fading light but less dangerous than staying on the ferry. The animals grew agitated, milling, snorting, and tossing their heads filled with white-lined eyes. Kicking at the side rails Quillon found them stoutly placed. "Mount up and ride them off," he yelled moving forward, dodging spooked horse hooves to remove the bar barricades. By the time he reached the raft's rails the first riders were already mounted. They spurred their frightened but reluctant mounts into the slow-moving water.

Another lurch proved the rope severed, and the ferry started floating down-river. Quillon urged the mounted horses off with slaps and shouts, working his way to where the duke helped riders with their unwilling animals.

"Mount now!" he demanded of Aurelias, throwing his body's weight onto the bridal of his employer's horse. Already the ferry accelerated with the stronger mid-river current. The duke threw him an angry and defiant look. "Now!" Quillon repeated. "I will help the rest off." At his shout, the duke jumped into the saddle. "Stay on his neck in the water and let him find his own way to shore!"

"I know what to do! Make sure you make it off, too!"

Quillon released the horse's head, already feeling the duke's strong contact with the reins. Spurred, the animal took two short hops and leaped into the water, sinking completely before the mount and riders' heads rose in the water. The animal made its way toward the far shore. Kissre's mount followed with a short leap. Water splashed back and over the raft.

"Hang onto their manes," Quillon yelled at the men still trying to mount skittish horses and slapped the horses forward and off the edge of the ferry. His own mount had already abandoned the now careening ferry. Quillon grabbed but missed the last horse. Its hind leg caught him, hurling him into turbulent water. He purposely dove deeper to prevent rising into hoof-flayed water before he kicked his legs toward the surface.

The strong current carried him downriver before he managed to make the shore, and it took a candlemark to walk back up the dark river's edge. He limped, his leg aching from the impact with a hoof. Aristo Aurelias and the troop waited, drying themselves around campfires.

"Are we missing anyone?" Quillon asked walking into the hastily made camp.

"One rider, who panicked, and two horses. I'm sending a man back with the body. We will camp here tonight. It will give us time to dry out," Aurelias answered. "I'm very glad to see you. I was about to send men down the river to look for you."

"You saw?"

"Yes. A trap. They garroted the man working this side of the ferry. The ferryman knew nothing." He nodded across the river. "They are rowing new lines across the river now. I have placed men with lanterns to guide them. We can question them when they arrive, but I doubt they know anything. It is obvious this attack was planned against me in particular. Did you recognize the man with the ax?"

"No. It was too dark. You received a message. Did its contents decide you on this hasty trip? Is there someone you suspect?"

"Yes, the message started this trip, and I won't delay it further. I would not suspect its author, but someone might have known the contents. They may have wanted me dead, as many do. There are suspects enough."

"The messenger?"

"Possible. We cannot discount the riders we sent ahead, either. There are others."

"You do not mention Kissre."

"After my most recent tragedy, suspicion has plagued me about my safety. I hired Kissre for her skill and added protection and doubt she had anything to do with this. Kissre values her horse too much to risk him in such a fashion. He took several hard kicks on the ferry."

"He took no serious harm and remained steady as a rock."

Aurelias smiled. "It's seldom I feel the sin of covetousness, especially over a horse, but after this, Kissre is safe from my greed. She pulled me from the water when the current dragged me from my horse." He sighed and looked at the sky. "Even if a trap, I am determined we will continue this journey tomorrow."

"Regardless, a wise man takes every precaution."

~ * ~

"I won't be forced into anything!" Warrick screamed at his oldest brother. His fury drove him to jump from the brocade-covered chair. He stood stiff with defiance. "Not when you get all the benefit." His throat felt raw from his screaming vehemence. Even his eyes felt strained and bulging.

"You owe it to the position you hold," Frederick said, as phlegmatic as ever.

They met in the suite of rooms given to the crown's heir. Decorated by Frederick's wife, the room's effusive and effeminate style provided the court much amusement. She worked at making over the entire palace, including the throne room. The only masculine aspect remaining in this room was the carved lintel, an engorged bull surrounded by pentacles, all Easure symbols, which were an unchangeable part of the room. Even then, the warm, life-like wood finish had been painted white. Frederick, a mushy sort of man to Warrick's mind, never cared. He merely smiled at the teasing and jokes. It made Warrick sick with disgust, embarrassed for his brother.

The reasonable tones of his brother's answer to his own tumult only infuriated Warrick more. It galled him that Frederick, ten years his senior, treated his younger brother as a brainless dunce, a court ornament good for political barter whenever needed. Frederick only spoke with him about his younger brother's numerous failings, his royal duty, his responsibilities, and his obligations. Frederick's very next words confirmed Warrick in his conviction and resentment.

"With privilege comes responsibility. At the Handfasting ceremony you are expected to ask Princess Pia for the privilege of her hand in marriage." Frederick hesitated one breath. "And you will do it." His placid brown eyes fell softly on Warrick.

Warrick sneered. *Weak. When did the heir turn into such a spineless worm?* Frederick, the great scholar, the estimable negotiator, the court's second star; even his appearance offended, the puce short jack over brown court breeches made him appear jaundiced. *Puce!*

"Privilege?" Warrick spat when the look that subdued his friends failed with his brother. "To Handfast and marry a foreign bride? A Sunderlune bride at that! Not a real princess at all! Does she even speak our tongue? What kind of horse does she resemble? Don't expect it of me. I do not intend to be a powerless lapdog in this court."

"Her grandmother was your great-aunt. You have never been powerless, but you need to fulfill your inherent duties and obligations. You will receive lands when you come of age and join the Aristo Court. You've enjoyed the fruits of your birth for a long time." Frederick flicked his fingers at his vest, swiping some crumbs fallen from the breakfast cake he ate. "It's time to pay for them."

"So you say. So Norbert, that stiff-necked, poker-faced, skinny-shanked Marshal, says." Grabbing his hat, Warrick stormed to the ornate door of the office. "But I don't take orders from either of you. I will take my petition to Father first," he sneered as he fled from the room, slamming the door as he left.

A candlemark later Warrick storm-sulked out of his father's apartments, unpleasantly surprised at his father's firmness and shortness. Now he found himself due at another appointment, this one with *the* Princess Pia. He scuffed his boots through the snow dusting the palace grounds. He wanted to cry but knew better. Someone always caught weak, embarrassing moments and spread them with vicious delight throughout the court.

His rampage from his father's presence doubtlessly made the rounds already. Who knew who watched from windows, doors, or walkways? His eyes roamed the two-and-four story buildings comprising the palace. Drapes covered most of the multi-paned windows in the ornate architecture to preserve what warmth the rooms held, but he knew prying eyes peered out. Even now, a sideways glance showed his servant Wen waiting outside the paved circle enclosing the fishpond. Warrick stamped his feet to bring them warmth. If anything, show temper. People respected temper.

He walked to the edge of the pool. Its waters still unsheathed by ice from the cold spell. The large fish moved with lethargic undulations, not even coming to the top for possible food. Warrick looked into the dark depths and saw his own future with dread. Everyone seemed to own a part of him. His father had his sworn allegiance, Norbert dictated his behavior, Frederick controlled his livelihood, his masters his mind and his time, and this princess his body. No one paid much attention to what he wanted. He was damned if he would let them have their way, not yet.

He stared at the sleeve braid decorating his jack. Two, his personal number, entwined itself in endless replication to form a bold pattern that concealed the number. That was the answer: to hide himself. The resolution and commitment of his number spurred him. Slowly a plan evolved. He smiled to himself. Every other fellow in the country had the right to choose when to handfast, and so, by the Holy One, would he! His blood craved challenge, freedom, and adventure, if only for a little while.

A short search turned up his cousins Tate and Emory. The two redheads were always up for any sport and agreed in short order. With energetic verve, they delved in, helping to finish the plan's details.

"They'll be watching me, so I'll meet you in town. At the Blue Aristo." He named their least favorite tavern, located at river level near the Rock Coast Bridge, a place serving a far more sedate fare than his usual taste. "That's the last place they will search for me."

Five

Cold infiltrated the austere interior of Queen's Library at Queen's University. After long candlemarks there, Ottillie considered the building more wind riven than Seer Mountain Pass, a site notorious for its violent breeze. Determined in her surroundings and mission and unrepentant of her resolve, she muttered a few words recently learned from her father's new under-groom after her horse not only bit the lad but also stepped on his foot. *Perhaps the gentle clerics held a desire to keep more earthbound types at bay,* she mused as the drafts cut through any normal mortal's clothing with absurd ease. Carefully she adjusted the folds of her floor-length brocade surgown for the uncounted time.

Looking between the stacks of books on her table, she found one cleric still watched her with benign aversion. With measured movements, she pulled the cuffs of her foresleeves down over her hands, covering her cold, stiff fingers. It helped little, other than to look pretty.

She admired her clothing with pleasure. The backsides of her cuffs were quilted in an apple green silk that matched the embroidered silk leaves adorning the gold stems that swirled up the sleeves. Pearls formed petals around topaz-centered flowers in a precise geometric pattern. Gold ribbons tied the sleeves to her brown velvet surgown while puffs of a fine linen chemise showed through the ties. The edge of the gown also hung heavy with gemstones, pearls, and peridot, and on this cloth, orange and amber silk embroidery embellished the whole. All in all, she knew, with the peridot winking from the fillet encasing her red hair, she presented an extraordinary visage in the somber, book-lined gallery. If they insisted that she wear what they considered proper 'women's wear' to enter their sanctified grounds, then she would dress to scream 'aristo woman' back.

Obviously, the misogynistic clerics had missed their mark. A bastard, true enough, but rich, and someone able to face down the haughtiest aristo in court. These clerics offered little challenge, especially at an institution where money spoke, if not more clearly than the Holy One's word, certainly louder.

She held a history of Kennetsure in her hands, but the book contained little about Aegis. Once expelled from court, history ignored them. Land records might trace ownership, except the family of the Vere Aegis was entangled within clan territory, making them unidentifiable. The families of the Wessure Aegis and Easure Aegis' were gone, dead and forgotten, and their lands reclaimed by the crown. Those on the western ocean coast in Wessure remained in crown hands. In Easure, Ottillie learned, Aristo Yonger had claimed the land by legacy. His claim, based on one of his distaff relatives from the Guthase family, went uncontested, and he had claimed the land from the crown.

Which left the Kennetsurean Aegis. Ottillie sighed to quell a thrill of anticipation that tickled just beneath her heart. *Egan.* One would think a supposed living talisman easier to track down as either fact or fiction.

She turned her focus to her father's problem. His men, the Kennetsurean brothers Corbin and Galen Napier, had unearthed no further clues behind the troublesome murders. Questioning guards and prisoners took time. No one remembered seeing anyone spend many candlemarks in the library other than herself, who nearly dwelled here. Neither of the Kennetsurean men knew anything about the existence of the Kennetsurean Aegis, which caused Ottillie some doubt of their intelligence or integrity.

Egan, like a litany, ran through her mind, disrupting concentration. The answers might be there. True, the aegis powers might be myth, but the library at Egan was reputed the greatest in all of Kaereya, perhaps the best in all the remaining world. Ottillie wanted to know all the past, even the forbidden secret history predating the Cataclysmic Centuries. She wanted to learn the truth of the Protector.

Rising to roam the stacks once more, she smiled at the cleric. Finally, she found books of interest and returned to her seat to read well into the afternoon. When no lamp was offered as daylight faded, she rose and picked up the books.

"No books allowed out of the library," the cleric said as she passed his desk.

"I am on the king's business."

"You have papers for this business?"

"Do you ask all the courtiers for the king's papers?"

"I am asking you."

"Send to the bishop. He will give approval."

"The bishop is conducting high service and cannot be disturbed. You must leave the books here until he can be reached."

How convenient. "I will return tomorrow," Ottillie said in the genteel voice her governess had ground into her comportment with the delicacy of a millstone. "Please hold the books until I return." She smiled a brittle non-smile and nodded with no response from the cleric. Once she placed the books on the desk, the cleric returned to his studies, ignoring her as she walked away.

She strolled in sedate steps from the library and headed toward her own apartment one floor below her father's rooms, a quarter candlemark away. Halfway there, Theodulf Gilchrist, Duke of Hearthron, stopped her.

Tall, black-haired, handsome, and exquisite, Aristo Gilchrist, as King Frederick's brother-in-law, exerted a powerful influence within the court. His courtier toads and hired men trailed him.

He demanded the fullest respect, for even with the death of his royal wife, his two sons, blood princes Emory and Tate, ensured his position at court, and the royal family held him in high regard. His expression mocked his gracious greeting, as did the smirks on his men's faces.

Ottillie assumed her ingrained poise and gave the curtsey Gilchrist's position demanded. His lazy eyes sharpened as she raised her head. He took her hand and raised it to his lips as he pulled her from her sunken position. "You appear, as always, brilliantly attractive, Ottillie." One of his retainers coughed to cover his snigger. With disciplined aplomb, Ottillie ignored it. The duke lowered her hand but kept it in his grasp, his thumb running over her smooth skin. It finally rested over the darker circle of skin as if to hide the blemish.

"Thank you, Duke Hearthron. Your well-known discernment in matters of beauty and fashion does me credit."

"Not at all. Perhaps if all... daughters... at court were as attractive, the court would be a far more elegant place."

Ottillie missed no nuance, but gave him her best simpering smile, and thanked him.

"Will I see you at the Handfasting Festival?" he asked.

Keeping her thoughts tightly guarded, Ottillie answered. "No, I'm beyond that now. Hopefully, I will be traveling."

"Traveling? This close to winter? The Earl of Rikon has given his permission?"

"Not yet, but he will. It's not bad if you head south."

"And where will your southern travels take you?"

"To the Zankiri coast. I am tired of the drafts in the Queen's Library and wish to spend the winter reading in warmth."

"Zankiri?" Gilchrist laughed. "Ottillie! You needn't go so far to stay warm. If you were in my care, you wouldn't spend so much time among the books and dust. There is more to life, you know."

Ottillie gave a silvery laugh. "I know that as well, Duke Hearthron." She gave him a sly look. "But I must confess I find myself lucky to remain in my father's care. I am thus assured of everything I want." With a subtle tug, she pulled her hand free.

"What, no desire to be a wife? That sounds premeditated, Ottillie, and I congratulate you on your machinations if they bring you all you desire. Just remember there is surely one other man who wishes to give you everything a woman could desire."

"The trick is finding him," Ottillie laughed. "I must not keep you any longer Duke Hearthron." She sank into another deep curtsy. "You are dressed for riding, and I would not wish to keep you from your horses. I know how you men are about such matters." She stepped back, allowing the duke and his retinue to pass. She kept the smile pasted on her face as she watched them walk down the hall. Turning, she made her way back to her room, all emotion firmly bridled.

~ * ~

The Duke of Hearthron stopped and turned to watch Aristo Rikon's daughter depart. Her gown swayed with her elegant movements. One of his companions made a humorous, foul remark about the lady. Others laughed.

"You are all very short-sighted," he said with a smile. "Lady Ottillie is the only child of the land rich, powerful, and wealthy Earl of Rikon, a prize that overcomes the few flaws his daughter possesses."

"If you can put up with the mouth."

"You don't let your dog bite you, do you?"

"Do you have plans for the lady?"

"I always have plans." Hearthron's smile deepened. Only he knew how much he planned.

~ * ~

Once in her room, with the door safely locked, Ottillie reached into the very deep side pockets of her gown and retrieved two books—rare manuscripts from the most restricted shelves of the library, two volumes of the witch Chloe's diaries. She knew her irrepressible smile unholy and felt the sullied feeling lingering from her return trip give way to her earlier elation.

Lighting a lamp, she opened the cover of one book. Her fingers lightly touched the inked words on the page.

*The Journal of the twenty-seventh year of my
life, Chloe, Sorceress from Kennetsure in service
to Monsignor Otto at Bishop's Infirmary through
the grace of His Royal Majesty, King Ewald III.*

The witch Chloe, creator of the Aegis Spell had written the hand-bound velum pages over five hundred years ago. She wondered if the witch had put a preservation spell on the books and laughed at her fantasy.

She read the first volume of the memoir through the night, reaching only a quarter way through the book's difficult to read passages. The account contained more than one year, each year change clearly designated on its own page with pen embellishments. Mostly it covered Chloe's training and service to her order and the Holy One in the infirmary, news of the court, and the progress of the war. The pages were brittle, the ink faded in places, and the hand was antique in spelling and style. One entry remained with her.

*I see the people who try to avoid me. I wonder
if only because of my magic? They don't see it
as a gift, and I often feel its weight like a curse.
I've heard the Cygnese have had many witches
born since the great changes of the Cataclysmic
Century, far more than here in Kaereya or any of
our other neighbors. Is that why people fear the
Cygnese? Reputedly, there are great numbers of
sorcerers in the far southern reaches of the Doane
Desert, too, but few travel there. They fear me,
too. It is an unhappy thought.*

What surprised Ottillie was how little society had changed. Aristos still aristoed it over Cliff City and the Eternal Palace with misplaced disdain and condescension. People still farmed, crafted, or worked in the same manner. The effects, she supposed, of the threat of the Protector.

That ancient tale told of a hidden, worldwide guard. The Protector supposedly had ordered universal prohibitions on certain types of weaponry, learning, industry, and land management. She sighed. Was this another myth from the Cataclysmic Century? She became lost in thought about the vagaries of life and society before falling into sleep.

As sunlight slowly drifted through her bedroom window, she rose and threw open the casement, leaning out over the wall. The chilled air braced her tired mind as she closed her eyes to the stiff breeze. Mist lightly clung to her skin in a refreshing salute. Opening her eyes, she looked about her. Fog cascaded down the island's cliff sides. Her tower window lay above the clouds lining the river. It allowed her to see the dawn-brightened sky, sparkling in crispness and clarity.

Ottillie looked to the south where only a writhing blanket of gray embalmed the horizon. Unseen, in that direction, lay the Doane Desert, that most exotic of lands where past and present melded, a land of mystery and magic. Somehow, she must convince her father the survival of Kaereya laid there. She needed to visit Egan. Already, she heard her father's arguments against such an undertaking and prepared her answers.

~ * ~

Entering the apartments given to Princess Pia with an entourage of courtier witnesses, Warrick assumed a nonchalant and dispassionate smirk. Wen, doling advice and platitudes with his service, had dressed him in an icy-blue short jack heavily adorned with jets and black embroidery and a matching silk vest. Knee trews with tall black boots finished his fashion. The valet told him the blue reflected his eye color, and the black contrasted with his dramatic blond coloring. Better yet, the black and blue matched his bruised mood.

Pia's maids greeted him and bid him enter the apartment's formal salon. Pia, a fuddy-looking girl, sat ensconced there. Her chalk skin, the frostiest of blonde hair, and eyes like the sun-bleached blue sails on the Thou River's older ships, disappeared into the pastel grandeur of the surrounding apartment, except for her clothes. An unfortunate surgown of orange and fuchsia brocade with old-fashioned slits displaying wisps of a turquoise chemise through the openings. It jarred the senses and turned her skin cadaverous.

One of her maids, a tolerably attractive girl, introduced him. Warrick swept into a flamboyant bow, flourishing his plumed hat. Picking up Pia's limp hand, he skimmed a kiss over the cool, ashen skin. He admired her only asset, a huge oval sapphire on the long, twig-like fingers. He placed his hat under his arm. Her mouth remained closed in a prim, straight line, but her empty, bland eyes flicked to him twice.

"My belated greetings, Princess Pia."

Her heavily accented voice was gauche and accusing. "I have waited long for this pleasure, Prince Warrick."

The reproving tones amused him. "My apologies, Princess. Duty detained me," he said, clicking his heels and performing a demi-bow.

The girl fell into sullen silence. The courtiers, his assigned watchdog underlings, took up a chorus, flattering the Princess in gushing accolades. Warrick did not even attempt to hide his amusement and added not one word of his own.

The visit lasted half a candlemark, his eyes marking the candle's progress in careless intervals. Before leaving, Warrick gave a naughty smile to the attractive maid. She blushed. The door closed. It was over. Warrick contained his sigh and hid his delighted relief under a cloak of arrogant disgust. While he brushed the suffering of the encounter from his sleeve like a speck of dust, his mind raced with other details.

~ * ~

"You will do as Eldin requires for your safety. I am not at all satisfied that you should take this journey. A misguided attempt to escape Handfasting, I am sure. If I promise not to make you stand, will you stay?" Norbert ordered and petitioned.

Ottillie recognized her father's mock sternness and his resignation. Only dim torchlight accentuated his face in the predawn, but she could see his concern for her in the taut lines around his mouth and shadowed eyes. Thus, he insisted on Eldin and his guards for her journey. Parents who cared for their children never gave over treating them like six-year-olds, no matter their age. Her father also knew how important this journey might be for the kingdom's sake, and how thrilled she was at its prospect. All she had talked about for the last few days was Tower Egan and the chance to talk with the last of Kennetsure's ancient aegis's family if he existed. That, and to travel to the southern deserts of Doane!

"You worry overmuch about me, Father. You might not have noticed, but I am much grown since childhood." She glanced at her escort. "Eldin nearly quakes before the daunting giantess he is appointed to guide."

A snort erupted from Eldin. Out of his accustomed uniform, he appeared a small man, slight of build, attractive, even a touch effeminate. Ottillie knew his ordinary traveler's dress hid a whipcord tough body and a fighter's soul. As a childhood friend, Eldin was unimpressed by Ottillie's rude humor. "If the aggravating giantess doesn't start soon," he said, "we shall not never leave."

Her father gave a soft chuckle at the Guard Captain's dry tones.

"There you have it, Father, it is time to leave. Say goodbye."

"Goodbye, Daughter. May your journey be safe, your arrival welcomed, and let the Holy One speed you home again."

With the last tightening of her clasp, she released her father's hand and took up the reins. She smiled over her shoulder, swaying with movement as her horse walked away. There were five of them leaving, and the horses' hooves rang hollow on the pavement. Her animal was a nice rangy bay with an easy gait and no flashy markings. It was hoped the numbers of the small company deflected harm, and the ordinary dress would escape attention. Each man, though out of uniform, was a Royal Guardsman. Ottillie loved her own Kennetsure style dress so different from court fashion.

Another glance at her father's cheerless expression nearly brought her back, but the tunnel through the south-facing Sphinx Tower cut him from view. He had been upset about the disguises, wanting instead to send her with a whole troop of suitably uniformed guardsmen, but her response "Why not announce the nature of my visit to the whole court, Father? Maybe that would draw out your conspirators," won the argument. The last thing her father wanted was his daughter becoming a target for a murdering pack of malcontents. Guilt at his distress assailed her.

She turned forward and nodded to the Royal Guards standing at the ornate iron-gated entrance. The men exchanged a few words with typical masculine banter with Eldin. Beyond them spread a garden shrouded in the morning mist so common at this time of year. The trees and shrubs lay bared to skeletal forms. The slope of the land fell toward the cliff's edge under the cover of a pristine fog blanket broken by large jutting rocks. Nearby, frostbitten plants created brown lace along the road's edge.

They followed the cobbled road, a track really, barely wide enough for two to ride abreast, turning back on itself repeatedly in order to reach High Bridge, the crossing off Hawk Island. It was a dismal start to the day, promising rain or worse.

"Would you explain where we are going again?" Eldin asked, adjusting his cloak.

"The Doane Desert," Ottillie said in a bland, provocative tone.

He made an exasperated sound. "That I know. I'm asking for details."

"To Egan." She sucked her inside cheeks to stop a smile.

"Ottillie! Beware. I am not overly joyed to make this trip as it is. It seems to me the books here are just as fine as those in Egan, if not, try those on Monastery Island."

"Not according to reputation." Ottillie's smile faded, thinking of her conversation with her father. They had agreed that no mention would be made of her real purpose: to visit the only person who might be a descendant of an aegis. In truth, her errand seemed a goose chase, but her arguments had been most persuasive, and her desire to travel was only part of it.

Aldous, the last known person to hold aegis blood, lived at Egan, the Aegis's keep. He might know why someone was so afraid of magic they were willing to kill. Heraldist Godfrey thought him perhaps the Kennetsure Aegis, but remained unsure, later admitting the old man might even be dead. He added Aldous had lived with an old, self-proclaimed witch named Leela. Ottillie had scoffed at her father's information, a witch indeed.

Something told her, though, that answers waited for her there. Since starting to read Chloe's journal, the urge to travel had become overwhelming. She convinced her father there was a good chance these two might know some lore that would shed light on all of the murderous incidents occurring in Kaereya. Maybe somewhere, in the yet unread sections of Chloe's diary, the author would write of her magic and of the aegises, but Ottillie doubted it. Curiosity drove her.

She looked at Eldin, an ambitious but good man. One who shared her predicament of bastardy. In the ever-changing political alliances of court, it was a common enough predicament. Any child of a terminated handfast could be labeled a bastard. After her father supported the king in a matter her mother's family deemed financially important, her mother withdrew from the handfasting. Finding his daughter pregnant, Ottillie's grandfather declared his grandchild a bastard. Norbert's ties to the king guaranteed him custody when her mother died.

Eldin was a childhood friend, but she had not seen him in at least six years. His career took him to a different social sphere. Unlike her, neither Eldin's father nor his mother acknowledged him. Norbert had helped him enter the Royal Guards. His own effort, not influence, had earned the captain's rank he held. In the past, she would have trusted him with any knowledge, but this long journey seemed silly for such an exalted escort. Especially when she could not give him an answer he would accept. Already she could hear his laughter and derision, *'Magic! An old man's stories. By the Holy One, Ottillie.'*

"The library at Egan is unparalleled," Ottillie answered. "Everyone of knowledge agrees upon that."

Eldin made a rude noise. "I know you are a woman of vast knowledge, and I know I am a man of limited learning, but what can you read there that you can't read here? You know, most men don't like a woman who is too well educated."

Ottillie laughed. "Don't underrate your intelligence with me, Eldin, I know better. Besides, educated or not, few men want to handfast with me. Luckily, I can take care of myself. Does that 'most' include you?"

Eldin shrugged. "Education in others never bothers me. It is not something to which I aspire. At least an educated woman may have something to talk about, even if I must endure a foolish journey to the end of the world. It would have been faster taking a boat."

"You sound misogynistic, bad dealings at your local haunts? Maybe you should raise your sights somewhat. Look for companionship from other than prostitutes." She glanced at Eldin who merely shrugged. When his face suffused with a suspicious darkness, she snorted a laugh at her accurate insight.

"What? An aristo?" He huffed a sound of disparagement. "I'd find more enjoyment coupling with one of the lake gulls. At least I know what to expect when they fly over."

"I said other than prostitutes. There are other women. As to traveling, you know I do not like going over water. Besides, the journey is the whole point! It is an adventure, Eldin! It is being away from the boredom of court and its stifling etiquette. It is seeing something you've never seen before."

"You're still afraid of water!" Eldin spoke the puzzle his mind must have been working on.

"My mother died at sea, and I nearly drowned."

"I'm sorry; I had forgotten you were with her." His warm brown eyes looked genuinely contrite.

"Your apology is accepted," Ottillie said with a smile to hide the tinge of pain the past always brought.

A light, misting rain started, and they fell into silence as they followed the seemingly endless turns in the road. The sound of the horses and shifting gear echoed off the walls that sometimes rose over their heads where the road cut through bedrock. Eventually they came to High Bridge. After an exchange of salutes, the men in her party all nodded to the guards at the bridge that led to the garrison home of the Royal Guards. Even with as far as they had descended, the bridge to the other island crossed at a high level from the river.

Guards Island loomed on the other side, a rounded outcropping of rock dressed in a seasonal garb of brown and yellow. White barracks and barns marched across the terrain between sawdust-covered training yards and paddocks. Everywhere blue-uniformed Guards moved over the ground. Ottillie knew even at this early candlemark the guardsmen worked at grooming horses, cleaning tack and gear, training and exercising horses, or training and drilling themselves.

"I wanted to join the Guards when I was little," Ottillie said to distract herself from the thought of crossing the appalling bridge. She suspected if a horse reared it could easily go over the low balustrade running along the bridge sides. She gathered her reins. Instead of signaling her mount to cross with her legs, she accidentally jerked his mouth. He pulled his chin back, then up as he got behind the bit, shaking his head. Ottillie saw white surround her horse's eyes, indicating his fear. She released her tight grasp on the reins, and her horse calmed, stretching his neck forward and down. Feeling him take the bit, she gently reassured him and resumed her self-control.

"Don't sound so wistful," Eldin said, taking the lead. Her horse fell in behind his with no urging. Halfway across the bridge, he looked over his shoulder and continued. "It's not as romantic as it looks. It is hard work, little pay, and just when you think you're done, an officer comes along with more orders."

Ottillie did not look down and tried to pretend the sway was due entirely to her mount's movement. "You seem to have prospered." A sigh of relief escaped her as her bay found firm footing on Guards Island. As the sun burned off the fog, the light rain stopped.

"I have, but I'm not sorry to be ordered on this journey, even if it means discomfort. It is almost like leave. All you felt was your love of horses. Just remember all those long-nosed nags have to be taken over to the low shores of Hawk Island for pasture."

Ottillie laughed, and Eldin gave her a wry smile, saying nothing about her poor horsemanship crossing the bridge.

Soon they passed the last row of barracks, leaving behind most of the activity. From the road, Ottillie picked out the infirmary and the few stores. A small town of officer's quarters, family homes, and the Commander's estate held the last bit of high ground. After that, the road started another descending serpentine path that took all from her view but the islands and water below them.

From here, she could see the jumble of crowded low islands, often separated by no more than a few feet, comprising the land journey through the Thou River to the plains of Wessure.

From her view, Ottillie followed the path of the Great River Road as if it were on a paper map rather than seen from beyond the cliff's edge. The main road from Hawk Island passed over another much lower bridge and threaded through the dense city on the island Alaric. It was a large island but at a far lower elevation. the road then headed west until becoming lost in the distant haze. She knew the Low Bridge off Guards Island to Alaric was just as low, thankfully, as the River Road Bridge from Hawk Island to Alaric. The track they descended would join the River Road traveling west to Wessure before turning south to the entrance to Kennetsure at Gotte City. This path saved them the scrutiny of travel through Cliff City and the court's curious eyes at the Eternal Palace.

The water surrounding Alaric Island sparkled in the sun, and the white tips of waves washed the shallow shores. Alaric looked pretty, still green with late autumn grass and the hardiest of plants showing a last profusion of bloom. She picked out Aristo Whiffern's palatial seat, its pink stone gilded in the morning light. As they descended, she saw below them the stone bridge speckled with the blue of Guards' uniforms.

They stopped to rest the horses and eat by the roadside. "How long before we get there?"

"A couple candlemarks."

"I think we should stop..." Both Ottillie and Eldin spoke at the same time, saying the same thing.

"Alaric Island is the last truly inhabitable city for many days of this journey," Eldin said. "Nearly all the low islands have tiny hamlets on the outer shores."

"Boat homes? I've not seen them before. We always travel north on Rock Road going home to Rikon."

"They are a necessity because they rise and fall with flood waters—"

"What about on the road?"

"—But there are few amenities on the road threading through the islands." His eyes glanced her way with her interruption. "We have already traveled far enough, and at this time of year, it won't be long before dusk sets in. The inns here will be the last hospitable place for quite some time."

"I've only traveled to Alaric from the shore route crossing at River Road Bridge." Ottillie pointed to the bridge below them crossing the river. "It takes a full day to thread through Cliff City and down the cliff cuts to follow the shore road to the bridge."

"Your father insisted we travel this way as it is safer." He was looking into the mouth of his canteen.

"It is a far less conspicuous way to leave the Palace."

His glance slid sideways to her. "Yes, safer too, even with crossing High Bridge."

"You are cruel to mention it." Ottillie laughed and blushed at his teasing and ignored the implicit question in his expression. "In a general way I am not afraid of heights, but that bridge always unnerves me."

"You did very well for someone who doesn't have to cross it every day."

"Ah, I see, daily experience is what I need. I knew I should have become a Guardsman."

~ * ~

"Is Wen going with us?" Tate asked as he slipped into the booth at the Blue Aristo. "That is a good costume! I hardly recognized you!"

Tate was dressed as a common groom. Warrick had chosen to dress as a traveling merchant. His dark-brown clothes were stolen from rooms at an inn many streets away. He had changed in a back alley after eluding the men assigned to keep track of him. It had been so easy. After escorting a tart upstairs for the evening, he had bound her as part of the play, locked the door, and left through the window. With any luck, they wouldn't miss him for a candlemark or more.

He took little with him, a few small gold and jeweled items for expenses. He thought of the plain casket in his saddlebag, found when he had explored the demolition done in the throne room.

He had watched the masons' work with interest, interested despite himself at his sister-in-law's changes. Building fascinated him, and tales claimed the palace riddled with secret passages. Each day when the workers left, he explored their efforts.

On the day they started taking apart the throne, he was especially interested. If there were anywhere to hide treasures or talismans, it was in the ancient throne. When they left, he searched the throne, digging through the rubble. The box he found did not look like anything important, filled with dust-dry dirt. Since what he found wasn't treasure as far as he could determine, he knew it must be a talisman.

He brought it along because he could not afford to have anyone find it in his rooms if someone searched them, and he hesitated to leave it unprotected. It might hold some ancient importance forgotten in modern times. It was best to keep it with him, keep it from unscrupulous hands. Besides, it already had brought him good luck—his escape.

"No. I am not sure I can trust Wen. You are well disguised, too," he said, inspecting the worn, laborer's clothing Tate wore. Where's Emory?"

"He thought it would look better if he stayed with the horses. He dressed like a servant also. Too bad about Wen, he is a handy fellow and knows all kinds of helpful things."

"Not if his help is informing my father or brother what I am about!" Warrick snapped.

"You think he would?" Tate asked wide-eyed.

Warrick looked at the younger of his cousins. Only fifteen and easygoing by nature, Tate possessed an open, innocent look that trusted everyone. Everything proclaimed him an easy mark. Warrick had a brief bout of uneasiness at his choice of companions and an even longer moment of shame at his planned escape from duty. "Yes, I think he would. Luckily, I'm saving him the trouble, for a day hence I will not be at the Handfasting, and he won't know where I am."

"Is that wise?" Tate asked. His eyes betrayed his nervousness.

More doubt filled Warrick as he finished off his ale. Tate was not nearly as game as Emory. It was too late, though, Tate must go with them, or Warrick chanced Tate spilling his guts to Frederick, or worse, Norbert. They needed to get off Hawk Island before anyone discovered their game. Eager to try, he grinned at Tate and led the way out of the tavern.

All went as predicted until they reached the North Bridge. Thick mist enveloped the river, rising in the cool night's air. All sound seemed unnaturally loud. Shouts and river noise rose from below, and the thunk of hooves echoed on the cobbled streets behind them. A torch burned near the guard's hut, its flame outlined by a hazy ring in the surrounding fog.

"Halt!"

At the guard's shouted warning, Warrick looked up from the shadow cast by his cowl. It was clear the command was meant for them. A guardsman held a lantern up as he stepped into the middle of the bridge, the flaps of his cape falling back from his arm. Warrick felt Tate's anxiety as his horse snorted and sidestepped. His own urgency spiraled.

"What is it?" he asked. "Why do you stop us? We have done nothing."

"You need to go back. It is too dangerous to cross tonight. Ice covers the bridge, and it is so fog-bound you can't see. We're telling everyone to spend the night in the city and cross tomorrow morning."

"I can see the lanterns along the bridge way."

"Yes, but once on the crossing, it is easy to lose the way. Don't want to end in the river tonight, do you?"

"We must be in Tatzk tomorrow before evening's fall. I've orders to fill."

"You're starting rather late tonight." His voice sounded faintly suspicious, and he swung the lantern to get a better look at their faces.

Warrick shifted uneasily in his saddle. "Unavoidable. Delayed by a tailor who haggled too long over cloth. My father has sold all his stock and needs more bolts from our weavers for a special order."

A grunt erupted from the man. "Aristo?"

Warrick shrugged his shoulders. "Yes. You must understand. We cannot fail to fulfill this order."

Behind him the noises of discord sounded, shouting voices, and running feet. Warrick heard Emory's soft exclamations of dismay.

"Mite young for traders, aren't you?"

"Our father fell ill, and we travel in his place."

"He might feel better if you stayed and arrived late at Tatzk."

"That might be so, but all of our livelihoods depend on this order. It is not only an aristo order but also a royal one. The cloth needed lies in Tatzk. It is not easy to find chartreuse silk shot with gold in time for First Day. That is less than three sennight from now, sir. I must be back with it in four days. We have no choice but to travel." He filled his voice with the whine and worry entering him as footsteps sounded closer.

The guard shook his head in disgust. "Then one of you must lead your horse across so the others may follow. It is unsafe else."

"Thank you, sir, for the warning and your understanding."

Warrick leaped from his saddle and quickly led his horse past the guard. The sound of the hooves on the bridge reverberated like drums telling his trackers, 'we are here'. Within a few heartbeats, darkness and fog swallowed them. Warrick walked faster, jogging, nearly running. Suddenly his feet slipped out from under him. The fall drove the breath from him, but he commanded his body to rise.

"Warrick! Are you all right?" Tate's voice carried to him, and he knew to everyone else on or near the bridge.

"Quiet!" he hissed. He heard voices questioning the guard, hesitated even as the guard answered. They had heard. Grabbing the reins, he regained his saddle. He pushed his mount to a jog and heard his cousins' horses follow even as shouts of 'halt' came from the island side of the bridge. The sound of horses following clamored on the bridge planks.

"I won't give up, not now! Come or stay as you wish." Spurring his horse forward, his mount hesitated and slid, would have shied had he not kept a tight rein. The animal slowly gathered itself into a cautious canter. Ignoring all else, Warrick guided his mount toward the lanterns lining the bridge. In the darkness between the lanterns, he murmured prayers that his horse kept its feet and that he did not lose the straight path. A lantern glinted off a bar crossing the way, and Warrick screamed.

The unexpected barricade appeared so late he doubted his horse saw it. He checked with the reins and urged with his legs, letting the animal know something lay ahead. He felt it gather itself for the leap and belatedly wondered if his mount would jump into the river. The horse's forefeet already lifted from the bridge planks.

His breathing resumed with the sound of hooves hitting the ground, not water nor plank. Loud male voices shouted, and figures rushed in his direction. Warrick laughed. He was on the Rock Road side of the North Bridge. He had crossed the bridge. He spurred his horse again, and the animal, with its footing secure, galloped down the dark road. He glanced back. Emory and Tate followed him. He shouted with relief and rode.

They laughed at the success of their strategy as they pulled their horses up four leagues down the Rock Coast Road.

"It was so easy!" Tate said his face flushed with humor, but his fright still evident.

"Hah, easy now, but you were scared enough at the guard's post," Emory said in a jeering tone of sibling bickering.

"Never mind," Warrick said unable to control his elation. "We are free!" He turned his horse and galloped westward on the Rock Coast Road, foolhardy, he knew, but exhilarating.

Six

"It'll be a frosty festival tonight," Freda said as she poured boiling water over herbs for a late afternoon tea. "It's fair cold, and this rain is like to turn to ice and slush before too long. It makes a good night for handfasting. It offers the snugglers an excuse to cuddle."

"So it is," Eudora said, lifting her eyes from the crust she prepared for dinner's dessert. "I don't expect the weather will keep many to home."

"Not like it would on any other night," Freda said going on at length about previous handfasting nights. "Fair many a virgin's last night." She sniggered. "Don't know why they call it the women's festival. Seems to me the men benefit most. Women just get bottom sore."

Eudora had failed to listen to Freda's babble. Her worried eyes kept attending Vesper's determined concentration on her dress these last candlemarks before the festival. Eudora straightened suddenly and looked over her shoulder at Freda. "Freda, enough of that vulgar talk."

Freda gave a snort. "The girl's not listening anyway. What difference it make?"

Vesper continued working with a skill and devotion that turned the dress into a new rendition of itself, oblivious to Freda. Eudora knew finding time to make her dress had been hard with all of Alvina's demands for Vesper's needle on her Handfasting dress.

"Way back when my sister handfasted," Freda said, "it was much the same as today, maybe somewhat worse. I remember icicles on the wagon coming home."

"Freda," Vesper said, jumping up. "Would you help me into the dress, a few pins remain, but I wish Eudora to pin the hem before I go any further. Would you please?"

"Sure as anything. Shiver out of that apron and work smock." She sighed, looking at Vesper standing in her shift. "Remember being as thin as you at my handfasting to my Marwyn. Ah, what a night that was!" She helped Vesper into the dress while she told the details of her story, saying as she finished, "Did I tell you Marwyn will bring the covered cart around for you to get to the festival?"

Vesper kissed Freda's wrinkled cheek. "Yes, you did." Jumping on her stool, Vesper overbalanced, and Freda needed to catch Vesper's arm before she fell.

"Be careful, child," Eudora said, wiping flour from her hands.

Vesper grinned, balanced herself, and straightened while pulling the dress into place. She turned on the stool. In the late afternoon light, the fabric fell into soft folds held in a glowing fretwork of silver ferns and flowers as the light reflected off the threads.

"Oh, child, it's a lovely dress," Freda sighed in unusual fondness. "Not much lace or beading, but an eye stopper, and you such a lovely thing with all that curly hair. Sure as anything, some man will be wanting your hand this time."

"If you're determined to settle for just any man," Dame Winnifred Kellsie said from the doorway. With a face gloating as much ferment as her voice, she walked over to Vesper and closely inspected the dress.

Eudora rose to stand next to Vesper and looked at her mistress. Dame Winifred smiled. "A charming dress. Where did you come by the fabric? You must have saved for a decade, Eudora." A brow rose in incredulity. "Surely not someone's old dress? I seem to recall… but no, it couldn't be. You've done a fine job Vesper and you look nearly as pretty as Alvina, not the accustomed mode, of course, but attractive all the same."

"Yes, Mistress, she looks fair beautiful. Does Alvina need help, Mistress?" Freda asked.

"Yes, she does, Freda, but I came to tell you the news. Brandt rode over to tell us that His Grace, the Duke of Lambere, has accepted his father's invitation to spend some time with the adjudicator's family. He attends the festival tonight. His wife recently died you know. I suppose it's never too late to start anew." She tittered. The flesh rising over the top of her stays quivered. "Heavens, I expect the age ranges of girls standing to greatly expand for a duke. Why, Freda, even you and Eudora could stand." She smiled, icy in derision.

"Not me, Mistress. My Marwyn's still living," Freda said.

"Well, yes, he is. I think Alvina could use your help now, Freda." Winifred turned as she spoke and moved to the door.

"Yes Mistress. I shall come immediately." Freda's sallow, age-lined face turned red with pent emotion. "The old besom-beast is bursting tonight, going to be a rare one, it is," she said, barely audible to Vesper and Eudora. "See if she don't explode tonight or I spit." Freda followed Winifred out of the kitchen.

"What is the matter?" Vesper asked, jumping from the stool, her skirt knocking it over with a thump in her rush to help Eudora. "You've turned so pale! Are you feeling ill? Do you wish me to get you a restorative?"

"No, no," Eudora said at last. "It's nothing. The heat. I must have stood too close to the oven." She smiled at Vesper. "You look so grown-up. So beautiful. I don't want you hurt." Tears filled the edges of her eyes and Eudora pressed her lips together to keep them from overflowing.

Vesper clasped Eudora's shaking hands as she helped her to a chair. She knelt next to the chair and looked at Eudora with concern.

"You think I'm jumping at the moon, don't you? You don't think Brandt will want me, do you?" She paused. "Perhaps not anybody. It's the gown, isn't it? It's too grand for someone of my station."

"No, that is, the gown is beautiful, and the embroidery on the chemise exquisite." Eudora forced a smile. "You've done a beautiful job on it, as good as any professional dressmaker I've known. And on Alvina's dress, too. Many men besides Brandt will want you, and not because of the dress."

Vesper's serious eyes studied her. "But not to handfast. Not for all his smiles, teasing, or his soft looks and faint touches."

Eudora's smile faded. "No, I don't think to handfast." She held Vesper's hand to her cheek and fell silent for a moment. Looking into her child's expectant face she said, "Vesper, do not go tonight. I promise you I will make it up to you. We will leave here and go to Kennetsure. You want that, don't you? I will even promise not to scold you for your visions and fantasies."

Vesper stared at Eudora for a long time before righting the stool beside her. The girl's shoulders slumped, and quick tears streaked her cheeks as she sat. "I know not to Handfast, Eudora. Not any of them. Not the one I want, not even any who might want me." Her back straightened, and she wiped her face dry. "There isn't any chance is there?" She asked. Her eyes begged Eudora to tell her otherwise. "He couldn't ask me, could he?" More tears filled Vesper's eyes. "Not with his family's expectations. Not with his father's position as adjudicator, not before a duke."

She bit her lip then smiled an astute smile. "It was a nice dream for a while, but I think I always knew it for a dream." Her hand smoothed the fabric on her knee. "I think I shall go anyway, just for the chance to wear my dress." Her hand floated over the fine fabric and with a choked smile, wet at the edges, said, "I promise you not to embarrass you with histrionics, and if Alfred shows up, I promise not to see him."

"You could not embarrass me; you are a good child. Go to the festival, as you want, and if you see Alfred, ask him to dance with you." Eudora smiled. "Always carry hope, Vesper. There is still a chance Brandt is true and not a fickle flirt. Who knows, if he asks, maybe you will do the smart thing and turn him down."

"You think turning Brandt down is smart? Don't you like him?"

"No, I do not. But we seldom like or love for another's pleasure." She patted Vesper's cheek in an old way of comfort. "Listen, my pet, whatever happens tonight, do not despair of your future. I promise you this, if you leave the festival alone, we leave for Kennetsure within a sennight. We shall enjoy a winter in the desert."

Vesper, unsure of what to say or do, hugged Eudora. As if the weather recognized their mood, the sky darkened, and an onslaught of icy rain clattered against the small window. Eudora rose to light a few lamps.

Awhile later, Freda's Marwyn arrived on schedule in the back courtyard. The Kellsie family carriage had left earlier. Eudora placed her own boiled-wool cape over Vesper's dress.

"There'll be more than one miss with wet, straggly hair tonight," Freda said as she coiled and tucked Vesper's long, dark hair into the hood. "But not your own. This cape of your aunt's may not be fancy but durable and waterproof it is."

"Oh, Marwyn," Vesper said as they stood beneath the back archway. He had stopped the cart under its protection. Her heart sank at her conveyance, then buoyed. She had no prospects anyway, so to be with old friends would help on the way home.

"Shilly and Shally look wonderful," Vesper said. Smiling, she kissed Marwyn and moved to pet the heads of his team. The old man had dressed the harness with brasses and bells, and carefully groomed and braided his carthorses' manes and tails, one a smallish gray and the other a massive piebald. As a youngster, she had played between the hooves and under the bellies of the two mismatched but utterly reliable animals. "And in this weather, too."

"You deserve better, Peeper, you do. Tonight will be the night, see if it's not." Marwyn using his pet name for her cheered Vesper in an odd way.

~ * ~

"Where is he?" King Frederick shouted his displeasure. His voice reverberated through the family chamber. Those able escaped his vicinity. "How could he disgrace his family, his country, like this?" He slammed a fist on a heavy inlaid and gilded table.

"I am sure he didn't mean to cause a disgraceful situation, Sire," Theodulf Gilchrist stated. "It is merely another of his pranks, a last adventure before settling into married life." He eased himself into a more comfortable position. This constant standing became tedious, and Gilchrist felt satisfaction at Warrick's snub of the Sunderlune princess. He could not have planned it better.

Frederick turned on his brother-in-law. "Disgrace? This is political assassination!"

The king swiveled on his heel to look at his King's Marshal. "Have you sent men to fetch him? What about his man? Does he know where the young scapegrace has gone?"

"No Sire. Warrick left without him. The man said Prince Warrick did not sleep in the palace last night. Those ordered by Prince Frederick to watch his brother failed through a stratagem of Warrick's. I have sent two of my investigators to try to track his movements, but it may take time. They believe the boy disguised himself to leave the city. If not dressed as an aristo, his presence may well go unnoticed by most of your subjects."

~ * ~

Entering the Adjudicator's Hall, Vesper was amazed at the crush of people, probably to see the Duke of Lambere and get a chance, perhaps, to talk with the great man. She smiled, *not much chance.* The room smelled of wax, perfumes, wet clothes, and dampness. The room, decorated by Norost standards, in festive ornateness, but Vesper surmised somewhat bucolic for anyone used to celebrations at the Eternal Palace.

Alvina was easy to find with her bright hair but Vesper did not approach her as Alvina held court surrounded by her young friends. Her ivory surgown was lovely, as was her golden hair, carefully curled and hanging below her waist, but the two together were not quite right. Vesper quashed her brief spurt of elation as uncharitable. Vesper's own wild, fly-away curls formed a tangle around her head and shoulders.

The maidens' dance was still some time away. Brandt appeared by her side with a sweet drink for herself and Eudora, smiling his charm in lavender silks with silver embroidery. He stood a short time talking to her before unspecified duties called him away. Eudora said nothing but watched Vesper and the crowd then turned after a few words of encouragement and removed to the matron's chairs lining the wall to wait.

Vesper gave Eudora a weak smile as she left and then looked around the hall. Lamps and candles lit the hall to a soft glow. She chose a spot where dripping wax from overhead chandeliers would not fall on her. The light changed her surgown, the pale green turned to misty gray, and the pattern shimmering in silvery shades alternating with charcoal reflections. If anything, it was even more beautiful, reminding Vesper of a forest glade in moonlight.

Brandt's father, the Adjudicator Otto Signus, stood at the far end of the hall in wine-colored velvets with multicolored embroidery tracing the knee-high edges of his long dress coat. Mayor and Winifred Kellsie stood with Signus along with a man Vesper presumed to be this affair's aristo guest, the most important Duke of Lambere.

The duke seemed an unprepossessing person from a distance even in his obviously rich clothing. He stood neither as tall as Mayor Kellsie nor wearing the weight of Adjudicator Signus. She noticed he wore boots rather than the dancing slippers of the other prominent men on the dais. Faint disappointment filled her. He appeared so ordinary, certainly not like an eminent and powerful member of King Frederick's Court. Vesper knew little of him except the tragic death of his family about a year ago.

Maybe Dame Winifred was right; maybe he sought another wife. When he spoke with Dame Winifred, Vesper wondered if maybe Alvina's suitor was at hand. With his time of mourning over, it was certainly possible. Maybe the duke wanted some of Norost's reputed handfasting luck.

Luck? Grief, just look at the designs based on number symbols in the elaborate surgowns and tunics tonight. Vesper puffed a soft snort; if one chose to believe in the representation of numbers as sanctioned by the holy fathers of the Church. The teaching master had gone on forever about number aspects, and yet he didn't believe in magic, couldn't see Alfred.

A pounding of the Crier's staff brought the assembly to order, and Norost's priest gave a long and elaborate prayer of thanks. Despite her scant expectations, Vesper could not help the curl of excitement and hope that fluttered inside her. Other agitated girls surrounded her, took her hand as they started chaining. As the prayer ended, most participants already formed the configuration for the maiden's dance. At someone's signal the music started, all soft strings and muted drums.

Her feet moved through the steps and her body through the motions of the dance without thinking. She felt her face flush and her heart pound but not with exertion. She prayed for what she believed could happen, both wishing to end the dance and hoping the music would never end.

As the music finished, the maidens dropped their hands, forming a large circle that filled the inner colonnade of the hall. The men participants filtered through their figures and took their positions for the suitor's dance, their numbers not near enough to pair every girl. Looking around, Vesper saw her own emotions reflected on the faces of other girls, girls with better expectations than her own. Suddenly she was ill with the spectacle, with her part in it and wished desperately to leave. Eudora said Kennetsure. Surely tomorrow, they could leave for the south. She dropped her head, closed her eyes, and waited for the music to end.

The last strains echoed, and Vesper heard the soft pad of slippered feet. Opening her eyes, she saw no feet in front of her. Pasting a smile to her face she raised her chin and swore, *I will not cry.*

Alvina stood directly across the circle from her. Before her, a silver and lavender satin-clad gallant bowed and placed a ring on her extended hand. The happy pair laughed and embraced.

Feeling a sickening crush inside herself, Vesper blinked and promised herself, *I will not cry.*

~ * ~

From the balcony of the Eternal Palace's Great Hall, Norbert watched the maiden's dance. Below, important matters of estate and family ties were at stake. The aristos were set on display, each vying to outdo the other. Some of the attire represented two or more years of an estate's profit. Only the uninhibited and Bishop-condemned Mask Night exceeded Handfasting in revelry and ostentation. The hall was equally grandiose in paint, architectural detail, and gilding, Prince Frederick's Princess having pushed for completion before tonight's event.

On the dais at the far end, King Frederick, his Queen, the Duke Hearthron, and other ranking aristos staged themselves. Beneath the scintillating light of hundreds of candles, bright colored silk and gold vests, braid enhanced and gem-encrusted surgowns, and foresleeves heavily embroidered with totems, numbers, and flowers displayed the pride and wealth of Kaereya's aristos.

From where he stood, the smell of wax overlaid all. It gave him a headache, though not as bad as the church scents induced. He rubbed his forehead.

Thank the Holy One Princess Pia was not present. Warned ahead of time of Warrick's absence, at least one part of this catastrophic political blunder had been averted. The court, though, tittered with the news and speculated in gossip.

After his interview with the Princess, Norbert felt some sympathy for the wayward Warrick. A more ill-favored and poorly dressed young woman would be hard to find. The other part of him sympathized with the colorless girl. Listening with increasing anger, the distraught Princess had threatened dire consequences when her countrymen learned of her humiliation by a Kaereyan Prince and the Kaereyan Court. Her heavy accent made her nearly unintelligible through her tears, hiccoughs, and wails.

Hard questioning of Warrick's servant Wen showed the man knew nothing, which was unusual, but showed how well Warrick had planned. The prince had taken little—some small pieces, readily saleable but unremarkable in themselves, no clothes, only horses and his cousins.

Norbert's gaze landed on the Duke of Hearthron, wondering what Gilchrist knew of his sons' participation in this ill-advised escapade. Damn Warrick. After the ceremonies, banquet, and later festivities, Norbert knew Frederick would call him to account for Warrick. An unpleasant night loomed.

The colorful ceremony continued in a highly ritualized form. Norbert grimaced as the middle-aged Aristo Geoff Yonger of Anatole entered the suitor's line. He stopped before Gilchrist's only daughter, who just turned sixteen. With a slight twist of the stomach, Norbert watched the unsmiling girl receive the token ring. His speculation roused like a charmed snake. *Two weasels sharing a warren? To what purpose?*

~ * ~

Vesper kept her head up, but lowered her eyelids, seeing only the slate floor surrounding her feet. Shrieks of joy heralded more pairings, but Vesper carefully tuned herself to indifference. This would be over soon. She waited.

Heavy steps clomped across the floor, loud and discordant among the whisper of slippered feet. Horsemen's boots, muddied, hastily wiped but still smeared, filled Vesper's view. Swallowing, Vesper looked up into a face not altogether unfamiliar. Golden eyes, glowing in a naturally darker skin than most and surrounded with disordered honey-brown hair escaping from a clansman's band, stared down at her.

She saw his lips move but couldn't hear the words for the pounding echo in her ears. Drew. That was his name. Drew Montoren, the little boy whom the town bullies struck with stones so long ago. She remembered him now, though the last she saw him was ages ago. He stood resplendent in an old clan short jack with elaborate piping, tight leather riding trews, and tall boots. Between his elbow and body, he clasped his soft clan beret.

Her ears suddenly opened to sound, the horrible empty, echoing sound ended, leaving a crystal clarity. She blinked her eyes, almost faint with sensation.

"Will you?" Drew's soft, low voice asked.

She didn't know how many times he might have spoken, but snickers from around her made her believe others watched this spectacle, and spectacle it must be, she realized. Clansmen did not come to a town Handfasting, at least not often. That they laughed at him in contemptuous ridicule, as they so often did her, roused Vesper's impulsive temper. He did not deserve it. A clansman reputed as poor as the rocky lands of Vere, so they mocked his choice—the housekeeper's foundling.

Drew's face alternately deepened and drained of color, and without thinking or saying a word, Vesper held out her hand. The gold ring felt warm from his hand and seemed to tighten on her finger. Several gasps surround her, but Vesper managed a fleeting smile.

His lips, cool and damp, touched her hand. He moved closer to her and she smelled the forest scent about him, wetness still clung to his jack and hair. He had only just arrived, she realized, with the cold of the night still upon him. It was nearly twenty leagues from his farm to town, and the weather frigid. Poor boy.

Her eyes flick up at him and her heart faltered. Not a boy of similar age as herself, but older by several years, maybe by six or more. A man, then, and one truly unknown to her. She looked and found she barely reached his shoulders. A snake of fear slithered through her innards. Without her notice, they moved to the music of the final ceremonial dance. Had the blessing, the contract, already been spoken? Was all completed? She shivered and dread formed in her mind. *What had she done?*

~ * ~

Drew watched Vesper, the most beautiful girl in the room, watched her emotions and thoughts flicker across her transparent face. She spoke no words, terror holding her in the unexpected grip of his choosing. She was his though, handfasted and bespoken by a priest and duly witnessed. It must have been a shock to her, but no one else had held the place he wanted. He had not been too late.

Of course, to her, it was a surprise. His eyes widened in his own shock and he looked down at Vesper. She had expected another.

Vesper had wanted someone else. He felt his throat tighten, his chin rose in defiance. Too bad, she was his, and he would not give her up. She feared him. It was clear, even understandable. He was unknown to her, a clansman about whom absurd rumors ran rampant. There was no fighting it. Who knew what type of heathen rites she thought he practiced?

He watched her. Only once she gave herself away, her eyes resting ever so briefly on the Adjudicator's son. Drew frowned, aware of the man's reputation.

At the end of the second silent dance, she turned so unnaturally pale it frightened him. He guided her to a darkened alcove in the hall, standing behind one of the huge columns. "You needn't be so fearful. I will not hurt you."

A gasp broke from her in sudden urgency. "I am sorry," she said.

"The contract is made," Drew said. "You cannot back out now."

"No, no... I mean, it's not you."

A woman approached. Drew recognized Eudora, Vesper's guardian from the few times he had seen her, unmistakable in her southern features. Eudora touched his sleeve, a look of concern on her face. "Is she all right?"

"She wants to back out," Drew said, defeated in the face of her parent.

Eudora looked with worried concern at Vesper, then her face hardened, though her eyes still held their concern. "She cannot back out now," Eudora said, repeating his words. "She owes you one year. Take her to your home, take her now."

"No, Eudora, you don't understand..."

"The rest of the ceremony..." Drew said, faltering.

"The legal part is over. Everyone saw it. Do you have rooms here?" At his negative headshake, she continued. "Take her now, it is reasonable. You have a long distance to travel in ugly weather. No one will remark on it."

"No, they've already had their say," Drew said with asperity.

Eudora gave him a look of sympathy. "Clansmen do not often come here. As you say, the words have all been said. Go."

"Eudora, no!" Vesper gasped. "It's so terrible, I see it and feel it, something dreadful. Please…"

Eudora's face turned to sudden dread, and she turned to Drew, "Take her out of here now before she creates a scene. I'll meet you in the vestibule with her cloak."

With some embarrassment, for tears ran down Vesper's face and a clansman could not move through the crowd unobserved, Drew escorted, nearly carried, Vesper to the entrance hall. Selwyn waited there, still disgruntled. He grew even more annoyed when he realized Drew had won his objective.

"Leaving so soon?" Selwyn asked rising to his intimidating height as he inspected Vesper. A fierce frown covered his face.

"It's so awful, can't help," Vesper said her voice barely audible, her head lolling as Drew took even more of her weight. "It's too late."

"By the Holy One, Drew, what is this? You'll not take her like this?"

"Yes," Drew answered in abrupt affirmative, not listening to his bride. "Now." His head swiveled once to check for Eudora, but not finding her, decided to leave. Seeing the words 'unsuitable' form on Selwyn's lips, he snarled, "don't say it."

"Only one left," Vesper said in a whisper.

Drew ignored Selwyn's renewed protest, grabbed his cloak from his cousin's keeping, and wrapped it around Vesper. Picking her up, he strode out into the rain. Icy wet seeped through his clothes before he reached his horse, but his heavier, waterproof cloak lay over his mount, warm and pungent with horse scent. Throwing Vesper onto the saddle, he mounted behind her, wrapping the cloak about his shoulders and forward over Vesper.

Selwyn, of all things, started laughing, his baritone a mocking refrain in the static chorus of icy rain. He glared at Selwyn before he pulled the hood over his head and turned his barely rested mount back towards Montoren.

Angry, Drew forced his horse into a jog until the animal slipped on the icy cobbles of the street. Belatedly afraid for Vesper's welfare, he slowed to a more sedate pace. The trip home would be bloody awful, more so than the trip in. At least Selwyn would not work so hard to delay the trip back, and Selwyn would suffer as much as he for his lack of planning. Drew smiled in grim revenge until the body in his arms reminded him that Vesper would suffer, too. His responsibility. Not an auspicious Handfasting and the fault fell to him. He glanced at Selwyn, maybe not all his fault, but he knew of the opposition he faced and had not planned well. It was too late to rent a room. By now, all would be taken. He swore.

Vesper huddled inside his great cloak, her heat, and the horse's heat slowly warming his body. She was quiet, unresisting. The gait of the horse rocked them both, and soon her body leaned into his, her head fell onto his shoulder in sleep. Better so. The whole evening could have gone better. His angry glance flicked to Selwyn, riding with no problem now, no loose girth, no broken bridle leather. His lips tightened. Swearing didn't do any good. Neither the clan nor Selwyn favored his choice.

Two nights ago Selwyn had ambushed Drew with a clan council held at Montoren. Eight of the clan chiefs waited when he entered the hall. Drew felt his nostrils and jaw seize as he recalled Clan Cader Chief Terril's words. Demands. "You'll marry within the clans, young Drew. It's the wisest course. There are several pretty girls, any of which would take you without a second thought."

He had refused and kept refusing during the interminable exchange. He had answered his clan chief, "I've already made my choice."

The panic of his late arrival, of the horrible ride to town with Selwyn's many delaying obstacles as if the rain and mud hadn't already caused enough, eased. Vesper snuggled for warmth between his arms, giving as much as she got, little enough on this forsaken night. Drew smote himself. Not forsaken but blessed, glorious night, thank the Holy One. His chest heaved in a deep breath of heartfelt relief. The thought warmed him with an inner glow not even his cold fingers and toes could diminish.

The furor his words engendered in Chief Terril had been intense and his mind replayed the scene. "An outsider! She'll never agree. Don't humiliate yourself and the clans before outsiders."

"I've waited long enough. If she won't, she won't. I'll still ask."

"And when she won't?"

"I'll take her anyway. Isn't that clan tradition?"

"You'd need help no one will give you!"

"Then I'll do it myself, and I'll fight any clansman who gets in my way." He had glared at Selwyn then. None of them knew he had made his choice twelve years ago.

It was over. He had her now, of her own choice. It didn't matter if she didn't love him today. With patience, she would come to love him in the future, and even if she never did, he had enough love for both of them. This would be no one-year trial.

~ * ~

Quillon, while waiting for Duke Aurelias, had just entered the vestibule in time to watch the tableau with the clansmen without time to divest himself of cloak and hood. The girl's distress did not alarm him. An unwilling Handfast was neither unknown nor unheard of even among his own people, let alone these strange tribes of the far north. He had come in to speak with the clansmen about their horses. The duke always looked for good stock. In his inspection of the animals, he found the fine leatherwork of the saddles impressed him as much as the horses.

He heard the girl, heard her low-spoken words, and stopped in shock. He saw her and took a step forward. The young clansman threw a defiant look in his direction, and Quillon realized his mind played a trick on him. Recognition was impossible. With awareness of a situation in progress, he stepped back into the shadows and watched the young suitor bundle his prize and leave. The taller man looked as unhappy as the girl did. Surely, the signs pointed to an inauspicious Handfasting.

Even as the trio rode away, a Kennetsurean woman entered the vestibule carrying a cloak. Quillon took another step back in surprised recognition, which drew her attention.

"The clansman, have they already left?" she asked, searching the shadows to see his face.

"Yes, mistress." This sudden trip finally fell into a pattern and Quillon reeled with the implication.

"With the girl?"

"Yes."

"But I have her cloak. It is so cold, and they have so very far to go." She stood there, but he had nothing to say, giving up, her face aged in resignation. She wrapped the cloak around herself and exited into the rainy night.

"May the night swallow you, harpy bitch," he said after she left, his fury overcoming his well-developed sense of precaution. Never did he think one from his own province would betray their calling. With another dumbfounded thought, he nearly took out after the clansmen, but his duty to the duke stopped him. Reflection on the incident told him what he imagined could not be true.

The duke didn't leave until the end of the celebration. Then, rather than join his hosts in their carriage as they bid, Aurelias rode back as he had come, on his horse with his armed men around him.

"You saw her?" he asked Quillon as they rode.

"Yes and recognized her. Recognized her... mother. I didn't believe it."

The duke didn't speak until they dismounted in the covered portico of his host's house. "Tomorrow I leave. I wish you to stay and investigate this matter. Find me the facts on this woman and her daughter." He slapped his reins against his saddle, spooking his mount into a side jump. One of the outriders grabbed the horse's bridle near the bit and calmed him. The duke apologized to his man and let him lead the horse away. He turned to Quillon. "Tell me if this town harbors a murderer but do not raise any suspicions of yourself, for I do not want her to flee to some new spot."

"And the girl?"

"I can make no move yet. With the threat this recent attack signifies, it is too dangerous."

~ * ~

The ride was as abysmal as Drew predicted. It took most of the night to get home. Selwyn swore long and freely but in calm, soothing tones to his horse, as Drew did when his mount slid and stumbled, waded through freezing streams and sucking mud. His hands were so cold he could not feel the reins, his gloves were unobtainable while he held Vesper. Vesper continued her silence, uttering no complaint though rudely startled, probably neigh scared to death, more than once as their mount stumbled and slipped, and suffered the cold perhaps more than he and Selwyn.

"We need to rest the horses," Selwyn insisted. "This is brutal on them."

"We cannot spend the night here," Drew answered.

Selwyn gave him a disgusted look. "I know. A token stop only, to let them catch their breath."

Reluctantly Drew agreed. Dismounting was painful, needles lanced from his feet to his knees. His hands moved slowly, and he was afraid to lift Vesper down, afraid he would drop her. She hopped down herself as though avoiding his touch. His unpredictable temper flickered at her independent move. He swallowed it, tired enough not to lose control. Selwyn took both horses' reins and moved them to stand under the shelter of a huge fir tree. He wore gloves and smiled maliciously at Drew's stiff hands as he turned away.

Drew threw his cloak up on one side and Vesper scooted under its protection.

"Have you no gloves?" she asked searching the pocket inside his cloak. Finding a pair, she lifted one of his freezing hands. Touching his hands, she ticked a sound of annoyance at their wet, cold state. She bent over and he heard a rip, then with the softest touch, she wiped his hands dry. Her hands were warm as she placed them around each of his hands in turn. Her silvery eyes looked into his as if hearing his unspoken question.

"Under my arms." With care she slipped his gloves over his now dry hands, then stood beneath his cloak. He rested his arm on her shoulder. Tired, she leaned into him.

"If we must make Montoren tonight, we better mount up," Selwyn said after too brief a break.

Drew knew Selwyn was right. When he went to lift Vesper, he hesitated. She pushed his hand away and mounted, flicking his temper anew. During the break, she had unlaced the skirt's front panel, allowing her to straddle the saddle. She pulled the skirt of the heavy surgown forward to allow him room to slide into the saddle behind her, slid herself onto the flat pommel of his saddle exposing a shapely leg soon covered with cloth. He hadn't thought of her comfort, not that this was much more comfortable, but at least she chose it herself. Drew urged his tired horse forward. When its movement pushed her back into his lap, he silently cursed and counted the distance to Montoren step by step.

The animals staggered to a stop, and they dismounted from the horses in the barn. Selwyn woke the smith's son to care for the animals while Drew lit a lamp to see them to the manse. Someone had laid a fresh fire in the larger fireplace inside the hall and left furs and blankets to warm as well. Drew took his dress cape from Vesper's wet surgown and then reached for the surgown.

"Stop it, you must get these wet clothes off," he said as she resisted him. He heard Selwyn's huffed snort of censure, but after that, his cousin ignored the situation and watched Vesper with critical eyes.

She slowly removed her surgown. Drew was too tired to react to anything by then.

Vesper, left standing in her hem-torn chemise, shivered, and Drew wrapped a blanket around her. Investigating the second fireplace, he found a dinner nestled in the fire's banked coals. He dished the stew into three wooden bowls and pulled the bread apart. Vesper tottered to the table from where she had stood since entering the hall. Her fatigue-white face and shadowed eyes stared at the bowl; the spoon shook in her fingers as she lifted it. Drew greedily ate his meal alongside Selwyn.

"A stalwart mate, for sure," Selwyn said in objectionable tones a bit later, his eyes full of sarcastic mockery.

Drew looked to where Vesper sat, sleeping, her head to one side of her bowl, spoon still in hand, the bowl still full. Grabbing two blankets, Drew first looked to the stairs of the solar and decided he could not do it. Instead, he carried her to one of the curtained-off bed chambers lining the hall. She lay, not waking, wrapped in the blanket. Shedding his wet clothes, Drew wrapped a blanket around himself and lay down next to her. He placed more blankets and a fur over them and fell into an exhausted asleep.

Seven

Ottillie groaned as she remounted the next day, sore and about to get sorer. Eldin laughed at her grimace and gave teasing advice. "You need to ride more."

"I ride plenty. Just not all day."

It took all morning to leave Alaric Island. It remained chilly on the island sitting in the shadow of the Guard Island's cliffs. Ottillie felt it oppressive. Not even Easure's customary bright color display could overcome the day's shadowed start.

Kites, banners, and flags flew overhead in wild abandon, many displaying the Dragon totem of Easure or the province's sacred numbers of two and seven. All the symbolic forms of the numbers were also prominently displayed. Bulls, bells, circles cut in half, figures caught in copulation, seven-pointed crowns, and scythes were all represented. Two represented commitment, seven faith, and mystery. Both symbolized air, an Easure element.

Buildings were painted in mixes of bright and pastel colors, and even the people outdid each other to dress in gaudy cheer. Noise distinguished the province as much as color. Chimes, wind harps, boats' rigging, merchandise hawkers' shouts and chants, customers' barter, gulls, and chirping birds, all added their bit of melody. It felt very familiar to Cliff City, and though Ottillie loved it, her expectant agitation for the coming change in landscape subdued it.

Their small troop wove single file through heavy traffic on the Great River Road in the city. Once free of the city, Eldin pulled his horse alongside for the rest of the long morning's ride. Ottillie knew the road snaked through islands bumping each other cheek and jowl at a few knuckle's length above sea level.

By afternoon, they reached the next island. Rock Island was a low flood plain of gravel, sand, and muck. Farmers still worked at harvesting all the crops, including marsh grass, off its flat surface. The traffic had thinned to cartage traffic over the rutted road, but they could still travel three abreast. Eldin insisted Ottillie remain between him and another guard with the remaining three riders behind them. "Have you ever journeyed this way before?" he asked.

"No, I have never been further on this route than Alaric Island."

"Well it doesn't get much more interesting than this. The next islands are all marshlands. We will have to travel single file over the bridges, and you will not cross while a wagon crosses. The Thou is low, so carters will be fairly constant along the road. They take full advantage of the season's dry roads and cooler weather. Their wide carts sometimes take up more than their fair share of road, and with double and treble teams of fen ox pulling, well, it can be a problem passing them. You will ride on the road's outer side at those times."

"Are the carters dangerous?" Ottillie asked in surprise.

"No. But not all carters pole their oxen. An ornery ox can horn you or your mount with a turn of his head. We are not traveling as an Aristo and Royal Guardsmen, so they won't be careful about walking a man alongside to keep the teams in line." He smiled. "The good news is your father ordered a local messenger to reserve us lodging, so we are assured of at least a few soft, dry beds, but I fear we may have to camp yet. The rider will continue west, so won't do us much good once we head for the Kennetsure crossing. You won't find the biting insects as romantically exotic."

The ox teams were the only things of interest on the road. She could understand why the carters were reluctant to dehorn their animals. On those teams where the oxen maintained their long, curved horns, strings of bells, whirly-gigs, or wind whistles enlivened their passing with cheery notes and bright colors. The animals seemed to appreciate their ornaments, nodding their heads more often than usual, setting the musical sounds free.

She kept up a general, light conversation with Eldin and the other guardsmen through their ride. As they crossed Rock Island, Ottillie found Eldin overprotective and wondered at his attention. She reconsidered the man grown from the boy she knew. Another side-glance proved him good enough looking, and he had already proven his tolerance and temper. For once, she allowed herself to consider how she would like someone in her bed, not only for lovemaking but also for a long-term relationship. Nothing bad happened, only a small tickle of anticipation.

Reaching the end of Rock Island settled Ottillie's initial journey jitters. The anxiousness for accomplishing the journey eased, allowing her to enjoy the travel. They rode through Easure's lowlands at an easy pace.

They passed fields where Farmers already cut rice stalks to sell to the papermakers. Water sparkled all around, even in the grain fields. Looking over her shoulder, Ottillie could see the high buttresses of the elevated islands behind her. They blended into one large shape from this distance with the heights of Vere and the Rikon hills sheltering them. Here the bright colored kites flew above the fields, boat sails filled the waterways, and mill sails turned in stationary circles over the land. At every floating house, porch, and window, the tinkling of wind chimes sang. Soon winter-brown fields surrounded by cold-gray, watery vistas replace the colorful signs of Easure dwellings. Not until Green Island did they reach lodging.

"This is the only lodge between Alaric and Left Together Island," her waiter told Ottillie as he handed her a cup of long-desired tea. "Most of the carters sleep in their carts," he said, his dialect thick and atonal. "Don't get much trade from them. Take care of themselves. Travelers been few lately, so it's a bit slow."

"Isn't this an unusual place for so fine a lodge?" Ottillie asked raising her eyebrows. The young man obviously found her attractive, and she enjoyed the chance for a harmless flirt.

"Green Island's got good hunting, duck and musk deer, some wild boar. Lots of birds in all that sea of marsh grass out there." He nodded his head toward the tiny window. "Quite a few aristos stay here for that reason alone." He shrugged. "That, and travelers like you, keep us going."

Eldin entered with a scowl on his face, gave the young man an order for ale, and sat down.

"What is the matter?" Ottillie demanded, suspecting a setback in their plans.

"Don't encourage his type. They are as rapacious scavengers as crows and with less intelligence."

"I wasn't encouraging him. He was just being friendly. He told me about the island."

"Something you haven't already read?"

Ottillie laughed and quoted. "Wise travelers always wear a hat traversing Bird Island. This royal sanctuary island, home to numerous species of birds, is one of the few islands where flying insects are not a problem." Taking her normal voice, she said, "I noticed you and your Guardsmen were prepared, too."

He gave her a slow, charming grin. "Traveled this way before. Any more pearls of wisdom?"

"That you don't already know?"

"Never read the guidebooks, don't know the particulars. Just the facts."

"Such as?"

"Stick to the bridges. Those little inlets between the islands you think you could almost step across are very deep and the currents very fast. And insects will bedevil us."

"Here," she searched a pocket and produced a small jar of cream. "Rub this on any exposed skin tomorrow morning. You can't see it," she said as he unscrewed the jar and made a face at the pungent smell. "And it helps for several candlemarks, then you have to apply more."

"More book learning?"

"Yes, and a visit to a good herbalist. Keep it, I have plenty. I'm surprised the Guards don't know about this. Here, give the other riders this one. They can eek-out enough to see them through the worst."

The waiter delivered Eldin's ale. Eldin raised it in a mock salute to her. "Anything else of interest?"

"Did you know those tree stumps we've been passing are really dwarf trees? The stumps are root knots that rise above the leafy stems. The actual trunk doesn't start growing until there is an adequate root system, and then they are harvested a hundred years later. The wood is very dense, hard, rot and fire resistant. Inside, they are a reservoir of fresh water. Another type lives in the Great Salt Marsh." At the pained look on his face, Ottillie laughed. "You asked."

"You'll enjoy Stump Island then, there are thousands of them there."

"Will all our lodgings be as comfortable?"

"No. This is the last comfortable stop until we reach Left-Together Island. That's at least two nights away." He looked at her over his ale mug. "I, for one, am always glad to reach high and dry ground. You don't happen to know Aristo Agino, do you?"

"I do." Something in her voice drew his attention.

"Not someone you would choose to impose upon," he interpreted. "Too bad. His estate looks most comfortable, especially so close to the Great Salt Marsh in Wessure. Oh well, that is a whole sennight away."

"He would, of course, give me lodging in my father's name."

"That way, is he?"

"Aristo Agino, Earl of Teeg and Agino, considers himself very high ranking. I will ask... if you like."

Anger crossed Eldin's chiseled face. "Very Aristo. I've met the type. The Holy One help me, my father is one, although not quite so high ranking a cuckoo. Well, there is a small lodge further into the marsh. We will plan our stop there."

"Thank you. Your father was a great fool, you know, and made an even greater mistake."

"Is my discontent so apparent? I'm sorry. I try to keep it under wraps. Your father not only recognizes you but also loves you. It makes a difference but thank you for implying my worth."

"My case is different. My parents were handfasted, but my mother's parents broke the promise before the year was up. She would not naysay them. I think Papa loved her to the end." She sighed. "Besides, your worth is no implication at all, but the truth. My father thinks so, too. He told your father he could not tell the difference between gold and dross.

"He did?" Eldin perked up and smiled. "It is true my half-brother is an idiot."

"That's stating it mildly," Ottillie said. Her dry tone drew a laugh from Eldin.

"As pleasant as this exchange has become..." he said.

"I know. Tomorrow is another long day in the saddle." Ottillie rose, rubbing her posterior in ever so delicate a manner. Eldin laughed. "Good night, Eldin."

"Good night, Ottillie, wear your herbalist's repellent to bed if you want to sleep."

She stopped and turned to give Eldin an amused grin. "Thanks for the warning. A reminder—book learning does not equate with experience." She dipped in a deep, court curtsey, and enjoyed his laugh at her departure.

~ * ~

Still groggy with exhaustion, Vesper woke slowly. She lay paralyzed in fear, not recognizing her whereabouts. Memory returned but did not release her paralysis. *What happened last night? Surely he was too tired... She would have remembered. Was this their bed chamber? A curtained-off alcove in a chamber wall? He was very poor then.* Hearing movement and the dull clunk of wooden dishes, she lifted the curtain and stepped out of the bed enclosure.

Only Drew stood in the hall, pouring water from a wooden basin into a pail. A glance told Vesper he had just completed shaving. With his back to her, he stood dressed in long leather riding trews and boots. A shaft of light entering a clerestory window gilded his honey hair and reflected off the small pedestal mirror before him. He must have heard her move for he turned and pulled on a tunic over his muscular torso at the same time. Undoubtedly poor, but at least he was attractive and well built.

"Good morning."

"Good morning," Vesper echoed.

"There is bread and cheese." He indicated a platter. "And cider."

Grasping the blanket around her shift, she rose feeling her skin heat with color at his regard. The floor was warm underfoot and she looked down in surprise. No sun shone on this section of floor. A nearby movement drew her attention and she stepped back in alarm as Drew approached, frowning.

"A tunic," he said, offering her a soft blue cloth. Vesper took the offering but waited until he turned away before donning the garment, even then she turned to face the bed. It fell around her in overly generous folds, but the length was only a little long. The sleeves were full, with tie cuffs. With practiced movements, she tied the cuffs close to the wrist. The excess fabric fell over her hands like great mutton sleeves. She ran her fingers through her hair, finding it less tangled than expected, but without pins she could not secure it. Turning, she found Drew watching her in an unnerving manner.

"Come," Drew said, and held a chair for her at the table.

Quick steps to the table reminded her of the warmness of the floor and she glanced down. The seamless rock floor was worn smooth under her feet.

"Your surgown is with Ramona. She thinks the wet has not harmed it. The slippers, I'm afraid, are beyond repair."

"Thank you. I had no thought of it last night, but it was my mother's surgown and is very dear to me. I expect the slippers were never meant for outdoor wear." She took a sip of the sweet cider, then another.

"It was beautiful," Drew said. He picked up his mug and drank. "I apologize for your discomfort last night, but I... I'm sorry anyway."

"There was a package in a pocket," Vesper said remembering the amulet with alarm.

"Ramona found it. She placed it on the sideboard." He nodded his head toward a huge, heavily carved sideboard nearly hidden in the darkness of the room.

Vesper rose and picked up the linen-wrapped gift. One of her forbidden folk hid deep in the shelf of the sideboard, startling her, his eyes gleamed in mischievous laughter. Vesper nearly shrieked in surprise. Alfred had never come indoors. Blinking her eyes Vesper saw the gleam was a reflection on a smoky glass ewer and closed her eyes briefly in chagrin. *Don't let your mind play tricks on you now.*

She heard laughter as she walked back to the table. It wasn't Drew, who watched her with a serious, perhaps unhappy, face. *Maybe now he regrets choosing the housekeeper's bastard?*

The ring weighed her finger as she placed the pocket next to him. Drew didn't touch it, in fact, he looked angry. Vesper hesitated before taking her own seat.

"You made it for him?"

"Him?"

"The Adjudicator's son."

"You know Brandt?"

"I know you made this for him. Did he know you?"

Vesper sat speechless, understanding his meaning too well. Outrage and embarrassment hit her at the same time, firing her face. "No. I never... I mean yes, I made it for Brandt." She sighed, giving over her irritation as she saw in her mind how it must look. "It was totally inappropriate. I meant to make... but Brandt chose elsewhere. He would not want this. He would hate anything so..." She searched for a word and admitted the truth. "Useless."

Drew had removed the plain linen square wrapping the pocket. Embroidered unicorns pranced through a forest of trees covering the cloth pocket. His thumb ran over the colorful threads as he inspected her stitches, and then he emptied the buckle amulet into his palm. "This is very old," he said, rubbing the freshly polished silver. "It is finely wrought and must have held great magic once. Did you embroider the pocket?"

"Yes. It was to be foresleeves." She half-laughed but it sounded more like a whimper. "He," her teeth clicked upon thinking of Brandt, "admired those I made for Alvina. The amulet was among my mother's things."

"Why didn't you make the foresleeves?"

"I don't know," she sighed. "Eudora asked me that, too. My fingers just fashioned this instead. It's a useless gift. No one believes in magic, mythical beasts, or amulets anymore. I'm very sorry. I didn't mean to offend you." She looked up into his face. "I have nothing else to give you."

"Then I accept your gift," Drew said. He rose and returned shortly to place a wool-wrapped object on the table before her and stood beside her while she unwrapped it.

Vesper found a spoon, its silver bowl emerging from a wood handle carved as a dancing unicorn.

"As a child you thought my pony a unicorn," he said. Looking at the embroidered pocket, he added, "I expect you must see them often. Happy Gifting Day, Vesper." His smile was beautiful, and Vesper realized how handsome her groom was.

Uncomfortable with his closeness, she still managed an uncertain smile, "Happy Gifting Day, Drew."

Sitting on the bench next to her, he regarded her with serious intent. "I know I'm not the one you wanted, and I will freely admit I've wanted you for a long time, but I promise you this—I won't hurt you. I won't touch you as a man does a woman until you ask me. But you must promise to give me time."

Blushing, Vesper agreed and thanked him, her voice barely audible. To keep her mind off his continued stare, she looked at her plate. The bread and cheese smelled more appetizing now. While she ate, she looked around the room with avid interest that turned to awe. It was immense. No farmer's croft this, but a grand hall, larger even than the Mayor's great hall, but very ill kept.

Curtains, torn and ragged looking, hung the length of one wall, covering sleeping alcoves lining the wall in an old-fashioned manner. At some time the clan probably shared this hall. Two fireplaces sectioned the walls on each side and the table stretched down its middle. Vesper thought at least twenty to a side could easily fit if it were cleaned properly and oiled. Now, like the straw, dirt, and noisome offal scattered on the stone floor, the table lay thick with dust, grime, riding gear, and anonymous stains. Eudora would have fainted. The sideboard, in a similar state, held many wooden tankards and bowls stacked on it. She also glimpsed the dull sheen of tarnished copper and the glint of what must be glass.

"Drew." Selwyn's gruff baritone sounded from the door.

His intense regard broken, Drew rose. "I must go, but I'll come back later to show you around." Vesper watched Drew leave, wondering if Selwyn was the clan chief and if this farm belonged to him.

Left alone, she slowly chewed her chunk of bread. Selwyn did not like her; that was clear. Why, because she was not clan? Or did he find her unsuitable? That boded ill for a lasting Handfast. She wondered how much influence he had over Drew. Not enough, apparently, if Drew still chose her. A moment's flicker of satisfaction drowned in the thought that she might not be any happier here than at the Kellsie manor. Her fingers crumbled the remains of her bread. At least someone had wanted her, even if he were a clansman. To be chosen mattered, and even being Drew's choice felt like salve on a seeping ulcer.

Her conscience rose screaming, *unfair, unjust!* She accepted Drew. To see him now as somehow less was contemptible. Even with no one to see, she felt the blood rush to her face; how ungrateful she was, being no grand prize herself. Drew seemed kind and admitted liking her enough to handfast, but how long would that last?

Unable to sit until Drew decided, or was allowed to return, she tore another section of the rich brown loaf loose and rose to investigate the hall. She counted seven bed alcoves along the sidewall. Five were filled with a jumble with every type of equipment, saddles, tools, leather hides, clothes, weapons, dirty dishes, even a book or two. Two held messed bedding, one of which she had slept in. She paused to speculate where Drew had slept if Selwyn also slept in the hall. She made the beds, making soft ticking sounds over the built-up candle wax in the wall sconces and the musty smell of the linens. Both stone fireplaces seemed in good condition. The grander of the two held a grime-encrusted emblem high above the fire pit. She could not make out the design, maybe an animal of some sort. Cobwebs strung from the wall to the ceiling and from rafter to rafter. Vesper gave a shiver of worry about crawly creatures that might descend on her unexpectedly.

At the far end of the room, she saw another table, smaller, and set crosswise to the room with heavy chairs lined behind it. A fine screen stood behind the table. Approaching it, she found the five panels of the screen carved with a leafy branch decoration. Her fingers ran over the relief, then down the satin smoothness of the table leaving telltale tracks in the dust. A low chuckle distracted her absorption and caused her to drop her bread, but a glance showed no one in the room. A second sound had her looking beneath the table. She heard a scurrying sound and thought of rats, but her attention was caught by the carved legs of the table, each leg seeming done at a different level of competence.

"I carved them."

Vesper knocked her head against the table's edge as she abruptly rose. Drew stood watching her as she rubbed the sore spot, blinking back tears of pain. His hand reached out and Vesper froze, but he only removed a dust ball from where her hair had swept the floor.

"How long have you been here?" she asked, unable to stop the petulant accusation from her voice.

Unperturbed Drew answered, "I just came in. Are you all right?"

"Yes. They're beautiful. I was just looking around, and I've dropped my bread." She searched the floor but didn't see it.

"I do better now. The legs were among my first attempts."

Vesper glanced at Drew as she continued to search. No use inviting mice. "The squirrels look very real. I should be afraid to sit here for fear they might bite. A dog must have taken it."

"Taken what?" Drew didn't smile, and Vesper felt uncomfortable under his gaze. Unable to hold its intensity, Vesper dropped her eyes and folded her hands demurely before her.

"My bread, I told you I dropped it, but I can't find it."

"The dogs are all outdoors with Selwyn. Come." He seemed disinterested in her reason and peremptory in his demands as he was already walking away. "There is an old pantry and buttery behind the screen, also a bathing room. From that passageway, you can get to the kitchen courtyard. Come, let me show you above stairs."

He waited as she approached the doorway and took her elbow, then hesitated and dropped it to lead the way to a stair landing off the main room. A stone circular staircase spiraled upward. Vesper followed him in silence up the rapidly cooling air of the staircase. Bright light flooded the upper end causing Vesper to gasp. It made it difficult to see the room beyond them. Shielding her eyes Vesper looked up into four windows lining the room's left, west-facing side. *Surely a costly extravagance?* A door at the far end and three others along the east wall lined the room. It was a large bower of a room filled with dusty old furniture and women's equipment. Two distaffs leaned in the near corner behind a web-covered spinning wheel. Rotting woof threads hung from a huge loom in the far corner, and the remains of what was once good yarn showed signs of mouse, or worse, rat infestation. Dust lined the wood floor. In a darkened corner, Vesper made out two sizable trunks. She looked at Drew. He blushed. "No one has been up here recently," he apologized.

"You've kept a bachelor's existence for many years," Vesper said. "How long has your mother been gone?"

Drew looked down at her. "She died three years ago." Changing the subject, he pointed to the doors running down the side. "One of these leads to an allure. The other two were used as bedrooms once, but they are full of furniture and other storage now."

"And no one has come up here to clean?" she asked astounded, changing the subject, to hide her bad manners, glad Eudora had not heard her. "What is in the far room?" Vesper asked nodding towards the wooden door opposite them.

"Your bedroom. Come and see." He took her hand and gently pulled her towards the door.

Whatever she had expected, it was not the room she entered. She waited while her eyes adjusted to the darker light. Heavy curtains fell draping most of the windows in the wall facing the door, but some light escaped their confines, bathing the room in soft color from three leaded-glass windows. As the room's furniture came into focus, Vesper saw it was as dusty and web infested as the previous room. This room, though, held charm and enchantment. She felt the rug beneath her feet and looked upon Southern knotting at its best, thick and dark, its pattern still faintly showing through a layer of dust. She could see that the massive bed, once cleaned, would be impressive. "Did you carve the bed?"

"No. It was my inspiration to start carving. My mother strictly forbade me from practicing on it. I was forbidden entrance if I had a knife on my person."

Vesper giggled, glad to hear the humor in Drew's voice, glad to know he poked fun at himself. Vesper slowly walked around the bed, then sighed. The once exquisite bedcover was gray with dust, and she could see signs of mice.

"What's the matter?" Drew asked.

"The bed linens. They should have been covered. I don't know if they can be restored." The sun shifted causing light to stream through an opening in the drapes. A glint caught Vesper's eye and she turned to find its source. Two finely wrought iron unicorn andirons held court in the stone niche. Their eyes glowed red as stray light caught them. Vesper turned to smile at Drew, still near the door, and gasped. A large circle mirror of blue glass held the wall next to the door reflecting the room and its occupants in a mesmerizing way. It grabbed her imagination. She had never seen anything like it. It had to be magical. Reflected in the mirror she saw more furniture, fine trunks, a chair, and a stool, tucked here and there. Vesper could not believe Drew meant this to be her room.

"I'm sorry it is so poorly cared for, but there has been no one with time to take care of it. Actually, I think we all avoided these rooms. It was painful to be up here knowing I would never see my parents again. I think the rest of the clan felt much the same."

"I promise to take good care of it, Drew. I know it is an enchanted room, and I thank you for letting me have it for my own." Both her embarrassment and her delight must have sounded in her voice, for Drew smiled at her.

"Come," he said holding out his hand for her to take, "I'll show you the allure. He pulled her from the room and Vesper gave it one more glance over her shoulder before Drew closed the door.

Outdoors, the air was icy brisk, but she didn't care. *The view!* It took her breath away. Fields and forest still covered in a white frosting of last night's sleet fell away from her in rocky terraces. On this, the northern-most border of the Vere Plateau, the Seer Mountains showed as great peaks of white piercing and hiding in snowy clouds that covered the dark gray sky to the northeast. Drew pointed to the left and she gasped. The Sunderlune plains extended forever, far below the elevation of the farm, emphasizing the unreal beauty of the scene.

The allure walk continued around the roof's slate edge. On the other side the view changed to a courtyard with the farm's buildings and barns, animals, and people starting the day's work, an old fallen stone wall trailed down one side of the farm, and a watermill's great wheel slowly turned at the edge of a nearby stream. Dense fog rose from the stream, hiding much of the landscape beyond, but she could see the ragged edge of the forest beyond them. She could imagine unicorns and fair people capering in such a landscape. *This was not the rocky farm of which the town-folk spoke.* Vesper only realized she spoke her thoughts aloud when Drew answered her.

"My clan, my family, has lived here many generations. In better times we afforded better. Times have not been so good to us the last few generations."

Vesper knew the items she had just seen were not just better, they were the best Kaereya had to offer. She looked at Drew, suspecting deception. She could not catch his glance, for it held fast to the glorious sight before them. The sun highlighted his fine profile, and the light wind blew the wisps of hair back from his forehead. The avoidance she sensed could be pride, and his cheeks could be red with the bite of cold rather than deceit. She could not gauge the truth. Vesper felt an unidentified stirring inside her.

"Poor or rich, it does not matter with such a glorious view." She wrapped her arms around herself and grinned. "Surely there must be Fair Folk and their creatures living here? Can't you almost see them dancing in the mist near that stream winding through the orchard?"

"You are fair-fey yourself, Fair Folk dancing in my orchard and unicorns disguised as ponies?" Drew said in an amused tone. "I've known you so for many years and do not believe you'll change, but we must go indoors now, for you are not dressed for this cold."

Although he sounded pleased, Vesper reigned in her imagination and followed Drew through the doorway. It was cold, and she did not want him to think her lost to common sense by romantic tales.

They returned to the main floor. Drew stopped to give her a pair of boots to wear and threw a long, thick wool cape over her before leading her through the buttery into a short walkway slippery with ice. They passed a garden gate that Vesper hurriedly looked through before Drew stopped at the kitchen croft, a low stone building warmed by two immense ovens.

Vesper held her hands out over the heat rising from one and looked around with curiosity. With relief, Vesper knew Eudora would approve of the kitchen, which meant the food would not poison. Two dark-haired women worked. One, at a wooden table scattered with flour, kneaded bread. The other tended a fire at the other oven. She saw their glances find her but there were no smiles of welcome.

Drew introduced one of the women as Berneta, the other as Ramona. Berneta spoke first. "I make the meals. Ramona makes our bread. You can pick Drew's meal up here at dusk and take it to the table or place it in the warmer."

"I will be glad to do so or to help with whatever you ask. Thank you. Thank you, too, Ramona, for Drew said you thought you could save my dress. It is very precious to me, as it was my mother's." Ramona gave a brief nod. Vesper thanked them again, and Drew, looking uncomfortable, returned the women's stern looks before he took her hand and led her out into the courtyard. She pretended not to hear the "help indeed," spoken in low tones.

Leaving the warm comfort of the kitchen, they entered the bitter cold of the day. The sun shimmered, frigid and pale between clouds, warming nothing but the spirit with its presence. Last night she had been unable to see anything in the dark. Now she saw the buildings neatly lined two sides of the cobblestone yard, the manor a third. On the fourth side, a massive, crenelated wall enclosed the courtyard, with an arched gate providing access. In the light of day, Vesper realized she was in a fortified keep. She looked at Drew who looked apprehensively back at her.

"This is no poor farmer's croft," she said.

"I have never considered it so." At her sharp look, he added "What the townsfolk think is no concern of mine."

"As this farm is none of theirs?" Vesper questioned-guessed.

"Exactly. In general, we do not welcome any towns' people here. They would raise their already high prices believing clansmen wealthy, when in fact we merely sustain ourselves. Are you too cold for me to show you around?"

"No, I would like to see your... farm."

"Well, not the farm, at least not today, but the courtyard. As you can guess from leaving the kitchen, the manor runs along this side. The stable is there."

"We entered last night from the archway?"

"Yes. There is also a forge, cow byre, poultry house, dovecote, and hawk mew. We are fairly self-sufficient. Grain and hay are sometimes difficult, but we trade other Clans for it."

"What do you trade?"

"Horses and their training, cheese, game. Besides baking bread, Ramona brews a fine beer."

"How many live here?"

"About seven families. Their houses run along that wall." He pointed to the far side of the courtyard. "The rest of the clan live on other farms in the surrounding area. "

"Just you and Selwyn stay in the manor?"

He gazed at her in amusement. "Yes—and you. He and I sleep in the alcoves. It is warm there. Even with the fireplace, I'm afraid it will take a lot to warm up your room. Did you believe we still slept 'en clan unite' as rumor claims?"

"Where is everyone now?" She ignored the heat in her face.

"Selwyn and most of the men left this morning to check the outlying farms. They will be gone tonight, or perhaps several days. The rest of the men and women are taking care of the stock or doing their regular chores."

"Am I keeping you from your work? Is that why Selwyn called you away? He does not like me. He didn't want me here, did he?" Vesper bit her lip, angry with herself. She could never keep her views to herself for long.

"It is enough that I want you here, and yes, there is work I must accomplish today, but you are not keeping me from it."

She did not like it when he stood so close, so tall. "What is your work? Can I help you?"

"I take care of the horses, breeding and training them. I don't imagine you cleaned many stables at the Mayor's house."

Vesper laughed in agreement. "No, indeed, but a few times. Show me your horses."

Drew took her to a wide door that led into the stable. Once the heavy wood doors closed behind them, the dark interior seemed warm with the scent of horses, leather, hay, and dust. Vesper could hear the horses shuffling and whiffing the hay in their stalls. As her eyes adjusted to the light, she and Drew walked down the central aisle. Several heads emerged from side enclosures, including two human ones.

"It's me, Gerdi, Hilde," Drew said, then introduced Vesper. "Gerdi and Hilde are helping today. Gerdi handles the dairy cows and goats. Hilde cares for all the poultry."

Vesper noted Gerdi's hostile gaze and Hilde's faint expression of welcome and tried to give a warm response and noticed their physical similarity to Berneta and Ramona. Drew and Selwyn didn't seem to fit clan form. Drew talked to them briefly before guiding her down the aisle.

He named each horse as he came to it, telling her about it while gently rubbing the animal's head. They were sleek and tall compared to the riding palfreys found in Norost, but not the massive heaviness of Marwyn's Shally. Their heads seemed to tower above Vesper as she raised a timid hand to pat their noses. Drew didn't seem to notice, lost in his rapture of telling her about them.

"This is Kuff," he said coming to the last stall. "He is the best animal ever bred on the farm. Hopefully, he will produce as many fine colts as himself."

The horse looked at Vesper with clear, inquisitive eyes. He looked like the others, his flaxen forelock falling over a long gray face blending into a black muzzle. Vesper smiled. A long thin white streak ran down his nose. It reminded her of a horn, and she trailed her hand down it. "You have a new unicorn."

Her comment pleased Drew. "We can go riding later if you wish." His enthusiasm was infectious as they turned to retrace the aisle.

"No, we can't," Vesper laughed, her spirits risen. "I never learned how. Your horses are very beautiful. I've never seen this color before. The hairs are actually gray."

Drew looked surprised. "Not many notice. It's what we've been breeding towards for generations. They are very gentle but strong and willing. I will teach you to ride. Are you cold?" He watched her as Vesper clenched her hands and blew warm air into them.

"I should like that very much, but you are right. I am cold. I will return to the manse to warm up and let you return to your horses."

"You don't wish to spend time together?"

Realizing too late the blunder she had made, Vesper blushed. "Of course I do, but daylight is short at this season. It is better to get your work done now and enjoy the evening together, isn't it? We can talk easier in front of a warm fire."

"You are right, I am sorry. You are cold, we will go inside." Drew said, but his face looked uncertain at her reasoning as he insisted on escorting her back to the manse.

~ * ~

That night as Drew walked into the hall, Vesper rose from her seat. "I've kept dinner warm. It is ready when you are," she said, her eyes searching his face. His face was red, probably from the cold, and the taut mouth was a sure sign of fatigue or anger. A sign she never liked to see in the Mayor. Even Drew's movements were stiff and quick.

"I'm sorry to have been so long... things kept me busy."

"No apology is needed. It gave me time to find my way around." Vesper said into his hesitation and looked at the noise behind him.

"Selwyn has returned early," Drew said in a rush as Selwyn entered.

"I'm sure he and the other men will find their own beds more comfortable on such a cold night," Vesper replied in a low voice aware of Selwyn's noisy return.

When Drew walked to the washbasin, she followed. As he finished washing his hands, she poured the warm scented water from the pitcher over them. She noticed a semi-circle birthmark on his palm, a strange place for such a thing, and she remembered first seeing it as a child. He gave her a strange look, expecting something from her. She smiled and gave him a cloth to dry his hands. Answering the doubt in his face she said, "It is a Kennetsure custom Eudora taught me. I always found it comforting. A touch of lanolin in the water helps keep the hands from cracking and chapping of cold."

"It is thoughtful of you. Thank you."

She performed the same service for Selwyn, puzzling over Drew's odd look and avoiding Selwyn's expression. He merely grunted before walking to the table.

"Sit, I will bring your dinner," she said as Drew remained standing.

"You have not eaten?"

"No, I waited." She went to the fire and removed the cover from the pot and dished up three wooden plates from its contents. Shortly she placed them on the scrupulously clean and oiled table. Vesper made the briefest of solitary graces before picking up her utensil. Through dinner, she remained silent as Selwyn told Drew of his day.

Afterward, she cleaned the plates and table with cleaning sand, then oil, and as Selwyn had already turned into his bed without a word, she smiled and gave a curtsey nod to Drew before taking a candle and heading to the stairs. Drew followed as far as the foot of the steps.

"You cannot sleep up there yet, I know the condition of the room and bed," he whispered.

She whispered back with a smile. "You know the condition of it this morning, but not how it is now. I am sorry I did not spend more time with you this afternoon, but I did not waste it. Don't worry about me. Good night Drew."

"I shall come and start a fire for you."

"No need." She smiled at the confused and dispirited look he wore. "But if you could bring up more wood?" He nodded and left. Vesper looked at Selwyn's expressionless face now peering from his alcove, his wordless appraisal accused her of some vile deed. She nodded and turned to walk up the stairs.

~ * ~

When Drew entered the shadowed second floor, he saw Vesper had swept the solar, pushing the old and worn equipment aside. As he entered the bedroom with his load of wood, though, he stopped.

Moonlight flooded into the room through windows now freed of their film of grime and heavy drapery. It entered the colored glass portions of the window and washed the bed and its white linens in stark evocative shapes of shadow and soft color. The great blue mirror reflected the night's stars. A fire burned in the hearth and flickering yellow flames framed the unicorn andiron's red-glowing eyes. Vesper stood unaware the light drifted through her tunic. The vision wiped his parents' ghostly presence from the room.

"I found an unexpected treasure," she said with a smile. "A trunk in the bedroom, here," she pointed, "it held clean bed linen that still smells faintly of lavender. The curtains and bed coverings I think can be saved. I took them down and placed them in the solar for cleaning later. I hope you don't mind."

With the heavy and voluminous cloth removed and only the snowy linens covering the bed, the room appeared austere.

"I don't mind, but it is very cold up here," Drew said, walking to the fire and placing the logs carefully to the side. He placed several more on the fire and stoked it to burn hotter, aware he needed desperately to escape.

"It will be warm enough once I am under the covers."

Drew turned to Vesper, swallowing before he said. "Then I'll say goodnight."

"Goodnight, Drew." Her soft confused voice followed his abrupt exit.

Eight

The next day Vesper stood in the harsh cold on the allure with a stinging wind blowing her tunic like a flag behind her. Enchanted, she didn't care, not until she saw a slow cavalcade make its way up the hill to Montoren Farm. Even from her height, she identified the team surrounded by Montoren horses and men—Shilly and Shally.

Vesper ran from the allure and down the stone staircase in a dangerous breakneck flight. Her hurried steps aroused attention as she ran to the arched gateway out of Montoren. Before she reached it, the blacksmith called Fulbert caught her by the arm, stopping her. "Nay, missy," he said in a deep baritone bringing her to an abrupt halt.

"Let me go! Marwyn comes, I'm going to him."

"You'll wait here," Fulbert said in implacable tones.

Vesper stared at him in shock. Never had anyone ever physically stopped her from anything. Looking around showed her clan women, some showing concern, others amusement. Vesper straightened, gathered what dignity she could, and waited. It was some time before she heard the jangle of Shilly and Shally's harness and the turn of Marwyn's wagon wheels on the ground approaching the manse.

Four clansmen jogged their mounts through the gate first, to quickly dismount, turn, and wait in a most threatening manner.

The escorted wagon came through the gate, Marwyn showing no concern—in fact, he looked most cheerful. Drew rode alongside, looking displeased and forbidding. It startled Vesper at how menacing he looked. Selwyn rode directly behind Drew. The huge rough hand holding Vesper released, and she ran to the wagon's side shouting Marwyn's name in joy.

Marwyn crawled in stiff and labored movement down from the wagon and Vesper's pleasure at seeing him diminished with the realization of how hard the long ride had been on the old man, already bothered by joint disease. The smile never left his face though, and he picked her up off her feet in an effervescent hug. She threw her arms around him returning the greeting.

"It's good to lay eyes on you, Peeper," Marwyn said. Vesper held him in a ferocious grip, closing her eyes to prevent and tears from escaping. At last, Marwyn put her down. With another start Vesper saw Alfred sitting on Shilly's rump, grinning at her. She looked around, but no one noticed as Alfred jumped up, danced a small jig, and used the harness for handholds to swing down to the ground. He laughed and ran, disappearing in an instant. Only Shilly showed signs of Alfred's presence, swishing his tail over his rump, and swinging his gray head around with a snort.

"What are you doing here?" Vesper asked returning her gaze to Marwyn. Both bewildered and frightened by the realization no one else saw what she did, she pulled herself back to reality. "You must have started out before dawn!"

"It's a long way, isn't it?" Marwyn said, puffing some in his accomplishment. "Brought you Eudora's gifting," he said grinning. "We three old-timers just ambled at our own pace. Can only stay long enough to shake out the kinks and unload. Freda will be looking for me before dark sets in."

"And your gift is surely this long journey. Oh, Marwyn, I'm so sorry, I have nothing to make the journey back easier."

"Ah, Peeper, don't worry so. Eudora took care of that." He slipped a flask partway from his jacket pocket and let it slide back. He looked around the courtyard at the watching clansmen.

Vesper's eyes followed Marwyn's, and she suddenly realized Drew had come to stand behind her. His heavy cloak fell around her shoulders and she realized how cold she had become. A movement from Drew and the interested clan dispersed to go about their business.

"Vesper?" Drew asked in a polite voice.

Vesper turned to him with a taut smile. "This is my friend, my uncle by assent, Marwyn."

Drew ignored her tone and stretched his right hand out to Marwyn. "I'm Drew Montoren," he said. "I'm the one Vesper accepted at Handfasting, and I apologize for the poor greeting you received from my clan. We have been bothered of late with trespassers having less civil intent."

"Ahk, I hear you," Marwyn said. "Much talk in town about reavers striking travelers while journeying hereabouts. Bad for business. It's a good thing you take precautions. Have you here a good man or two to help me unload Vesper's trunk?"

Selwyn alone lifted the trunk from the back of the wagon and took it to the hall's entrance.

"Come in, warm up and have a drink before you resume your return journey," Vesper said. "Are Shilly and Shally's blankets in the wagon? I'll cover them." While Vesper talked, she walked to the horse's heads, petting them with gentle strokes. Shally, the huge piebald, closed his eyes and lowered his head to Vesper's ministrations.

"That sounds welcome," Marwyn said.

It was Drew though, who got the blankets and threw them over the tall backs, rubbed their withers and neck, and born horseman, checked them for strain. Vesper ignored him. A sullen fury still knotted in her stomach.

"They are a fine team," Drew said, finished with his task. He came to their heads and scratched Shilly's neck just behind the ears. Shilly gave a snort of pleasure.

"Thank'yu, lad. It's nice to see someone who can still appreciate them. Far past their prime. Eh, now, so am I," Marwyn said looking around him. "You know horses, you do. These are fine mounts you and your men ride."

Vesper glared at Drew, who, while he remained civil in affirming Vesper's invitation, did not lose his stony look. Marwyn had his ale and chatted to both Vesper and Drew non-stop. His eyes roamed the manse hall under the frowning presence of Selwyn. All too soon he was on his way. Vesper watched his departure from the courtyard, then walked to the allure to watch the wagon disappear in the distance. She heard Drew come up and stand next to her.

"Do you greet all your guests in such fashion?" Vesper asked.

"Anything unexpected is suspect. Your friend was unexpected. I'm sorry if it has upset you. The clansmen will escort him all the way to town. Will you receive more visitors? I brought your trunk up to your room."

"Thank you," Vesper said, her voice as stiff as her posture. She turned her head and looked at Drew. "Am I a prisoner here?"

His lips firmed but he continued to watch Marwyn and the clan escort disappear over the crest of a hill. Vesper waited. At last he spoke as if choosing his words. "It is not safe for you to leave the confines of the enclosure. As I said earlier, we have had unwelcome trespassers. You know nothing of the surrounding land and trails. I only asked that you not leave the manse while I am gone. For your own protection."

"I know the way to Norost. You had me stopped from even going outside the gates to greet Marwyn."

"Yes. This is a different life from what you are used to. You promised me time, and you will do as I say." A slight jut of his chin backed his words.

"I promised you time, but not to be your prisoner." Vesper turned away and left him standing alone. Once in her room, she closed the door, threw the lock, and stood with her back against it. It struck her Drew was not like Brandt at all, but stubborn and perhaps the owner of a fine temper. She heard his footsteps enter the solar and approach her door. Turning she backed away from the door until she caught her image in the blue mirror.

Its depth's misted, showing her an image. Within the sapphire glass Drew slumped over a horse's mutilated carcass. An arrow's shaft pierced his back. Blood seeped from his mouth and nose. His blank gaze told her his condition. She threw her hand over her mouth to keep from screaming and squeezed her eyes shut. Opening them she found the mirror reflected only her own horrified visage, but the former scene was burned in her mind.

Outside her door she heard Drew's steps descending the stairs and opened her door. By the time she reached the steps, he was already gone. As her heart slowed, she returned to her room and noticed Eudora's gift sitting at the foot of the bed.

She recognized from the mermaid on top it was her mother's trunk. Vesper ran her hands over the carved surface then unlatched the clasp with anticipation. Inside were all her clothes. She sighed in relief at having something of her own to wear. What she found underneath clutched her heart. Several beautiful chemises and collars, embroidered with exquisite white on white embroidery, lay on top of folded yards of fine linen. Wife's wear. In a smaller box lay threads and needles and a small scissors. Vesper sighed in pleasure to be able to sew again. She lifted another matching box from the inside. The smaller box also held treasure—the gift of healing. Bottles filled with the herbs Eudora had taught her about, plus ointments and elixirs of Eudora's mixing, and more, a book, a copy of a rare herbal.

It was a thoughtful gift. A gift of knowledge and love, mixing old with new. A gift telling Vesper she was a woman and ready to make her own way. Tears burst from Vesper and she cried in longing for Eudora's calm presence.

~ * ~

After a sennight spent in the revelry of wild escapades, Warrick woke hungry, his head aching and with an urgent desire to ride. Anywhere. Shaking Emory and Tate awake, the three climbed onto the still saddled horses. "Do you know where we are?" Warrick asked Emory.

"No. We've just followed the sun."

"Well, then," Warrick grinned through a headache, "let's continue." He turned his horse hard and shouted over his shoulder. "But let's find some food first." Emery and Tate rode behind him. Nine leagues down the road a village woman offered them fresh bread and boiled eggs. They asked where they were. The woman laughed. "You're in Lycon. Where were you headed?"

Warrick thanked her for her direction and trouble on their behalf. As they left, he said, "I thought you said we followed the sun? Only if it traveled south!"

"I can't remember having seen the sun that much, to say," Emory said. Tate gave a feeble laugh, still feeling his wine. The boy looked green and soon puked up his meal, but then perked up.

By noon they were twenty leagues west heading toward Konoch. Sometime later Warrick pulled up. Smoke and screaming ahead forewarned of trouble. Riding all out they crested a small hill and saw six wagons, two burning. Several bodies lay scattered about, and reavers looted the wagons. Screaming in anger, Warrick charged toward the beleaguered travelers. Hearing them approach, the outlaws were gone by the time they reached the wagons.

Warrick chased them but lost them in the surrounding hills. "Too late. Too damn late for the only adventure at hand!" he shouted. He pulled his horse around and headed back to the wagons. Tate looked white with fright but had followed gamely. Emory had come, but his girth had loosened and dumped him several hundred yards behind.

Five men lay dead around the wagons. Warrick rode to each. They had been dragged to death behind horses, trampled and stabbed, mutilated either before or after their deaths. It was the first time he had seen dead men, and his stomach heaved in protest. Emory, still fixing his saddle, didn't observe this fault, and Tate was too sick himself to bear witness to what happened around him.

Cries from the wagons drew his attention. Six women huddled there, their clothes ripped or missing, their eyes dead in pain-filled exhaustion. One old lady, maybe a grandmother, and perhaps her daughters with their three daughters, he guessed. One child, who appeared near the age of one of his half-sisters, huddled in her mother's arms with blood smearing her naked legs. *Raped.*

Unable to speak, Warrick turned his gaze to Tate, but the younger boy ran to the last wagon before throwing up. With no one around to follow his bidding, Warrick searched the debris from the wagons and found blankets he placed next to the women. They cringed when he approached, so he kept his distance as much as possible.

Gathering wood, he made a small, inadequate fire. Tate approached. "Do you know how to build a proper fire?" he asked. Tate shook his head no. "Then see if you can find cooking utensils or any food left about." Tate searched the wagons, then walked the perimeter avoiding the bodies. He returned with a small pot.

"We cannot leave the bodies. Look in the wagons for something to wrap them in. I will help you after... One of us will have to set snares for some small game, find water." Tate nodded and backed away, not looking at the women.

Going to his horse, Warrick found his flask filled with wine, not water. He filled the silver cup from his saddle pack and took it to the women. The three older women sipped, but the younger girls, now wrapped in blankets, stared at nothing. Tate finally reappeared with water. With inept difficulty, Warrick kept the fire lit.

"What are we going to do?" Tate asked. Emory stood behind his brother.

Placing the flagon of water near the women, Warrick returned to his companions. "Tate, you ride back to the last village. Bring help. Emory and I will stay here to protect the women. Be careful. Do not mention who we are. Is that clear?" The boy nodded in relief and scooted to his horse.

"And what are we going to do?" Emory asked, also avoiding the women.

"We will wrap the bodies as best we can and pull them behind these wagons where the women will not have to see them."

Warrick said nothing when Emory puked several times during their oppressive task. When they returned to the makeshift camp, the water was still there, unused. Warrick picked it up and slowly forced some liquid down each resisting mouth. They remained like that all night. Tate arrived with villagers and a priest in carts the next morning. A woman came with them and went to the victims by the wagon. Warrick presumed her a healer. The villagers dug the graves. As the men were placed in the ground, their women moved to the grave. They remained dry-eyed and quiet while the priest intoned the death rites in a soft voice.

"Will the women return to our village?" the priest asked. His parishioners' expressions varied from dismay to astonishment at the possibility.

Warrick looked at the women. One of the younger women looked up.

"We will continue on our way."

Warrick slowly walked to her. "It would be wise to stay and refurbish your wagons before moving on."

"We have no option, sir. We are traveling players and have four more engagements before we reach Mel Snecte for our winter camping. If we do not make these engagements, we will lose them to some other traveling troop. The lost income would be impossible to replace."

"But your menfolk..."

"Everyone knows the stories and the words, sir. We will find men willing to play as we travel."

"We could, Warrick," Tate said. "If they're the same plays we see yearly at c..." Tate stopped at Warrick's look. "You know the words, so do Em and I."

Warrick stared at Tate. Emory cuffed his brother.

"No, he is right, Em," Warrick said at last. "We cannot let them travel unprotected." He turned back to the woman. "With your permission we will travel with you, see you safe to Mal Snecte, fill in for you how we may." He was not prepared for the woman's tears or for her falling onto his chest. With discomfited reluctance, he put an arm around the woman and let her cry. The woman pulled herself together and went back to her remaining family, Warrick went to the village men who were preparing to leave.

"Is there any place nearby where I can replace the horses and provision the wagons?" It took another day, and Warrick paid with a gold hat ornament and a jeweled belt kept from when he changed from Prince Warrick to the merchant Warrick.

~ * ~

During the journey, Ottillie often read from her purloined diaries far into the night wrapped in robes and blankets. At her journey's start, she was still on the first volume, but a delay of two more nights at Green Island because of sleet and ice let her finish it. Once past Chloe's first observations on the court and her new life there, she began to write of the war. The sorceress described her work at Bishop's Infirmary.

It became gruesome with accounts of the various patients, their injuries, and how they were wounded. Reports of small children with hands or feet cut off, of women raped and beaten and dealing with the aftermath, of soldiers wounded in battles. The day in day out depiction of unspeakable cruelty, deprivation, and evil wore on Ottillie. It described war not as the heroic stories told of it, but in the terrible cost individuals paid. Ottillie spent as much time thinking over Chloe's words as she did in deciphering the writing.

Now, in their eighth day of slow travel and constant delays, Eldin, already disturbed, berated her. It was predawn and Ottillie was too tired to assist in breaking camp. "What keeps your lamp on so late?" His demand came at the end of a long harangue, one of several the past days.

"I'm reading. It's hard to sleep in the cold and damp." His angry eyes lanced her with guilt.

"Reading! You goose! You're the one who chose to travel in winter. Two more days and Last Day is upon us! And we have not yet reached Gotte City. If we do not reach it by then, Ottillie, we will be delayed further! We must reach it by tomorrow or wait in the city. Kennetsure observes year's turn for ten days!"

That night they camped at the edge of the Great Salt Marsh, forty leagues distant from the ferry across the south branch of Thou River and Gotte City. The push to cross through the drier section of

Wessure's Salt Marsh tired Ottillie and no candle burned late in her tent that night.

Even with an early morning start their journey was doomed. Eldin's horse stepped into an unseen sinkhole, stumbling to his knees, throwing Eldin into cold water. This far south, it was not frozen, but the days never warmed to comfort. Luckily, the horse didn't break his leg, but he was lame. They stopped for Eldin to don dry clothes, and they had a cold lunch of dried meat and hard biscuits. Ottillie insisted they light a fire to warm him and heat water for a soothing drink, but all the men just laughed. There would be no fires while in the salt marsh as they carried no dry wood or kindling and wouldn't leave the trail to find any.

They traveled through the night, leading their horses through the darkness, down a mushy, sodden road. They made Gotte City too late on Last Day to arrange for desert guides. They were lucky to secure rooms. Ottillie, too tired to care, slept through the night's long religious ceremonies of the year's last day, then through most of First Day.

On Second Day, she gave a thought for her father's speech and missed him, if transiently. The cold rain had stopped, and Gotte City was bathed in warm sunlight, with squat, two and three-story balconied buildings lining the streets. She broke fast in the street, buying from a local vendor. The old peddler told her each building surrounded its own private garden where painted tiles enlivened the eye, fountains the ear, and colorful flowers the spirit on warmer days, but the weather had been unseasonably cold for the area. "It will warm in a few days," he promised.

Escaping to explore, Ottillie found the paved streets barely one cart wide with small walks that led behind the buildings, often showing a glimpse of the private gardens through wooden doors left ajar. Yet all Gotte City's activity took place in the streets and public squares. People talked, met, played, worked, and shopped, filling the streets. Few carts traveled the city's narrow streets. Long lines of donkeys, always piled high with merchandise and packs, tread behind their handlers. The sights, noises, and smells were new and irresistible to Ottillie.

While Eldin hunted for a guide, she investigated the city, and luckily, she was back before Eldin returned, gruff from his fruitless inquiries. "I've learned a guide comes back through this way in a fortnight. They say he knows the route well and leads a large troop who will guarantee our safe arrival."

"There are worse places to be stranded, Eldin." She could not understand his barely controlled rage.

"I would have thought, with your desire to reach Egan, the news less welcome," he glared at her, turned on his heel, and left.

~ * ~

"Tonight is Last Day. For the first time, I won't be in chapel with Eudora." Vesper shrugged. "I don't know why I confide in you. You never speak to me." Vesper talked at Alfred as they walked around the walled garden where fresh snow defined the garden beds from the stone walkways. She sniffed at him as he kicked snow off shrubs, then bent to pull a few dead weeds from between the bricks of the walk. Alfred enjoyed the garden. Low growing shrubs bereft of leaves and badly in need of shaping outlined the beds. It had become a daily habit to walk here, once in the morning, and again in the late afternoon before picking up the night's dinner.

It was a place of comfort and hope, a place to think and reflect and talk out her problems with Alfred, although he was not always present. Often she heard the tinkling sound of laughter, but it also might have been ice cracking as the wind whipped the trees.

With bold nerve, Alfred had walked into her solar the day of his arrival and taken up residence among the looms. Within a few days he had sorted threads and formed a small woven hammock. She watched him bounce on it several times before lying down with a grin and falling asleep. Later she had taken several small fox skins and left them by the loom after draping one over his sleeping form. They would allay the cold.

Even in its dormant and unkempt state, Vesper could see the beauty of possibilities in the dormant garden. Now was the time to prune, the time to plan. Soon she could plant seeds. Her fingers felt buds swelled ever so slightly on some branches, promising renewed life. She recognized the dried seed heads and stalks of several useful herbs scattered willy-nilly through the beds. Alfred found it all of great interest, too.

No one had tended this garden in a long time, and Alfred marched around with a disgusted face at broken branches, fallen stone ornaments, and overgrown thickets. Still, with pruning, the fruit trees and the roses would come back. There might be other plants still waiting to show new growth in the spring. As Vesper planned how to save the garden, it filled her with purpose and Alfred's antics often brought laughter.

Before she left the garden to enter the courtyard, she stopped and placed the remains of a loaf of bread on a flat stone, as she did every day in offering for the other Fair Folk. She knew they were about, sensed them, though they never showed themselves.

"Have you made new friends?" she asked Alfred, but he ignored her while he ran hands over the rusted ironwork of the gate. It, too, needed repair.

If anyone saw her, they would assume her mad, tell her the dogs took the bread, but how could the dogs get past the garden's gate? Besides, before she returned this way with dinner, her offering would be gone. Alfred watched her, made no comment, but followed. He would help himself to the dinner she brought nightly from the kitchen and kept warm in the coals of the hall's fireplace.

She sighed in both content and discontent. The manse, like the garden, could be made beautiful. Her explorations had proven its comfort, even to a bath with hot and cold running water. That discovery had amazed her until she discovered the door leading down below the rock floor of the hall. The manse sat on a cave filled with a great pool of hot water.

Vesper frowned at the memory. Before she could explore too far down dark tunnels, Drew had found her, grabbed her elbow, and marched her upstairs while forbidding her to return. "It is dangerous," he said, his face filled with ferocious anger. "A source for heat and water, but it is a maze of tunnels where you could easily become lost." She had to concede it might be. It had been scary entering that shadowy abyss alone. Even with her small lamp, it had been very dark and frightening.

Drew, though, had not stopped at that prohibition but started listing others. She must tell someone if she left the manse. She was not to wander the farm fields alone and never to enter the forest.

"I can leave the manse enclosure now?" she had asked.

"Not without an escort."

"That is ridiculous. Who will go with me?"

"I will."

"You are always gone."

"I will make time. You need to learn to ride anyway. We will start tomorrow."

She had disliked how he spoke as if she was some unwelcome encumbrance or duty. Drew had kept his promise to her, but maybe it was easy for him. Maybe wanting her meant something other than physical desire.

It was so confusing. On one hand he said he wanted her, but why? He did not show any of Alvina's signs of love. He watched her, but seldom talked to her, or did anything with her, except give her daily riding lessons in the freezing cold. And his clan hated her. Of that, she was sure.

She closed the iron gate of the garden and moved toward the courtyard. Dressed now in her own clothes, she felt more comfortable, more confident. She recalled Eudora's gift and what it must have cost her both in coin and time. In secret, too. It was a pleasant thing to think on in a home where most of her new family, even the few children, made her unwelcome clear. A place where her visions ran wild.

As she walked the courtyard, she said good morning to all with a small polite smile. Most gave a grudging, "Day, Miss." Only Drew, when he looked upon her, gave any indication of welcome, but Drew was kept singularly busy. She seldom saw him except at dinner and always in Selwyn's presence. *Patience and time*, Vesper could almost hear Eudora's words, *win more than rage and war*.

She kept herself busy in the manor. The Holy One knew there was enough to do there. At least the entire upper floor was now scrubbed clean, the linens and rugs were beaten free of dust. She worked on the allure where no one could remark on her labors. She could even dry linens there with no notice. Most of the hall was clean too, not that Drew or Selwyn noticed. By standing on a small table brought from the solar, all but the highest areas were now cobweb free, and she had not felt comfortable invading the alcoves full of their possessions. The medallion over the fireplace turned out to be the Clan's device, a great unicorn of carved white quartz, recumbent on a gilded quarter moon, the motto blazoned across the top, 'Faith, Courage, Fidelity.'

It was enough to clean their sleeping alcoves, change the linens, place fresh candles. One of the clan women collected the laundry. She never introduced herself and Vesper, in an unusual tinge of offended pride, refused to ask.

To finish her job, she needed a ladder, and although she searched the hall, pantry, and buttery, she had found none. In her investigations, though, she found old soaps and bathing salts and thick drying linens soft with age, a wonderful luxury with a hot-water bath available. It was another contradiction to all she had heard about clansmen and how they lived.

Contemplating her problem, Vesper watched Gerdi herd three of the small, tan mountain-bred cows common in the Vere plateau through the archway and toward the cow byre. Beside her Drew led one of his horses, still blowing hard clouds of vapor from its nostrils. The horse's hooves clopped rhythmically on the cobblestones of the court. Two of Drew's huge rough-haired hounds heeled at his side. Gerdi talked animatedly with him and Drew laughed at her remarks.

Gerdi was a young woman, perhaps Vesper's age or a little older, confident in her person and attractive with the dark brown eyes and hair of most of the clan. Only Drew and Selwyn had fair hair. Standing nearly as tall as Drew, but more plump than thin, Gerdi smiled and waved to the other clansmen in the courtyard. Vesper took a deep breath. *Patience.*

Catching sight of her, Drew waved and walked over, his horse and hounds following.

"Good day, Vesper." The exhilaration of hard exercise in cold weather showed in his face and smile.

"Good day, Drew." Her fingers ran through the coarse hair on the heads of one hound, his head butting her hand. "It looks as if you've ridden far and long."

"Not far. Selwyn and I have been practicing arms down in the lower pasture."

For the first time, Vesper noticed the sword hilt emerging from near the saddle's pommel and a buckler hooked near the flap. Noticing her gaze Drew lifted the buckler. Underneath, the amulet buckle was attached to the strap. "It has brought me luck already. I unhorsed Selwyn today."

Vesper's mood lightened and she smiled. "I am very glad then, that you accepted my gift. Can I help you with your horse?" At his look of surprise, she said, "I use to help Marwyn with Shilly and Shally when I was younger. I know how to groom a horse."

Drew indicated his acceptance. "Shilly and Shally?"

"The man with the mismatched draft team who brought Eudora's gifting." She thought Drew turned slightly darker. He repeated his apology for the poor reception given her friend but obviously didn't remember Marwyn's name. Apologetic but unrepentant. The protection and privacy the clan insisted on were forbidden subjects. If she asked, the subject was changed or ignored. In her ambiguous situation, she hadn't insisted on an answer.

"Marwyn is Freda's husband. She works with Eudora. Shilly and Shally are his draft team." Drew grunted a reply.

"Marwyn loves them." She giggled. "Maybe more even than Freda. When I was a little girl, he let me ride the wagon with him to collect stores from town. Do you and Selwyn practice often?"

"Daily." He looked away at Vesper's look of inquiry.

"Do you expect to do battle soon?"

"No, but the clans stay ready."

A non-answer for another forbidden subject. "Today is the Holy One's Last Day. Do you have plans? May we go into Norost tomorrow for First Day's Blessing?"

"No." After a pause, he mollified his harsh refusal. "We have not celebrated First Day in many years, and we have no priest to give blessings either this eve or tomorrow."

His tone suggested she not ask more. Annoyed, she decided to burn a month's worth of candles tomorrow to celebrate the day.

Inside the stable he tied his horse and loosened its girth and pulled the heavy saddle in one motion from the horse's back. Vesper picked up a brush and started work. This one had black legs, face, and neck that worked into a mouse gray body. The animal gave a horse sigh and groan when Vesper ran the brush along its back. As she worked Vesper talked.

"You seem to stay prepared for battle. Is this just your clan or all the clans?"

While she brushed, Drew took care of the riding tack. At her question, he turned and gave her a brooding look, then raised his brows and shrugged, still rubbing the bridle bit clean. "All clans, I suppose. With ever more travelers coming to Vere, the clans have suffered from pillaging. We have already lost much land to outsiders by land laws." At her look, he explained. "By law, anyone settling on land for six months owns it. We stay vigilant to keep squatters from encroaching here."

"I didn't know. Is all of Kaereya like that?"

"No, only Vere."

"Vere law, or clan law?"

"Clan law."

"And you follow Clan Montoren?"

"No, Clan Cader. Clan Cader ceded the farm to my family when one of my ancestors married into the clan. We kept our family name by clan consent." Finished with his task, Drew took another brush and started on the horse's other side.

"Is Selwyn clan head?"

Drew laughed. "No. Neither am I. My claim is only head of Montoren Farm. Selwyn is my cousin. We are both considered of Clan Cader, as you are, now."

"Do you owe obligation to the Caders?"

"Yes, but outside of occasional council meetings, social occasions or chance encounters on borders, I don't see either my clan or the other clans that much."

"The people in town think you a reclusive lot. I see you have some cause, but why have you ordered that I cannot leave the compound without an escort?"

"I am cautious by nature and training." His eyes avoided hers. "My duty is to protect the clan from any further encroachment by outsiders. The clan stays ready to do so by force if necessary. As for you not leaving the compound, you do not know this land. It is dangerous country. I would not have you lost or injured."

"I do not lose so easily," Vesper snapped, feeling very much an outsider. "And you practice more than caution, you practice deceit." She looked at Drew over the horse's back.

"What do you mean?" Drew's voice held a subdued snarl that matched his expression as his eyes fastened on her at last.

"You wear the meanest clothes whenever you enter Norost. You purposely make the townspeople think you desperately poor. It is a lie. You are no poor farmer. This 'farm' is not the barren rock you let the world believe. The storerooms are full of the produce of your orchards and fields. There is no shortage of wild game or domestic meat and dairy animals. Your hens lay well. Paupers do not stable twelve and more horses. So why the pretense in town?"

"Because it is necessary, and you will not question it or accuse me of lying," Drew said with a forceful swipe of the horse brush that matched his voice. His horse snorted in upset. Drew's sudden calming words to the animal inflamed Vesper's temper anew.

"Do not think you can control my thoughts or words or hide the truth when it stares me in the face!"

She straightened. Her hand balanced on the horse's back as Drew rounded the horse's rump in obvious temper. Before he said a word, Vesper turned ready to battle, but the horse sidestepped into her and as Drew pushed it away, his hand landed on top of hers. Time stopped, then restarted with several slow jolts.

He withdrew his hand. She blushed at wanting that warmth and stepped away, her anger dissipated. "I think I better collect our dinner from Berneta," she said in a tight voice and fled the stable.

Vesper regained her composure by the time she collected the platter of roasted meat and root vegetables. Passing the garden gate she saw the stone empty and produced a cheerless smile. Alfred sat on a stone at its entrance. He sniffed and followed her inside the hall. She placed the platter on the hearth and watched Alfred help himself and go up the stairs to his bed. Recovering the pot, the low flames drew her eyes and she sat staring into the fire.

Dizziness warned her, quickly followed by reality dulling shadows. She could see the flames and hear their crackling, but as if from a distance. Another view overlaid her vision. Fierce pain gripped her causing her to clutch her stomach and squeeze her eyes closed. A swirling darkness filled with wailing overcame her senses. Opening her eyes, she saw lavish bed curtains and well-dressed maids crying in anguish and wringing their hands above her. She could barely speak for the pain and fear engulfing her. *"The baby, is the baby all right? Poor Edith, my poor baby,"* a voice said, *"Tell me the baby is fine."*

"I am sorry. I did not mean to cause you distress." Drew's voice sounded far away.

Half aware, she heard her voice suddenly, moaning in anguish. *"The poor baby. Dead, they're all dead."*

Drew's voice and the touch of his hand on her shoulder brought Vesper from her vision. She still knelt, gazing into the fire. Vesper shuddered, feeling cold with sweat. Steadying her shaky legs, she rose and turned to Drew. His hand fell to his side.

"I'm sorry," she said, feeling the tears on her cheeks and rubbing them away. Biting her lip, she said, "You caused me no distress, I was... I was lost in thought." She could not control her voice or her shaking.

"Your thoughts do not seem pleasant. Who is dead?"

Still shaken, Vesper looked over Drew's shoulder and saw Selwyn staring at them from near the table. "I did not hear you enter.

Are you ready for dinner?" She collected the ewer of water warming in the fireplace and walked to where Selwyn washed. As she poured the rinse water over his hands, he asked, "a lover's quarrel?"

She handed him a towel. "Wishful thinking?"

Selwyn laughed. It was not a pleasant sound. He straightened with a smug look and walked away. Vesper became aware of how much Drew and Selwyn looked alike, Selwyn being a taller and older version.

He did not grin as Drew followed her upstairs later. Entering the solar, Drew appeared most self-conscious as he looked around the room. Vesper found it hard to breathe.

"You've done much work here."

"I've had plenty of time and never expected to live without some purpose."

"There are reasons I do what I do."

"I do not doubt that. I am sorry I questioned you. I had no right."

"You have a wife's right."

"I am not a wife."

"You will be."

The look he gave her made Vesper shiver, unsure if that was what she wanted. Drew looked just as doubtful about the prospect, but there was no escaping her owing him a year. Vesper forced herself to relax as she exhaled. "I am sorry to have started an argument with you. It was not my intention."

"What did you want?" Drew asked with clipped, gruff words, his voice an insinuation.

Vesper tried to smile. "Some conversation, a chance to know you better. This is all very strange for me, and I am homesick."

"For Brandt?" There was no doubt now of Drew's snide and disparaging tone.

Holding her temper Vesper answered in truth. "For Eudora. She and I spent most evenings together, talking and reading."

"You are lonely? Then it is my turn to apologize for leaving you to yourself so often." He did not sound very apologetic. "You need only ask to have that change."

With his sarcastic jab, Vesper raised her chin. "You must do your work. Your clan would dislike me even more if I took you from that, too. Besides, missing the past is part of all change."

"They do not dislike you," Drew said.

She would not call him a liar, but he read her face.

"They wanted me to Handfast within the clan that is all."

"Then why didn't you?"

"I told you why already. I wanted you."

"How can you say so? You don't even know me."

"I do." His defiant tone and past tense didn't escape Vesper. "Down there, by the fire, were you thinking of Brandt?" Drew demanded in a harsh voice.

Surprised and offended, Vesper answered him back in tone. "No, I wasn't. Why would you think so?"

"You loved Brandt, you expected him to ask for you at Handfasting. You say you are lonely for Eudora. What about Brandt? Are you lonely for him, too? What dead baby did you speak of?"

She could not speak of her vision. It was too painful, and she was afraid to tell anyone, especially Drew, of her curse. "I already told you I was not."

"No, you didn't. You sidestepped and only talked of Eudora. Tell me then, what upset you so?"

"It is of no importance, and I do not wish to think on it."

"Something upset you, certainly not our argument. I'm the injured party there. I'm the one you named liar."

His face displayed the anger her words had inflicted, and Vesper felt guilt over her insinuation. "I was not thinking of Brandt."

"Then was it because we will miss the First Day Mass in town? Are you angry about that?"

"No, how could you think so? It is twenty leagues even in good weather."

"You keep to yourself here making no attempt to join us. If we are to succeed, you must let go of thoughts of Brandt."

"What do you mean by that?" Vesper asked growing cold.

"I'm saying that I accept anything that passed between you and him."

Anger shot through Vesper. "I was never with Brandt in any way." His look clearly told her he didn't believe her. "What? Now you think me a liar? Did you think I spoke of a child of my own? You think me a whore? Why, because I'm labeled bastard? What right have you to accuse me? Tell me what secrets you keep, then I'll tell you mine." Her voice spiraled to a shrill demand that made her throat ache.

"I have not accused you of anything, quite the reverse," Drew said looking offended. He turned abruptly and left, leaving Vesper in an inflamed, speechless state. That soon released in tears but left her with many unanswered questions.

~ * ~

Chloe's Story

A sennight after receiving the golden dragon, Chloe walked along the cliffs reveling in the warm day. It was her first walk in days. Wounded soldiers and citizens flooded into the Royal City from what had been a calamitous battle for both sides. Chloe did not know the details. Only the Bishop ever had reliable war news, then, not often. She only dealt with the aftermath. The wounded usually only knew about their own segment of the battle. From them she knew it bad without learning more.

Fresh green showed under winter's brown along her path. The shrubs and few stunted trees also displayed signs of growth, and her shoes squelched in soft, melted earth. Wildflowers, tiny and brilliant yellow, bloomed in clumps at the cliff's edge. Even the air seemed revitalized.

Galloping hooves drummed the ground and Chloe looked behind her. A large cavalcade of aristos approached. The horses were pulled to a halt next to her, and with recognition, Chloe sank into a curtsy.

"Mistress Chloe." His voice blasted from atop his horse. "Stand up, girl!"

Chloe stood and spoke without looking up. "Your Majesty."

He swung down from his horse, as did several courtiers. "Is it your habit to walk along the cliffs?"

"Yes, Your Majesty. From here I can sometimes see my homeland."

"Please, no 'Your Majesty.' We have had enough of that formality today." He motioned her to walk and took her elbow in his hand, his horse followed behind. "You miss your home?"

"Yes, Your…" Chloe stopped, unsure how to address so exalted a person if not by respect. This was a difficult situation, and his marked notice made her uncomfortable. As if reading her mind, he spoke.

"Call us Ewald. We give you permission. It seems you are a lucky charm. After all, you have saved our heir, and after meeting you, this blasted war is finally going our way. You are a good witch, indeed. It seems the least we can do for you."

At first she didn't understand. Then closed her eyes and gave thanks to the Holy One. "Truly? Will it end? What a wonderful gift you will give your subjects."

"What else would you have?" His eyes slid to her.

"Nothing, Sire. That is enough, and you have already rewarded me."

The King laughed. "A trifle, believe me. Others would have asked for an estate, or a title, or greater riches."

"I am a healer, Sire. It is my duty to save lives. Your notice and reward are undeserved treasures."

"You make me feel ungenerous!"

"Nay, Sire. Too generous."

"Ewald, Mistress Chloe, remember."

"I cannot, Sire. It would be improper. You are the king. I am only one of your subjects."

King Ewald frowned and stopped. Chloe thought him about to argue, but then he laughed. "This interlude has taken us from weighty war worries, Mistress. We must thank you again." He mounted his horse and with a nod of his head, galloped away with all his retainers following him. Once back at the infirmary she heard the news. Sunderlune had withdrawn from the western province.

Chloe caught a sigh of relief, then smiled in private pride at the King singling her out. It was a happenstance but a flattering one. The

King was an attractive middle-aged man, powerful and personable. It affected her.

She did not expect it to happen again. But it did. Like he knew when she left the infirmary. Three times was not coincidence. He also visited the infirmary and spoke with the wounded. It was then Chloe realized with horror the King was interested in her personally.

He continued to pursue her until everyone already assumed she had given in. By then it was too late. For the first time, Chloe found herself in love, and gave of herself. Spring turned into a wonderful, sparkling time.

"You cannot do this," Chloe said. They met in an apartment in the Eternal Palace, but she knew not in the king's suite.

"If you are the Court's Sorceress, no one can remark on your presence in the Eternal Palace. I can give you rooms here."

"No sneaking in through the lower caravans? No. You would only set me apart further. It is not just my gift or my Kennetsurean appearance. You will rouse the entire court against me. I do not think I can bear that. What I do is enough."

"What? Loving me is a burden?"

"Yes, Ewald, it is. One I gladly carry."

"Because you love me?"

"Yes, and because you gave me little choice."

"By destiny's stones, Chloe. You are not at all flattering. You will do it anyway, then. You will be made a Lady by my command."

"Please don't."

He rose from bed. "And I will give you no choice in this. On Bull's Day during Summer Festival. In thanks for your service to the wounded of the war. You will see, Chloe, no one will remark on it or disparage you."

She did not speak her thoughts. A woman was not allowed to refuse the king. Everyone understood that. No one would disparage her. It was an honor to be the king's mistress. But no one would respect her.

<h1 align="center">Nine</h1>

"I have little enough to celebrate this Last Day, although I am glad of your presence, Raymond"

Raymond Aurelias sat next to his friend glad Norbert had recovered enough to speak. This was their first chance to talk since Aurelias arrived back at court, but nothing could be said that might be overheard. It limited his desire for any conversation.

Their silence separated them from the rest of the Aristo revelers. Most had not dressed in sober comportment for the long prayer vigil but in anticipation of this first banquet of the new year. The participants proved Easure's reputation as a province of color and wind, amply justified. Easure's fish and bull motifs adorned cloth, jewelry, and headdress, along with its sacred numbers of two and seven. Although both he and Norbert had changed, it was only into finer quality fabrics.

He noticed Norbert averted his eyes from the kaleidoscope of color cavorting through the hall. Around them the steady unintelligible clamor of unchecked voices, the clank and bang of food service, and the musicians' woodwind efforts in the gallery vied with the Princess Edith's piercing whine. The child should have been in bed hours ago, but all the Royal children were present, save Warrick. Luckily, the tedious banquet was nearly at an end and Aurelias sensed Norbert's cringe as the entertainment started. Acrobats hurdled into the hall.

"I did not bruise my knees through the night in prayer for myself," Aurelias said, answering at last.

"I know." Norbert sighed then snorted softly as he admitted, "We are both worried. It seems that dread overrides all I do. What is the cause of your unease?"

"The same." Without looking at his friend Aurelias knew the truth. Anxiety dressed Norbert's frame. When he returned to court just before yesterday's religious observations began, Norbert's changed appearance had struck him. Always thin, he now looked gaunt and haggard, his clothes hanging on him like shrouds. Something major harried Norbert. With his own worries snapping at his heels, he knew they'd both have to wait for airing. Ottillie usually took better care of her father, but he hadn't seen her. Perhaps she had handfasted at last. The thought stabbed him.

Looking around at the indulgence surrounding them, Aurelias said, "It is good Court convenes tomorrow, if only to give many a chance to recover from the sparse sleep and drink indulgence of Last Day." He lifted his drink flagon in a quiet toast to Norbert.

Norbert did not return the toast or eat much of the meal. Taking no offense at his friend's snub, Aurelias smiled. The scent of worship always afflicted Norbert with megrims, making the Holy One's glorification services more torture than cleansing ritual.

"I am averse to a day of weary formality and custom, renewed oaths, and sober duty. It is as long and as uncomfortable as this evening's service," Norbert grumbled. "But even more so when I must report what none want to hear. It is a perfect day for others to suffer with me." Norbert kept his eyes closed.

"You still suffer from the afflictions of the service, so I will disregard your ill-humored complaint."

Norbert swore. "My head is ready to drop off, although the worst seems over. At these times I swear I would willingly have it severed and stuck on the Holy One's staffs."

"You must be popular with the clergy," Raymond said.

"Afterward, I cannot taste any drink without getting ill. The Queen suffers from the headaches the candles give her also, so I have a sympathetic company."

"Are you ready for the Royal Court's opening tomorrow?" At Norbert's curt assent, Aurelias continued. "Frederick seems to be enjoying the evening's celebration, although the queen looks ill."

Norbert snorted. "The family is to enjoy the night wonderfully well, by Frederick's order. It is a great performance considering Princess Pia remains in her room, and the Queen suffers from the service and worries about Warrick. If no one mentions him, it will continue so. For once, the entire family behaves, filled with lectures of duty and terrorized by His Majesty's tantrums."

"All except Edith, who should never have been allowed to attend."

"Frederick insisted."

"I've heard the gossip," Aurelias said. "Since the year turned two candlemarks ago, I don't expect this to last much longer."

"Thank the Holy One," Norbert muttered. "After I recover from this agony, I have a problem to discuss with you." Aurelias nodded.

"I miss Ottillie," Norbert said.

A knife of anger stabbed Aurelias' heart. He took a deep draft from his flagon and slammed the vessel to the table.

"What have I said?"

"Nothing. Later. Where is Ottillie? Did she Handfast?"

"No. She left Handfast eve, for Kennetsure. In Egan."

"She refused to even attend?"

Norbert's face tightened into even harsher lines, his lips seeming to disappear. "I doubt she would get any decent offers. She is of an age to make the decision, although so doing indicates she never plans to wed."

Norbert's long face softened in amusement at the face Aurelias wore. "You may well look surprised. She wanted to go. Supposedly to do some investigation for some of my problems—to do some research in Egan's library," he added before Aurelias could ask, but his eyes strayed to where the Duke of Hearthron chatted with Frederick.

Frederick held his youngest, the toddler Edith, on his lap. The tired child was nearly asleep. Servers walked about with communal vessels of honey wine. The king's tasters offered drink to the royal family after performing their duty.

"I wanted her gone for her own safety."

"You think someone would harm her here?" Aurelias asked, watching the king and his brother-in-law.

"The Eternal Palace is no haven. Many predators roam here. Holy One, may this end soon."

Aurelias glanced at Norbert, who seemed to shrink in upon himself, then at the opening doors. The second entertainment entered—players for a drum story. "Can you leave?"

"No. I must attend the king's disrobing, and newly back at court, so must you."

Aurelias swore. "I know, but we don't need to sit in the line of fire. Come, let's escape to one of the galleries. We can watch without all the noise."

Norbert rose, but also kept watch on the Royal family.

Much to the Queen's obvious dismay, Frederick offered his little daughter several tastes from his tankard. Aurelias knew that after ten days of rampage Frederick had resigned the problem of Warrick to his Marshal to find a solution. Now the king watched his court in an almost playful mood.

"Stop it, she's a baby!" The Queen's voice overrode the soft buzz of voices surrounding lower tables. The Court stilled at her strident voice, and the drums came to a merciful halt. Aurelias settled back into his chair. The taut lines around the Queen's mouth and eyes, her pale complexion and glassy eyes told of her condition.

"Drink your own," Frederick rebutted his queen with a wink. "I choose to share mine. She shall sleep well tonight. Won't you Edith?" He asked the toddler sitting on his knee.

With a huff of exasperation, the Queen glowered at the king and signaled a waiting-woman. A woman came immediately and took the small princess in her arms. The king gave the child up willingly with a wicked chuckle. The Queen also rose and left the assembly, her retinue of maids mirroring her movement. Frederick watched his Queen's withdrawal.

When Frederick showed no sign of leaving, Aurelias rose, as Norbert did, and withdrew to one of the galleries, escaping the resonant drum notes reverberating off the walls.

Norbert listened as Aurelias told a page to watch and alert them when the king decided to leave the hall and ordered some distilled essences brought. Subdued laughter filtered into the room where they sat, but the overwhelming din ceased, and the sickening sea of color and smell were gone. Shortly the drink arrived in two carved horns set in silver stands. Norbert refused. "It only makes it worse. The Queen always manages, but I don't know how she does it." After a quarter mark in the relative quiet, he revived and for the next candlemark he found relief in talking of the problems of Kaereya.

"There is a network of conspirators. My agents Corbin and Galen have found some of the tendrils and untied some of the knots, but few know more than their immediate contact, and when those men are found, most times they are dead. Whoever leads this group is ruthless. Any liability is immediately destroyed. It is most frustrating. There has to be a court-tie."

"A traitor?"

"Yes."

He questioned Norbert until there was nothing left of the topic. Soon afterward Aurelias related his trip to Vere.

"I did not expect to find her so soon. Indeed, I really had no idea where to look. The message came from Norost, so I started my hunt there. It was only chance that brought me to the Handfasting Ceremony."

Knowing his friend's feelings about another marriage, he gave a soft laugh. "That must have given rise to expectations."

"Yes." Aurelias shook his head to reinforce his friend's sour confirmation. "Adjudicator Signus asked me to attend. His son handfasted the Mayor's daughter." Aurelias closed his eyes. "But there she was, looking so much like her mother, it was like seeing Lorelei alive, even to the surgown. I..." He opened his eyes. "I gave no sign of recognition." He sighed. "I relived, too, my last view of

Lorelei, her maid lying backstabbed to the heart, Lorelei and my infant son's throats cut. All supposedly by Lorelei's hand. She still held the knife, poor woman. How could I have known there was a second child? Known Lorelei gave birth to twins?"

"You could not," Norbert said. "Let the past go, Raymond, don't let it haunt you. Now you know not by her own hand. And now you know a second child was born, and that she lives."

Aurelias swiped his face with a hand, rubbing his eyes as he did so. "It's hard to believe. Two wives and two sons dead, and by the Holy One's grace, a living child, but one stolen from me." He sighed. "Anyway, with the attack on me, I could say nothing, show nothing. It was too dangerous. Whoever knows, has kept her alive this long, they must have a purpose. I felt I could not have my own peril descend on her."

He paused, reliving the horror of the past, finding Lorelei, then years later finding his second wife Mantha and their son dead in a road accident. "Then, a clansman claimed her hand, and before I could intervene, she had accepted him. The Handfast was much to everyone's surprise. The Adjudicator Signus didn't think she even knew the young man. They thought me there to seek another wife. They were lucky my hands were tied. If it were a trap, I refused to spring it. It was a total disparagement for her, but those hill-bound clansmen should keep her safe enough. I left a man to investigate the housekeeper and keep an eye on my daughter. If he thinks her in danger, I'll take an army up there and pull her out."

Norbert ignored Aurelia's exaggeration. "Do you know who sent the letter?"

"At first, I thought it was the housekeeper, but it doesn't make sense. If she killed Lorelei, why would she let me know she has my daughter after all these years? If she planned the river incident, she must have known it risky. Why would she want to kill me anyway? I had no notion I had a daughter."

"Maybe the two are unrelated. I've already told you of my suspicion of a long-term plot against aristos. If Lorelei had magic in her bloodlines, she was a target for these nameless assassins." He shrugged at Aurelias' indrawn breath.

"More likely, one of my enemies has long planned my downfall. Someone desires for me to see all my work and all the important people in my life end in the most painful way before destroying me."

"Do you have so many dedicated enemies?"

Aurelias shrugged. "No. A few hate me, hate my politics, but wouldn't lift a hair, let alone a weapon, to destroy me."

"This housekeeper, she kept your daughter from you, it's true, but maybe she came upon your murdered wife before you, found the living child and wanted to protect her, or desired the baby for herself. Barren women have been known to steal children. Now the child is grown. She brings your daughter to your notice wanting Vesper restored to her proper position." Norbert shrugged and continued with his speculations. "Maybe she held a grudge over some past incident unknown or forgotten by you and drew you with the letter to see your daughter disparaged, knowing the clansman would claim her. She might have some reason we can't discern. Maybe she didn't send the letter. You don't know all the facts, Raymond."

Aurelias slammed his hand on the side table and rose in agitation. "My daughter, now my only child, and I can't even acknowledge her for fear someone will try to kill her."

He picked up the tankard and threw it. The horn shattered into tiny pieces against the fireplace rock, the remaining alcohol essences burst into flame from the fire. The flash echoed his anger. He took a deep breath and clenched his jaw.

In the quiet that followed, he finally said, "I'm sorry. I thought I was past this." He stood looking at the fire. "As I said, Signus didn't realize my interest, my mixed elation at finding my daughter, my pain at seeing her left standing, then worse, handfasted to a clan farmer. At first, Signus said no townsman one would claim the girl, a housekeeper's bastard." He took a deep breath and clenched his jaw.

Aurelias struggled to control his temper and wondered if Signus knew how lucky he had been. "Even Quillon recognized the girl from her likeness to Lorelei."

A knock on the door and a low voice informed them the king was withdrawing, ending their conversation. Within another candlemark Aurelias was in his bed.

~ * ~

His valet shook him awake. Norbert woke groggily, finding it hard to confront reality. That ceased when he entered his drawing room. The presence of a Royal Guardsman triggered his sense of disaster.

After listening to the message, Norbert ordered his valet to find Aurelias, then quickly dressed.

Walking into the Royal Apartments, Norbert ordered extra guards brought to bring order to the King's Hall below stairs and to honor the king. Already rumor spread throughout the Palace, and he cursed. Theodulf Gilchrist sat with his head in his hands on one of the chairs near the fireplace. Norbert heard his grief. Aurelias had already arrived and cast a haggard look at Norbert as he entered. He turned to the King's Seneschal and the Royal Equerry and asked them to show him the King. The Equerry started babbling, his horror, anguish, and fear apparent.

"The effects of the alcohol he consumed at the banquet helped him fall asleep faster than usual," the man said, his eyes red-rimmed and his motions jittery as they moved into the bed chamber. The vile smell of vomit assailed the senses. Norbert hardened himself against what he would see, feeling his own illness.

Beneath the heavy curtains enclosing the bed, the King lay in a spew of vomit, his face contorted with pain. Norbert tested his monarch's pulse, but the corporeal part of His Most Royal Majesty was beyond help. Aurelias looked as stunned and appalled as he felt, realizing part of their world had ended.

"Has the physician seen him?"

"No, it was already too late," the seneschal said.

"Call him now. Let him determine the cause of death."

Word came back within moments that the physician was with the Queen. Norbert gave orders for three of the Royal Guards to make sure no one touched anything within the room. Sent another to get Prince Frederick, now the new king.

"But we must take care of His Majesty!" the equerry said.

"The Holy One is taking care of His Majesty. Another few moments as he is will not harm him now."

The Royal Guardsman attending the king pushed the reluctant retainers out of the bedroom and took up his post. As Norbert and Aurelias prepared to leave, Norbert's men Corbin and Galen Napier arrived. Norbert ordered one to interview each servant, from the Aristo retinue, to the common palace workers. Ordered the other to seek out the royal tasters.

Gilchrist stirred and rose, his face tear-streaked, and asked to accompany them to the Queen. "I must be the one to tell her of this tragedy." The Duke of Hearthron walked from the room. Aurelias spread a hand in invitation for Norbert to lead the way, showing the usurpation of power did not go unnoticed.

In the Queen's apartment the physician still tried to help Her Majesty, but when Gilchrist asked, the man looked at him with a hopeless shake of his head. The same vile smell filled the room. The Queen's low moans were barely audible, but she worried over her children, especially the youngest. Norbert looked at the physician. The man shook his head and mouthed 'dead'.

One of the attending handmaids pulled on Norbert's sleeve, an older woman and longtime friend of the Queen. She led him back into the sitting room. "If you mean to question Her Majesty, sir, it is impossible. She is unresponsive to questions. Her life is now measured less than a candlemark."

"You have tried?" When she nodded, he asked, "and the younger children?"

"Dead. The poison acted faster on them."

"Poison?"

"Yes. I came here from the nursery. From the symptoms I suspect monkshood."

At a sound, Norbert turned to see the drawn face of the man sent to Prince Frederick. "Earl Rikon," the man stumbled over his words, nodded a frantic bow to Aurelias. "Aristo Norbert, Aristo Aurelias... Prince Frederick and his Princess are dead. And one of the pages who served the king's dinner was found dead below stairs, his neck broken." The Guardsman broke into tears and covered his face with his hands.

Gilchrist suddenly sat in one of the decorative chairs lining the room. "By the Holy One!" he moaned with obvious distress. "Such calamities, such evil. Who? Murdered. The entire royal family. Murdered."

"All but Warrick," Norbert said, with dread shrinking his skin. He turned to one of his men. "Go to the boy's body, keep everyone from touching or moving anything, then send a servant to show me the way. Go!" He turned to Gilchrist and put a hand on the man's shoulder. "I am most sorry to intrude into your grief, but I need your assistance."

Gilchrist raised a stricken face to him. "What can I do?"

"Someone must tell the Court."

Awareness came into Gilchrist's eyes. "Yes. It must be done, and you are correct, it should come from me, as family." He rose and left.

Norbert and Aurelias waited, but the Queen passed within the candlemark, never regaining sensibility. Norbert used the time to send messages and give orders. In the corridor outside the Queen's apartments wails could be heard. Already word seeped out to the general court and populace. The noise of mourners gathering on the courtyards outside the palace soon became audible.

Norbert passed through several corridors before he reached the page's body. Walking through the unnaturally quiet halls, many detained him, both servant and Aristo, asking if the news were true, Norbert tried to contain his own disquiet. He had sent Aurelias to gather the other Aristo Council members and missed his company. Others took care of the bodies of the royal tasters, found dead among those sleeping off their celebration.

At the base of the lower-level steps, the last body lay. He recognized the boy. The freckles now stood out on the ashen skin, the sandy hair lay in a pool of blood and the impertinent eyes stared dull and sightless. It was the youngster from Master Godfrey's workrooms. It seemed like the boy had slipped on the stone steps and fallen to his death, but pushing the shirt aside, Norbert noticed fingerprints on the boy's shoulders and on his neck. No accident, then. Someone broke his neck before flinging him off the steps. He looked around but found neither a platter nor a pitcher, nor any sign of spilled food or liquid. He walked up the steps. There, on the upper landing, drying liquid puddled in a few worn indentations in the stone. It was wine. A search showed no other traces of the crime.

Before he finished, Master Godfrey came, still in his nightdress, his feet slippered, and his face in torment. His hand held a candlestick, its wax catcher dripping and spilling to the floor.

"Tell me it isn't true?"

"I'm sorry, Master Godfrey, he is below."

In an unexpected display, the heavier man staggered and reached for Norbert. He helped Godfrey keep his balance. Anguished eyes stared into his. "He was a good boy, full of faults, but not evil. He wasn't, truly, he wasn't! I won't believe he intentionally poisoned the king. His killing himself must prove that!"

"No, I am sure he was duped, like many others. He didn't commit suicide."

"An accident?"

"No. He was murdered. His neck broken."

Godfrey fell silent in shock, his face displaying his state. Norbert patted his arm. He walked the Master back to his rooms. The wails of other mourners seeped through the walls of the palace. Servants already dressed the palace in the black and red of mourning.

Within the king's apartment, Aurelias waited with what seemed a crowd but resolved into the king's counselors. A cold, pale winter dawn entered the room through the window, mocking the tired, bloodshot eyes, the unshaven faces grim with grief, fatigue, fear, and in some instances, speculation. Gilchrist and the others had already changed to mourning dress, but he and Aurelias wore the formal attire they had thrown back on in the middle of the night.

In lieu of direct authority, Gilchrist presided, answering questions, and receiving condolences. Noticing Norbert, he asked for his report. Norbert looked at Aurelias, who held equal rank, but his friend stared out the window.

"With your permission, I would like to lay out Frederick and take care of his corporeal remains," Aristo Marshon said, making his request of Norbert, not Gilchrist.

Norbert gave permission, noting Gilchrist's frown. Marshon's next question halted him.

"Who reigns over Kaereya?"

"Warrick," Aurelias answered, turning from the window. In the brief silence, no one protested his assertion.

"Are you sure he had no hand in these events?" Aristo Agino asked. "It seems suspicious that he is conveniently absent while his family is murdered. He is an impertinent, discourteous wastrel, unworthy of the crown."

"He is our monarch until evidence proves him otherwise," Norbert said.

"Regardless, I will contact Master Godfrey and have him research the family lines for other possible heirs," Agino responded.

"My God, all of them. It is unthinkable. What can you tell me, Wilhelm? You must have some idea? Does anyone know where Warrick is?" Gilchrist asked.

Norbert could offer nothing.

~ * ~

Within her solar Vespe, cut cloth for a shirt. Why the impulse to make something for Drew overtook her, didn't matter, she needed to stay busy. Alfred, present most of the time, watched with patent pessimism. Keeping her hands occupied helped ease her mind and using her needle talents to save what hangings and bed linens she could, was practical. A groom's shirt was another matter. In the days since her argument with Drew on Last Night, she had avoided everyone.

First Day had started with a cold, early morning riding lesson, given in an impersonal calm and critical manner by Drew. Following that, she cleaned, took air in the frigid garden, and picked up dinner. The day ended in the evening with the men at the table. Drew carved, Selwyn worked leather and she plied her needle. Mostly in silence.

Now it was Second Day. As she picked up scissors to cut the fine linen fabric, dizziness overwhelmed her and she stopped, putting both hands on the table to steady herself.

Three young men rode their mounts hard, fleeing or chasing through drifts of powder-dry snow. Blood filled the tracks they left, bleeding out onto the snow until all turned vermilion. Beneath her feet, swift as nimble swallows, indigo lines cracked the ground, spreading and separating into smaller and smaller fissures until she fell through the empty night-blue. Fear and alarm hung in the air with the floating snow.

Voices drew her back to herself. At first, she thought them part of the vision because she didn't recognize them. Then she heard Drew's voice shouting. She roused and stood, hoping her legs would support her. Never had one of her visions been like this—part reality, part illusion. Curiosity finally drove her down the steps.

Walking into the courtyard, she found chaos reigned with Kennetsure riders mixed with clan riders, their horses filling the yard. They all moved around three great wagons. Clansmen not already assembled arrived with welcoming expressions of joy.

Drew and Selwyn talked with a Kennetsure rider near the barn doors. The coldness of the day had turned Drew's skin russet over honey and the wind fluttered his hair about his face. Vesper caught her breath at the tumult about her. The Kennetsure man handed Drew an envelope and she could see they talked in earnest words. Looking up, Drew glimpsed her, and without a welcoming smile, beckoned her to him.

Threading her way through the milling people and animals, Vesper walked over.

"Leander, this is my Handfasted, Vesper." He did not tell her why a Kennetsurean stood in the Montoren Farm courtyard. Vesper noticed the emblem on the man's shoulder, painted onto his leather hauberk, and recognized it as belonging to the Zekarac Order. His silver belt buckle held the image of a sphinx. Her gaze returned to his poor face. Seeping sores corded his dark skin wherever scratching fingers had spread the poison.

The knight answered her unspoken question after she greeted him.

"Montoren Farm has a long-standing trade agreement with my employer, who was a very good friend of your espoused's grandfather," Leander said in the melodious southern voice.

"You must be doubly cold then, for Vere is seldom as warm as your own clime, and your country never as cold as this past sennight's snow-laden way. You and your riders must come into the manse hall and get warm." She turned to Drew, "Have Ramona and Berneta something already prepared?" At Drew's nod, she smiled. "Have them serve it inside," she ordered and turned to Leander. "I have never had the privilege of meeting a Knight of the Zekarac Order."

Taking Leander's arm, she walked toward the hall, asking him about his journey. As they crossed the courtyard, the other riders slowly dismounted, and clansmen led the animals away. Others unloaded the wagons and took the boxes away. The Kennetsureans followed Leander as Drew, walking behind her, repeated her invitation to them.

Leander wasn't the only one inflicted with the rash. As the riders entered and divested themselves of outdoor wear, Vesper noticed the seeping sores and scratching of many. Vesper went to her solar. Only a sennight ago she'd had an uncontrollable itch herself but was unable to find the cause. She did find, however, a chest filled with dried nettle leaves left long ago in the solar. A day spent following Eudora's recipe made a huge batch of ointment. By the time she finished, her own itch had disappeared. Now she took the ointment back to the hall.

Of the ten men in the group, eight were affected. One had eyes nearly swollen shut, and the others itched and scratched at their clothes, but she saw Ramona led several clansmen carrying heavy trays of roasted meat into the hall. *An expected visit then.* Vesper fumed.

The men lined up to wash their hands, and Vesper, realizing hunger would win out over itching, took a pitcher, poured scented water over their hands, and presented each a clean towel as he finished scrubbing. As she poured the water, she told the afflicted she had ointment for their sores when they finished eating. To the man with swollen eyes, she added, "I have a tincture of hazel that will ease your eyes. Come to me after you have eaten."

Several things turned her temper. Ramona's face when she saw the cleaned hall and the expressions of thanks from her Kennetsure guests as she performed the wash ritual with each of them. Each bowed in deep courtesy at her service. Clansmen entered and sat down directly to feast with their guests. The table sat near thirty before all was done.

It was hard work, and unexpected. Then came the cleanup. While she cleared the tables, clansmen brought in boxes and crates. They accumulated in stacks. Vesper could smell the mixed aromas of oranges and lemon, cinnamon, and ginger.

In the morning they repeated the whole process in reverse. The wagons were loaded with items from the farm: fine goat fleece, cheese, smoked salmon, trout and pike, dried northern berries and fruits, leather saddles and goods of Selwyn's making and carved items of Drew's work, iron items from the smith Fulbert's forge, and what she suspected were ingots of silver and gold, recognizing symbols on the boxes and the labor needed to lift them.

"Surely you and your men can stay a few more days to recover from such a long journey?" Vesper asked Leander as she helped serve breakfast.

"Thank you," Leander said with a wide smile. "But we would all rather travel and be able to rest in warmer places. We are later arriving here than we like, and it is better if we start back. Drew says the weather might turn worse soon."

As the men assembled to return, each approached Vesper and bowed, giving her a Kennetsure sign of thanks. "For your gracious hospitality and for the salve of relief." To one of the wagon drivers, the man with the swollen eyes, she gave a precious glass bottle filled with hazel water and a wooden tub filled with nettle ointment. "Your eyes look better today, but you will need to use this twice a day until the itch is completely gone. Everyone will need more of the salve before long. Good journey to you." The man expressed his thanks.

As Leander mounted his horse, she took him a cup of hot sweet cider. "For your safe journey," she said. For the first time, Vesper had requested help from a clansman. She had asked Fulbert to carry a tray of cups to all the Kennetsure men. Drew and Selwyn helped pass them out. She grabbed Leander's saddle flap as dizziness assailed her and only half-heard herself speak. "Make haste. You are needed in Gotte City."

Leander said nothing of her odd behavior but handed her his cup, saluted her, and urged his horse away. She turned away as the cavalcade left the arched entrance. She felt a thread of worry enter her and sensed someone watching her. Turning she found Drew, standing alone near the arched entrance, staring at her. His face wore its familiar austere look, but her stomach flip-flopped, and she fought to get her breath. Entering the manse, she found Ramona and Berneta already working to clean up the hall. She helped them as they set about opening the crates. The oranges and limes smelled heavenly, but the other two moaned there were too many.

"They always send so much," Ramona lamented. "They will spoil before we use them all."

To Vesper's surprise, they didn't know many uses for the spices outside of a few culinary uses, so she asked if she might have some.

They shrugged their shoulders. "If you have a use for them, Miss, use them. They will just go to waste here."

"If we store all in the buttery, it is cool there and will keep the fruit longer, plus you will have easy access to them when needed." They shrugged and helped her move the crates of fruit, the stoneware jugs filled with olive oil, boxes of medical salt, table salt, pepper, rosemary, ginger, clove and cinnamon, figs and dates, precious coffee beans, tea leaves, and lastly, dried sea fish packed in kelp filled the boxes. When Ramona went to throw the box filler out, Vesper saved the dried material. She earned strange looks and more shrugs, but they never said nay, and Vesper knew the dried kelp made a worthy medicine. What the boxes not brought into the manse held, Vesper wasn't told.

~ * ~

"Have you located Prince Warrick?" Gilchrist asked.

Norbert didn't immediately answer him.

Grief reigned throughout the Eternal Palace, its somber silence bled into Hawk City and beyond as the news traveled. As he took reports from his agents, Norbert kept track of the undercurrents of court and city, searching for signs of impending danger. Black and red draped not only the palace but also the city. Overnight Easure's bright flutter of kites, flags, chimes, and whistles had vanished, only the lamenting bell Rigel in Aron Cathedral rang. Already lines of mourners extended beyond the entry courts and parade route to the Palace's front entrance.

The atmosphere inside the place felt as cold as outside. In the palace chapel, Frederick lay in a coffin made especially for him during his long reign. The Queen also had an elegant coffin, but the Crown Prince, his wife, and his younger sisters all lay in hastily finished and furbished boxes.

Norbert knew Gilchrist handled the crisis within the court with adept charisma. His calm words steadied many hysterical and distraught courtiers and ladies, and for that alone Norbert kept a deferential manner despite his dislike for the man. Everyone kept deep mourning, gathering in quiet and somber groups. As Gilchrist's grieving expression and soft words calmed the fright-filled, disbelieving conversations of the past two winter days, Norbert lost charity. It soon dawned on him that the man had manipulated the situation. Gilchrist's sons had a certain claim to the crown, among others. Unfortunately for the Duke of Hearthron, they were apparently larking with Warrick.

Norbert wished he could handle his job as adeptly. Within Cliff City, alternate bouts of disheartened misery and violent panic ravaged the populace. His men and Royal Guardsmen patrolled the streets, for reassurance as much as keeping the peace.

"No. He has not been located. Have your sons sent any messages?"

Gilchrist gave him a look of loathing but gave up his pretense his sons weren't with Warrick. "Do you suspect foul play keeps them away?"

"Are you asking if I think Warrick planned this? No, he only had an ill-timed rebellion. The murderous plotters could not have known Warrick would skip his own Handfasting or be gone so long as First Day." He sighed, rubbing his hand over his burning eyes.

"We need Warrick. We need him now," Gilchrist said. "Kaereya needs a king, even such a wayward one as this. What about Princess Pia? Have you considered one of her agents might have wanted revenge for Warrick's spurning?"

"The Sunderlune retinue has always been under scrutiny, Aristo Gilchrist. They could have done this only with Kaereyan help. Help from someone within the court."

"You're sure Warrick had no hand in this?"

Norbert took a deep breath and slowly expelled it. "Warrick is a spoiled and recklessly wild young man, but he is intelligent enough. I will never believe him capable of what has befallen the rest of his family. He held his stepmother, the Queen, in great fondness and truly loved his little sisters. I pity him when he finds out, and hope he rushes back. A man I trust is trying to track him and the Royal Guards are sending riders to search, but we do not want the country more alarmed at this point."

"He better hurry back, or he will lose his crown. Kaereya cannot remain kingless."

To Norbert it sounded a threat.

~ * ~

Aurelias came to his rooms at his request. He looked as haggard from the previous day as Norbert felt. For the first time Norbert realized how old he was getting. It was not a comforting thought. He invited Raymond to sit before the fire with him and share a noonday meal.

"I need your help. Someone must hold Wessure steady for Warrick. We cannot afford any uprisings."

"Wessure will remain loyal to Warrick."

"Not if some of your Wessurean aristos get power hungry. You are the ranking Aristo there. Under your banner, most would hold loyal, or support you in putting down any disloyalty."

"I'm going back to Lambere to comfort my people after Frederick's funeral. I could speak with the Wessurean aristos at Court before leaving."

Relieved, Norbert asked, "What about Quillon? Who will ride with you?"

"I've a new outrider. A mercenary. She has proven her keep."

"She?"

"Yes."

Aurelias seemed distracted and remote. He digested what his friend didn't say. "What is your difficulty?" Norbert asked.

"I want to settle the issue with my daughter. Now the royal family is murdered, it becomes imperative."

"It might be better to ignore her."

Aurelias glared at him. "I want her out of Vere and under my protection."

"You never finished the story of finding her."

Aurelias twitched in agitation. "I've thought about your remarks about someone wiping out magic. It seemed ludicrous at the time." He sighed and looked away. "I never spoke to you of it, but at the best of times, Lorelei was unsettled, at the worst, she verged on insanity. She saw things she couldn't explain. She claimed they were future messages."

"I wish you had. I'm sorry."

Aurelias sighed. "The pregnancy seemed to unbalance her. In the end, she feared everyone and ran away from me, from her life, from all protection. All she said was she feared for her child." He scrubbed his mouth with a hand. "As if I would have harmed a child of mine. I tracked her. I was so proud, so filled with my importance. I tried to keep her disappearance secret, thought such gossip would dishonor the family's name. If I'd been more concerned about Lorelei, maybe I would have found her in time."

He looked at Norbert with sad eyes. "In the end, I believed her insane. I've paid over and over for my arrogance, for my failure to protect my wife. Pride is a sin, after all, and it seems I must ante-up once more. I fear for my daughter. This is the message sent to me." He pulled the yellowed paper from a vest pocket and handed it to Norbert.

Norbert did not like the shamed self-contempt he saw in his friend's face, then studied the letter. "I'm sorry, but, Raymond, at least now it appears your wife didn't commit suicide. Her signature is shaky here, but the wording sounds like her. Whoever wrote this, must have put down exactly what she said. The sentences, well, they don't exist. That could be from the exhaustion of the birth or the writer's talent. But she is happy, not despondent. Thrilled with her babies. She trusted you enough to let you know about them. Whoever stole this letter—that is the deranged criminal."

Aurelias remained silent, drinking his ale. Norbert's mind wandered. "Who was the clansman?"

"What?" It was clear Aurelias had been lost in his thoughts. Norbert repeated his question.

"A young man from Clan Cader, but a different name. Drew Montoren."

Norbert sat back mentally going over his reports, then rose and shifted through some sheets on his desk. "Maybe not such a disparagement, Raymond. The clans are notorious for keeping to themselves, hiding their wealth with all kinds of subterfuge. They like to perpetuate a fable of poverty. Don't believe it. They are a canny, parsimonious people who can wring the last drop of juice from an apple and feed twenty people on one rabbit. It drives the Vere tax collectors mad." He gave a loud sigh of satisfaction as he lifted a page. "What do you know of the aegises, Raymond?"

Aurelias stared at him, then started laughing. "What? By the Holy One, Wilhelm, you take the most illogical leaps in topics."

"Leaps of intuition," Norbert answered. "What do you know?"

"What every schoolboy is taught. A myth surrounding four men once appointed to the peerage by the king. Supposedly they safeguard the borders. The story says they are magical, sacred protectors, with the power to preserve Kaereya from any invasion. The station didn't take, displeased too many aristos. The families have all died out."

"Do you believe in magic?"

"What? No. Well, not the hocus-pocus kind practiced by so many charlatans."

"Well, I can tell you've never been to Cygna. They practice a very real magic. I've seen it at work, and you're right, it's not the sleight-of-hand used by so many scoundrels preying upon the unsuspecting."

"You can expect anything from Cygna, including deception," Aurelias said. "You're right, I haven't been there, nor wish to, not after they tried to attack Kaereya. What has that to do with Lorelei?"

"Have you ever considered Lorelei might have been a seer?"

Raymond laughed, then sobered. "A seer? You mean a witch?"

Norbert sighed. "I was involved in the negotiations in the dispute with Cygna. I assure you it's not deception, but a mental thing. They believed the reason they couldn't complete their attack was our aegises, more precisely they named the Vere Aegis."

"How can they believe that when we don't?"

"It's only been the last hundred years that belief has failed in this country and only among the more educated. Cygnese minds work differently from ours, and they claimed they felt him. Anyway, as I said, someone in Kaereya does believe in the old magic and has systematically tried to remove all traces of it from our bloodlines, including those of aegis descent. Ottillie is traveling to Egan Keep to speak with the last known member of that aegis family. It might surprise you to know, although the location of the Vere Keep disappeared along with knowledge of that aegis family generations ago, records here at court list the surname Montoren marrying into the historical family of the Vere Aegis."

Aurelias looked at him as if he had lost his mind, then with dawning horror. "You mean my daughter is living with a man who is hunted by the butchers you fear?"

"Well," Norbert said, looking up from shuffling his papers, "what I thought to do was relieve you of your anger over Vesper's disparagement, but the other connection is there as well."

"Do you think it an attempt at subterfuge by the Cygnese? To make sure we cannot attack them with magic like you claim they use?"

"No, no," Norbert said, sorry he'd mentioned Cygna and didn't add he had asked King Frederick to send messages asking to open talks with the witches about their common threat, Pertelon. That effort would come to naught now. "They only fear for their own country, their own land. They are suspicious, anxious, and very conservative but not land greedy. They thought we planned to close Seer Pass. What few traders are welcomed there must travel through the pass, especially since Pertelon has all but blockaded their port of Guerestu. No, an internal attack killed the king."

"These traitors are here at court?"

"I believe so...or have very strong ties to it. They are more than traitors, they are insurgents wanting to affect a new monarchy, or possibly, to hand Kaereya over to another country. Someone used the Heraldist's students to investigate Aristo history. Master Godfrey didn't believe it at first, but one of his apprentices was involved in the Royal deaths. It makes sense. All Kaereya's notable family history is there in his chambers.

"If your suspicions are true, Warrick is in extreme danger if his location becomes known."

"If we don't protect him, he will lose his crown or die. At best, some Aristo such as Gilchrist will take the throne." Norbert agreed with the face Aurelias made. "Exactly, or at worst, we become puppets of the king of Pertelon, or the Cygnese, or some other agent."

"Over my dead body. Do you have any idea who is behind this?"

Norbert sighed. "Do not speak so, Raymond. There seems to be too much willingness of late to fulfill such oaths. That's why you must be in Wessure. As for who committed the murders, no, I don't know. Certainly, someone within the court. This tie to the Heraldist's office confirms a conspiracy. My biggest fear is someone acting for Pertelon's King Clement. Whoever it is, they are cunning and cover their tracks well. The list for those wishing to gain the throne, many—starting with Warrick's uncle."

"He is not blood, but family by marriage," Aurelias said. "May the Holy One protect us if such a power-hungry incompetent as Gilchrist comes to the crown."

"He can't, but he could become Regent. Until Warrick returns, it is almost inevitable. Don't underestimate him. He has many devoted followers and works at building his power. His sons are eligible. For that matter so is your Vesper. Lorelei was Frederick the First's granddaughter, wasn't she? And you also claim descent from another, more ancient line."

"Yes, but," Aurelias waved off the notion with his hand, "it means nothing, both lines are too distant and both through the female line. Gilchrist's sons are with Warrick, aren't they?"

Norbert huffed his disagreement. "Those with far lesser claim seek the crown. There are not many blood descendants left. If Warrick, Emory, or Tate becomes ineligible, Vesper might be the only one remaining with blood of direct descent. A good reason to kill the offspring of the Duke of Lambere."

"The others are all ineligible?" Aurelias asked him with a worried look.

"The others are all dead."

He saw the dawning belief in his conspiracy conjecture on Aurelias' face, joined by an expression of anxiety. "What of Warrick? Any idea where he is?"

Norbert sighed. "No, and if we don't find him soon, he'll lose his right to the throne. It could happen anyway, with him running away from duty and not returning, even after the death of his family. Those with any hint of expectation are scenting power and lusting after the crown and scepter. We must find him."

"If anyone finds out about my daughter... I must protect her, Wilhelm."

"After finding Warrick, Raymond. I need your power in Wessure to track him down. We both swore to his father, and I will work my hardest to protect his birthright if only for his father's sake, and the loyalty I still feel towards him. But the truth remains, my heart is prejudiced against this last twig of the family tree."

"No, Wilhelm. First. I must make sure Vesper is safe. I will have her out of Vere with all possible speed." In the end, Norbert talked him into compromise. They devised a plan to get Vesper out of Vere while allowing Aurelias to keep Wessure steady.

~ * ~

Aurelias went with him to Princess Pia's apartments at her request. At first Norbert was not sure he talked to the same young woman. Her maid took them to the pale-colored princess, but now her face was flushed with youth's health and she dressed in soft shades of lavender-gray that made her eyes more colorful. Aurelias advanced and took her hand, bowing low over it and placing a light kiss on its back.

"Earl Rikon, King's Marshall, and Your Grace, Aristo Aurelias, Duke of Lambere, the circumstances here in Kaereya are most tragic, and I offer you my personal condolences as well as those of my country."

Her voice was so different, the heavy accent gone, that Norbert's suspicion rose, then an inner humor settled him. The Princess must have read his look, for she blushed.

"I asked you here to tell you that, under the circumstances, I have decided to go home," she said without preamble. "The situation here is much changed, and I feel it best for both our countries' interests if I return where I belong."

"The situation is much changed," Aurelias said, his eyes measuring the attractive woman before him. "You could become the queen of Kaereya. We came to assure you of your position here."

"Thank you, sir," she said with a smile, "but I find myself guilty of duplicity. Prince Warrick left court because of me. I never wanted to come to Kaereya, never wanted the betrothal, and tried everything to discourage Prince Warrick, to drive him away. I don't think he wanted the alliance either.

"As a political pawn I knew our desires were of no importance, and my actions were childish and irresponsible. With Prince Warrick missing, the court in mourning, and the royal family... the situation has changed. I find myself guilty of depriving Kaereya of its heir to the throne. If and when Warrick becomes king, if he wants an alliance with Sunderlune, he will make one, I am sure, with someone more to his liking. In the meantime, my women and I will leave and take the encumbrance of our presence from your shoulders."

"You have been no encumbrance, Your Highness," Norbert said.

"If you drove Warrick from court, then you just as surely saved his life. When Warrick becomes king, he could find no better queen," Aurelias said.

"Not Your Highness or Princess, sirs. The title was only honorific as a state position to make me eligible for this alliance. As you know, my father is the Chancellor of the City States of Sunderlune."

Norbert bowed. "Your suggestion is probably best under the circumstance, Your Highness."

"Once Warrick is crowned, I will recommend he seek you out," Aurelias said, as the Princess curtseyed.

~ * ~

"It was a mistake to act without Warrick present. Norbert does not suspect him." Yonger moved in agitation around the small room in Gilchrist's apartment. "I have planned this for too many years for him to escape."

Gilchrist sipped some wine and looked about him. Yonger looked hysterical. He prowled the confined quarters like a wild thing. These rooms were much smaller than those of the Royal apartments. He would not have to put up with them for much longer. "Remain calm. This action will make him ineligible. Even if he returns, such a taint of mistrust will cover him, he will never rule effectively. With all his liberal use of insults, none will support him."

"Norbert?"

Gilchrist smiled. "Has to hate the young man. I tell you, Warrick has made no friends."

"And your sons?"

"Emory knows his duty. When he learns of the Royal family, he will find a way to contact me. Then we can easily track the boys. A convenient accident could take care of our last problem."

"There have been too many accidents. Norbert watches."

"If you had listened to my advice earlier, there would be no suspicions, no investigation. You were clumsy, as with killing that page. Trying to eliminate magic is ludicrous. There is none in Kaereya." He smiled. "Although I should thank you, I suppose, for eliminating so many potential rivals."

Yonger stiffened and turned to give him a patronizing look. "I follow Clement's orders, as you do. When he wanted you included, you knew. He will make you king."

"What has he promised you?"

The Aristo looked over his shoulder at him. "Anatole."

"You're stupid if you think he will fulfill his promises. No, we must see to our own expectations. First is to place blame for all that has happened where it belongs—on Clement and Warrick. I will make Emory king, and through him acquire the power I need. You will become a great Aristo." He gauged Yonger's acceptance of his offer.

"I want Eminence in Easure and all of Anatole."

"You wish equal rank with Aurelias and more land than the King?"

Yonger's face suffused with hate. "Aurelias! I want to see him dead."

"You hold a grudge against Aurelias? So do many. Don't worry. That thorn will be removed from our sides, as will the King's Marshal."

"They are harder to kill than you think."

"Not when you hold the king's power and have eyes in every camp."

~ * ~

"We must have a king," Aristo Yonger said to the assembled Aristo Court. "Warrick is either dead or too cowardly to return. We must call his claim forfeit and elevate the next in line."

Norbert listened as various voices broke in one over another.

"Where are Gilchrist's sons? Where are Emory and Tate? Are they not next in line?"

"They are of the female line. Is there no heir through the male line?" the Earl of Teeg asked from nearby.

"Who else remains?" Aristo Wiffern asked simultaneously.

"Nonsense." Theodulf Gilchrist said in disgust. "Warrick's absence only shows his acumen in staying away from those who have sought his death."

Norbert overhead a low voice, "Everyone knows Gilchrist's sons are with Warrick. Whom does he think he fools? The Holy One help us if any of them gets crowned." Norbert recognized Aristo Marshon's voice.

"The good uncle talks different out of court than within," the Earl of Teeg said in an equally low voice.

Norbert also knew Theodulf Gilchrist spoke differently out of court. The man actively politicked for his son Emory's right to the throne. Daily Norbert made the rounds of the old king's loyal vassals, ensured their support of Warrick, but he knew the boy must show up soon before it was too late. He prayed Warrick knew of his danger. His eyes fell on Theodulf. He claimed that his sons were on his estate on Crone's Island. Norbert had not exposed the lie publicly, at least not yet.

"Or speaks of Prince Warrick's culpability in the deaths," A voice shouted from the other side of the room, answering Gilchrist's comment.

"Outrage!" Aristo Marshon shouted, rising to his feet. "Warrick left long before his family was so foully murdered! There is no proof for such heinous accusations." More voices sustained this viewpoint.

The outcry of voices made the accuser back down. Norbert thought of Yonger's recent betrothal to Gilchrist's daughter. His bride now held the possibility of having the royal line descend through her, or of even becoming queen, making Yonger...

"Now is a time for calm," Norbert said from his position near the empty throne, putting aside his conjecture for future reflection. "Warrick has been on a mission for the crown." He made the statement, knowing few believed it, though none questioned the lie. "But the prince may well have sought shelter when he learned of his family."

~ * ~

Chloe's Story

Everywhere within the church candles burned, filling the air with heavy incense. It was Star Day, the first day of Summer Festival, the day of the single eye of God. A day given to the celebration of creation and spent in prayer to give thanks for the sanctity of the Holy One's making of man. The bells rang periodically, sometimes singly, more often in chorus, from the deepest bass of the huge bell named Rigel to the silvery Lillith. From above, in the side and rear balconies, choirs sang, one all male, the other female, their a cappella voices chanting in soft melodies, sometimes separately, sometimes in question and response, sometimes in union. They brought her spirit the first peace since coming to Cliff City.

Kneeling during the long series of litanies in the great sanctuary of Aron Cathedral, Chloe prayed for forgiveness for her sins. She had not come into church while she still committed adultery with Ewald, but now she knew it over. A new conquest walked publicly at his side.

She grieved, but common sense had told her their relationship would be a brief thing, soon forgotten by the king. She shed a few tears anyway because it hurt.

Tomorrow Ewald would make her an Aristo. She would be Baroness of Charm Island, a small holding in the Thou River off the coast of Kennetsure. She wondered if he knew the cruelty of his gift, the inherent joke, then guessed not. Ewald would only see it as proper reparation for her services and see a connection between charm and witch. He'd never understood her gift, no matter how often she tried to describe it. She readily forgave him.

As evening fell, she rose and left the cathedral. Already the sounds linked to a night of excess brewed. The scent of beer and wine permeated the air with grilled meats and spiced sauces. Laughter, talk, music, and singing filled the evening. Chloe sighed; even walking through the celebration seemed like participating, which she didn't want to do.

It was to be expected with this first Summer Festival since the war's ending. This year, in a rare set of celestial occurrences, Fire Day, the longest day of the year, coincided with a full moon, and that transpired in a year of the Wheel Day. The holy day of zero, a day occurring only every three years, an ill-omened day for birth or death. This year the celestial events were acclaimed as part of an extraordinary festival.

Somehow, she felt Kaereya's troubles had not ended with the war, but others saw it as a good omen. Chloe thought both the king and his subjects looked for a further reason to indulge in life's pleasures.

"Hello, Aristo Chloe. Having missed you here much of late, I am glad you came to celebrate the holy number one."

Chloe came out of her self-contemplation and found Monseigneur Otto standing next to her. "Just Chloe, please, Monseigneur. Circumstances of guilt prevented me from cleansing my soul." Screams of laughter drew her attention.

Monseigneur Otto also looked at the early revelers. A group across the street shared tankards of ale. The woman's dress was indecent, exposing most of her breasts. When she drank from her tankard, the men's hands felt her. Chloe turned away.

"That has not stopped others from coming into the Holy One's house," Otto said in a dry voice. "It is over?"

She didn't pretend to misunderstand him. "Yes—or almost. He still insists on the investiture tomorrow."

"Don't feel too much guilt. Even if you had a family here to protect you, you could not refuse without serious repercussions." More squeals of laughter interrupted him, and his eyes drifted to the scene across the way. "So much excess. I fear for Kaereya."

"They've seen too much war, too much death," Chloe said. *Even King Ewald acts so.* She did not say that, though, but "after Summer Festival, I might leave for a while."

"Where?"

"I don't know yet, but I've seen myself traveling."

"Seen, Chloe?"

She looked at him through eyes blurred with unshed tears. "My gift seems to have changed."

"You foretell? Do not let anyone know."

"I know. My visions might be only my own desires fooling me, but if not, I do not think I can bear another of Bishop Thidrek's comments on the evils of magic."

"Not all Kaereyans feel that way, and the commoners still believe in special gifts."

"That may be, but times are changing, my friend, and witch-bred gifts are abhorred. In Kennetsure I knew nine others who had gifts of one sort or another. Here, I am the only one. It is not comfortable, especially when I already look so different."

"There are many here in Cliff City, even among the Royal Guards and the Army, who live because of your gift. They know your goodness. If you have any need of help, come to me."

The next day was even more difficult than Chloe anticipated. Bull's Day, the day of commitment, was considered a good day for signing contracts and making investitures. The darkness of night would bring the duality aspects of lust, caprice, and falseness. She knew she would not be called to Ewald's secret apartment tonight with both a pang of loss and the relief of freedom.

King Ewald saw no problem in their parting, expected to remain friends. He remained adamant about raising her to the rank of Aristo and gave her Charm Island for the title's support. The ridiculousness of the situation struck her, especially when expressing gratitude to her king for his benefice. In lieu of her tangible token, he took her prior service as pledge. Chloe cringed but swore her fealty.

It was the first time Chloe had moved as a social equal among the aristos. Most showed the same fear as the monks at Bishop's Hospital, revealing the effectiveness of Bishop Thidrek's continued postulating. They might be rich, wellborn, and spoiled, but Chloe saw they were much like any other group of people. Some men wore bullhorns attached to their headgear; some of the women also wore horns or antlers. Many carried bells to celebrate the number two. They often rang them as she passed. Chloe wondered if in well-wishing her new status, or to ward off a witch.

King's Hall was grandly decorated for Summer Festival with festoons of flowers and all the tokens of Kaereya's four provinces. As usual, the air and wind symbols of Easure predominated.

The night before Ewald had surprised her. His valet had come to her apartment, led her to the king for a night visit. This last time, she had sensed his indifference, but she had been prepared and smiled. "I have a gift for you."

His expression had perked with interest. "A gift? What for?"

"Because our time is over, and yet your concern has led you to make me an Aristo."

He opened the small pocket and a buckle slid into his palm. He fingered it and looked at the celestial objects decorating its surface. "Is it magic?"

"No, Your Highness. It is only a silver buckle. It is the design that is important."

"The sky?"

"No." She had laughed as her gesture missed its mark. "The sun, the moon, and the stars. What I wish for you, what I would give you if I could."

"You know?"

"Yes, Sire, I know. I will go now, and I shall not stay at court, it would be wrong. But, if you have need of my gift, send and I will come."

"Can your charm protect me?" He asked still holding the small buckle in his palm.

"No, I only meant it as a gesture of goodwill."

He turned it over. "What does it say on the back?"

"Ancient signs of luck."

"Then it is an amulet. Thank you, my witch." He smiled and Chloe had left.

"Lady?" A servant offered her a cup of wine, drawing her from her reminiscence. Chloe gratefully took it, stopping to sip. When she looked up, she froze. Across the room, Queen Sophia sat at the dais, her son, young Prince Ewald, stood beside her.

The boy Chloe had saved on the cliffs outside the city stared at her with hatred. Their chance meeting had started this whole chain of events. Queen Sophia also stared at her. Her face looked calm but filled with pain and humiliation. With a sudden pang, Chloe realized the Queen knew of the liaison. Shame washed over Chloe, and she perceived the enormity of her sin.

The sooner she left, the better. Chloe loathed herself, despised what she had done. She nearly cried out to the Queen, 'I'll give it all back.' She knew it not only impossible but also untrue. Deep within her, an abiding love existed for a man unable to share it. She sensed Ewald's goodness, his concern for his people. Right now it was submerged in the desire for the reckless excess almost everyone in the country seemed to share. She would not regret one day or one night, but she must move on.

"Lady Chloe?"

Chloe turned to the voice. A dark-haired, pale-skinned man looked down at her. He wore sober dress, dark conservative clothes, unusual in Easure. "Yes?"

"I am an emissary from Cygna, my name is Dustyn. The rumors state you are a Kennetsurean witch?"

"No witch. I do not place hexes or conjure the unseen."

He smiled. "I sensed your Talent before I approached, Lady. I noticed your countrymen tend to treat you as they do me—with an arms-length of caution. I have never met either a Kaereyan witch or a Kennetsurean before. There are not too many of you here at court."

In his eyes she saw the spark of appreciation, a look once seen in Ewald's gaze. She stiffened, suddenly feeling his hands caress her body, though she could see them in plain sight holding a silver drinking cup. She blushed.

"Only myself, and my dark skin singles me out among so many with light."

"Your loveliness would do so in any crowd."

A wave of dizziness assailed her, with views of mountains and this man. His arm caught her. She smiled. "An emissary, and a gallant, just what I need for company. Tell me, Dustyn, what do you mean talent?"

"Your Talent is what makes you a witch. In Cygna, we are called Talents."

Piqued, Chloe's mind filled with questions, tearing it away from guilt, humiliation, and shame. "Talent? You must tell me more."

"We share a Talent, Lady."

"Chloe only, please. How?"

"Chloe. Earth. You have a sizable Earth Talent. I also am an Earth Adept. This is not the place to speak of Talents, but if you would permit me to accompany you tomorrow, we may talk of gifts at leisure, and you may tell me of Kaereya's Summer Festival celebrating numbers."

Chloe gave her first genuine smile in a long time. "I accept. You know we have eight more days of Festival."

"An excessive country."

"You do not believe in the Holy-One's numbers in Cygna?"

"Yes, but less fervently. We have a sennight of Spring Rites, but it is more of a fair than a celebration. Even that would be too conservative for your countrymen."

"Yes, it would. No place is more extravagant than Easure. Tomorrow is Fire Day."

"Longest day of the year."

"Then Wolf Day to celebrate four, the Holy-One's feminine aspect. Hawk Day celebrates the learning aspect of five, Key Day the choices of six, Crown Day is for seven's miracles, Staff Day for eight's justice, and Soul Day for nine's religious observances."

"All too confusing. I never did well in arithmetic."

"This year Wheel Day ends the celebration, but it is the first in years."

"A calendar day?"

"Yes. I will tell you all the major and minor significance, the positive and negative aspects. Our festival is also tied to a merchant's fair and you must not miss that either."

"I am intrigued."

Ten

By the time the small mummer's troop reached their winter home, Warrick was well pleased with his adventure. Here on the furthest western edge of Kaereya, things were clearer in his head, as if the Peace Ocean's breezes had swept through his mind.

The women all seemed recovered, except for the little girl, who remained quiet and withdrawn. At his or Emory or Tate's approach, they no longer shrank away. He and his cousins played their well-rehearsed parts in the short morality plays favored in Wessure, and they worked after the little dramas setting camp or taking it down. They had enjoyed the playacting and did a good job of it, if he did say so himself. No longer was making a fire a difficult chore. He had even liked the physical labor, but he was now ready to return to being Prince Warrick.

Four days after Last Day, he found pleasure in sighting the low buildings of Mel Snecke. His money was nearly gone, everything of worth sold to reestablish the women, so it was time to return to Hawk Island, make his apologies, and pay his punishment.

Leave taking was not difficult. The women found others they knew who welcomed them. That night he and his cousins would sleep in beds, but before then they would have a final revel, the first since their wild carousing at the start of their adventure. Entering the tavern, they found a table and ordered drinks. After several ales, his cousins needed to seek relief. Sitting by himself, Warrick listened to the conversation at the next table until he broke in.

"What do you mean the king is dead?" He grabbed the man behind him by the sleeve and tugged.

The man pulled Warrick's hand off his arm. "Where you been you haven't heard? Yeah, dead. The news came by riverboat yesterday."

"Then Frederick IV is King?"

"No, by the Holy One. They're all dead. Murdered. The whole family. All except Warrick, who they say was sent on a special mission and hasn't been heard of since. Probably dead, too. Sorry business."

"Who is king then?"

"No one. That's what has all the Aristo's sniffing. They're like hounds—all baying to become the new king. May the Holy One help us! To Good King Fred!" The man saluted his companions. They gave a cheerless laugh, but they looked glum as they drank.

"Look at him," one of the man's table-companions said. "He looks stunned as a poleaxed ox."

Without speaking, Warrick rose and left the tavern. An eternity later, Emory and Tate, their faces stricken, found him roaming aimlessly around the small city.

"They're dead. My family. All Dead."

"We heard," Emory said and dropped his gaze. Tate cried. They took him back to their room. Warrick sank to the floor, buried his face in his arms, and loosed the agony crushing him.

Toward morning he sat with leaden eyes looking out the window as the first glimmer of light spread across the horizon. He listened to the soft snores of Tate, asleep only a few candlemarks. "What should we do?" Emory asked.

Warrick glanced at his cousin. "Go back to the Eternal Palace, hope I have not been disinherited. If I have, well, I can become an actor." He forced a weak, crooked smile to show he joked. Then his eyes wandered back to the window.

"Is it safe? Whoever murdered your family, they might be hunting you."

"So what? I really don't care. My little sisters... what did they do to deserve such a fate? Edith was just a baby. Frederick. He was a good brother, never purposely mean, studied, and capable."

"You must care! You are the king of Kaereya and have been for days. It is my duty, and Tate's, to protect you."

Warrick bit his lip, hoping to still his wobbly chin. "Some king."

He heard Emory draw in a long breath. "I'm taking you to Pertelon. King Clement will protect you until we sort out who can be trusted in Kaereya."

"I swear to you Em, I will find the ones responsible and kill them. Somehow, we need to get a message to the Earl of Rikon. He will know what to do."

"No. You cannot. It could be an act of Rikon's—who had more access to your father than his Marshal? I say escape until you learn whom to trust."

In the end, going along with Emory was easier than facing himself. They traveled eastward to Karn to take the ferry across the Northern Thou River and head east on the Rock Coast Road. Traveling hard, riding at night, avoiding hamlets, villages, and cities allowed Warrick moments without thought.

~ * ~

A sennight into the new year Vesper walked into the stables searching for Drew. She woke at daylight to catch him before he left the manse, only to find him already gone. Her night had been saddled with dreams and now, edged with the sharp spur of anxiety, they drove her to find him. She found the stall of his favorite mount empty, but Selwyn worked in the manse stamping designs on leather.

Her worry grew. She had hoped to confide in Drew, to end the past few days of unspoken dissension. Each day she suffered new visions, a reality dressed in the language of symbols. A falling dagger, a shattered shield, and blood-covered land. These ill omens created a desperate sense of loss within her.

Each new vision induced an undefined fright, and now they invaded her sleep. Last night's dream focused on Drew in desperate danger. He searched for something lost, unable to tell her why. Their search ended when a spear pierced Drew's back in a mortal blow. The expression on his face as he looked at the point emerging from his breastbone, propelled her from her dream.

Now she fumed in frantic agitation as she sought Drew. *Selwyn.* Vesper marched with purpose back to the manse.

"Where is Drew?" she demanded.

Selwyn looked up from his work with a distracted look, his face hardening as he considered her.

"What? Concern?" he asked in a jeering voice. He huffed lightly. "Norost." His attention returned to his work and he tapped the stamp he held with quick precision.

"Drew never goes anywhere without you. Why is he gone and you here?"

"He left me to protect you." Selwyn threw his tool on the table, giving her a hateful look.

"Why?"

"Reavers are about, someone needed to stay. He thought you might try to run away." His fingers ran over the leather where he worked.

"No, why did he go to town?"

This time Selwyn's nostrils widened in obvious anger as he searched for another tool. "To provide you a bride's gift."

Vesper held her ground against Selwyn's intimidating disapproval. "How?"

"He is selling the younger stud."

"Kuff? But that is his best one! And you let him?"

"I still follow his orders." His temper radiated like water ripples.

Rising her chin, Vesper demanded, "Take me to town."

Selwyn gave a sour laugh. "Not likely. I said I still follow orders."

"Only when convenient." Vesper clenched her jaw, whirled, and left. She stood in the garden with her fists clenched. Alfred stood before her with his hands on his hips, his look daring her. She snapped her fingers at him and left. Watching the courtyard, she found it empty. Everyone stayed close to warm hearths today. She slid into the kitchen unobserved. There, in the heat from the ovens, Ramona and Berneta gossiped and kneaded dough in apron-covered tunics, their lace-covered caps hiding their view of Vesper.

A quick search showed Vesper their outer cloaks hung nearby. Grabbing Berneta's brown cloak Vesper left as quietly as she came.

Once outside, she threw the cloak over her and pulled up the hood. Berneta often left the manse grounds to meet with her husband, a forester. No one would question her leaving the farm. Wearing the stolen cloak she easily left through the arched entrance to the courtyard and then ran until the manse disappeared behind her.

Two leagues down the road she heard hoof beats drumming behind her. A glance showed Selwyn riding a horse down on her in a full gallop. Fear stilled her heart, and she turned and fled from the road through the adjacent field. She could not outrun a horse though, and when Selwyn's arm scooped her off the ground she screamed.

"Shut up, you silly chick, and stop squirming before I drop you." His horse had slowed to a jagged trot as she fought Selwyn's arms. The horse jumped suddenly and threw Vesper against the pommel with sharp pain.

His gruff voice continued shouting. "Stop it, I tell you! I mean you no harm and you certainly can't walk all the way into town." His actions did not calm her, and his horse twirled in nervous circles as Selwyn pulled back on the reins trying to control them both.

Vesper stopped her movement. "You will take me to town?" she asked as her dizzy vision steadied.

"Damn you! Yes," Selwyn said, his rein holding hand moved to guide his mount. They moved toward town. "What Drew does to you will appease having my hide chewed."

Vesper didn't quite believe him because it always seemed Selwyn roared at Drew, not the other way around. But as the horse remained headed in the right direction, she gave a self-satisfied sigh and relaxed against Selwyn for the long, and she suspected speechless, trip into Norost. Vesper tried not to fidget with worry, but it was difficult. Selwyn's arms held her in an uncomfortable, tight lock.

How long had Drew been gone? What if they were too late? A sense of doom penetrated her, filling her with the dreaded dizziness and the blankness that followed. *Not now!* She fought it but it did no good. The unreal views and strange actions started of their own accord.

> *As from a cliff she saw the land below her and realized it was Kaereya. Armies marched. She recognized Kuff moving through a mist, his single long horn softly gleaming. Drew rode him but dismounted. "No" she screamed. There were too many enemies around. Only Kuff could carry Drew to safety. The horse was talisman bred. Anyone could see that. She sensed Drew waited for something, searched for it. A messenger of death, a single crow, cawed and darted through the gray sky. Drew watched it. Rain began to fall. "Remount Drew, get back on Kuff," she pleaded. Soon, she knew the spear would fly again. Intuition told her Kuff was Drew's security, and only he could carry the shield. She shouted but Drew couldn't hear her.*
>
> *A dark figure, a faceless shadow, emerged from the surrounding forest and took Kuff's reins from Drew's hand and mounted. His laugh sounded like thunder. He pointed at the land and it heaved and belched fire. He pointed again and a tree, leaning, close to falling, burst into flame. Drew watched it but didn't move. Selwyn shouted and ran, trying to save Drew, but fire encircled him, wrapped him in a fiery embrace. He screamed, but she couldn't make out his words. Kuff was spurred into a rear, he squealed and aimed his horn-crested head at Drew. This time the blow*

*came from the front, displaying Drew's agonized
face. Blackness came, distorting time and reality.*

Selwyn's baritone in her ear woke Vesper. "We near Norost." She startled awake unaware she had fallen asleep. As they neared Norost's outskirts, she said, "He will go to the market."

He snorted at her idiocy. "I know."

When they entered the yard, Vesper pushed at Selwyn's arm until he released her. She slid off the side of the horse to land in an ungainly heap on the ground. Jumping to her feet, she rushed through the market searching for the Montoren horse. Catching a glimpse of silver and gray she ran and grabbed Drew's arm just as he extended it for the end-of-deal clasp.

"No," she said, louder than she meant, out of breath and fighting dizziness. She turned to the hooded buyer, surprised to see a man of Kennetsure beneath the cowl. "I am very sorry, but the horse is a bride's gift and not for sale." Vesper turned to Drew to explain, but he and the buyer talked over her explanation.

"You let your woman belie your bargain?" a bystander asked. The buyer demanded, "Is it true? It is her animal?"

Drew, astounded and fumbling in surprise, gave feeble apologies, saying he did not know his betrothed valued the animal so much.

"The sale clasp has not been given, the deal is not concluded," Vesper said. "Go find another horse, you can't have mine!"

The tall Kennetsure man, his hazel-gold eyes glowing in the shadows of his face, said, "As you wish, of course, gracious lady." He performed a hand gesture of deference and backed away, but his eyes pierced Drew with vexation.

Someone watching the proceedings said, "Eh, now you know why the clans are so poor, they let their women do their haggling." A bout of general laughter and talk flowed through the market. Vesper and Selwyn held Drew, who was prepared to physically confront the heckler. She remembered grasping his jacket to hold him back, then to remain upright as the ground undulated beneath her feet and events whirled around her.

She roused in a strange place. "Where..." she started to ask.

"The Sated Beast," Drew said, his hand dabbing at her face with a cold cloth. "You fainted."

"Pickling vespiary," Vesper said in feeble, horrified tones. "I never faint." A quick peek showed the tavern more sedate than her imagined image.

"What?" Drew's voice rose in panic, "Selwyn she is raving again."

"Not raving." Vesper pushed Drew's hand away as she started to rise from the bench where she lay. Selwyn sat across the alcove from her. He watched her, a disturbed look filling his eyes. Vesper sighed, another failing. Achieving a sitting position with Drew's help, she took a quick breath. "That's what Eudora calls this place."

Liquid spots lay down the front of Berneta's cloak and a strong smell of beer and alcohol permeated the air. She took the wet cloth from Drew's hands and rubbed at the spots. A glass with clear liquid sat on the table. Picking it up she sniffed. "You gave me distilled vapors?" she asked, shocked. Before Drew could respond, she demanded, "Where is Kuff, where is your horse?"

A satiric expression crossed his face. "I believe Kuff is your horse. Tied outside."

As she opened her mouth, he added, "He is well watched." Then, "I even used coin." She took the words as a subtle reproach for her comment about his former appearances in town. Today he appeared neat and well dressed, if somewhat flustered looking. She, in a borrowed cloak and old tunic used for cleaning, and Selwyn with stains of leather dye and oil on his vest, looked like paupers. "I could not allow you to sell him."

"Is your woman feeling better?"

Vesper looked up to see the tavern owner standing nearby.

"Yes," Drew said. He laid more coins on the table. "Thank you."

"Looks like your handfasting was successful. When do you expect the little one?"

Vesper felt her face flame. She heard Drew's denial of an impending child. He spoke about the recent sad news. The man nodded.

"Ah," He frowned. "Such sad, disturbing times," and turned away to serve his other customers.

Keeping her face turned away from Drew, Vesper pretended to inspect the interior. It was not so very bad, certainly not what she expected from Eudora's contemptuous comments.

"Are you feeling better?" Drew asked. "If so, we should start back to Montoren soon."

"I feel perfectly well," Vesper stated and rose. It was Selwyn who grabbed her elbow as she wobbled and escorted her before Drew could move. Her eyes widened in astonishment. As they left the tavern, the Kennetsurean from the market stepped from their way with another respectful, near courtly, motion to Vesper. The eyes were calm and gentle now. He didn't smile but cleared a way for their exit from the crowded room. Selwyn's habitual frown deepened, and his eyes narrowed at the man. Drew reacted in a similar fashion to the man's courtesy.

"What sad times? What has happened?" Vesper asked and without stopping added, "Oh, dear, Eudora will hear where I have been."

Drew followed her gaze, and she felt his movement next to her. Brandt walked with Alvina towards them. Vesper could feel Alvina's eyes sizing up her appearance in a familiar disdainful way as she walked past them. Unable to help herself she called out. "Hello, Alvina, Brandt." She thought Alvina wouldn't answer, but at last her friend stopped and turned with a vague smile. "Why, Vesper, I hardly recognized you. Are you well?"

"I am fine, thank you."

Brandt's eyes stayed on her in a way that made her uncomfortable as well as embarrassed. Heat entered her face.

She watched Alvina place a perfectly clean and manicured hand on Brandt's arm. "Me, too. Things have worked out very well. We were married a sennight ago. Have your nuptials taken place?"

Vesper felt herself blush, but before she could answer, Drew placed an arm around her waist. "I'm sorry to interrupt your conversation, but as Vesper's friends, I'm sure you'll understand when I tell you she has been ill this morning, and I need to get her home." He nodded to the couple and pulled Vesper away.

Drew made no more comment but picked her up and placed her in his saddle while he mounted behind. She knew him well enough now to realize he was angry, but she couldn't tell why. Selwyn took Kuff's lead rope after he mounted his own horse. Drew's arms circled her while he held the reins, not like Selwyn's hard grip but in a gentle enclosure. She leaned back, exhausted, and was soon lulled to sleep by the horse's movements.

~ * ~

Quillon watched the trio leave town. This was the closest he had come to the clansmen since they left Norost at Handfasting. Getting the Sated Beast's clientele to talk was easy, and rumors ran wild about the Clans, but little of substance emerged.

That the young man cared for his women was undoubted. He had seen Drew ride into town and followed him, and when his purpose became known, felt a covetous desire for the stallion. He had covered his avarice with the idea it was an opportunity to assess the man up close. The duke would have wanted the animal, too. Here, in this small community, its true value went unappreciated, and his disappointment at Vesper's interruption in his deal was near keen, but quickly brought him back to his sense of duty.

Vesper's unexpected appearance had startled the young man, as did her fainting spell. Quillon had followed them to the tavern and heard the girl's rambling voice speak of strange things from murdered babies to horses that were foundations. To him it was clear. The girl, like her mother, was a seer, and in certain jeopardy.

~ * ~

Drew rested his chin gently on Vesper's head as they started the long trek home. The night was cold, but the sky clear and the ground hard. The trip would take only a few candlemarks, not like the first dreadful ride home with her. Not long enough for him to hold her warm body with the soft rose scent she wore rising in fragrant waves.

He had loved her since he first saw her on his twelfth birthday. It had been so long ago. He had ridden into town by himself on his new pony, an act for which he would pay dearly twice, once by town bullies and again when his father fetched him home. Even then clanfolk were heckled in town for their dress, for their manner of speech, for being clansmen.

Some young boys, seeing a young clan boy ride proudly into town full of foolish bravery, had taken the opportunity to taunt him by throwing rocks. One of the boys threw with accuracy or luck, for his projectile hit Drew in the face. Another hit his pony. The scared animal had reared, dumping him on the ground with one unexpected side lunge. Dizzy, his vision blurring, and sure his end was at hand, he had been slow to rise. Over the roaring in his ears, he heard a small whirlwind jump to his defense, standing over him, daring the boys to throw one more rock.

"I'll tell your fathers," she threatened, "Better, I'll tell the Mayor and he'll tell your fathers."

Her high, shrill voice brought storeowners to the front of their shops, and then out to grab truant sons and drag them away.

"Holy One, you're a mess!" She had said looking down at him, her face scrunched in study, a line between the misty gray eyes. His first response had been anger and embarrassment that such a little girl, a child much younger than himself, should save him. As his head cleared, he had wiped his face and found his hand covered in blood.

"You've a bloody nose and a scraped chin and a big gash on your check. You need to see Eudora." She had helped him to his feet, dusted off his feathered cap, its jaunty feather broken, and ushered him to what he came to know as her personal safe haven, Eudora. He'd been completely at ease with the tall dusky woman once he realized she was from Kennetsure.

Eudora, without a word, tended his nose and cleaned his face, anointed his chin and cheek with ointment. All the time her daughter held his fingers in a friendly grasp, jabbering about Fair Folk and magical beasts despite Eudora's urging her to cease her prattle and hush. She called his fat little pony a unicorn. Her curly dark hair and silvery eyes enchanted him. Opening his hand, she had looked at the mark there without fear or disgust. "Look, Eudora."

He had looked at the older woman then, in panic. "It is not a mark of evil."

"Of course not," Eudora said. "It is only a birthmark."

"Then the Holy One gave him the moon to hold," Vesper said, her finger tracing the crescent shape.

He remembered taking a deep breath in relief. Vesper had smiled up at him. She was the first girl he had ever liked and became the only one he wanted. His hand traced the now small scar on his cheek and smiled.

He could never think of the next twelve years of waiting without feeling the anxious torment—the infrequent unauthorized, jaunts to Norost, sometimes only to catch a glimpse of Vesper and knowing he must avoid detection. Excursions to find out everything he could about her. Trips he paid for with stringent punishments. He refused explanations to first his father, then Selwyn, then his clan. The year she came of age to join the Handfasting ceremony, his parents were killed, and it was impossible for him to make the Norost ceremony.

The unusual circumstances of their death alerted the clan. Too many others in the Montoren family had already died in accidents. Only Selwyn, his grandfather and he remained, and, unknown then, his grandfather would soon pass, too.

Clan Cader had held a council, calling all Vere's remaining clans to attend. They concluded protection was needed, and that Egan needed warning. It was too late for the Seward Aegis and the Ward Aegis. Their families were already gone...

Last year he had stated his choice. Selwyn and the clan scoffed at his pick, and openly decreed he could not make it. Before Handfasting, the clan found urgent duties for him elsewhere. During those two Handfastings, Drew had panicked. The relief he felt when he heard her left standing both times defied description.

When they arrived in Montoren's courtyard, Vesper still slept. Selwyn appeared at Drew's side and lifted Vesper from his arms. Before Drew could dismount, Selwyn already walked toward the hall. Leaping off his mount and leaving all three horses standing, Drew followed. Several clan members stared at the unusual event, but

Drew didn't care. Selwyn continued up the stairs and into Vesper's bedroom to lay her down in the huge bed, demanding Drew pull the covers back first. He then pulled Vesper's boots off, covered her, and left the room without looking at Drew, telling him to undress her as he left. Drew watched him walk away, astonished at his cousin's behavior.

Vesper slept through the whole amazing event. Drew looked at her peaceful sleep, then remembered the horses left standing and rushed from the room. Others, seeing the untended animals, had already unsaddled them, and now groomed them. Selwyn worked on his horse. Drew took a brush from Gerdi and worked on his, or rather Vesper's, Kuff. Fulbert took care of the third horse. Gloominess hung in the atmosphere informing Drew the news from town was known. Gerdi, with a mournful look at Drew, wrapped her shawl tight about herself and left.

"Is the little miss all right?" Fulbert asked. The huge smith's voice seemed subdued from its usual baritone boom.

"Tired."

"Shocked." Drew and Selwyn spoke together.

"The news you bring is shocking. The king is dead and no one has yet been crowned. What is to become of Kaereya?" The big man's lower lip trembled as he finished talking, and he wiped his eyes. After a moment, he looked at Drew over the horse's back. "What is to become of us?"

Drew felt his own dread reflected in the smith's face. He had no answer. Selwyn also looked sober and drawn. Leading the horse into a stall, the smith closed the rail door. The clang of the latch sounded unnaturally loud in the quiet barn. With another good night and an even sadder smile, the smith left. Finished with Kuff, Drew put him in his stall. By the time he emerged, Selwyn waited. They walked together back to the hall. Word of the atrocity had spread, and a sense of mourning hung like a blanket over those left in the yard. Drew more than once was stopped and asked if it were true.

As they reached the door Selwyn said, "She knew."

"What?"

"Vesper. The night it happened, Last Day Eve, in front of the fireplace when you two argued, I heard her. She spoke of the child Edith, the poor dead baby. The Queen's youngest child was named Edith."

Drew scoffed. "How could she know? Edith is a common enough name, and she could have spoken of some memory."

"I have thought of little else today. She knew, and it was not the first time. Did you listen to what she said in town?"

"Of course I did," Drew said, exasperated.

"When you thought her raving today in the tavern, did you listen to what she said?"

Drew stood and thought, but knew that in his concern for Vesper, he had listened but hadn't heard. Selwyn read his face.

"She spoke of the foundation, the horse that would become the symbol of Kaereya, talisman bred by talisman. The clan's mountain unicorn, the battle mount of the Royal Guard, and the king's pleasure and parade horse."

"She was talking nonsense, dreams of her fantasy about this animal."

"Do you remember what she said that night kneeling before the fire?"

Frowning in concentration, Drew said, "Just something about the poor baby." He shrugged.

"And, *'dead, they're all dead'.*"

He didn't want to remember, but it came back to him anyway. A chill of disquiet ran up his back.

"Then remember what she said as we left the Handfasting Ceremony?"

"No."

"I do. I've had all day to think about it. She said, *'Can't help, it's too late.'* Then, *'Only one left.'*"

"That proves nothing."

Selwyn shrugged. "She was up before light looking for you, very agitated." Selwyn gave a rare smile, this one tinged with irony. "The Little Bit demanded I tell her where you were, demanded I take her to town. I ignored her. By the time it was brought to my attention, she had fled a few leagues down the road."

Selwyn waved away Drew's anger. "Nothing happened, I found her straight away. Fought me until I promised to take her to town." He looked at Drew. "She had a spell on the way into town. Spoke of the tragedy to the Vere Aegis, the loss of the foundation sire that could carry him throughout Kaereya. She could not know who you are, Drew, unless you told her."

Drew shook his head at the unasked question. "I did not want to scare her."

Selwyn went on as if he hadn't spoken. "It started me thinking."

"So what do you think?" Drew asked, knowing the answer, reluctant to hear it.

"I think her a seer. That's why you've been obsessed with her for so long, far longer than you let anyone know. I think she holds magic as great as your own."

Fear ran through Drew. Seers of legends were unstable, known for taking their own lives or becoming crazed because of the images they endured. No, not Vesper. "Your imagination has gone wild. Everyone knows there are no seers in Kaereya."

"As there are no aegises in Kaereya?"

"Magic myths crop up here as often as in the south." Drew scoffed at Selwyn to relieve his own anxiety.

"That's because we believe and accept."

~ * ~

Chloe's Story

As they prepared to leave on the journey to Cygna, Chloe felt some trepidation at traveling so far from Kennetsure. Now she would not even have a distant view of her home. No one seemed interested in her departure, except Queen Sophia and her son Ewald, who eyed her coldly while she asked formal permission to travel of King Ewald. Monsignor Otto had come to wish her fair journey, but no others.

Dustyn must have sensed her uneasiness for he smiled at her.

"You will be comfortable among those who share your gifts."

"Your Talents are so easily accepted in Cygna?"

"Not at all." He laughed. "Even after so many generations Talents are uncommon and held in suspicion, but we make gains. Talents now hold many positions within our government. We have proven our value."

"You seek to comfort me?"

"I know you will come."

"You do? Foresight?"

"No, I have no Chronos Talent. I only speak of what I want and find myself eager to start our relationship."

"You are optimistic."

"I'll give you time to get over Ewald, but we'll be together before we get to Cygna."

It was what she saw. By the time she reached Cygna she was glad she came.

Eleven

"We waited for you," Drew said to Vesper before she even reached the bottom step into the hall. Selwyn stood by the table. It was clear they delayed their morning's work, as breakfast lay on the table.

Vesper swallowed, afraid of the portent of this unexpected assembly. They were sending her back, she realized, the handfasting ended. Defying both of them yesterday, interfering in clan business, was the last straw. Lifting her chin, she walked to the table.

Of all things, Selwyn pulled the bench out for her to slide in. Her eyes watched him in startled suspicion as she thanked him. After yesterday, she expected he was happy enough to see her go to even perform a common courtesy. They would breakfast, then tell her, she was sure.

They ate in silence. Vesper drank her cider hoping to open her constricted throat. Between sips from her wooden mug, she tore her bread into ever smaller pieces. She noticed neither Drew nor Selwyn made a full meal.

"The king is dead," Drew said.

"What?" She swiveled her head to Drew, unprepared for his words. Her fingers tightened into fists and her innards seemed to shrink in upon themselves with a cold ache.

"There is no other way to tell you. Selwyn and I learned of it yesterday, but because you were... ill, I decided not to tell you then. There was nothing you could do, anyway."

"Dead?" Vesper repeated. "Then we have a new king?"

"No. They are all dead, murdered, even the children. On First Day."

Vesper felt the tears flow from her eyes in unrestrained streams. "No, no, no. It can't be so. By the Holy One, who would commit such a horrible crime? Was there no one who could protect them?" Her body started shaking. "What will happen?"

"No one has been crowned. There is a dispute. It seems Prince Warrick is missing. He must be crowned soon, or the council will choose a new king."

"That could cause civil war," Selwyn said. "There are several aristos eligible. They will tear Kaereya apart."

Vesper heard the trouble in his voice. "What will become of our poor country?" she asked in real fear. "Can they not find Warrick? Or do they fear he has been murdered, too?"

Selwyn's rough voice spoke to her distress as he laid a gentle hand on her arm. "We are strong in Vere. You will be safe here."

She stood up, with a sudden desire to escape. "I need some air." When both men protested and comforted her in jumbled sentences, she said, "I will be in the garden," and fled.

~ * ~

A day later she was still fleeing to her garden at odd moments. Walking there helped calm Vesper's ragged nerves. Alfred followed her steps looking very glum, his arms clasped behind him, and she drew comfort in the presence of even an imaginary person. His brown and dried-leaf tunic looked tenuous for withstanding the frigid air. The garment trembled like the few oak leaves remaining on the trees, fluttering in a breeze beget dance. He stopped and looked at her, but never spoke, not since years ago when at Eudora's insistence, she had denied the existence of her childhood friend.

She sighed, feeling her desperate loneliness. Drew left with a few of his clansmen after breakfast and would be gone on some unstated business to the outlying farms for several days, most likely to inform everyone of the king's death. He left Selwyn in charge. It didn't matter; she could not have talked with Drew anyway. She just missed the thought of his presence.

Light snow fell in slow, feather-soft flakes onto the shroud that had covered the ground during the night. It was as if the snow was as sad and as lethargic in its grief as Drew's clan as they moved about their daily tasks, talking only in somber, low exchanges.

She stopped pacing and sat on a stone bench placed beneath a winter leaf-naked tree. She pulled her cloak tighter against the chill, such sad news, such fearful news. The king and his family, murdered, even the baby. An unimaginable tragedy survived only by a missing prince.

Devastating news because she knew, had known for a sennight from visions seen in reflections of the blue mirror. No longer could she gaze in its depths without one of those terrible awake-dreams striking. In desperation she had covered the mirror, wanting to see no more. It made her wonder if her imaginings had caused the tragedy. It fired more wraith-like visions that shadowed her consciousness with fear and guilt.

"I knew, but refused to believe," she said to Alfred. "It is a curse. I might have saved them! Warned them!" Alfred's expression didn't change.

She jumped up and walked to the gate but turned around before reaching it, rubbing her forehead. "Why fool myself? Who could I have told, even if I'd acknowledged what I saw? No one who could have made a difference." She flopped down on the bench with a sad huff and placed her chin in her knee-braced hands. Cold tinged her fingers and cheeks, but where they met, warmth returned, but not as warm as the tears on her face.

She looked at Alfred who now sat before her on the stone walkway, a small, scrawny, and grizzled-looking man. "They're getting worse, not going away like Eudora said they would if I ignored them. She said, *'you must live in reality,'* but what is that, admitting I experience these visions or denying them? Denying hasn't worked too well. Now I say things that make people believe me crazed. Maybe I am. I see you." She laughed while still crying, "Holy One, now I'm even talking to you. Something I promised not to do years ago." Her laugh ended with a sigh.

"There is no one else who sees, and denial never made you disappear. Every day, I live in fear these visions will escape me, take over my life, and leave me to wander forever in a phantom-filled world where what is not is as real as what is. If this is foresight, I don't want it. How can I live knowing the terrible things that will come to pass and be unable to change any of it?"

Alfred rose and danced a circular jig, shaking his fanny at her and making obscene gestures that candidly mocked her sincerity. He sniffed and sat down with his back facing her, his face looking out over the garden.

"Alfred, Kaereya needs its last Prince. The court needs to know where he is. Perhaps, if I could control these visions, I could find him. But how could I do that? How do you search out something that comes of its own accord even while fighting and denying them? If I seek them out, can I get lost in their presence? Will I be trapped in that vision or make it come true? What if I never emerge to myself? I tell you true, the thought terrifies me."

Alfred's head turned and he looked at her out of the corner of one eye.

"You could answer me," Vesper said. He made a mocking, insolent face. "You think I must find the courage to try, don't you? You think me a coward, afraid and denying what I know. I promise you, from now on, I will accept my... visions, try to understand what they mean. If denial won't keep me sane, maybe acceptance will." Alfred remained quiet. Denial and a broken promise to Eudora lay between them. Why should he believe her?

"I swear it, Alfred, with my heart's blood and by my soul's salvation." She gave the age-old oath. He remained unmoving and

Vesper's eyes left him to wander her surroundings. It was not his problem, but hers. A choice to make and abide by, no matter the consequences.

The garden looked beautiful even under the snow. The gray stems of parterre shrubs seemed to form a cleaner pattern. Its framework was more distinct. The hard work of pruning them had provided visual results. Swaying branches of the fruit trees, striated in smooth bark, created moving mosaics on the clear blue sky. Patterns in the wall were picked out with bright snow and the air held a frigid scent of promised renewal.

With fresh resolve, she rose at long last and shook the snow off her cloak and skirts. A bright color unseen at the side of the bench caught her eye. A small purple and yellow crocus bud emerged from the snowy blanket. The sight cheered her. Beyond the wall she heard crows cawing, and feeling different somehow, she left the garden.

~ * ~

"You should consummate the Handfasting, wed or no," Selwyn said as they rode down to the practice field.

Drew firmed his lips and kept his focus straight ahead. "Not unwed."

"Then marry as soon as possible."

Drew cast Selwyn a poisoned looked. "Fine talk from you, who never wanted the Handfast in the first place."

"I've changed my mind. She is a seer..."

"She is no seer!"

Selwyn ignored him. "And a healer. She will be good for you and good for Clan Cader. Take my advice, end this. You want her. It's obvious every time you look at her. Take the final step. You don't want to lose her through inaction."

"I can't. I promised."

Selwyn snorted. "You think she will care?"

"I will care. It's my word."

"Wait until breeding season and see where your word gets you."

Drew groaned at the thought and Selwyn laughed.

~ * ~

Chloe's Story

Dustyn was dead. Killed by someone without a gift, someone who hated the Talents gaining power or any authority within Cygna. Intolerance reigned in Cygna, too.

It still stunned Chloe. For days she had sat doing nothing but gaze at the cold winter snows outside her window, her arms holding her young daughter, Bliss. Talents here called her their black swan. The one Kennetsurean in the country, the only one most had ever seen. Who would have thought she could live in this cold country for twelve years?

Until Dustyn's death, it had become her home, the place she wanted to be. Two loves had she, one made of gauze, more of awe and respect, easily rent. Tight-woven silk composed the other, a cloth with the substance to last an eternity.

No visions came to comfort Chloe, but in late winter her destiny changed with the delivery of a message from the Kaereyan Court. King Ewald III commanded his witch to return to his court. It was such a funny idea Chloe had laughed. Laughed until a desire for her childhood home, for Kennetsure, struck her so hard it brought tears and took her breath.

Even during the long journey back to Kaereya, her mind mourned the loss of her beloved, but time dulled the ache and a slow acceptance came to her. At the Eternal Palace, a Royal Guardsman helped her dismount. As she climbed the stone steps to King's Hall, she looked about her. Not much had changed, and she sensed signs of neglect. One of the Guardsmen must have sent a messenger to tell of her arrival, for a page met her before she reached the end of the first corridor.

"His Majesty asked me to show you to him, Lady Chloe."

"May I have a chance to clean myself of journey grime before I greet the king?"

"He asked to see you before you entered the Palace, Lady."

Surprised at the immediate summons, Chloe followed the young page. Inside the disrepair was more noticeable. She thought of reasons while she walked and realized an unforeseen result of the war—lost tax revenues. Kaereya had been hard hit.

As she entered the king's anterooms Chloe recognized one or two faces from her sojourn at court but couldn't put a name to them.

"Lady Chloe!" Ewald's voice had not changed although she hardly recognized him. Her own black hair held streaks of gray, but Ewald's russet had turned a dingy gray. His face was lined with worry and pain above a portly body. "You look exactly the same, as beautiful as I remember you, but far too tardy in attending your duties in that I must recall you from Cygna."

Chloe rose from her curtsy. "You flatter me, Your Majesty, with the most pleasant of falsehoods. If my absence has caused you any distress, I am most troubled."

"I need you, Chloe. I need my witch."

"I am not a witch, Your Highness, I know no magic."

Ewald threw a hand in dismissal of her contradiction. "Your gift, then. I need it. Kaereya needs it."

"How may I be of service to Kaereya?"

"I want you to protect her. Make her borders impenetrable to foreign attackers."

Chloe felt her face stiffen. Her mind stumbled. "Your Majesty... I cannot. What you ask is far beyond my meager Talents."

"Chloe, I have sought of everyone for a cure to the curse that has fallen on Kaereya. You left for a pleasant life in Cygna, but everyone else has had to live through the consequences of the war. They are many—poverty, widows with no support, orphans, beggars, the lack of skilled workers."

"The last I knew everyone was lost in wild excess."

"They still are, Lady, they still are." Ewald turned around, but not before Chloe saw the tears run down his cheeks.

Her eyes widened. Something more bothered him, and Chloe sensed his sadness, his regrets.

"My only good luck I attribute to you, to the amulet you gave me. Through three overthrow attempts, I've worn it. Through the days of endless negotiations, I've worn it. I swear it has saved my life. Always, it served me well, as you have always served my realm.

Strife still tears this country apart, Lady."

"It is but a buckle, Sire."

"A magical buckle, from a magical woman, and one that has cursed me."

Chloe started at his words.

"Yes, you may look at me that way, but curse me you did. I used to think war such a glorious occupation, an honorable thing." He turned around in sudden accusation. "Until I met you. I went to Bishop's Hospital twice during the war, both times on your account. The first time I just walked around and found the sights and sounds oppressive. A king, you see, doesn't witness the battlefield except from afar. Then I saw you working, helping those for whom the war had shown what a merciless bitch she was. It shamed me and it has haunted me ever since. You did this, and now you shall remove the curse. I command it."

"I will do my best, Your Majesty." Chloe hesitated, dumbfounded, then lowered into another deep curtsy. She backed away from King Ewald's presence. Once free of the Petitioners' Chamber, Chloe's mind raced. She sensed his disease and felt sad with the love she once held for him. She sensed another presence and looked about her. A page showed her to rooms in the Palace. It seemed Ewald would not give permission to leave until she found his cure. She sank wearily into a chair, her mind blanked with this new dilemma.

"Should I unpack for you, Lady?

The voice and the Talent she sensed earlier drew Chloe from her stupor. An attractive woman with golden hair and wearing a servants' dress waited for her to answer. She looked up at a woman.

"I am Melissa, Lady Chloe. I am to serve you while here at the court."

Twelve

Warrick pulled his mount up just above North Bridge to Hawk Island. The urge to cross the bridge, ride to the Eternal Palace and find his family alive and well was overwhelming, and defied logic. "It is wrong, I should go back."

"Whom can you trust?" Emory cried. "Rikon hates you for all the trouble you've given him. No one has sworn fealty to you. They will kill you."

"Father," Tate said. "He would help."

"Shut-up, Tate. You know nothing." Emory turned back to Warrick. "Yes, he would help, but whoever killed the king will make sure we die also, probably before we reach the Palace. They must have people watching for you. Think of how many you can't trust. We must find the perpetrator of this crime before you can reclaim your throne. Come, Warrick, we cannot hold here, you are sure to be recognized."

"Not like this, unwashed, unshaved, and rough dressed. There is another answer," he said. "We can go to the Royal Guards."

"You propose to go all the way back to Wessure to pick up the Southern River Road? That's risky. Everybody must be looking for you, enemies as well as allies. We need to find your allies."

He grinned with acceptance. "Probably more enemies than allies. We can send a message to your father and wait for him to meet us. We will be safe then."

"No messages until you are secure. Anyone could intercept it."

"Not if you or Tate delivers it."

"We cannot leave you unprotected."

"There is a guard outpost close, up north of the cutoff for Seer Pass. They will have the latest news, and at least I might not be murdered in my bed."

"Maybe. Unless someone has taken over the government and has put a warrant out on you."

"We will do it anyway."

Emory began to argue but Warrick held steady. He really had nothing to lose except a kingdom.

At the turnoff to Seer Pass, they came upon another group of travelers under attack. Emory warned Warrick they could not interfere; it was too dangerous. Warrick looked at Emory, wondering at his sudden cowardliness. He reluctantly agreed maybe it was time to be less reckless, more prudent, but his stomach could not contain the bitterness, burning with the acid of deadly anger. His sword hissed from its sheath even as he wheeled his horse and spurred it into a full gallop. This time, with rage driving his sword arm, he was not too late. The cowards saw three of their number slain before running for the cliff trails twisting through the ravine.

He did not follow but pulled his horse to a walk and approached the wagons. No men's bodies lay scattered around the wagons and no raped women wailed among fallen bodies. A pale young woman stepped from the recesses of the middle wagon holding a short bow and waited for his approach.

"Prince Warrick?" She spoke with a soft accent that added distinct precision to her words.

He didn't recognize her, but she must have seen him at court. A complication he didn't need. Dismounting, he took her raised hand and kissed the fingers. Her soft, sweet voice continued.

"Your rescue was deeply appreciated."

Only when he stared into the deep blue sapphire on her second finger did recognition come.

"Princess Pia?"

Her hand curled around his. A rueful laugh tinged with recent terror welcomed him. "Indeed. It seems we are both much changed." Her blue eyes searched his face.

With a stupefied gaze, he searched her face, not at all what he remembered. She was beautiful. "What are you doing here?" He looked around, horrified. "With so few retainers? Have you no idea in how dangerous a position you've placed yourself?" Images of the other women entered his unwilling mind. Pia's face reflected the horror he felt.

"I am safe. You saved me. I am on my way home. Enough guards remain to see me safely there." Her retainers worked around them moving the bodies, checking the teams and wagons, shouting to each other.

Handfasting. His eyes swiveled back to her with ashamed and flushed understanding. "My actions were unpardonable. I humbly beg your forgiveness."

She sighed with a sheepish grin. "Not too humbly or I shall have to apologize also." The grin faded. "We both played our little games. Your family... I am so sorry but so glad to see you alive. What are you doing out here?"

"Emory thinks we should go directly to King Clement in Pertelon. But," he nodded to his cousins. "We are instead on our way to the Royal Guards' outpost up the road. We plan to reach safety, then send a message to my uncle, the Duke of Hearthron."

Her eyes grew large and worried. She pulled on his hand and led him away from those working around the wagons to a private spot some distance away.

"It is true you are in grave danger, and it is even more true you must not go anywhere without knowing who waits to meet you. But you must not leave Kaereya, especially not to go to Pertelon. It would appear you abandoned your country, your crown. Please believe me, I understand politics." Her eyes searched his face in serious intent.

"Pertelon is not an answer, Prince Warrick. The usurper who holds the crown of Pertelon will not help you, even if he says he will."

"I felt that, too. It seemed wrong."

"It is also true that the Palace is a dangerous place. Whoever killed your family... they abide there. I do not know your uncle, but I have had dealings with the Earl of Rikon. He let the court believe you were on a mission for your father. He is a good man and I know he works very hard on your behalf."

"He is at court, where you tell me not to go," he said with a grin, even as his skin bristled with prickles of caution.

Warrick watched Emory talking with one of the Kaereyan guards escorting the Princess. He probably planned to send a message.

Pia's gaze followed his. "Trust must be earned, even from those closest to you."

The implication made him try to jerk his hand from her. She held onto it. "I am sorry to tell you this, but remember, I have nothing to lose or gain in telling you what I know."

"My cousins? My uncle?"

She sighed. "I don't know the truth, only rumor, and nothing of your cousins. One of my maids overheard your uncle say you were not fit to rule, even if you were alive. Don't go to either the Eternal Palace or Cliff City. Don't go anywhere you might be expected. If recognized, you might die before you arrived."

Her words echoed Emory's advice, except in the solution. Whom should he believe? As she said, she had nothing to gain in her advice, except revenge for a lost betrothal and the humiliation he caused her. It made him suspicious.

Her look changed to one of inspiration. "Aristo Norbert trusts the Duke of Lambere. Go to Aristo Aurelias. He has a look I trust, also. Please do this, I beg it of you for saving my life."

"It looked to me like you saved your own life," Warrick answered. He noted how the sun formed a halo on her pale head. She looked innocent and trustworthy like one of the angels in the glass windows of Aron cathedral. His heart wanted to believe her.

"I had an unusual upbringing. But surely you saved the lives of my retainers and my lady maids."

"Then," he said, raising her hand to his lips but keeping his eyes on hers, "I must do as you say. Promise not to hold the past against me? I can promise you nothing at this juncture in my selfish, misspent life, but if you try and forget my previous behavior, my rudeness, arrogance, and ignorance, I think I would like... I would like you to return to Kaereya."

She smiled. "Not only you behaved badly. You have not mentioned the orange, fuchsia, and turquoise gown."

"Or your much-improved speech? You have a very sweet accent." It seemed somehow inappropriate to feel anything but anguish and grief, but he did.

She laughed, a joyous sound to his ears. "Exactly. But it would be improper for me to return to the Eternal Palace, and it could put you in jeopardy. Sunderlune is not on the other side of the world."

"Just the other side of the Vere Plateau."

She smiled. "A short route exists through the Seer Pass. A courier can easily make the journey in a few sennights. Send me a message of your safety and your desires." She looked back at her wagons. "You will go to the Duke of Lambere? Promise me, please?"

He looked at her. "Yes. I will take trails through the Rikon Hills. We can be there in little more than a sennight. And you must promise me to keep yourself safe."

"It is a favorite occupation of mine."

~ * ~

The message stunned Norbert, even suspecting it. The timing was disastrous but explained so much. "How?" he asked the courier.

"They were on us before we knew it, sir. The Pertelon troops overran the island before a proper defense could be mounted. Aristo Delphine ordered me to deliver this. One of the boatmen rowed me out to one of our merchant ships and I made my way here. It has taken just under three days. The Aristo and his family were to take another ship and should arrive soon."

"Have you told anyone?"

"No one, but the ship's crew knew."

"So word has already begun to spread," Norbert said aloud, then composing himself, dismissed the courier to seek food and rest. It had been a well prepared and thought out assault. The Guard's unique system of mirror and light communication usually flickered news through the island garrisons to Guard Island. No messages had come.

Now he knew why. The garrisons were taken, Pertelon already far into Kaereya, moving along the Southern Thou's banks westward toward the Peace Ocean. King Clement wanted control of the river.

Gilchrist, by default King Frederick's closest kin, held charge in Warrick's absence. While Gilchrist dithered about taking any measure, Pertelon chose to make their move, probably King Clement was well informed of events in the Eternal Palace.

Turning to his window, he thought of all he must accomplish and the scant time to do it. Warrick. They had to find him. He quickly sent his scribe for courier riders and wrote a message to Aurelias. Saying a brief prayer to the Holy One, he sat down to his desk and started writing messages. His pen paused. Ottillie was caught right in the line of the advancing enemy. If at Egan she would be safe, but how would he get her home?

A servant interrupted him, saying that Master Godfrey wished words with him. Dismayed at the untimely interruption, Norbert nevertheless told him to show the Heraldist into his antechamber. Puffing with exertion from the trip, Master Godfrey entered holding several oversized books in his arms.

"Bring some wine and two goblets," Norbert told his servant. "Master Godfrey, this is unexpected. Please be seated."

"Marshal Norbert," the portly Heraldist gasped, "I have information."

"Recover yourself first, sir. The information won't disappear."

"Such perfidy." Master Godfrey's cheeks worked like bellows with his breathing. He drew a last gulp of air and grabbed the goblet of wine handed to him, taking a long swig. He exhaled before speaking. "In my own people! Since the death of my youngest apprentice, I have been questioning each of my masters and journeymen. When you first came to me before, I disguised my dismay at the state of my records," he said. "I have my own very precise way of filing. The folios were not in my order. Other folios were missing. I knew then someone had gone through them. I should have told you, considering the information you sought. I should have known then, but who expected an attack on the king?"

Norbert, sitting in the opposite chair, took a sip of his own drink. "What has this to do with the king?"

"One of my journeymen has been selling family histories, was hired to find those with magic in their background." His breath returned to normal as if unburdening his message gave him ease.

"Your information is most valuable."

"Too late," Master Godfrey moaned, tears escaping his eyes, "too late."

"We've all been too late, too complacent."

"Not you."

"Just not successful. What have you here?" He opened one folio looking at the exquisite painting. A blood-red dragon stood rampant, balanced by its out flung-wings, floating over a rising sun. He knew it rising because these were Easurean symbols. Easure's other symbols, pentacles, two bulls, and seven fish were woven into the device. The motto, 'To Serve with Humility and Joy,' flowed on a banner around the base of the emblem. The family name Guthase was scrolled in elaborate lettering on the bottom of the sheet.

"These are the folios of the Aegises. Yes, I know, no one believes, but King Ewald the III gave each land in perpetuity. Therefore, the Court Heraldist has kept track of the families, as best they could, through the ages. My master illuminator still held these. I will dismiss him, but right now he is locked in a closet. I thought you might wish to speak with him."

"That was good thinking. Why bring these here?"

"You will need to look at them, then I wanted you to keep them safe until this trouble is over. I wish no more deaths attributed to my negligence."

"Take me to your man, I have some questions for him."

The walk back to his rooms showed him rumors of the invasion had spread. When he returned, Norbert was near ill. There had been several men inquiring of the Heraldist's staff, and Norbert presumed, had been doing so for years. The man identified two courtiers with ties to Aristo Yonger, one of Norbert's own staff, and one Royal Guardsman. Eldin. The confession dealt Norbert a blow for which he wasn't prepared. His thoughts flew to Ottillie. He shook his head to dismiss them. He had to decide how best to use this information. So far none of the men was guilty of anything other than seeking information.

He sent a page for two of his senior staff. "You will question our man, find out who gives him orders. Then ask Aristo Yonger if you may question his men." Before he finished with his orders, Gilchrist sent a notice for an emergency convening of the King's Council for the next afternoon. Norbert fumed. Aurelias, delayed longer at court than he originally planned, had left town a day earlier and the dispatched courier had not returned. Without Aurelias he knew Warrick's chances of keeping the throne ebbed.

~ * ~

As the aristos gathered Norbert noticed many still wore mourning, but just as many had already put it aside. It didn't surprise him with all the scheming taking place within the palace.

"Kaereya is invaded! My lands are threatened. It is intolerable," Aristo Yonger of Anatole Island shouted before the preliminaries of the Court's Assembly even finished. "We need leadership now, not when Warrick finds it convenient to return to his duties." A loud chorus of agreement followed. "Listen to the people in the street," Aristo Yonger yelled. "They grow restless and upset with their kingless state. They ask for the king. And where is he? No one knows! Set aside this vagrant youth and replace him with someone of proven steadiness!" The court erupted into clamorous talk with Yonger's declaration, the volume escalating as others voiced their opinions.

Norbert ordered the Court Minister to pound his heavy staff on the stone floor, and the thud echoed over the shouting. When the aristos quieted, he spoke. "It is true we are in a perilous time. Our king is dead, and the new king remains uncrowned. We are invaded. Pertelon is moving troops through the southern islands in an effort to reach the Peace Ocean in a move that will cut Kaereya in two. It is not hard to guess the invader's purpose, control of the southern branch of the Thou River. Through the last years Pertelon has ravaged our country through subterfuge. I have the proof here." He held up his report. "Their agents did this with the help of some of our own countrymen, even those standing among us now. Some aristos denounce the heir for not coming forward. Can they blame him when his father's killer lingers unidentified amongst us?"

"It's your job to identify the culprits, Norbert," Theodulf Gilchrist said, jumping from his seat on the dais. All eyes fell upon the Duke of Hearthron, still dressed in deepest mourning. "Your duty is to find my brother's murderer."

"That is true, sir," Norbert said, noting Gilchrist's dropping 'in-law' in his brother reference. "But our traitors covered their tracks well. This report outlines their craftiness. I say these betrayers did more than disrupt our monarchy, they sold Kaereya to the Pertelon usurper, King Clement!"

It was an uphill battle. Naysayers and disbelief met his every argument. He outlined step-by-step the attack against Kaereya of the elimination of whole Aristo families, targeting those with any historical vestige of magic.

With his accusation, those who held their lands through such deaths disclaimed any knowledge or involvement, especially of the elimination of the royal family. He raised his voice to be heard but was drowned out as cries of panic, disbelief, laughter, and outrage rose in cacophonic waves.

Cries for order, impassioned pleas for restraint, and the court minister's pounding staff failed to bring order, let alone quiet. In the tumult, Aristo Yonger's voice rose to promote Theodulf Gilchrist, Duke of Hearthron, to king. More noise arose. Screams of protest erupted with shouts of support. Surprise, though, eventually brought an agitated semblance of order.

"But his sons are missing too, and they hold the blood," the Aristo of Marshon exclaimed in outrage in an unexpected moment of silence. "He has no blood right to the crown!"

"Regent, then," Yonger screamed over raising voices. "Regent until this impending crisis is over! Then we can determine the next course to follow!"

A gust of frigid air blew through the hall from the main doors opening. Heads turned to see what disturbed the council, and the turmoil diminished.

"Or until the rightful heir, Warrick, is crowned," a voice spoke from the back of the room. Norbert thanked the Holy One. Raymond Aurelias stood inside the doors.

"Warrick has lost his right to the throne!" Yonger yelled his fury evident at Aurelias' appearance.

Raymond Aurelias, Duke of Lambere, strode forward still armed and garbed in muddy riding clothes to stand before Aristo Yonger. In his drab and dirty clothing, shorter and ordinary looking, he seemed a less than daunting presence to stop the exquisitely garbed Yonger, but silence followed in his wake. It was Yonger who fell back a step at Aurelias' expression.

Saying nothing to Yonger, Aurelias turned to the group. "I, like all of you, gave my oath to Frederick, our deceased king, to support him and his heirs. I have not seen Warrick's body to quit my oath. To my mind, it is a wise son who hides until murderous hunters are uncovered. I know. My family has been killed. I have been attacked. I no longer believe these circumstances either fate or accidental. Who among you hasn't been touched by the loss of family or friend by an unexplained incident or unfortunate accident?"

"How do know you he still lives?" Yonger sneered.

"How know you he doesn't?" Aurelias snapped back to a low chorus of yeas. Aurelias turned and looked at his fellow aristos and Norbert smiled. Yonger had discounted the respect accorded Aurelias. "I agree we need a Regent. That is enough for now. Let us protect the crown and the country for its rightful successor. If Warrick is dead, then Master Godfrey, the Court Heraldist will know who holds the line."

Accepting the Aristo's demands, Gilchrist, Duke Hearthron was appointed Regent. Norbert brought up the last subject. "We need troops." His speech started a new torrent of argument.

Regent Theodulf Gilchrist finally spoke. "Each Aristo must raise his people to fight for their own lands. The king's soldiers will protect the king's properties."

Stunned speechless, Norbert listened in fury to the general round of confirmation.

"But what about those who have already suffered loss of home and land?" Aristo Delphi asked. No answer came, and not even Aurelias's pleas could move Gilchrist or the aristos to a more aggressive stance before the council ended.

"They're scared," Aurelias said as they walked together to Norbert's apartments. "They will not move until the king commands them." He sighed. "They also smell a chance at power."

"I know," Norbert said. "Those not checking their heredity for the taint of magic right now, are politicking for the throne or with whomever they sense will win it. I expect I have sent Master Godfry more work than he would like." A sour smile crossed his face as the image of the Heraldist at their last meeting arose. He checked his thoughts and closed his eyes. "By the Holy One, where is Warrick?" They reached Norbert's apartment. "You returned precipitously."

Aurelias sighed. "A premonition of my own. Halfway to Tatzk, possibilities entered my head. I talked with Kissre."

"Kissre?"

"My mercenary. Within minutes she determined Clement's threat and possible tactics."

"You came back on a mercenary's whim?"

"A woman mercenary, too, but one who has fought Clement on his eastern border. Yes. It seemed logical. I felt you needed the warning."

They sat in the chairs in front of the fireplace. "I've already spoken with the Commander of the Royal Guards," Norbert said.

"They will batten down Easure as much as possible."

"Are you sure the boy is still alive?"

"No. But we must still hold out for more time."

"It has been over a sennight and waiting grows more dangerous."

"If he is dead, someone will bring forth the body. Whoever planned this outrage will see to that. It is the fastest, simplest way to move forward."

"Do you think Warrick participated?"

"No. Warrick is headstrong, disrespectful, wild, reckless, defiant, and truant. The list is endless and much of it provoked, but he is not deceitful or evil. Even I suspected he meant to miss Handfasting.

King Frederick had him watched but he evaded his guards." Norbert shrugged. "For all his bad behavior, he truly loved his family, particularly his younger sisters. I will not believe he participated in their deaths."

"Do you have any suspects?"

"Suspects? Certainly. You heard them in court. My men are watching the dissidents and those most vocal about disinheriting Warrick. Aristo Yonger causes the most ferment; he constantly pesters and petitions for the Aristo Court to declare King Frederick's line dead. Aristo Gilchrist's followers promote the appointment of a new monarch. That will not happen. There are candidates through the female line still viable. Gilchrist petitions for Emory's rights. The problem is Emory disappeared with Warrick, so is in no better position. The thing I found most interesting is Aristo Yonger handfasted Gilchrist's daughter. I found out today that two men hired by the Aristo Yonger worked to find magic-tainted families." His hand pounded on the chair arm. "According to Aristo Yonger, the men were dismissed months ago. There are a few others with motive."

Aurelias sighed. "Yonger thinks to take the throne through the female line? Are there not others with a clearer claim?" He was silent a moment. "I do not like leaving you here in this... wasps' nest... of intrigue and betrayal. They could take you out as easily as anyone else."

"They've tried, but I also have a network of friends and supporters. You are the strongest arm in Wessure and the only one sure to hold fast. Plus you own a fleet of merchant ships and have interest in keeping Pertelon from your shipping lanes."

"That may not count in the end."

"Still, you will serve Warrick best there."

"Right now, it is where I want to be, too."

"Your daughter?"

"Hopefully. I've cast a lure. I will spend the night here and leave tomorrow to ferry down the Northern Thou as far as possible. What other news comes?"

"Kennetsure is already invaded, but my sources say the invaders stick to the Thou's shoreline, not venturing into the desert. In Vere, the clans and the rugged terrain will provide an adequate defense."

Within days news came from Orveka, Anatole Islands' largest city. Norbert read the missive with a sinking feeling. Aurelias had left for his home—too late to recall. Pertelon troops had breached the eastern end of the island. A message came to the court beseeching the Aegis Yonger to return to the island. Under the circumstances, Norbert started laughing at the ridiculousness of the situation. Aristo Yonger might have seized the lands where the Aegis's Ward Keep once stood, but he was unrelated to the old Guthase family, he lacked their reputed magic. According to the Heraldist's records, the last of the family had died twenty years ago.

A day later Regent Theodulf Gilchrist called him. He was dismissed as King's Marshal for his inability to solve the murder of the Royal family. There was nothing he could do. "I will need time, Regent, to clear my rooms."

Gilchrist waved his hand. "Take as much time as you want, I doubt the next Marshal shall want rooms in such a shabby section of the palace."

Norbert nodded and left. He would need to be extra careful now, and how could he get word to Ottillie? Later, Corbin, his Kennetsurean investigator, returned. Norbert's former employee answered the questions put to him. When Norbert heard the name given up, his face froze. After a minute he said, "I am no longer King's Marshal."

"That rumor spreads through the court."

"Do you need help with our former employee?"

"No. His body was found earlier in the alley of one of the city's less-safe districts, a victim of the city's violence. I have another message. It is a copy of one from the guards sent to protect Princess Pia."

Norbert read the message. "Will you accept another assignment from me?"

"Galen already packs. We are full of discretion, Earl Rikon."

"We border treason."

"One must always choose one's sides with care for the future, sir. We will find Warrick before harm comes to him." The typical Kennetsurean reply gave Norbert some comfort.

~ * ~

The guide finally arrived sixteen days after Last Day. He introduced himself as Leander as he stood with Eldin and Ottillie in the main business plaza of Gotte City, only recently reopened.

Ships had brought the news of the royal family's demise within two days of Last Day's Eve. Deep in mourning for King Frederick and his family, the city's usually noisy market area had lain closed and quiet.

Eldin was edgy, eager to continue the journey. A uniformed Royal Guardsman approached where they stood settling the transaction.

"Lady Ottillie," the man said and handed her an envelope. "Your hotel directed me here. I will wait for your return message. The news, I fear, Lady, is not good."

Ottillie looked at her father's seal on the dispatch. Breaking the wax, she read the contents.

"Ottillie, Ottillie!" She only became aware of Eldin shaking her. "By the Holy One! What has happened?" Eldin asked.

She looked at him totally distracted, mindless of what went on around her. In disbelief she repeated the message to Eldin, her eyes imploring him to prove it untrue. "Pertelon invades and we have no crowned king. The Duke of Hearthron has been made regent. My father is dismissed." With her words, she burst into tears and handed Eldin the paper. She heard his inward gasp, and his cry, "No!"

People around them had heard her, and with the presence of a royal messenger, a whispering followed by a wailing spread through the crowded trade plaza. It was much later before any of them came to themselves enough to talk of business.

"You must go," Ottillie said. "The signal line is broken, and the remaining eastern garrisons must be put on alert."

Eldin whispered in urgency, "I can't leave you here!" He looked around, obviously deciding what to do with her. "You must take the men and return. I'll get you some additional escorts." His edict failed to move her.

"No. I'll be all right. You will need the men, and that is what my father has ordered. The news must be carried to them. Only you can do that. Go do your duty without worry for me."

"I will take very good care of the Lady Ottillie," Leander said from nearby. "I've traveled the route to Egan often and have many outriders to keep her safe."

"How much?" Eldin asked.

"No cost. I must journey there to make a delivery. It would be my pleasure to escort her." He performed the Kennetsurean deferential bow to Eldin. Eldin looked dubious, but Ottillie smiled.

"I agree," Ottillie quickly accepted Leander's offer.

"I don't like this."

"Eldin, you are insulting a Knight of the Zekarac Order." She indicated the emblem on the guide's shoulder. "That rank alone guarantees my safety."

With a little more argument, Eldin agreed. With his capitulation came a look of profound relief. He turned to go, and Ottillie unexpectedly felt a pang of privation. She barely controlled the tears filling her eyes.

"Wait," Ottillie put a hand on Eldin's arm. She removed a pendant from around her neck, the put it over Eldin's head.

"What's this?"

"A gift of friendship and thank you, an amulet to see you safe. The Easure Dragon, a protective symbol of good luck. And I do thank you, Eldin. May the Holy One travel with you."

He looked at the cloisonné pendant for an instant and slipped it under his jacket with a smile. "Ever a good friend. I shall treasure this, Ottillie." Giving her a desolate smile, he kissed her hand and left.

She stood next to Leander and watched Eldin slip through the crowd, wondering at her friend's last expression. Leander gave instructions for the gathering of her and her belongings for the final leg of the journey to Egan, and with a finger gesture, two of his men followed her until she returned ready for the journey. Leander helped her mount her horse. The Kennetsurean guide was the least inquisitive man Ottillie ever met.

"I thought we traveled by camel?"

The man smiled at her assumption. "Not until the very last, and if the weather holds, not even then. We are taking the easier river route. We follow the Gotte River to Cethair then take the Egan Road. Horses travel that way very well."

"No camels." She took a disappointed breath. "Too bad. I'd looked forward to it."

"We only take camels when we travel a more direct route and actually go through some very harsh terrain."

"I won't see the desert?"

"Lady Ottillie, you will see more of the desert than you wish."

"Sir Leander, I look forward to it, and even more so if you would call me Ottillie. Rank is necessary for survival at court but a nuisance on most occasions."

"Then let us do without rank and titles during this journey." He gave her the Kennetsurean salute of obeisance and stepped to his own horse.

Nothing met her expectations. The mornings and evenings were cold, and the days cool enough to require long sleeves and cloak. A long train of packhorses stretched behind them. She rode behind the laconic Leander. After her gambits for conversation disintegrated like charred wood, Ottillie gave up and watched the scenery. The countryside around Gotte City changed gradually from cheek-by-jowl buildings sharing stucco walls to more dispersed dwellings, and finally, isolated houses. The lack of a wall separating the city from the country surprised her only because she was out of the city before she realized its absence.

By the third day of travel only large palm trees grew in the river's flood plain separating large fields of grain where farmers labored.

Occasional boats floated past, with shouted greetings between the water and land travelers. Only children paid them any attention. Unlike her earlier journey, the view remained essentially the same throughout the days of travel. By the time they reached Cethair the weather had turned warm as summer in Easure.

Masses of flowering shrubs surrounded the city and grew in large containers throughout, but the town itself consisted of small, nondescript, single-story houses shaped like haystacks. By then Ottillie didn't care. The people were friendly, and she fulfilled her most recent fond wish, to sleep in a bed. The longed-for comfort lasted but a single night, but it was enough.

That night, with decent lamps available, warm and comfortable, she started the second diary postponed for this leg of her journey. It started in the forty-first year of Chloe's life. It was not the next volume, but more than a decade later. The war was over, and the middle-aged Chloe lived in Cygna with her husband Dustyn and their daughter Bliss. With Dustyn's death she moved with Bliss back to the Kaereyan Court and took Melissa as an apprentice. From then on, Melissa was often mentioned.

> *I found the honeybee in impure Amor again. This time with one of the Royal Guards, and right here in my rooms. They were both much surprised, as I was. Such immoral and decadent behavior billows through the Eternal Palace, through Cliff City, and into the country like bad gas through a bowel. I think it has to do with those who survived the war. Everyone had endured so much death; seen so much desolation during the war. I told her she had to mend her ways.*

A sennight later, another entry said:

> *The honeybee appeared before the magistrate for indecent acts today. I argued it wasn't her fault that a seam should rip in such a way. I've lied and must do penance. How am I to train this shameless young girl?*

Chloe's observations of the royal court continued, too.

> *The king is morose, even this long after his great victory over Pertelon and Sunderlune's unholy alliance. I see the changes in him others seem to miss or ignore.*

And a few sennights later:

> *I heard from the Earl of Anatole, that yesterday, during the trade negotiations, the king shouted in the presence of the Cygnese Ambassador, 'Appease Cygna for what? The damn Cygnese Council claims they didn't know Sunderlune troops moved through Seer Pass. How, sir, do I believe that?' He blames the Cygnese, and certainly, public opinion believes the Cygnese should have done something to help. After so much time in Cygna, it hurts me. The king distrusts everyone, even his councilors, but he cannot continue to alienate all around him, and I have not yet found a solution for the task he has set upon me. A notion nags at me though.*

At that point, pages in the diary were missing. With careful inspection, Ottillie found them cut out with a consistent precision that made it impossible to even guess how many pages were cut. In the last pages she read:

> *I leave tomorrow. My sorrow is great, so much work undone, but I am useless here. No one understands or believes except for four marked men. They are mocked and so am I. Tonight is Mask Night, the eve of Blood Day. The city is wild in revelry. I can hear the celebration through my one small window. The excesses scare me. Tomorrow, harvest ends with the blooding. I do not wish to see the slaughtering of animals. It reminds me of too much. So I leave the Eternal Palace in the autumn of this year and go to Charm Island to spend my remaining years.*

Slowly closing the book with dissatisfaction, Ottillie turned out the lamp and lay down. *Egan, the answers are in Egan.*

Leander had them up before first light to head into the real desert. "You are in luck, Ottillie." Leander had decided to ride next to her. "It is a good time to travel the desert. The ascetic Lady Doane often decides to bloom at this time of year. I have heard she has dressed for your arrival."

"I thought it was all sand, like an ocean?"

"That happens only much further south and deeper into the continent. Those barren areas are traveled only with great risk. The trek to Egan can be dangerous, especially in the heat of summer, but at all times for those unprepared for Doane's vagaries."

Ottillie, glad he decided to talk, didn't question the reason, but responded with perfect serenity. Later they left the arable lands of the Gotte flood plain and moved into the desert.

Strange, often scraggily, dried and withered-looking plants bloomed with bright yellow flowers. Red blossoms seemed to emerge from the rust and buff striated ground by themselves. Leander named the plants and went on to describe the desert habitat. The vibrant colors contrasted with the muted bluish and grayish foliage. More, the change was discernable not only by sight but also by feel. The breezes held grit that stung her eyes and the light seemed brighter and more intense.

"Do you hunt in the desert? Are there animals?"

"Certainly. Some few are dangerous. Do you hunt?"

"Yes, but I'm sure not with the skills needed here." With slow patience she drew him out on any number of desert subjects, then moved on to Egan itself.

After days of unending uniform landscape, even the flowers and the unusual colors of the landscape palled. All that was left was talk, and Leander kept his willingness to entertain her. Three days after entering the desert he pointed to the horizon on their left. "See? That's Egan."

Two bumps on the undulating surface appeared. "I thought there were three?"

"From this angle Singing Rock hides the middle promontory, Spring Rock. Bastion Rock is on the left. You have read about them?"

"Yes. I know Egan Tower was built on Spring Rock. They seem awfully small."

"Wait until you arrive to judge their height. The Aegis Kennetsure resides there."

"Aldous, Aegis Kennetsure? I wasn't completely sure he was the aegis. With a great library."

Leander laughed. "Yes, with a great library among other things."

"When do we arrive?"

"Another five days."

It was four days before they arrived at the base of Spring Rock, days with the Guide Rocks growing ever more prominent in the landscape, great towers of rust stone layered in diagonal streaks of blue, gray, and buff. Excitement entered Ottillie affecting everything. She looked upward and said, "They seem impregnable."

"This road ends at the top of Spring Rock. Even now we traverse a slow upward incline. The last part is not for the weak of spirit. Indeed, the Guide Rocks both inspire and measure courage."

He was right. The road rose slowly up the side of a butte then disappeared into the shadows at the base of the towers cresting the prominence. Once there, Ottillie saw it undulated up the side of Singing Rock, clinging to both natural and man-carved ledges. The rock sides ascended higher and steeper than the cliffs on Hawk Island. She swallowed a qualm of alarm, but this trail led where she wanted to go. It was the fifth day of travel as Leander had promised. The surprise lay on top. The road leveled out into a small city built of brick and the natural stone that supported it.

On the far end of the summit, a keep soared four stories higher and the road abruptly ended right at its gate. A tiny gray-haired woman stood there in typical Kennetsurean attire. Soft gauzy cream-colored cloth draped over her aged body and emphasized her dark coloring.

"Lady Ottillie. At last! We have been expecting you for days. Leander, help her down. Aldous? Aldous, Ottillie has arrived."

Leander moved to Ottillie's mount despite the fact she had successfully mounted and dismounted by herself from the first day. He took her elbow and guided her to the woman, where he performed the Kennetsurean motion of deference.

"Leander, it is good to see your mournful self." The woman's shining brown eyes inspected the line of packhorses. "I see you've completed your mission and brought me work. Your trip was uneventful and safe?" the old woman asked Leander. "There were no problems encountered, what with the royal family's death?"

"No, Mistress Leela. The trip was fast and uneventful except for the sorrowful news. We all had succumbed to an itchy rash, but the Aegis's handfasted saw to our relief."

'You got to meet her? Good. You can tell me all about it. There is tea and a meal prepared for you. Come in, come in." Leela motioned Ottillie forward. "You've so much to learn and so little time, you don't want to spend it gawking out here. Aldous, come from your books." Leela's suddenly shouted command startled Ottillie.

"I'm here, I'm here." A voice came out of the deep-shadowed entrance behind Leela before the Aegis arrived in person. He was short, shorter even than Eldin, heavier in age, with long white hair pulled into a braided tail surrounding a dark-skinned bald crown.

"I didn't know the Aegis had a handfasted." Ottillie, confused, blurted out her thoughts, then felt the crimson flood her face.

Aldous and Leela laughed. "Leander spoke of Vesper, Drew's betrothed," Aldous spoke, his voice a friendly tenor.

"Drew?"

"Yes. The Aegis Vere."

~ * ~

Chloe's Story

"Tokens are important, Melissa. They tie the spell to the common mind, build the belief that holds the magic," Chloe said. Images formed dreamily in her mind.

"I plan to use ancient creatures, long extinct, but full of mystical revelation to represent my talismans, my Aegises. In the north, I see a unicorn, wild, unfettered, and loyal, stomping among the moonlit forests of Vere. To protect the waters of the thousand islands of Easure, a fierce and devoted dragon will soar in the thermal winds of the sun's first rays. In the west, a strong and crafty mermaid Aegis, seldom seen but at dawn or dusk, will swim deep to protect her treasures, and entice the unwary to their doom. To the south, under a blazing desert sun, a sphinx Aegis, inscrutable, wise, ageless, and poised, will destroy those who cannot answer the enigma of the desert. These are symbols of ageless magic."

"How do you carry out the spell?" Melissa asked, patently unimpressed by Chloe's flight of fantasy.

"We must find men of magic, Earth Talents."

"In Kaereya?" One of Melissa's eyebrows rose in skepticism.

"Yes. They are here. I know they are. Do you believe in predestination, Melissa?"

"Lady?"

"I was thinking it a good, but unusual circumstance, that I, of all Kaereyans, have spent so much time in Cygna. Else, I would not have had the idea for this *spell*. With my healing gifts, my own Earth Talent, and what I learned in Cygna, I can tie our four Aegises' Talents to their home province, through many generations."

"What good will that do, Lady?"

Chloe laughed. "An Earth talent, Melissa, feels the land. My Aegises will know when something or someone trespasses on their domain. We consecrate them with symbolism and ceremony to implant the image in everyone's mind, then let nature take its course. I must contact the king. We will probably be traveling."

"If you say so." Doubt filled Melissa's voice.

Thirteen

To say the request was odd put aside its very tempting promise. His clansmen found the courier and his escorts, in full heraldry uniform, headed for Montoren Farm with the message. Drew read it twice and handed it to Selwyn. Selwyn viewed it with suspicion. Drew saw it as a dream fulfilled. What breeder and trainer of horses doesn't like his efforts appreciated? He took the letter and reread it. Aurelias' own ducal crest topped the letter. The thick smooth feel of the paper told of its expensive nature. The Duke of Lambere probably didn't write it himself, more likely the fine hand belonged to a scribe.

At the Handfasting Ceremony in Norost, the duke had noticed Montoren Farm's fine horses. He wished the use of a stud horse to improve his own estate's line. If clansman Montoren could also bring three or more trained geldings and perhaps two mares, the duke might be interested in their purchase. The Duke stated an exorbitant financial advance for the trip with an added sum for the inconvenience of bringing the animals south, and more for each of the Duke's mares that took in foal. He mentioned Drew's handfasting and invited his espoused to come also, as so long a separation during the Handfast often caused distress. The missive ended in the Duke's flourished name. His wax crest sealed the paper.

"Take the request before the Clans' Council," Selwyn said. They stood in the stable. The sounds and smells of horses surrounded them in the frigid air. Selwyn had tucked his hands into his cloak to warm them. The courier waited for his reply in the kitchen where he had been offered food and drink.

"No."

"Then you have to take it to Clan Cader. You need his permission to leave."

"No. The horses are my business, not Terril's nor the clan's. The money would provide Vesper with a decent bride's gift plus provide the means to build and make the changes we've wanted to make to the farm for years."

"Your safety is involved. Besides, you know you can't leave Vere."

"We have eight mares and six geldings, young but well trained. The older stud's get are always fine colts, although for a duke, maybe Kuff. He is not proven by get but is the finer animal. Maybe both, let the duke choose."

"You're not listening."

"I am. It is you who are not. You will have to come. Maybe one more clansman. Do you think I should take Vesper? It might not be safe, but I hate to leave her alone for so long a time."

"You may not have noticed, but several have taken Vesper to heart, not the least being Fulbert. He would let no harm come to her, neither would Ramona nor Berneta. But if it is safe enough for you, it is safe enough for her. You will be quite close. Maybe that will take your mind off leaving Vere."

Drew threw a hateful glance at Selwyn.

"It's what you want," Selwyn answered his offensive look with a complacent one. "You're so itchy to bed her you're jumpy."

Drew huffed and stomped out of the stable without another word to Selwyn's deep-throated laugh. In the manse a time candle burned on the sideboard. He pulled a drawer out and hesitated. Vesper's industry showed in the neat array inside. *Take her or no?*

He wrote a reply that took nearly a candlemark. Although Drew was an excellent scribe, he had never written to so exalted a personage. Composing a suitable answer for an Aristo was his main concern. He withdrew a long-unused crest and debated at its usage, then sealed the letter. Unicorns were ubiquitous in Vere. None could know this the original. Done, he went to the kitchen shed and gave the courier the letter, its fold protected by a properly wax-embedded crest.

Vesper waited with the courier, her hair pulled back by a beaded net caul, its curly length hanging down her back. Her work tunic was of dove gray, held in place with a pain corset. She looked beautiful. He suddenly changed his mind. There was no way he could take her. It would kill him.

"I'm going with you." She said upon his closing the kitchen shed's door. The warmth of the kitchen spread through the cold sheath surrounding him from outside. Everyone went very silent. Bread was baking, and lamps lit the dark interior highlighting shadowed faces.

"How do you know I'm going?" He looked at the courier.

"Not from me!" the man said. "I was only told to deliver, not told the contents."

"I know. I will not be an encumbrance. You know I ride well enough to go."

"You've never ridden for so extended a time. It will be cold, and we will be out in all weather. You will be safer here."

Her determined chin firmed in defiance. Drew handed the courier his response. "If you wish, spend the night here. It will make your journey easier."

"Thank you, clansman. I will do that and be off with first light. I've the coin for your travel, too," the man said. From the saddlebag he carried he produced a pouch. Offended, Drew began to disclaim any need.

"His highness, Duke of Lambere, said to give it to you if you came."

Selwyn took the bag, hefting it in his palm.

"Come here before you leave, your breakfast will be ready," Berneta said. She looked at Drew, her face a study of concern, but only turned back to her work with no comment.

Vesper turned on her heel and left. Drew added a few comments and questions about the courier's journey, then left. He had worries of his own. Selwyn was right about one thing, leaving Vere would be hard, maybe impossible for him, but he needed to try.

~ * ~

Persistent argument won her way, with surprising support from Selwyn. She hardly slept the night before afraid Drew would not wake her. They started at dawn, Drew and Selwyn dressed in heavy brown riding clothes. Drew rode Kuff and Selwyn the older stallion. Vesper's gelding, chosen for temperament rather than value, followed Kuff without much direction from her.

Vesper wore a dark blue riding tunic and cloak that had belonged to Drew's mother. The heavy wool cloak was very full and covered her horse's rump as well as her legs. Rabbit fur trimmed its hood and front closure, but winds whipped frigid air up her legs. Before they started, Selwyn had wrapped fur around her feet and ankles, causing Vesper to blush. He also lined her saddle with lambskin, for which Vesper was now very thankful. Unrolling the fur cuffs of her cloak sleeves down over her hands helped keep her fingers from freezing, but they were stiff with cold.

"If I'd known you had no proper warm clothing, I'd have never agreed to let you come," Drew said soon after they started. His fuming face and fierce eyes filled her vision, his face close, whispering his fierce anger.

Vesper offered no excuse or apology. "I will be fine," she said and swore to herself to mutter no complaint. Now she drew strength and endurance from self-imposed pride.

The first leg of the journey took them to the outskirts of Norost, then they followed the southern road west of the town. Three geldings and one mare had been deemed worthy of sale, and each man had two lead ropes tied to their saddles. Both Drew and Selwyn were completely unaware of Alfred perched on one of the packhorses Selwyn led. He was not heckling her today, but sat, blanket-wrapped, in one of the open pack pouches. His head, covered with an unlaced fur legging of Drew's, peeked out of the loose pouch flap. He seemed content and interested in viewing the countryside and looked remarkably happy. If so, he was the only one.

Besides the effort of controlling three horses each, Vesper sensed anxiety between the two men that translated into Drew casting worried looks at her, and Selwyn's watching them both. Drew and Selwyn's concern for her only stiffened her determination to survive the ordeal without whining, but why did Selwyn worry over Drew?

It made her fearful of her dreams concerning Drew. To distract herself from her discomfort, she carefully examined every detail from those visions, but too often got sidetracked with other thoughts. The visions had made her insist on this trip, but they had changed since Drew kept Kuff. Fear remained, and the falling dagger and shattered shield remained, but Kuff and Drew's shadow extended across the land. Sometimes she saw an arrowhead without a shaft strike Drew, and more terrifying, a sword that she shoved through his heart, blood spraying back to cover her hand. In other visions she felt herself drowning, or saw Selwyn eaten by fire. It was not pleasant. What she saw frightened her, but she knew she wouldn't harm Drew. Where the danger came from, she didn't know, but it was there, and she would face it.

Drew was right about the length of riding. By the end of the first day she was very sore. Their frequent stops along the way only made each mounting and dismounting slower. Walking helped. When they stopped to camp, Drew had to help her dismount. He actually pulled her from the saddle, and then she could barely stand. He looked so severe, she escaped by kneeling to hold her hands to the small fire already started by Selwyn. It was very humiliating after her brave words.

When Drew saw her stiffness remained the next morning, he threw a vicious look at Selwyn. She smiled as Drew blamed Selwyn for her presence. She had gone to Selwyn with her request to go. What he said to Drew, she didn't know, but it had worked. Knowing her good luck, she counted any pain or discomfort a small price, and let Selwyn deflect Drew's anger.

Eudora had always said to focus attention on other than the affliction. The long ride gave Vesper ample time to reflect on her actions and sort out her confusion. She tried to recall all her encounters with Brandt. It was a humiliating exercise. Reflection forced her to realize she fantasized most of Brandt's feelings for her. With hindsight she realized Brandt was an incorrigible flirt, and desperate to escape the Kellsie household, she took it as encouragement. His actions could be read both ways, but she had chosen to ignore signs that he played.

Then there was Alvina, her best friend, her only friend, who upon reflection failed in friendship. Vesper saw how her own desperate desire had made the friendship. That was Alvina's way with all her friends. It was very lowering. How could she ever trust her judgment when she constantly deluded herself?

These revelations quashed her spirit. She had been a fool, blind and deaf to everything but her desires, immersed in dreams and impossible what-if wishes. Her eyes fell on Alfred who returned her gaze with a contemptuous twist of mouth and eyes. How could he not exist when he was there, in front of her?

What of Drew? What did she know of him? Her attention focused on Drew's broad shoulders in front of her with an appreciative sigh. He was not attentive like Brandt, but secretive and more likely to look at her in anger or with no emotion at all, than with a smile. His self-assurance and steadiness attracted her. He never shirked hard work, and she had no doubt his clan respected and loved him. He loved his horses with intensity and passion, and when he stroked their necks, she felt shivers tingle along her back.

Her developing feelings for him made her fear her terrible visions of him, visions that increased in frequency and intensity. That was the true reason she insisted on coming. Whatever it took, she would not let harm come to Drew. It dawned on her that she felt that way about all those she loved, Eudora, Freda, and Marwyn, but what she felt for Drew was very different, involved her body as well as her spirit. The two were tied together whenever she looked at him.

On the second night of their journey, they camped on the shores of Moon Lake. The lake had not yet frozen over and a vast silver cloud hung over its hidden surface. Walking into the mist to find privacy, she found herself cut off in the viewless murk. Vesper saw to her personal needs, aware of or imagining dark shadows moving around her.

Looking up, branches from otherwise unseen trees appeared overhead, poking from the wall of fog-like black, thin fingers. She twirled around once trying to find the stars but saw none. Lowering her gaze, she slowly twirled once more, unable to select the path back to the camp. With effort, she forced herself to stand still, to remain calm, to not call out and prove her ineptitude. Dark shadows seemed to wheel around her within the obscuring fog enmeshing her, menacing, and threatening. She closed her eyes. In the crisp air she heard faint sounds of wood breaking, then the crackle of a fire.

Relieved, Vesper followed the trail of sound, soon joined by the scent of burning wood. Both men looked up as she rushed into the camp. Their faces were inscrutable, and their eyes lowered to their appointed tasks as she froze in embarrassment. Alfred stood on the other side of the fire, backside to it, looking over his shoulder at her. A shiver ran up her back, but it didn't tickle; only chilled. "Ghosts are playing," she said to them. "I felt them. Saw them watching me." It was an inane remark but Drew started.

"We are in Clan Oran territory," Selwyn said as he broke a wind fallen branch and placed the wood on the fire. His eyes watched the flames while he talked. "They have a tale about a girl from their clan who fell in love with a young man from rival Clan Eklin. They eloped and handfasted as right and proper, but their clans tried to disavow the ceremony. Rather than be separated, they mysteriously drowned after praying to the fallen moon held in the Lake's depths. Superstition says their spirits were changed into the wild geese who summer on the lake, but in winter, when the geese leave, the ghosts of their unhallowed bodies walk the shores together, sharing in death what they could not in life."

"Does the tale say if they hate the living?" Vesper asked.

"No, I don't believe so," Selwyn said, his eyes moving from the fire to her.

Vesper glanced at Drew who remained silent and intent on cooking a dried meat stew. She noted the humor hidden in Selwyn's eyes and sensed his dismissive mockery as if he had laughed out loud. Somehow that calmed her more than words of concern. "Somehow, I don't think they would." She pulled her cloak tighter against the cold. "The ghosts I felt were evil, lurking and waiting to take advantage."

"Advantage of what?" Selwyn asked.

"I don't know. Of us. They scared me, but I frighten easily."

"And perhaps it was just your imagination in the fog," Drew said.

"A wise traveler pays attention to gut feeling," Selwyn said. "Imagination often comes from the gut."

Drew snorted. "You probably sensed small animals moving about. If it frightens you, I'll go with you next time. That might be safer, anyway. You don't know the area."

"I wasn't that frightened." She knew her protest fell on deaf ears. They ate dinner in silence then she arranged the oiled wool blankets they slept within at night. Tired, she did not sleep right away. The fog continued to roll in unfathomable depths, the edges defined by the light from the fire's hypnotic flames. Long after Selwyn snored, she watched. Her eyelids finally became too heavy to stay open. As sleep came, she thought she saw a single horn undulating like glinting, silvery ice through the darkening haze, patrolling the camp. An old voice floated into her mind, and she heard Winifred Kellsie tell Eudora, "too imaginative, too excitable. She will certainly have brainstorms." Vesper slept.

The next day the fog remained and spread until Vesper couldn't determine how Selwyn found the trail. She refused to think about her sore discomfort or contemplate her many failings but watched the trail's edges. Evil lurked there, prowling, pursuing, and ready to pounce. As she watched Drew's back appear then disappear in the gray wisps, she wondered that he didn't see it. When the mist lifted in the early afternoon, she saw Drew's face as he threw back his cloak's hood. He had fallen back to ride beside her, sometimes a little behind her during the thickest air. Now he looked pale, his lips tight, lines crossing his forehead, his bearing tense.

"What is wrong?" Vesper asked in alarm, drawing Selwyn's attention.

"Nothing," Drew said, brusque and cold.

"He just worries about Montoren whenever we are gone," Selwyn said, but his glance lingered on Drew.

~ * ~

"There is an inn ahead, I think tonight we should stop there. The last few nights have been very cold. Too cold for Vesper to sleep out," Selwyn said.

"She hasn't said anything," Drew said, his own gut tight with torment.

"Like you, she hasn't said anything about any discomfort, but she has never traveled before, never slept outdoors, and never been exposed to the cold constantly without warm clothes to endure it. You watch her when she dismounts, she is saddle sore."

Drew looked behind him where Vesper's horse followed. She looked wearied and depressed and didn't even attempt to guide her horse. Oblivious to all about her, she didn't even notice his scrutiny until he moved to her side. "How far is it?" she asked, with a rickety smile.

"We should be there before darkness settles in."

They were, but only one room remained available.

"You will have to protect Vesper. I will sleep in the barn with the horses," Selwyn said.

"You get only one stall," the innkeeper said.

"We'll leave all the horses outside in the corral. I'll take the stall," Selwyn said.

"You have this all worked out?" Drew asked, knowing the tantalizing agony he faced. Selwyn's smile answered him and widened at the obscene word Drew called him. Following Selwyn out of the inn, he helped Vesper off her horse and told her they had a room for the night.

During dinner Vesper seemed to revive and talked of some of the herbal plants she'd seen along the trail. Drew watched her shift in her seat to relieve her discomfort. She asked Selwyn questions about the route he followed, how he had come to know it so well. If Drew had come to know anything about Vesper, it was she prattled when nervous. Selwyn answered her with smug humor that escaped Vesper's notice, but Drew knew it aimed at himself. Then she asked them both if they believed in magical beings.

"Like what?" Selwyn asked.

"You know, unicorns and Fair Folk," Drew said. "Vesper does. She believed my old pony was a unicorn."

"Don't make fun," Vesper said.

"I'm not making fun," Drew said. "I believe you see them."

"Then don't grin so at Selwyn."

"Believing in a thing often makes it so," Selwyn said with a shrug.

At long last, but all too soon, Selwyn said goodnight. Drew counted the steps to his chamber of torture, twenty-one to the stairs, twelve stairs, fifteen to the room. He unlocked the door and let Vesper enter. A floral scent mixed with horse wafted by him. He swallowed and closed his eyes. Closing the door, he leaned against it and opened his eyes. Huge crystal eyes regarded him from a pale face, and he swallowed.

"You're staying?" Vesper asked. Her rose-flushed face blanched, then bloomed pink.

"It's the only room. It would not be safe to leave you in the inn while both Selwyn and I stayed in the stable."

Her mouth worked but no words came out. He couldn't force a word of comfort so just stood and stared back. Turning her back to him she stood frozen for a moment. Then she carefully placed her folded cloak over the end of the bed—then started disrobing. As the laces untied his breathing suspended.

"Don't," he gasped as she started to step out of her chemise. She turned back to him, her face stricken, her hands stilled. Blood flushed heat through him. Drew moved to the window and opened it to take several deep gulps of freezing air. At a click from the door he turned. It took three quick steps to stop Vesper's half-dressed escape. She still struggled with her clothes, then struggled with his detaining hands, a sheen of tears covering her face.

"Let me go. If you don't want me, it is only right."

"You can't go anywhere."

"I can leave."

"No, you can't," he said wrapping his arms around her shoulders in a restraining clamp. "You're my wife."

"No wife." Vesper buried her face in his shoulder and the cloth of his jerkin became soaked while she sobbed words of which he caught little—doesn't know—she has always liked him—no experience.

She continued her babbling confession as he pushed her away to hold her at arms' length.

"How will I know? I've fooled myself before." She burst into renewed sobbing.

He pulled her close again. Petting her hair, Drew waited until she stopped with a gasp and a hiccup.

She tried to break contact, but he held her firm.

"I'm so sorry. This is very embarrassing. I'm so sorry."

"You've not asked." He prayed he'd read the situation right.

Drew kissed the top of her head, tilted her head back, and kissed her forehead. "Do you remember what I said on Gifting Day?"

"Gifting Day?" she asked.

"You were frightened then, too. I made you a promise."

"A promise?"

"Yes. That you had to ask."

Another deep blush covered her face, and a speechless, confused look followed. Turning her face away she said, "Then I release you from your promise."

"That's not the same. I have kept my promise at some personal cost. You must say the words, Vesper. I need to hear them."

More tears spilled from the edges of her eyes and her chin firmed. She took a deep breath and he felt the tremble ripple through her body. "I want you... I want you to..." She stopped. "I want you to love me."

"You are content with me and want no other?"

"Yes, and hope you are content with me."

"Well, I won't be."

Shock opened her eyes to glassy circles, and she bit her lower lip.

"Not until your eyes seek only me, your lips thirst only for mine, and not until your body burns with a passion that sears the soul." Drew slowly set about showing. As her surprise faded and enthusiasm grew, he lost himself to all else—including the open window and the unlatched door.

Selwyn, cursing himself for forgetting the blankets taken to Drew's room, took the steps two at a time to the second floor. He pulled up short at the door opened a slit, and the sounds of a struggle. He pushed the door open, but the inhabitants didn't notice him. Filching a blanket from the pack by the door, he backed out as quickly as he entered, softly closing the latch. He could not lock it from outside, so wrapped in a blanket and a smile, he sank to the floor outside the door.

~ * ~

They had ridden for days through the forests of the Rikon Hills in as direct a route as possible. Of all the things Warrick had been forced to study, his favorite was geography and cartography. It seemed impossible. In less than three sennight they had come from the western edge of Wessure to the furthest reach of Easure and returned through the Rikon Hills to Wessure. Within a day's ride they would reach Aurelias' manor.

For once he could take pride in his dead reckoning and his memory of Kaereya's surface, but it was an empty conceit. It struck him as he traveled. There was no one left who cared about his success or failure. Not his father, not his brother, not his stepmother. They were now dead like his long-passed mother. Even his small stepsisters, those sweet little girls who always worshiped him, were gone forever. There were no courtiers around to heap false praise on him, no Norbert or other court-appointed Aristo to tell him his faults or show him a better way. Only Emory and Tate followed him, silent with their own thoughts. When Emory asked that they stop to rest, he knew they must.

The days were little warmer than the nights, which were freezing. Winter seemed as eternal as the ice inside him. His cousins lit a small fire and heated some water while he gazed at the terrain and the position of the weak sun.

The two brothers bantered between themselves about some nonsense. He paid them no attention. Hearing the crackle of wood burning, Warrick returned to the fire to warm his hands. It was hard to keep warm outside and nothing seemed able to melt his frozen interior. Emory poured hot water into a wooden mug and handed it to him. Sipping the tasteless warmth, he watched the flames. They seemed symbolic of his future.

"I think we are but a day from Aurelias' estate," he said at last.

"Will he help us?" Tate asked.

Warrick looked at his young cousin, his face etched in permanent perplexity, stamped there by the events in which he was embroiled. Tate's eyes begged for his safe world to be restored.

"Yes. The Dukes of Lambere are reputed for their loyalty. Aurelias stayed ever a faithful servant to my father." Warrick watched the strained eyes lighten with hope, keeping his own doubt silent.

His father was no more. Would Aurelias remain loyal to the self-centered son? Warrick's gaze returned to the fire. *Had there ever been a more unworthy heir?* "We have enough daylight to ride hard for some time. We will be out of the Rikon Hills and down into Aurelias' land. The snow ought to be less there."

"Why don't we camp here tonight?" Emory asked. "The horses need rest. More or less riding tomorrow makes little difference."

"You always want to stop," Tate said. "I'd just as soon go. Travel further today and arrive earlier tomorrow. I look forward to sleeping in a bed and having someone else cook my food." He looked at his cup of water. "Just to have a decent beverage will be a joy."

Emory, come from the horses, cuffed his brother bringing a weak smile to Warrick's face. His misery didn't allow feelings of fatigue, but he could see the effects of cold and exhaustion in his companions. Like him, they were too long without bath or change of clothes. He envied them. They still had each other and family to return to.

A branch snapped in the trees behind him and one of the horses snorted. Warrick froze and motioned the other two to silence.

"What is it?" Tate asked, his voice a sharp whisper of worry.

"Shush," Warrick hissed. His hand felt for the hilt of his sword and he slowly rose. He sensed Emory pulling Tate toward their horses. *A good idea.*

Backing he felt for his horse's reins, then backed to the saddle. Placing a foot in the stirrup, he mounted. The whole saddle gave way, sliding to the horse's side and throwing him to the ground. He jumped up and looked in stunned confusion at the heap of riding gear on the ground.

Men suddenly burst from the woods, entering their glade from three directions. Free of restraint, his horse bolted. Left in the open, Warrick slid his sword out of its scabbard. He stepped forward to engage the first to reach him.

He felt someone take his back and saw a glimpse of Tate's cuff and heard his younger cousin's sword sing free of its scabbard. None of the men they faced showed even the sword skill Tate possessed, but they outnumbered them three to one. Warrick slashed through the neck of the man he faced and braced for the next to take his place. Tate took another down even as Warrick finished his second. He quickly glanced around him. *Where was Emory? Had he already fallen?* Two more men engaged Warrick and he turned his full attention to the fight. Anger added incentive to his arm, and he cut his foes down in short order. Those who remained backed off, wary, circling. Two more men emerged from the surrounding trees carrying bows.

"Tate," Emory screamed as he pulled two horses forward. "Mount!"

Tate ignored his brother's command as a man charged. Even as Tate's arm rose armed in defense, Emory screamed, "No!"

Turning Warrick saw the arrow pierce Tate's chest. Warrick grabbed Tate around his shoulders, supporting him. His cousin looked so surprised, so disbelieving, even as his legs folded to the ground. "Emory," Warrick called. He twisted his head and saw Emory wheel his horse and spur it to a gallop. "Go, Em, getaway," he said softly, but it was too late for any of them. An arrow took Emory in the back. His cousin rode on, slumped over his horse's neck. Warrick looked at Tate. The boy's eyes were vacant, and he knew him dead. He stood, sword in hand, to face his attackers. They had held back but now advanced. There was no escape, but he would not surrender. It was time to join his family.

~ * ~

Chloe's story

"Another friend has died today, Melissa. Few remain."

"Do not fall into the doldrums, Lady. I will most likely outlive you. So will Bliss and her children, so you will have mourners. You got your Aegises situated just in time."

"Consecrated. I am glad King Ewald lived to see it."

"The court is not in mourning for long. Ewald IV is king. His coronation is planned for the day after tomorrow, in Aron Cathedral, it should be a joyful occasion."

"He hates me, Melissa, doesn't believe in my spell. Well, as it is not a spell as he understands it, that at least shows his acumen. My poor gentlemen are already tormented by the aristos. It was a mistake to bring them to court."

"They'll leave. They received their land in perpetuity by decree of his late grace."

"Mark my words, Melissa, I'll be sent from court in a trice once the new Ewald is crowned, and the Aegises will exit with me."

"Before you, Lady," Melissa agreed. "But you've wanted to leave for a long time, and everyone knows you set the spell. Time will prove you right."

Chloe looked at Melissa, still young enough not to have looked at her own mortality. "I will not live to see it. You should study harder. Your Talent could be much improved."

"Why should I want it improved? To have everybody make ward signs at me and avoid me..."

"Like they do me?" Chloe sighed. "You're right, of course. People fear me, and the boy I once saved now hates me. Life takes strange corners. Help me pack, I will seek passage and permission to leave. Let us find out at long last what Ewald III gave me for a home."

Her answer came from the new king two days later while Melissa shopped. Thidrek, the King's Abbot, entered her apartment with a few of his Templar Guards for support. Their stern visages intimidated Chloe.

Stopping before her with the swish of ecclesiastical robes, Thidrek posed, appearing more a character in a play than something real. "Your time at court is through, witch." He handed her some papers.

"I heard the son valued his father's advisor." She took the papers and read them.

"You are dismissed from court."

"So I read, but I keep my land?"

"It is a small price to pay to get rid of you."

"I thought a knife in the back would accomplish that easily enough."

The priest took a step back from her. His expression arrested Chloe, and she looked behind him at the Templars. They stood in threatened stillness. *You're afraid of me.* Her surprise kept her from uttering the words. Her gaze returned to the papers.

"King Ewald demands you relinquish your account of the spell to me."

"What? Why?"

Thidrek seemed to have regained a semblance of courage.

"Your writings. He knows you keep them. Your accomplice wished to save her soul."

"You questioned Melissa?"

"Information is easily obtained from the purveyors of evil." A sneer crossed Thidrek's face.

Chloe immediately understood. "She slept with one of your agents? She always talked too much."

"Your evil launched her into whoredom."

"No. Melissa is no whore. She indulges freely, and you must acquit me, as she was that way before we met."

Thidrek made a warding sign. "Foul blasphemer. The writings."

She gave him her journal. He searched through it, roughly turning pages until he came to the dates he sought. With soft mutters he read the passages, the explanation of the spell, and its execution. "Talents, gifts, magic indeed. Euphemisms for corruption."

Feeling sad, she watched the abbot. He did not want to believe, saw her only as the enemy. He would either destroy her journal or hide it as he chose. It didn't matter. He could not undo the spell because it was not a spell as everyone thought of it. It was a matter of using the gifts bred into four bloodlines.

With a small knife he cut pages from the book. With a satisfied look, he watched her as he tossed the sheets in the fireplace as if that ended the magic. With a spurt of flame. the sheets blackened and curled into glowing ash. His eyes glowed with righteous fervency.

"None will ever learn of your evil from these self-indulging inscriptions. I will see to it that your name is expunged from all of Kaereya. History ignores those never mentioned. I advise you, witch, to leave Cliff City." He put the journal under his arm and walked from the room.

She took his advice. It seemed strange to be traveling again, this time by ship to her home. "Better to let me dwindle in obscurity than risk public fervor or martyrdom status at my death," she said to herself. She assumed Charm Island a miserable piece of land if King Ewald IV had not taken it from her. There was a building of some sort on it. Hopefully, it would be habitable.

She stood on the ship's deck overlooking the watery view. She enjoyed the sound of the wind catching the sails, the jangling of the ship's rigging, the sight of the sun on the water, and the crisp air flowing steadily into her face. The feeling of peaceful contentment felt good. Too often of late her thoughts had turned to despair.

Haral Lake was the only open water on the Thou River, but even here some islands rose to stately heights. Others emerged as low marshland, submerged in the present high water. The submerged lands and strong currents made navigation difficult.

"We are coming around Dream Island now, Lady," the ship's captain said. He had been very deferential since she had stepped aboard. "Charm Island is just behind it."

"Thank you, Captain. Is it a good place?"

"You don't know?"

Chloe smiled. "I spent much time studying in Cygna, sir, and never have had a chance to visit my home."

"I don't know, Lady. We have never stopped there." He shrugged. "The charts show it a fair harbor and it doesn't lie in the shade of other islands, so it might be good for crops. The shoreline is covered with palms, but it has highlands for storm protection."

"Palms. I have not seen any since leaving Zankiri as a very young woman."

"You have given many years of service to Kaereya, Lady. Many will remember what you have done for us."

Chloe looked at the scarred and tanned face of the Captain. He was older, perhaps just over her age. "You served in the last war?"

"Yes, Lady. Those you served are grateful for your care of the injured. Your magic to save Kaereya will not be forgotten. Wonderful magic."

"Thank you, Captain." She gave him the best smile she could muster, knowing she fostered a lie.

Fourteen

A deep contentment tinged with rekindling desire made Drew's ride both agreeable and uncomfortable. The wait for the ferry had allowed closeness and the touching of hands. That small touch now doubly reacted on him. Even Selwyn's harangue about forgetting safety precautions could not quench his satisfaction. Yes, it had been a mistake, but nothing had happened, unless he counted Selwyn's knowledge of the night's events. His cousin's self-satisfied smirk would wear out even inexhaustible patience. Drew turned in the saddle to check Vesper as she followed. He was greeted with a shy smile. He smiled back and turned forward to hide his accompanying expression of pain. He groaned. Riding was most unpleasant. He heard Selwyn's laugh but ignored it.

By the end of the day, they would be out of the Rikon Hills and into the Lambere lands. He had felt a shiver run down his spine when they had left Vere lands, which had nothing to do with legal boundaries, but it was not so very bad. He glanced back at Vesper again, just as Selwyn threw up a fist in warning. The sound of clashing metal conveyed the type of trouble ahead. A quick glance at Selwyn and Drew dismounted. He tied the extra horse leads to a stout branch. He turned to Vesper at the same time he reached for his bow. "Stay here, do not come near!" Selwyn joined him and together they headed for the turmoil.

They stopped at the edge of a small glade, knocking their arrows. One set-upon traveler, wounded by arrow and sword, still stood surrounded by six brigands. Rather than closing for the kill, they taunted their target even as he fell to his knees. One raised his sword to behead his victim. Drew and Selwyn's first arrows struck together. Both pierced the swordsman's neck clean through.

The assailants turned to their new opponents. Another of Selwyn's arrows took a toll. They did not run away but charged Drew and Selwyn with blades drawn. Arrows took down two more as they came, but the third's blade swung for Drew's head.

Another horse broke from the surrounding wood. Vesper. Her horse plunged into Drew's attacker even as she brought a branch down on the man's head. He staggered but recovered.

The man turned on Vesper. Drew screamed and thrust his blade. It hit chainmail and slid. Drew threw himself bodily on the man taking him to the ground. He saw Selwyn's horse bull its way between their falling bodies and Vesper, heard Vesper's scream and knew their actions too late. With rare savagery, he twisted the man's head, breaking the neck. He rose gripped by fear, but Vesper remained upon her horse, pale terror covering her face.

Selwyn grunted and moved to check the bodies. Drew watched Vesper, quite unhurt, ride directly to the fallen traveler and dismount.

After a brief numb pause, anger consumed him. He followed her screaming, "What were you doing? I told you to remain with the horses."

She knelt and didn't raise her head from the man lying beneath her searching hands. "He is still alive but needs help. Restart this fire. The scuffling has put it out, but I'm sure it can be stoked into renewal." She moved to the body next to the traveler. "His companion." A gasp escaped her. "He is young! Poor, poor boy. He is dead."

Drew stopped, startled at his dismissal.

"Close your mouth," Selwyn advised with a sour grin. "It makes you look witless. All the others are dead. Tracks show one horse and rider escaped. Someone cut this girth," he said kicking the saddle. "They fought a hard battle." He looked at Vesper. "That was a very foolish and dangerous thing to do."

"He would have harmed Drew," she said as she worked on the man. "This one is young, too. Are you going to start the fire? Why did they attack with swords if they had arrows?"

"I don't know, a grudge perhaps. They baited this one, wanted him to see his end," Drew said with a shrug.

Selwyn swore and spoke to Drew. "I'm going to get the horses. You tend the fire. While I'm gone, feel free to beat some sense into her."

"I have so little to help him." She jumped up and pulled items from her saddlebags. "I'll need hot water." Vesper didn't even look at him while she tore some clothing into strips.

Drew had never felt the desire to hit anyone, but now an overwhelming urge to smack his wife possessed him. He didn't care about the wounded man, didn't care about the surrounding bodies. He took a deep breath and decided another scold would do no good. He ignored all and restarted the fire. As threat and danger passed, his lingering fright fueled fury at Vesper. Satisfying thoughts on ways to punish her filled him.

"Cattails," she muttered. "Cattails and willow bark. Help me."

Drew muttered some curses below his breath before he answered. "What can I do?"

"Get blankets from his saddle gear and make a place for him by the fire."

"We will not be spending time here," Drew said. "It is too open."

"I must treat him before we can do anything." The patient reasonableness of her voice drove Drew to his feet. He tore through the packs of the saddle lying on the ground, taking his fury out on the contents. A heavy box fell from some soiled clothes. Drew could not catch it before it hit the ground. It contained nothing and he threw it back in the bag. His eyes flicked up at the sound of hooves, and he reached for his sword. It was Selwyn bringing the remaining horses. Vesper sprang to her feet.

"Alfred, you must help me. I need cattails and willow bark. Help me, please! Ask your friends. Surely you've seen them?"

Selwyn looked at Vesper with as bewildered a look as Drew felt. "Alfred who?"

"Can you not see him? He has been with us the whole way! Please, Alfred." She started running to the glade's far end. Drew quickly followed her, catching her with his hand pulling her to a stop.

"No, no, it's there—see? Alfred's friends knew. Thank you, thank you! Have you a knife?" She grabbed the blade from his belt and turned, continuing her flight.

By the time Drew caught up with her, she was bent over, walk-sliding, flatfooted on the marsh ice, cutting the spikes with split catkin ends spilling tan-fluff. Drew looked up to find Selwyn guarded nearby from atop his horse. Vesper handed Drew the stalks, filling his arms. An incautious step and his foot broke through the ice and into the cold muck below them. "Vesper, the ice is not solid."

"It is all right. I think I have enough." She still talked in an abstracted manner. "There is always willow around," she said and scanned the edges of the pond. Finding what she wanted, she cut the yellow branches emerging from brown shrubs on the pond's edge. Carrying an armful of willow branches, she hurried back to the wounded man and the fire. She scolded Selwyn as she passed. "You should not have left him alone."

Later she rose from where she stooped, having cut out the arrow's head, sewn the several wounds, and bandaged them with the cattail down and her own shredded shift.

While she had worked, Selwyn had contrived a litter for the man, shredded the bark from the willow, and stewed it how she asked. She thanked him. "For it will ease his pain later," she told him.

As she finished washing and drying her hands, Drew handed her journey bread, dried meat, and fruit he had unpacked.

"I seem to cause you to tear up good shifts. I shall buy you another, I promise."

"It was cleaner than anything in their saddlebags."

Drew snorted. "Even the bag was filled with the dirt of their journey." He scooped a hand through the bag, showing her the dusty soil. Wiping his hands off, he asked, "Who is Alfred?"

Vesper raised trepidation-filled eyes to him. "He is Fair Folk. I've known him all my life."

"I see no one."

"He is there. I don't know why no one else sees him. I renounced him once before when Eudora said I was too old for imaginary friends. He has not spoken to me since. But please believe me, he is as real to me as you are."

"Eudora wouldn't be familiar with Fair Folk because they do not live as far south as Kennetsure," Selwyn spoke with conviction. Drew looked at his cousin, surprised at his easy acceptance of Vesper's invisible friend.

Vesper continued to gaze at him in apprehension. It didn't matter to him whether she saw Fair Folk or not. The truth was she found what she needed with no idea of where to look for it. Something had guided her. He touched her cheek. "I believe you. Why is he traveling with us?"

"I don't know. Alfred always manages to go where he wants."

"That is their way," Selwyn said, nodding.

As they remounted, one of their spare horses pulling the litter, Vesper asked, "But what about the bodies? Should we just leave them like this?"

"We will report to the duke when we arrive, but this is a dangerous place and we have lingered here long enough." Drew, his anger and fright evaporated, he only sought to get Vesper to safety and away from this grisly scene. He would save his acerbic words for later, sure of Selwyn's support.

~ * ~

Quillon rode upon the glade and inspected the havoc. For days he had tracked the duke's daughter. Today a lamed horse had delayed his travel. Afraid of what he might find, he checked the bodies littering the landscape. He recognized none. From the tracks and blood and the carefully doused fire, he reconstructed the events.

Someone had lived through the carnage, badly wounded, and from the hoof prints, taken off in a litter by the clansmen. He stooped next to the youngest victim. With some surprise, he recognized an Aristo. Not by dress as his were those of a trader but by a gold signet ring on one thin hand.

Always alert, he felt the hooves before he heard them. Rising, he pulled his blade ready for confrontation as two riders rode into the glade. They slowed their horses as they approached him. He recognized the two Kennetsureans and slid his blade back into its sheath. They recognized him also.

"Quillon, have you been ambushed?"

"No, I just came upon this place. What do you here, Corbin? It is too damn cold for desert blood."

"Service often demands discomfort. Galen and I search for Warrick. We had heard three young men traveled this way."

"Warrick, here?" Quillon looked around as if trying to find the heir.

"You knew the boy missing?"

"The rumor has spread wide."

"Have you checked all bodies?"

"All are too old to be Warrick, except this one whom I don't recognize."

At Napier's silence, he looked up. "You know him?"

"Yes. That is Warrick's cousin Tate, son of Theodulf Gilchrist, Duke of Hearthron. We must search the entire area to make sure the other boys are not here."

"There are tracks of one horse leading off in that direction," Quillon said pointing southeast. "Others appear to have taken someone from the field by litter."

"Where, what direction?"

"Settle, Corbin. I know their destination. They are clansmen making their way to Lambere with horses for His Grace, the duke. I have been following them for some days at Aristo Aurelias' behest."

"They might have Warrick with them, we must follow."

"No. If they have him, he will be safe. I will continue my watch. Someone must take this young man back to his father and warn Norbert, another must follow those tracks of the one who escaped. That also might be Warrick."

Napier turned a suspicious look on Quillon. "Why were you tracking clansmen delivering horses? It does not make me trust their motives over much."

"I follow them to protect Aristo Aurelias' daughter."

"The Duke of Lambere has no daughter."

"Yes, he does. It is a long story, and one I'm neither free to relate nor have the time, to tell."

Napier looked at his traveling companion. "You follow the clansmen's tracks. I shall take Tate back to Regent Gilchrist." He looked at Quillon. "If your clansmen carry Warrick…"

"Aristo Aurelias himself will send the message. I expect they shall be at the duke's seat sometime tonight. I don't expect they will stop to camp."

<h1 style="text-align:center">Fifteen</h1>

"It's a glorious sight."

Ottillie didn't turn from the balcony at Leela's voice.

"I marvel in it daily, but you wouldn't like it in the heat of summer."

"This is perfect bliss." Ottillie continued enjoying the morning desert turn iridescent in purple, red, rust, and gold as the sun rose.

"Come, take a seat. The coffee is ready. We used to have only pillows to sit on, but now my old bones make it too difficult to get up and down."

Ottillie took the chair indicated, reveling in the freedom of her loose translucent turquoise layers of diaphanous fabric. Freedom, too, from the excesses of court. She raised the cup Leela poured to her nose and inhaled the aromatic brew. "It smells so delicious." She sipped the bitter liquid. A long soak in a Kennetsurean bath and a good night's sleep had restored her travel-worn body. She looked at Leela enjoying the contrast of her silver hair, dark skin, and yellow garment. "You knew I was coming."

"I am a touch sorceress, not a seer." She laughed at Ottillie's expression. "Leander travels with messenger birds. Part of his service is the delivery of the birds to friends we keep in touch with. We may be at the ends of the known world in Kaereya, but we stay informed." She took a sip of coffee. "He returned at unheard of speed. Drove his men from before sunrise until long after dark. One sennight from Norsot to Gotte City."

Ottillie expressed her surprise. "Why the hurry?"

"He heard from a seer that you waited. Leander said you came to see our great library, a worthy cause for travel. And having an Aristo lady such as yourself seek us out, honors us."

The first part of Leela's statement gained Ottillie's attention. "Sorceress? Seer?"

"Yes. Kennetsure nomads and the Clans of Vere are more accepting of the unseen. Then, too, the great sorceress Chloe came from Kennetsure. So magic is part of our heritage."

"Chloe? Who set the Aegis Spell?"

"You've heard about her?"

"I came across some references to her in the Queen's Library on Hawk Island." Ottillie felt surprised her teeth didn't fall out with her dissembling.

"Really?" Intelligent brown eyes smiled at Ottillie. "There is little written about her, but I seem to recall the monks somehow managed to keep some of her diaries. The rest, of course, are here." Leela sipped her coffee.

Ottillie smiled. "Is that so?" She talked to a witch who almost seemed to know her secrets, but she wasn't ready to reveal her perfidy. She had brazened her way through such situations previously. "I should like to see them if it is permitted."

"Of course it is permitted. Unlike Queen's University, learning is for all in Egan. I might teach you something of your own Talent."

"My talent?"

"Certainly. You will make a very credible sorceress."

Ottillie's mouth snapped shut. The suggestion was totally outrageous.

"Nonsense, Ottillie." Leela rose. "It is what drove you here. Can you deny you had an irresistible urge to come here? Many great Aristo ladies have been witches and worse, but few had true Talent." Her mouth tilted into a wicked smile. "You've been under the influence of the clergy of the Acolyte Mission, very strict and old-fashioned misogynists whose beliefs forbid magic—all in Easure are. Come, let me show you the keep then what Egan became. Like the northern clans, the people of the Doane Desert have protected their Aegis. Our people have built a cult around his presence and a city around his keep." She sighed. "Unfortunately, Aldous seems to be the last they will have."

"I find it incredible that the Vere Aegis still exists. No one knows about him."

Leela laughed. "Those who do swear oaths to not discuss it. The clans told us, you know, to safeguard Aldous. Too many lamentable accidents warned them drastic measures were needed."

"Why? Surely no one still believes in their magic?"

"That is the other reason you have traveled here isn't it? To find out what is going on? Only now it is too late."

"How is it too late?"

Leela looked at her in surprise. "The king is dead, the monarchy sabotaged, the Seward Aegis and the Ward Aegis are gone, and Chloe's spell damaged. Clement Neville, the Usurper, has planned well for many years."

"You think this King Clement's doing?"

"Without a doubt. Do you think yourself the only one to seek answers here? Clement studied here before he seized the Pertelon throne."

"You let him come here?"

"That is the catch to free access. You don't always know the reason behind the desire. Only later did we learn that he had tested the magic of Cygna, and that of the last Aegis Ward, then came here seeking solutions."

"Do you really believe in magic?" Ottillie bit her lip, a dumb question to ask someone who believed herself a sorceress.

Leela smiled. "Magic isn't something mysterious, Ottillie. It is a Talent some people possess. Just like some run faster, or jump higher, or have blond hair or dark skin, so too is Talent. You are born with it."

"Then why don't we know about it? Why are we afraid of it? Why is Clement killing everyone with historical ties to magic?"

"Kaereyans don't believe because they've been taught to disbelieve. Most people don't understand 'magic,' think of it as a mummer's entertainment, or worse, evil tricks. Not long ago they were so afraid of those who showed signs of it, they thought them evil and hunted them. Fear and ignorance are powerful social motivators. Those with Talent were held suspect, called witches, and often ostracized, even Chloe. It wasn't long before those with Talent hid the fact. Denial doesn't make it vanish. Murder does."

"Then he hired someone to systematically destroy those suspected of having it? How could he know?"

It was Leela's turn to look disconcerted. "What has happened? We knew through the Vere Aegis someone hunted aegises. It is easy enough to find the blood if you know the key. We thought some outside agent sought to prepare for an invasion. We sent word to the court, but obviously, no one believed."

"What key?"

"All those of aegis blood have birthmarks. It is a trait, like blue eyes."

"Many have birthmarks. Even I have one. They cannot all be aegises."

Leela laughed, taking Ottillie's hand and inspecting her mark. "Many have aegis's blood, but few have the talent to go with it."

"My father thinks it someone at court. Someone wanting the Kaereyan throne for themselves." She told of the families that had suffered losses.

After a minute's thought, Leela looked at her. "If it is Clement, it explains much, doesn't it? Make sure magic is eradicated in Kaereya, kill anyone who could oppose him, murder the royal family to throw the country into chaos, then attack. Luckily your father is a strong organizer."

"My father has been dismissed. Do you have messengers that travel to the Eternal Palace?"

"You wish to get a message to your father?" Leela looked sad and sighed. "Our only remaining correspondent in the court has died. They let all her birds go. There are others but they don't have court connections. We can try."

Ottillie followed her through the ancient stronghold, still eminently defensible from sheer location, but far more open with arched balconies and open alleys allowing breezes to ventilate the keep. The Knights of the Zekarac Order occupied one tower, with a training yard outside where the clang of arms was often heard. In a second tower, the members of a Kennetsurean religious sect devoted to learning and service resided. They performed the menial tasks of the keep, cleaning, food preparation, and general upkeep. Leela and Aldous occupied the third tower with guests allotted rooms in a fourth. Everyone gathered in the main hall for meals and community.

From there, Leela led her into the town atop the rock's summit. It seemed a small community as everyone greeted Leela and she, in turn, introduced Ottillie to a bewildering array of citizenry. They had every convenience—foodmongers, bakers, tailors, shoemakers, leatherworkers, smiths, jewelers, weavers, papermakers, bookbinders, printers, and healers. As the day's heat increased, Leela took her to the converted cave that was the library.

The library was also part of a school, many of the students lingering outside the columned entrance. She listened with interest but couldn't contain her excitement when Leela finally led her into the depths. Inside the cool entrance, she saw the library was cut into the rock with light coming in through small vertical tunnels. Painted and gilded relief sculptures ran above the filled bookcases, covering the wall from floor to ceiling. Ottillie uttered a soft "oh" that echoed through the vast edifice.

"Egan's second mission has been to preserve knowledge. We have a school that also incorporates a fine infirmary."

"Where are all the books from?"

"We receive items from all provinces in Kaereya and beyond. Things come to us from beyond the Doane Desert, from the Eastern Empire, and lands far away across the Peace Ocean."

"You actively trade that far away?" Curiosity consumed Ottillie. She wandered the shelves running a hand over volumes, scanning titles as she went.

"Yes. The nomadic tribes travel far. Sailors come to other ports than those on Kaereyan shores. Here, these are what you are looking for, to complete those already in your possession," Leela gave her a quelling look, one brow raised.

"How did you know?"

"By the Holy One, Ottillie, you don't even blush."

She gave an unrepentant grin. "I never claimed to live up to everyone's expectations for an Aristo lady. The strictures are tedious and often ludicrous."

"Melissa mislaid one journal when Chloe left the court. The King's Abbot, Thidrek seized the other. They were not found until many years later."

"Someone has cut out all pages dealing with the spell, but why did they keep the rest?"

"I remember Clement was most interested in that passage and disappointed when he didn't find it here."

"I thought it was probably destroyed long ago."

"Unfortunately. We won't ever know how Chloe set the spell. You can start reading them tonight. Tomorrow you and I can start your lessons."

"You think I have Talent?"

"You have what is called Touch Talent. Untrained, of course. You sense the presence of others, their mood, and I would guess, occasionally, their thoughts. You will see, it is not as abhorrent as you have been led to believe."

"I may take these?"

"Certainly, but we do hope you return them."

At that, Ottillie did blush. "Perhaps I should give you those from the Queen's Library."

Leela chuckled. "Maybe you should return them from where you found them."

~ * ~

"Hello, Ottillie, come sit."

The Aegis's voice came out of a dark corner of the library. Strong sunlight, flooding an open archway between them, hid his presence. As she came closer, she saw it wasn't so dark, and that Aldous had a large volume open on the table before him. His head, free of a sun protective hat was shiny bald with wispy white hair askew around his ears and nape, escaped from the longer hair braided into a tail. Ottillie had not expected to see him. So far their encounters had only been at social moments and meals. He had seemed congenial but reserved. "Good morning, sir."

His hand waved. "Just Aldous, please. No one calls me aught else." One hand smoothed out a color-laden page as she took the chair opposite him. "This was printed before the Cataclysm. We have nothing that compares to it. Here look."

Ottillie gazed on the silky smooth, hard page, with breathtaking pictures that matched gazing on reality. She could not understand the written words.

"Language and the symbols for word have changed. They are always changing."

"What is this one about?"

"Geography. What the world was like. Very little is recognizable today."

"These illustrations look so real, so like things we see every day. Well, not here in the desert. What caused the change? The Cataclysm Century?"

"Everything you know about that event probably isn't true. Laws, society, culture changed afterward, along with how history was recorded."

"Why don't we know? Is it kept secret?"

"Not secret but concealed from easy discovery. The last international meeting of nations banned certain learning and manufacturing. Some now seem ridiculous, but at the time fright made judgment poor. That's when the Protectors were set in place. This is an example of the prohibited arts. Through the ages, facts have changed and the stories with them. Few cared about it."

Ottillie, stunned, sat for a heartbeat. "You know this? Why tell me if it is prohibited?"

"More than a century ago one of my relatives traveled to seek permission to learn the history and let it slowly disseminate through the population. It was established then that those who made the pilgrimage to Egan in search of knowledge were deemed worthy of learning. Few enough do."

"Where did he go to get permission?"

"There are other centers of learning, older, some nearly untouched by time. A few have more authority over the remains of this world than others. One exists far to the Southern extremes, one in the Eastern Empire, another on an island in the Peace Ocean. If you believe it, they tell me one exists in the sky."

"The Protectors?"

"Not quite, although the Protectors are supposed to circle the world in a day." His warm brown eyes, slightly hazy, lowered to his book. "Did you come to learn about the Cataclysm?"

"Among other things."

"Yes, yes. Kaereya's more recent problems." The Aegis waved a wayward hand. "Messenger birds arrived this morning. Pertelon troops are moving through the southern islands in the Thou's South Branch. We sent messages, yours included, to your father, but it might take some time to reach him."

A sense of dread and relief flooded Ottillie. "Thank you. I worry about him. Can you keep Pertelon out of Kaereya?"

"No." She felt the sorrow in his words. "The spell is badly damaged. The Seward Aegis is gone, as is the Ward, and I am the last of my line. Still, Pertelon will have a hard time. I do from here what I can to help, and I doubt they know I still survive. A few years ago we let rumor of the last Aegis's death to circulate. However, the Pertelon army will still not find the Southern Branch of the Thou River friendly."

"Do you have any idea what is happening?

The old Aegis shrugged. "The usurper king thinks he has destroyed the magic left in Kaereya. I suppose Cygna gives him enough problems without allowing their kind to develop here. He probably has a grand plan for an empire and needs to capture all trade routes and access to ocean commerce."

"Are we facing our own Cataclysm Century?"

Aldous chuckled. "We are facing something very minor to that. The Cataclysmic Century is a misnomer. It took several centuries and was the culmination of human error mixed with natural phenomenon."

"That ended the world?"

"It didn't end, we are here, aren't we?" He leaned back in his chair. "It was a terrible time where life was tenuous, but not the first such time. They started burying more than birthing. Buried so many they lost four-fifths of the population within two centuries. Our world seems to go through such oppressive times in cycles, the cause of each a different crisis. This last one was the worst."

"And that's when the Protectors were set in place?"

"That's when the Prohibitions were drawn up. Prohibitions thought to save people from committing the same mistakes."

"Have they worked?"

"They have, but times are changing. Man is a curious animal, always looking back, thinking he is smart enough to handle what his ancestors couldn't. Feel free to look at anything you want. We have only a short time for your study."

She gave him an inquiring look.

"The Aegis of Vere is in Wessure. It means the spell has weakened or somehow Drew has surmounted his limitations. I want to see him, feel the need to join him. Leela agrees. We leave in two sennights." He smiled. "That seems to be the bare minimum of time Leela needs to pack."

~ * ~

"Have you had enough of study?"

The deep voice drew Ottillie from her pages. She smiled at Leander. His dark skin with the startling gray eyes looked both ghostly and stately against the white of his robe. A wide sash of cloth in bright-colored stripes fell from one shoulder.

"Not yet. There is so much to read, to learn."

"Leela says you have been indoors too much."

"I have not advanced far in her teachings."

"She says it is because you don't believe it. If you wish, I will take you desert hunting."

Ottillie opened her eyes wider in delight. "Really? I've used a spring bow but not a short bow. Can you teach me?"

"Assuredly, and to track, too."

"Now?" She jumped up prepared to change. "What shall I wear?"

Leander answered, "Not now, it is too hot. There is good hunting at twilight."

"I would like to see the desert at night."

"Go to your room. Rest this afternoon. Someone will wake you and bring you proper clothing."

Ottillie quickly cleared her table. Once in her room, she lay down and picked up one of Chloe's journals. The afternoon heat made her drowsy.

A knock on the door roused her. A feminine voice asked entry and Ottillie gave permission.

"I've brought you clothing for tonight. Leander sends it with his regards."

Rising, Ottillie stretched noticing the light was fading. Her hands ran over the soft leather clothing. A long tunic slit up the sides with trews and boots proved irresistible and she slipped into them feeling exotic and free of court strictures. Excitement for the coming hunt drove her to the hall early.

~ * ~

At night the desert came alive with faint chirpings, howls, squeaks, and squeals. It was marginally more comfortable, not near so hot. Everyone went without the daytime hats and wraps as the sun no longer painfully beat on skin and mental sinew. Ottillie stood at their camp's edge. The fire threw soft shadows as she watched the horizon after the dramatic setting of the sun. Streaks of pink-lined purple filled the sky. Different, fascinating, new scents assailed her nose.

"We go soon, Ottillie, here is your bow."

Ottillie turned, Leander stood with four other nomads ready to hunt. He handed her a bow and showed her the differences between the bow she was used to and the Kennetsurean short bow. The arrows, too, were shorter, almost bolts, but made of wood so hard it felt like metal. It was not difficult, and she had managed to hit an improvised target twice before they were walking into the desert.

Pointing into the sky, Leander picked out stars one by one. "That is the hunter," he said, finished showing her the discernable star pattern. "It stays on our left going out and on our right returning." He pointed to the horizon where three black shapes rose from the desert floor to dominate the night sky. "Always keep the Guide Rocks in sight. Be careful, sometimes the desert can play tricks on your eyes and turns you about. The rocks can disappear behind hills or not appear as shadows on a dark night. If that happens, look for the hunter."

"Do you expect me to get lost?"

"No, Ottillie, I will hunt near you, but it is better to be prepared than dead."

Ottillie raised her brows but agreed with the sentiment. "What are we hunting?"

"There are small desert antelope. The wild dogs who hunt them are not good eating, but if they hunt you, kill them."

Something curdled inside Ottillie. "Dogs hunt people?"

"Often. We are usually easy prey, especially lost children."

She had come this far and wasn't going to miss out on an adventure for so small a reason. She was no child, being taller than most of the men present. Flashing an unintimidated smile, she said, "Let's go."

"At first you will follow me, but as I think you learn, I will move off to your left. Remember I will be listening, if you have trouble, shout."

The other hunters had already gone off alone. In low whispered words Leander showed her the stalking methods. She realized why they didn't hunt in groups but chose areas to hunt. Her clothing not only allowed her free movement but also, its color let her disappear into the darkness of the vegetation. The leather trews protected her legs from the hard, spiky stalks of desert vegetation. She smiled. Only Eldin wouldn't be surprised that the always elegant court lady would wear such simple commoner wear. Stopping as taught, she listened. Eldin had called her a duck in peacock's feathers before.

It surprised her. Arresting her movements, stilling her own natural sounds, made her more aware of the world around her. Closing her eyes, she felt she could almost hear ants walking. Close by she heard a small rustle and opened her eyes.

As her vision adjusted, what had appeared meager moonlight now flooded the desert floor with light. Motion caught her eye. A long-tailed, mouse-like creature sat washing itself on a fat branch sprouting large white flowers along its length. The creature froze as Ottillie heard a faint rhythmic flutter. She could almost sense the creature's alarm. Without moving, she searched the night with her eyes. A bat pirouetted just about the foliage level of the shrubbery. The mouse relaxed and went back to its cleaning. Within a heartbeat, a large form, white and black striped, feathered, and with grasping claws fell on the mouse. With a squeal, the small shape disappeared with another flutter of quiet wings.

Ottillie took several slow steps from the site. Quieting herself once more, she loosened her senses. Off a short distance to her left she heard a soft bow twang followed by a thud. In her mind she felt the animal's pain, the sting of the arrow, and the instinct to run on legs that stumbled and refused to work. She shook her head to dispel the emotive and imaginative mind pictures.

A reflection caught her gaze. Close and to her right, opalescent green spheres watched. She froze. It examined her. She felt it, felt its hunger.

"Leander," she whispered. He said he would stay close. The animal moved through the undergrowth and the unearthly reflection disappeared in the shadows, followed by the long shadow of its tail caught on the ground as the moon emerged from a light cloud cover. She sensed the predator circling.

"Leander?" She spoke his name louder.

She backstepped. A branch crunched beneath her boot. Afraid to scream, afraid to give in to panic, she remained still, listening.

The noise of the desert clamored in her ears. A cool wind fluttered grasses. The click and buzz of insects saturated the air. Far-off howls of wild canines induced quivers that rippled over her skin. Closer, the soft, cyclic, four-footed gait padded on the coarse gritty ground.

The feet stopped and Ottillie held her breath, aware of the creature's stench. She sensed its interest turn, swivel in another direction, hone back on her.

A biped step approached. Leander. The creature took a step in the direction of the approaching man. A sense of confusion overcame her, shame. She could not let him walk into a trap.

"Leander, stop! Danger, straight ahead!" She screamed as she raised her bow and aimed by intuition. It was still there; she heard its breath, its readiness to lunge. Her fingers released the bowstring and the arrow sprung free.

She heard the thud of impact, but no other sound except running feet. Pain squeezed her heart and bolts of sharp, hurtful light shot through her head. By the Holy One, what had she done? "Leander! Leander!"

"Ottillie! It is all right I am here." Strong arms circled her shoulders.

"Leander, I shot, not waiting to see my target. You were so close, I thought I shot you!"

"Shot? Shot what?"

She felt the shock in his words, saw it in his face. How could she have been so stupid to break such a cardinal rule of hunting?

"The animal stalking me. I heard you approach and thought it would attack you."

The rest of the hunting party crashed through the brush to where she sat having fallen on her butt after her horrified belief she shot Leander. Two of the men had heard her, and perhaps at a motion from Leander, trotted into the dark.

"I'm better," she said, pushing herself to her feet and disengaging from the comfort of his protective arms, her hand pushed against her heart. "It was such a relief to see you alive and unharmed. I promise you—never again will I commit such a stupid mistake."

One of the hunters returned. He spoke to Leander in such an agitated Kennetsurean dialect Ottillie could not understand him. The second man crashed through the shrubbery, staggering from the weight on his shoulders. He dumped his burden at Leander's feet. The moon's soft light reflected the soft sheen of fur on a long, muscular feline animal of indistinguishable color. The muzzle still curled over vicious fangs.

Leander walked around the animal and squatted before its forequarters. He picked up one huge, clawed forepaw. After a moment he looked up at Ottillie. His face was shadowed, but his eyes night-glowed in an eerily familiar way to Ottillie.

"No apology or promise is necessary. It is I who must apologize. Never would you be allowed on a hunt if we knew such had invaded our territory. Your bolt flew true to the lungs. She probably dropped in her tracks. How did you know the silent one stalked you?"

"I did what you told me and listened. I heard it shortly after I heard you shoot your antelope."

"Ottillie, I shot nothing, I have followed next to you to make sure you ran into no trouble. And no hunter ever hears the silent one. She is feared throughout the desert for her soundless stalking, but usually she sticks to the eastern edges of the desert."

"But I heard you."

Leander looked around.

"I shot an antelope," one of the hunters said. "But I was not within hearing distance."

She heard the soft murmurs before Leander's hand motioned them quiet. She knew that Kennetsurean word, Leela had taught her. Witch magic.

~ * ~

Chloe's Story

Chloe sat at her desk in the front room of her small house on Charm Island and slowly opened the volume titled *Journal of the 69th year of my life. Chloe, Earth Adept.*

All the other journals of her years were in this room, except two. One confiscated, and one misplaced while packing to leave the Eternal Palace. Melissa had spoken of her speaking to the wrong lover, who informed King Ewald IV of the Aegis Spell's written existence. Neither Thidrek nor Ewald IV would kill the aegises outright for the same reason they let her go into obscurity. To prevent an uprising among his subjects, citizenry unsettled by the last war. Too many remained knowledgeable in weapons' use, of her service, and the Aegis Spell. Perhaps Thidrek had served her well in that respect.

She sighed. So much time had passed so quickly. A lifetime.

Oblivion had best served her Aegises. In the years since most spoke of her shields as nothing more than tales. Both Ewald IV and Bishop Thidrek were dead. Young Ewald from a riding accident barely three years into his reign, Thidrek from apoplexy before then.

Her mind rambled. She sighed again. It was a sign of her age. She focused her attention and read a previous entry.

> *Fifth day of the Fourth month. Arrogance is a sad failing, especially when combined with a lack of foresight, both of which I have practiced, much to my shame and regret. I am at the time in my life where looking back is more pleasurable than looking forward.*
>
> *There are not many years left to me. The spell has failed, as has my promise to King Ewald III. Not the Aegises. They protect their land as planned even if without the prestige and status I originally envisioned. That was in my thoughts, but not in my design. Nothing, though, protects Kaereya from inner defeat.*
>
> *My failure weighs on me. I invoked the power of four, the Holy One's number for woman, the compass, and the land, but I needed to invoke the power of one also. Outer safety without consideration to inner protection is useless.*

Her mind had dwelled recently on King Ewald's request. She picked up a pen and wrote.

> *25th day of Sixth Month. I have been remiss in writing, too despondent and preoccupied with myself, holding my faults before myself as a mirror of failure and reason to retire. No more. I had a dream three nights ago. Since I have done nothing but pace and think. Perhaps I have found a remedy.*
>
> *One, the Holy One's number of man, and four, his number in women were both needed: male and female, His aspects of engendering. I've given Kaereya protection without internal power and I know because of that, I have failed to give Kaereya the protection asked for. Magic needs faith to survive, and numbers represent faith. Four and one combined into the aspects of five, the gift of knowledge. An Aegis of Five must come, one tied to all of Kaereya. I think I have a remedy.*
>
> *Melissa has been quite concerned with me. The honeybee finally having lost her buzz after eight unplanned children. Who would think so many ships would shelter in this small harbor? I hear the children shouting outside even as I write, my grandchildren run with her children. None show Talent. I will need Melissa. I will need time. May the Holy One grant it. The spell can't be changed, but a second spell can be set in place. Whether it will work or not, I'll never know.*

Sixteen

Raymond Aurelias was wakened by his own command when word came. His riders had met and escorted his expected guests. His valet held his heavy robe for him to slip into. Fastening the closures, he left his room. "They arrive very late," he muttered to the messenger.

"They carried a wounded man with them, Your Grace."

"A wounded man? They ran into trouble?" Terror seized him. Someone tried to kill his daughter. They knew of her existence and it was his fault. He rushed down the remaining stairs.

They stood in the entry foyer, two of his men just setting down a litter. For a brief eternity, all he could see was her. She stood there wrapped in a common oiled-wool cloak, her hair still hidden beneath its hood, cold-red hands clasped nervously together. His daughter was home at last. Some small movement from the man by her side brought him up. He was going too fast. The movement also caught her gaze. As she looked up at the man, her hood fell back to show the beauty of her smiling face. He looked around and saw his oldest retainers suddenly stop and gape. They recognized her.

Beyond the gathered trio, Kissre stood in the doorway. He nodded and she backed out, closing the door. Taking the last few steps to the floor, he took the Clansman's hand in a greeting of peace.

"It has been a long trip for you, Clansman Montoren. I thank you for making it. You ran into trouble?"

"Yes, Your Grace," the young man said. "We came upon outlaws beleaguering a traveler. My wife has tended him, but he needs more help."

At the clansman's words, Aurelias controlled his impulse to strangle the man. Wife indeed. He knew them unmarried. To conceal his anger, he walked to the litter, asking if the healer had been called.

"Yes, Your Grace," his housekeeper answered. Aurelias finally looked down into the face of the wounded man. Blond hair lay in dirty strands around a gaunt and deathly countenance that emphasized a strong and tenacious jawline. Irises shadowed the huge, nearly translucent, closed eyelids. The mouth lay slack and colorless, its sharply bowed upper lip no longer set in a sneer over its thick, pouting lower partner.

Aurelias fell to his knees. "Get that healer here, now!" he shouted. He laid a hand on the pale, hot forehead.

"He is sore wounded, Your Grace, and I fear from your reaction you know this man. He is very young and very strong. I did the best I could for him but had no proper healing herbs with me." She had stepped forward. "If anyone can survive such wounds, he can."

He looked into his daughter's moonstone eyes, wide with concern and kindness, and nearly cried. "Then, we had all better believe so, and pray to the Holy One to make it so, for you and your clansmen have saved the life of your uncrowned king, His Royal Highness, the Crown Prince Warrick."

~ * ~

The night seemed infinite to Raymond. He needed to attend to too much to allow rest. His healer insisted on moving Warrick to a suitable bed chamber. Vesper went also and had not left the sickroom since then. Aurelias offered belated hospitality to the clansmen then questioned them on the day's events. The two men insisted on seeing to their horses. Afterward, he placed them under the auspices of his housekeeper.

Quillon arrived surreptitiously and reported, even while Aurelias sent couriers with a message to Norbert. He called Kissre and gave her a new assignment and swore her to secrecy. He brought his own men to heightened security and made sure the housekeeper and staff knew of the situation with his daughter and with Warrick. They left under threat of dismissal if anyone spoke to Vesper before he did. Then there was the endless waiting, the planning, the pacing, and the distress. It seemed but an instant before the gray light of an overcast day lit his window.

The healer finally entered his office. "Your Grace."

"Well?"

"His Highness is sleeping naturally. He awoke during the night, asked after Emory and Tate, but I had no information to give him. He asked where he was. He has a very good chance of surviving. The next few days will tell. The young clanswoman did a fine job."

"Thank you. You will stay with him?"

"Most assuredly. I will sleep in the room with him and have several maids to help watch during that time. I believe the young woman will help, too."

"No, I wish her sent to her room. Make sure one of your maids shows her the way. She has had a long journey and needs rest."

"Yes, Your Grace." The man bowed and left.

Too tired to sleep he decided to go to the stable and see the unnecessary horses he was buying.

In the stable he had assigned for the new horses he found the two clansmen already at work grooming and feeding their animals. He was as unprepared for this surprise as he had been for the one the previous night. At first look, he fell in love with the proud animal standing in the aisle. His to be son-in-law, Drew Montoren, brushed a fine stallion, smaller than most heavy warhorses, but of better proportion and a refined bearing. The mane and tail were long and silky. Its unusual color, intelligent eye, and elegant head drew attention. Beautiful lines promised easy gaits. He ran a hand down the muscular neck in admiration, envy, and excitement.

"Dare I ask if he is for sale?"

"No, Your Grace. I brought him for stud only. He does not breed color true the first generation except for like, but the second generation bred to each other will often carry the color."

"If the others you brought are of half the quality, I shall count myself lucky."

"You shall have to judge for yourself."

They talked for some time about the horses, about the trip. Aurelias had them show him each horse's gaits. Well pleased, Aurelias congratulated Drew on his animals. "I will take them all. I would buy one or the other of your stallions, too. Think on it."

"Kuff belongs to Vesper."

He looked at the young man. Taller and more handsome than himself, with as proud a bearing as any Aristo. "The two of you recently handfasted in Norost, did you not? I was there and remember."

"Yes, Your Grace."

"And you've wed? I heard you call her wife."

A blush ran over Drew's face. "No, Your Grace, not yet."

"Why not?" he demanded. Both clansmen seemed confused at his poorly concealed anger. "Do you find yourself dissatisfied with your choice?"

He watched his daughter's lover's face fill with rage, but the man maintained his demeanor. "My bride did not know me," he said, civilly enough.

"But you've bedded?"

The young man's posture stiffened. "It is custom in the Clans and in most of Vere."

"In Wessure the wedding takes place within days."

"I don't know how aristos, or those not of the clans, handle their handfasting and marriages, but clansmen must have different customs. Clansmen need love. They have little else. I've only given her time to learn to love me."

"And has she?" Aurelias snapped.

The second clansman put his hand on the other's shoulder in warning. Aurelias also heeded the unvoiced command to control himself.

"I do not see how that can concern you, Your Grace." The honorific was spit out with a nice degree of veiled contempt.

"Then you plan to marry her?"

"As soon as we return home."

"Why wait? You must stay here, now, for several sennights, maybe more. When Warrick heals, he will want to speak with his rescuers. Let me make preparations for you. You can be married here. No," he held up a hand. "Don't object, it is no problem, and certainly you deserve some thanks for your chivalrous duty for Kaereya.

"Thank you, Your Grace, but I must decline. My clan will want to be present, and in truth, Vesper and I need no grand ceremony in our station."

"Nonsense. We will talk more of this later. Were your rooms comfortable?"

"Very much, Your Grace. We expected nothing so splendid."

"Well, since you are not yet wed, you will not mind so much. I gave your betrothed a room in the wing near Warrick's room. The healer said she intended to help in the sickroom." He nearly laughed at the deflated, displeased face turned to him. Clansmen were a surly lot but invariably stoic and polite. A handfasting could last a year without marriage; a year permitting disavowal by participants, including parents. Separation from his daughter might not be that hard and a better choice.

~ * ~

Drew's surprise at not even sharing a room, let alone a bed with Selwyn, was over. That the duke separated him from Vesper he found intolerable. The man had no right to judge clansmen by their differences of handfasting. He wasn't even sure he believed the Aristo Aurelias about any prohibition on prenuptial bedding. A handfasting lasted a year. It was law. Besides, he was here only on business and he wanted Vesper next to him at night even if only to sleep.

He searched until he found a maid and asked her where Vesper's room was. He knocked on her door, his anger mounting with humiliation at having to find his own betrothed. She was not in her room. He went to ask at Warrick's room, but Aurelias's men-at-arms guarded the entry. Asking if Vesper were inside heaped further humiliation on him. Totally frustrated he made his way back to his room.

Vesper waited there and rose when he entered.

"I thought I should never find your room. This place is too large." She slid into his arms and laid her head on his chest.

"I missed you last night."

"I missed you, too," she said. A blush spread over her cheeks. "I want you to kiss me."

"Like the night before last? You're not too tired?"

"I slept this morning."

"How is Prince Warrick?"

"He has survived the initial injuries. If no infection sets in, he will be fine. Aristo Aurelias told the healer that the King's Marshal shall be here in three sennights and that he must be kept safe until then."

"Is there aught Selwyn and I can do?" He said, placing nibbling kisses on her neck as he unlaced her corset.

"Only help to protect him while we are here."

"Did I tell you how glad I am that I relented and let you come? I have not suffered any... homesickness, not with you along."

"Then I am glad, too. For now I know how much I love you."

~ * ~

"She won't stay out of his room," Aurelias said, throwing a sheaf of papers on his desk. Quillon stood listening to his Aristo's seething ire.

"Your Grace, they are betrothed. After all, this behavior is common among the Clans. Even in my home province of Kennetsure a woman often must prove her fertility before becoming a wife."

"You think he will discard my daughter? By the Holy One, he will rethink that when I'm through with him!"

"Neither he nor she is aware of the relationship. I believe separating them was your desire?"

"Not now!" The duke shouted at an interrupting knock. It was repeated. He ran a hand over his head. "Enter." Kissre stood there, mud-spattered and disheveled.

"Your Grace, there is a large troop of men approaching. They are presently ten leagues east on the Northern Road."

"How many?" Quillon asked. "On the road? That's unexpected. Did you recognize them?"

Aurelias reached for his sword belt and cloak.

"At least sixty men-at-arms, traveling fast. They're clansmen."

"Clansmen?" Aurelias asked. "Are you sure? Was anyone able to recognize what clan?"

"Clansmen, yes, sir. From many different clans."

"Get the two clansmen. They can ride with us. Why would they save Prince Warrick only to bring this threat down on him? It doesn't make sense."

They all made for the door, outside of which, those very same clansmen waited, pointedly staring at Quillon.

"Why are the clans threatening my land?" Aurelias asked with his temper in his voice.

"Why is this man with you?" Drew Montoren asked, his voice as uncompromising as his posture.

Aurelias looked at his man. "Quillon? He is my deputy. He is Knight of the Zekarac Order and completely trustworthy."

"Why did you set him skulking and spying on me in Vere?"

"Your Grace, I believe Clansman Montoren recognizes me from some dealing we had in the city of Norost."

"Clan Cader and others reported all the questions you asked about Montoren and what went on there." The young man said looking at Quillon, his hand lay on his sword hilt.

"Call off your clans now!" Aurelias ordered, putting his hand on Quillon's sword arm. "Any petty argument you have with me can wait until I am assured of Prince Warrick's safety!"

"No clansman would harm Prince Warrick," the older of the two clansmen said.

Looking at the two belligerent men, Aurelias said, "Prove your words. Ride with us to prevent an armed contest between my men and the army of clansman headed here."

It was not an equally large troop that rode from Lambere Manor, but Aurelias thought better armed and trained. He ordered the Montoren men to ride between Quillon and Kissre where a close eye could be kept on them. The two forces met head to head at the four-league stone from the estate. Aurelias threw a look at the clansmen in his party. He ordered them to silence until he requested they speak. Drew nodded.

"Why do you come armed to my land?" Aurelias shouted as the assembly quieted.

"We follow a man who asked questions about two of our clansmen. When we found our clansmen gone without a word, we followed. That man rides with you, Duke Lambere. Do you hold Drew and Selwyn Montoren hostage?" He pulled a sword from its scabbard with the echoing sounds of his followers reflecting his actions.

"Hostage to what?" Aurelias yelled. "What could I want with a clansman?"

"That remains to be known!"

"Cader Chief Terril," Drew said, riding forward from where Quillon and Kissre guarded him and Selwyn. "I came to sell my horses that is all. I am not a prisoner but came of my own free will."

Chief Terril's face pinched in anger. "Drew Montoren, you had no right to act so rashly! You know all the clansmen would ride to protect you." Aurelias listened with relief and amusement to the humiliating harangue rung on the young man next to him. That Drew did not appreciate his public chastisement was obvious.

"Cader Chief Terril," Aurelias said. "Tell your men to sheath their weapons."

"How did young Drew come to sell you horses? How did you know he breeds horses?"

Looking at the clan chief who had still not sheathed his weapon, Aurelias took a calming breath. It did no good. "Yes, Drew and Selwyn Montoren are here at my devising, and here Drew Montoren will stay until he marries my daughter."

"You have no daughter, and I am already betrothed!" Drew shouted, his head snapping in Aurelias' direction.

"Yes, I have a daughter," Aurelias said, swiveling to look at Montoren. "You've bedded her, and now by the Holy One, you'll wed her. I'll not let you disparage her further by using cagey clan tricks to end the handfasting! You will not abuse her further!"

"But I'm handfasted to Vesper." A look of sheer confusion covered the face staring at him.

"Vesper is my daughter!" Aurelias shouted, then forced himself to calm. His declaration astonished the clansmen. It surprised his own men, and the shock on Montoren's face would have been funny under other circumstances. He turned to see more of his men riding to join them, making his force outnumber the clansmen. He settled, knowing how outrageous he sounded.

"It is a long story," he said in resignation, "and I don't know all the details, but you will marry her on Spring Day two sennights hence, clan custom or no." He turned to the clansmen. "Stay and see your clansman married if you wish. Then, if you love Kaereya and your home province, Vere, stay and help us protect King Warrick. The South Thou and Easure are invaded and others seek to claim the Kaereyan throne."

They held their mounts to a slow walk on the return to the Lambere estate. Aurelias looked at his future son-in-law. It was seldom he so badly mismanaged his affairs. He spoke with some embarrassment and umbrage. "You must allow me to tell Vesper. She does not know."

Drew gave him a nasty look and opened his mouth, but Chief Terril, riding on the young man's other side, said, "That sounds fair, Your Grace. It'll be shock enough for her no matter who tells her."

~ * ~

Regent Theodulf Gilchrist looked down on the body of his youngest son. "Was Emory there?" He already knew the answer but needed to keep his façade of ignorance. Word had come earlier. Emory lay sore wounded at the Hearthron manse east of the Rikon Hills. The boy had to live—else all was a disaster. His voice shook.

He looked at the Kennetsurean as he demanded information after his other son and the prince from Norbert's agent. Corbin had brought Tate's body back.

"We believe so, we believe he escaped. We did not find Prince Warrick," the man said in a flat unemotional voice that matched his face. Gilchrist wondered what knowledge hid behind the impassive expression.

He dismissed Norbert's Kennetsurean tool. Aristo Yonger stood next to him, with a few of his closest allies. When Corbin's footsteps had faded away, he asked his Marshal Wiffern, "Is it possible the Prince is held for ransom?"

"No demands have come, Regent Gilchrist."

While Wiffern spoke, Gilchrist's gaze fell on Yonger's confident serenity and suspicion flared. *The traitor, he never meant for any of the three to survive. My daughter, Yonger's wife, would be Queen, making Yonger Consort Ruler...*

Wiffern pattered on, unaware of his Regent's inattention. "Aristo Aurelias must not have known of my appointment. His message went to the Earl of Rikon. It arrived this morning."

Gilchrist looked at Wiffern, a tool he was now sorry he chose in expediency. Norbert would never have been so unaware of the undercurrents swirling around him. He swore. "What message, and why did Norbert not come to me directly? What does he suspect, or was this just an insult to my authority?"

"I don't know, Sire," Wiffern said, looking alarmed at the look Gilchrist gave him in intent interest. "He left Court before the message was delivered by the Royal Guard Commander."

"He left? How dare he?" Gilchrist's temper rose. No one left court without his permission. He would not let all of this be for naught.

"Yes. He rode out with most of his retainers this morning. To protect Warrick. That was Aurelias' message. Warrick has been found. I was on my way to you when you summoned me."

With supreme self-control, Gilchrist reigned in his temper. "Has anyone else left court?"

Aristo Wiffern had taken several steps backward toward the door. "I've had reports that about twenty other aristos and their troops have left the Eternal Palace. The Archbishop also left."

"And you kept this to yourself? You did not think this important? How did they all steal from the palace?"

"The Royal Guard Commander notified the Archbishop, who felt you would be grieving for your son. Besides, as Regent, you are obligated to remain here in the present unsettled state of the country. The Commander came to me before he left. He rode to protect the realm but left three contingents to protect the Palace and City."

"Without advice or leave from me?" *This was very bad.*

"They go to protect the King," Wiffern said, bewildered.

"Leave me, I wish to be alone with my son."

Wiffern bowed and left. Aristo Yonger remained, but the smug satisfaction had fled him.

"You promised me a kingdom. With all your plotting and conniving, all it has accomplished is my son's death."

"Hold firm. Admit nothing. You can still be king. We know Emory lives."

"Alive, but wounded, and may not survive. Thank the Holy One he had the sense to go to the Hearthron Seat rather than here."

"He showed good judgment. You'll see. I can still make you a king."

Gilchrist swore. "Liar. You attacked Warrick, tried to kill my sons at the same time, so the line would go through my daughter and you would rule. Your plot is foiled. Warrick will be king. And should Pertelon win, Clement will take the throne."

"I have ambitions like any man." Yonger looked at the dead boy. "This was not by my devising. Emory sent the message to you telling you where they traveled. Warrick had luck on his side, but not for much longer. Clement will make Warrick's rule short. We will plan for that event." His gaze came back to Gilchrist. "Do not think to turn on me. I have proof of your involvement. As I said, hold steady, we can still prevail."

Seventeen

Vesper looked around the room the housekeeper led her to, feeling a little nervous and very out-of-place. The room shouted luxury without obvious ostentation. She didn't dare sit on the fine fabrics with their shimmery brocades and walked around the edges of the beautiful rug. Tapestries on the walls caught her attention and she inspected each, absorbing the story they told about fishermen, sailors, ships, and mermaids. The numbers of three and nine repeated through all the themes; three the number of beginnings and births, and nine the number of the Soul, of mental and spiritual attainment. Both numbers signified water. The doorknob clicked startling her. She turned to face the Duke of Lambere. He smiled at her.

"Good afternoon, Mistress Vesper. My healer speaks very highly of you and the help you've given him in Prince Warrick's care. I thought to offer you my thanks also."

She curtseyed. "No thanks are needed, Your Grace, it has been my pleasure."

"You are wrong. Thanks, indeed, are due you and your clansmen. You have done Kaereya a great service. You've saved the life of our king. I've been assured Prince Warrick will live, that he improves daily. I'm sure, when he is better able, he will want to thank you properly."

"I don't believe we will be staying that long, Your Grace. Drew wishes to get home to Vere, to Montoren Farm."

The duke snorted. "You say Vere and Montoren Farm like a clanswoman."

"I am, Your Grace."

"Well, your Drew and his cousin Selwyn have agreed to stay awhile longer. The horses, you know," he said at her puzzlement. "His stud and my mares when they come into season. It takes time. Please sit," he said pointing to one of the chairs. "I knew your mother."

"My mother, but..." The duke suddenly frightened her. "I am sorry, Your Grace, no one knows who my mother was."

"You look a great deal like her. It was quite a shock when I first saw you. Growing up without your parents must have been very hard."

"I was very lucky to have Eudora. She is the housekeeper to the Mayor of Norost."

"Still, any loss is difficult. I've lost two wives, an infant son, and a son almost a man."

"I am very sorry, Your Grace. I knew of your last wife and son, but not of any other." Vesper wondered why the duke would confide in her but didn't know what to say.

"She was carrying our child, afraid and alone. The physician said madness gripped her. She was afraid of everything, even of me in the end. There was a celebration, for my birthday, it was the last time I saw her alive." His look became distant. "Afterward she left, ran away. Took the gift she gave me with her. I searched for her. It seemed like forever. It was forever." His gaze found hers. "I found Lorelei, my wife, and the baby, both dead, by her hand. Her maid was dead too, apparently killed before Lorelei took her own life. That was eighteen years ago. They say time heals, but that day, what I saw and felt, lives in my mind."

Vesper sat at a loss of what to say. "I'm... so sorry. It must have been a terrible time for you, but I don't understand why you are telling me this."

Aurelias rose. "I'm telling you this because you are involved. Come with me." He presented a hand to help her rise from her seat.

Bewildered, Vesper rose and followed as he placed a hand beneath her elbow, guiding her. The main hall was empty.

"As I said, you are involved. I've only told you the first part of the story." He led her up the stairs. "Several months ago, a sennight before last Handfasting Day, I received a message. One from beyond the grave—a letter bearing Lorelei's seal. You can imagine my surprise, as I am certain I buried the seal with her. It was a terrible shock. The letter was not in her hand, but she had signed it, probably candlemarks before she died. In it she described her happiness."

Aristo Aurelias stopped in the long wide hall. "She told me how sorry she was to have doubted me, how confused she had been. She told me the danger was over, and that I could rejoice in the birth of my son." Aurelias looked at her. "And of my daughter." He turned to look at a portrait hanging before them.

Vesper gasped. "This was not here before," she said inanely.

"No. I had it removed before you arrived. It has only just been replaced. Your mother."

In the painting a dark-haired Aristo woman stared back. Her hair was arranged under a proper coif, but loose curls escaped. The painter had captured the beautiful fabric of her rich clothing. Vesper instantly recognized the fabric. Aurelias kept talking but Vesper didn't hear what he said. Her hands felt like leaden weights falling at the sides of her skirt, weighing her down until she could barely stand up.

Mesmerized, she could only stare at the woman in the painting. Aurelias finally said something that penetrated her daze.

"That is not possible," she said sounding as confused as she felt.

"But it is. You are my daughter."

"But Eudora..."

His voice hardened. "We will talk of her later."

~ * ~

"No. I will not believe it. Eudora could not possibly have murdered my mother and stolen me. There must be another explanation. You said yourself someone has hunted your family, caused your terrible misfortunes." Learning so much before strangers only increased Vesper's sense of unreality. This must be just one more of her fantasies, particularly as Alfred perched on a book table watching her. It was too quiet for so many men, adding to the dream essence. They all stood, too few chairs for all in the room she supposed.

"Your family now," Aurelias said.

Several of his men stood behind Aristo Aurelias. Vesper recognized the one he called Quillon from Norost. His tiger's eyes shifted from her to Drew then to the clansmen lining the other side of the room. She turned to Drew. Behind her betrothed stood Selwyn and many strangers she didn't know except they wore clan garb and tokens.

"It is a possibility you must consider," Aurelias said. He turned to Drew. "You will have to doubly guard her. I think you should leave her here until it is safer to travel."

"She will be safe with the Clans," Selwyn answered for Drew. Chief Terril seconded Selwyn's claim. "We take care of our own."

"I do not like the thought of my daughter immured in the wilds of Vere. How will I ever get to know her?"

"Although it is not as grand as your estate, you are always welcomed to visit Montoren Farm," Drew said.

Aurelias threw him a disgusted look but turned his attention back to Vesper. "I've had my housekeeper look for your mother's wedding gown. On such short notice, it is the best choice. She will have the maids alter it however you like.

"Wedding gown?"

"Your father... Aristo Aurelias," Drew said in a voice filled with the doubt she felt, "insists we be married. In a fortnight."

"What? We cannot do that!"

"Of course you can. It is already planned."

"I cannot! It is too much to accept. Drew and I will be married in Montoren before his clan."

She became alarmed at the look on Aristo Aurelias' face. "Your Grace," she said belatedly.

"Not Your Grace! Your Father! I realize it is a shock, but anyone looking at you knows the truth. All here have seen your mother's portrait." He seemed to recollect himself and lowered his voice. "You inherit Lorelei's dower lands. You are my heir. You should have been married within days of handfasting."

His face pinched in controlled anger. "Learning you were stolen from me was devastating! Imagine my torture at finding you too late, already handfasted to a Clan... Vere man, at my learning that my family has been under an insidious attack for years. I was horrified. Now I find you are not only unmarried but also sleeping together! It will not go on! You didn't know, but you do now. Now you must uphold your name. It is his choice, either he can marry you a fortnight hence, or I will disavow the handfasting!"

Drew bellowed "No," in an outraged howl, as did Selwyn and Chief Terril. "You would not dare!"

Vesper looked at her betrothed's angry face and felt her stomach twist. Everything felt unreal since viewing the portrait in the upper hall. She had no experience in dealing with enraged men. Her glance darted between one, perhaps her father, and the other, her love.

"I fought my clan for her, and I'll fight you!" The threat in Drew's voice was unmistakable. Chief Terril placed a hand on Drew's arm, restraining him. Drew shook off the hand, and in his anger, unwisely pulled his knife blade. Quillon's sword blade matched the movement and the knight moved to protect his master.

A scream broke from her throat. "No."

Several clansmen forcibly pull-pushed Drew back against a wall, disarming him. He struggled against them until Selwyn shouted, "Drew!"

"Then you'll marry her as is proper!" Chief Terril glared at Drew, then turned to look at Aurelias, his face changing. "I know the pain this situation has caused you, Your Grace, and to have it proclaimed before strangers must surely cast you anew. Our young Drew and his handfasted are also most distressed at this revelation. I stand as Chief of Clan Cader. The boy has been unyielding about the girl for years. He won't back out of marriage now. Any marriage." He said with a glare at Drew. "If marriage gives your father-in-law peace of mind, then Clan Cader makes no objection. It's what you've wanted all along. Eight other clan chiefs can stand witness that the nuptials occurred within clan tradition."

A chorus of agreement met Terril's statement. "Yeah, I think it a good thing," Chief Terril said. "We will stay the fortnight to the wedding." He nodded to those holding Drew and they released him.

"Then we agree." Aurelias turned back to Vesper. "You must start dressing according to your station."

"I will buy my own wife's clothes," Drew said.

"She is not your wife yet, and how I wish to gift my daughter is my business!"

"Your daughter but a day!"

"My daughter, stolen from me these past eighteen years!"

"And now my betrothed bride, duly handfasted and witnessed by yourself!"

"Selwyn," Chief Terril said. "Remove him until he can calm himself."

Vesper watched through stricken eyes while Selwyn and several men pulled Drew, unwilling, from the room. "Lady Vesper," Chief Terril addressed her. "If you might retire?"

"Not to his room!" Aurelias shouted.

"She had another? Then she may go there." Chief Terril put his hand on her arm as she passed. "Lady, I must ask you to stay away from Drew. You will not help the situation if you go to him."

"But we have been..."

"I know, but it does not seem the custom here. I remind you that you are in your father's house."

Still confused by it all, Vesper nodded and left. As she reached the door, Duke Lambere shouted, "Kissre!" A woman dressed like one of the duke's men-at-arms came through the door. "Vesper, this is Kissre. She will guard you against harm."

Vesper whirled on her supposed father. "You have no cause to doubt me, to set a guard upon me!"

"I have lost two wives and two sons due to a lack of diligence. I will not lose you."

"I am not in harm's way here."

"I will take no chances. Not now. Not even once you are married. Clansman Montoren may husband you, but he will understand I will not relinquish a father's interests in your protection."

"The clans will protect them both." Chief Terril nodded at Vesper. She at least knew that part of her duty to clan. She curtseyed to the duke her father and the clan chiefs and left. Closing the door, she looked for Drew, but they had taken him further than the hall. Men-at-arms and servants filled the hall. They nodded at her in deference. It caused an urge for hysterical laughter, but in this dream, she forced herself to calm.

~ * ~

Cold water shocked him, pushed up his nose. Selwyn's fist on the back of his shirt pulled him from the trough. Drew came up sputtering. He twisted and swung at his cousin. Several hands grabbed his upper arms and he plunged underwater again. This time they held him until his lungs burned. When they pulled him out of the water, he emerged gasping.

"Settle down. Get that temper under control," Selwyn said. "Cader Chief Terril sees to your interests."

"He has no right! None of you have. The handfasting is consummated. She is my wife!" His words emerged between gasps for air. Water streamed from his hair and face, leaking down the neck of his jacket to wet his shirt. The discomfort of cold and damp against his skin rekindled his frustrated rage.

"Not your wife yet, and he is her father. You marry her in a fortnight. What is to argue about that?" Selwyn's hand had not released his grip on Drew's collar.

Drew forced calm while he caught his breath. He swore to get back at them. Restraining hands released their hold and he shrugged away the last touch. "No one has the right to interfere—not Cader Chief Terril, not Aristo Aurelias—and not you. The handfasting was witnessed. He could have intervened then."

"Did you not listen?" Selwyn's voice was full of irate exasperation that he expressed in shaking Drew. "He was attacked. He feared for himself and for her. He had just learned her mother might have been murdered. He was still mourning his second wife and son. Very wisely, he decided on her safety."

Chief Terril walked up. "Taking it hard? You'll be able to bed her before you know it." Several clansmen offered suggestions of how to relieve his frustration until then. Laughter followed. "You've done well for yourself and the clan, young Drew. The duke will do right by his daughter, and we could not have found a better alliance for you." He looked around at the other clan chiefs, smiling broadly. "Even if an Aristo would have consented to Handfast with a clansman."

"Does well for all the clans," Clan Shea Chief said. A chorus of yeas agreed.

"I've dispatched men to ride and return with clan dress for you. It'll be a proud day for us, boy. A proud day."

Drew flung away and went to find dry clothes. He heard their talk while he escaped.

"Has he suffered land sickness?" Terril asked Selwyn.

"A little, up until he bedded his seer bride."

"Then other concerns occupied him?" More good-natured jokes and laughter followed. "You said she was so. Well, well. A very good connection for the clans. Luckily, Clansmen understand such things better than most."

By then Drew was out of hearing range. He entered the back entrance and took the steps two at a time, disgusted his position destroyed every vestige of privacy. Once in his room he sank into a chair and put his head into his hands, covering his eyes with cupped palms of darkness. He had noticed, and what Selwyn said was true. Leaving Vere he felt none of the usual shakiness, not the feelings of dread and panic, nor the wrenching pain of cramps in stomach and muscle.

~ * ~

Warwick felt too tired to move. A pretty girl changed his bandage. She had dark curly hair and clear gray eyes shifting green. One of Aurelias's maids he assumed. Under normal circumstances, he would have been interested, but nothing engaged him. Everything

271

was beyond his caring. All he could think about was Tate, all he could see was his cousin's death eyes. The look of stunned surprise on Tate's face turned into his father's face, then his brother Frederick, then those of his baby sisters. Warwick wondered if one could die of guilt. It felt like it. He hoped so.

"You need to get up and walk around," the girl said as she finished her chore.

He turned his gaze to the wall. "Go away."

"She is right." The healer walked in. "Lady Vesper and her betrothed saved you, brought you here."

"I do not think Prince Warrick is interested in that," Vesper said. "He has not had a chance to mourn for his family." She laid a hand on Warrick's arm. "You must not feel guilty that you survived. Kaereya needs you. Your father would have wanted you to carry on."

"How do you know?" Warrick spat the words out. "He considered me irresponsible. I was." To his shame, tears trickled out the corners of his eyes.

"No! You played a prank, but that alone caused no one serious harm. How could you know someone would poison your family? You saved yourself, maybe by the Holy One's design."

"Was it the Holy One's desire Tate and Emory die?"

"You were hunted. They tried to save their monarch. Do not besmirch their honor in your guilt at living." Warrick looked startled at his nurse, no girl this. She watched him in concerned quiet, then turned away. He heard her speak a few soft words with the healer. The door closed.

"She is right. You must concentrate on getting your strength back. The Earl Rikon is on his way."

"You called her lady."

"She, as it turns out, is the Duke of Lambere's daughter."

"He had a son who died. I've never heard of a daughter. She has never attended court." The healer explained the extraordinary circumstances.

"She handfasted a clansman?"

"Yes, the one who saved you. They marry in a fortnight. He must be important among the Clans. He came to sell Aristo Aurelias some horses. An odd story," the healer said pausing and straightening, "But fine horses, at that."

"What is so odd in that?"

"A horde of clansmen followed him out of Vere. It seems, Your Highness, you have an army assembling."

~ * ~

Drew found the darkness of his room welcoming. It let him escape the watchful gazes of Clansmen. There was more Selwyn didn't know. Without much effort he could feel the land around him. Vere had always been a familiar part of him. This land was like meeting an unknown relative. It lay in well-defined flat, fertile fields of loose, deep soil, heavily cultivated and peaceful on the surface. Not at all like untamed Vere's craggy dangerousness with forest-lined rock faces that suffered frequent rockslides and avalanches, streams prone to flash flooding, icy lakes, hot springs, and hard-earned pockets of fertility. Vere underground was stable, ancient rock filled with rivers and deposits of minerals, water, and air.

In Wessure the serenity was all on the surface. Far beneath its flat top, he felt-saw the tense bedrock, fissured and unstable, grinding and pushing. Everything felt different and yet vaguely the same.

Was this due to Vesper? He groaned. Two sennights without her. If they hadn't touched, he might have endured; but what they felt was too new, too intense to make the time acceptable. He stayed in his room through dinner. Unable to face the bed, he stayed in the chair well into evening's darkness.

The doorknob clicked softly, and Drew rose, instantly alert. Soft steps took him through the pitch darkness to the door as the intruder carefully closed the door.

"It's so dark! Didn't you light a candle?" Vesper whispered to him. She started as he touched her.

"What are you doing here?"

"Where else should I be?"

"I was told you couldn't come."

She giggled. "What such a new father desires, a clan chief demands, and what I chose to do, can differ. They can't really know me or expect my obedience. I am sorry I acted a simpleton earlier. It was all too much, too fast. I should have supported you."

"There was no need. I understand. He is your father."

"There was every need, for you have become my heart." Drew wrapped his arms around her and held her tight.

~ * ~

A maid helped Vesper into her wedding apparel. A traditional tight Wessurean surcoat of crimson and purple embroidered with gold threads and garnet beads. The cream lace of the chemise emerged through the neck and fell overall. More lace fell out of the sleeve cuffs of the surcoat to nearly touch the floor. Vesper had never worn anything so obviously expensive. Its heaviness made her shakily aware of the cost. The servants had bathed, perfumed, dressed, and primped her. She was unused to so much attention, to others performing the most personal of services.

Her father, the word sounded so curious. It was strange. Unbelievable. He wanted her to believe Eudora guilty of an awful crime, of stealing his daughter, maybe even murdering her mother. How could she reconcile herself to such a story? She could not. Soon she and Drew would be married, soon they could travel home.

A knock sounded on the door. Her father, the Duke of Lambere stood before her, staring at her. She heard his words as through a fog. "You look beautiful. Your mother would be proud." He took her hand and placed it on the sleeve of his luxurious coat. "It is an auspicious day for marriage in Wessure. A day of three and nine, the Holy One's aspects of beginnings and creativity—it bodes well for you."

"I am already lucky. I have Drew and find I have a father." She walked next to him. Outside the front door, they stopped. It was a beautiful day with a light sprinkling of snow, the last day of Second Month.

Even as they stepped from the last stone step leading from the manse and onto the courtyard across from the chapel, the massed sound of horses approaching broke the stillness. Aurelias' head swiveled, and he shouted to one of the men walking the parapets. He seemed relieved at the answer and distracted as he spoke to her. "I'm sorry, wait here. He's early. He must have ridden all out."

Others had heard the clamor. Clansmen descended from the chapel's porch. They made a colorful lot in clan garb. Prince Warrick also emerged, looking pale and weak, but with Quillon supporting and protecting him. Several clansmen took protective positions around him, and she saw his eyes widen in surprise. Her eyes were drawn to Drew as he emerged looking tall and distinguished. His eyes caught hers. She smiled, but he didn't return her greeting, remaining somber looking.

It seemed mere moments before horses poured into the courtyard, mounted men carrying multi-colored banners and pennants. Many she identified as Royal Guardsmen. Aurelias left her at the base of the steps to greet those dismounting.

"You made good time," he said to a gaunt man still atop his horse.

"Hello, Raymond. Did you think I would not? I see you expected us." The man watched an army of servants pour from the manse's lower level-doors to help direct the disorder as men dismounted.

"Not really. Today we hold a wedding."

The stranger looked at Vesper. "Your daughter?" The stranger came to her and took her hand in a courtly manner, kissing it. "It is a pleasure to see you here, Lady Vesper, safe and where you belong."

Vesper felt her mouth open, but no words emerged. She felt heat creep over her face in a furious blush.

"Vesper, this is my old friend, Wilhelm Norbert, Earl of Rikon and the King's Marshal."

"I'm glad for Prince Warrick's sake that you are here, sir."

"I am glad, also, but King's Marshal no more. I have been relieved of office." He turned to Vesper. "You shall be glad too, Lady Vesper. I bring a Bishop to marry you." He looked at Aurelias. "For a wedding today and a coronation tomorrow—a coronation day that combines four's stability and one's creation and unity. Lady Vesper, can we detain your nuptials for a candlemark?"

They did not wait on her answer. Her father led her back into the house while his man Quillon shouted orders in the courtyard. Vesper sat in a side room listening to the turmoil outside. It finally diminished, and her father returned. "Shall we try again?"

While they walked, he talked. "Did you know another coronation took take place here in our Adoration Chapel? It's true. Your great-great-grandfather on your mother's side, King Heinrich the Second. Your mother once gave me an amulet she said came from him. She believed it held magic and good luck, she took it with her when she ran away."

"One with the sun and moon on it? I gave it to Drew as a first gifting," she looked at him with concern. "It was with my mother's things. Eudora gave it to me."

His hand patted hers. "I won't demand it back. It was yours to gift."

~ * ~

Drew watched Vesper approach from the carved and gilt chapel door. He took her hand from Aurelias. Every time he looked at her she grew more beautiful. He gritted his teeth with a sudden desire to provide her the beautiful things her father could, but that thought faded as she looked at him and smiled. He wore a black jacket bound with a Clan Cader sash of argent, azure, and noir, with his Grandfather's silver crest pin attached to his Cader sash. Even wearing clan dress, he felt Vesper's pride in him and hoped he could make his vows emerge through the tension clogging his throat.

He had never wished for so grand a ceremony, with so many exalted guests. The chapel's ornate architecture and colored glass windows fashioned a dreamlike state, so different from the clan's outdoor ceremonies. He walked with Vesper to the altar, Aurelias following through the small, over-crowded church. Clansmen mixed shoulder to shoulder with the most eminent aristos of Kaereya.

Terril's riders had returned, which meant they had ridden day and night to arrive with formal clan dress and his stave. With their return came thirty more clansmen, with more to arrive within the next few days. The Clans had committed to Warrick. Fourteen clan chiefs were now present, only five staying in Vere to keep the peace there.

He took Vesper's hand and turned to face the Bishop. At first Chief Terril and the other clan chiefs had objected. They had spent time with the chaplain explaining the intricacies of clan weddings. Unruffled at the refusal of his services, the Bishop simply said, "Nonsense, I know clan ceremony." He did, and Drew managed to speak after Vesper gave her vows in her soft clear voice. With their kiss, a thumping of clan staves reverberated through the church.

With the ceremony completed, Vesper kissed her father. Aurelias swept her into his arms and whispered loud enough for Drew to hear. "New family we might be, but never more desired a child or dedicated a father. I swear by all I am and all my honor, he best treat you as you deserve."

He let her go, and Vesper sank into a deep curtsey to Prince Warrick, now surrounded by the Earl Rikon and other exalted aristos. Prince Warrick took her hand and raised her placing a kiss on the tips of her fingers in what Drew recognized as a very practiced manner. The Crown Prince's eyes sparkled in an appreciation that set Drew's teeth on edge. Warrick then held out his hand to Drew in a clan sign of friendship. Drew returned the gesture, but Rikon's hand shot out and grabbed his, turning it palm up.

"Your palm is marked." An uncomfortable, shuffling sounded through the church.

Drew flushed. "It is not a sign of evil."

"I know," the earl said. "It is the sign of the Aegis of the North."

Chief Terril stepped forward in a belligerent step, "What do you know about Vere's Aegis?" Drew felt the tension among the clansmen and the surprise among the aristos. Vesper's hand trembled in his. He lifted it to his lips and kissed the soft skin on the back of her hand. Her eyes smiled back at him.

"Enough Cader Chief Terril," Drew said. "I owe service to Kaereya and the crown, not just Vere."

"You are the Aegis? Then I am glad to hear you say so and very glad to meet you, sir, Kaereya needs your service."

~ * ~

"Earl Rikon, I am glad to see you," Warrick said. He didn't know what else to say.

They stood together in the Duke of Lambere's study after the wedding. Outside the muffled sound of celebrating clansmen entered the room. The drums of a Wessure wedding pounded counterpoint to Vere's string instruments in compelling music.

"I did not leave my father with a good memory of me. Not any of my family."

"Your Highness, I am glad to see you alive. And I am sure Frederick, as both your father and the king, would have been pleased and heartened that you survived. Let me express my deepest sorrow for your loss. I know it is difficult. It was a great loss for Kaereya. Your father was a good king. But I fear I don't bring much good news. You are still in danger."

The sudden weakness that periodically overtook him assailed Warrick. "I am sorry, I must sit down."

Norbert helped him to a chair. "Please sit, also." He waited until the older man sat. Dressed in black, Norbert looked more like a crow than ever. He checked his wayward thoughts. "I must apologize to you for my past behavior. Before coming to Aristo Aurelias, I met, by chance, Princess Pia. She is the one who advised me to come here. We were afraid to enter Hawk City. It was on the way here that my cousins were killed."

"With all the danger about you, it was a wise decision. I fear your enemies might hold more power in both the city and palace than even I believed. Tate's body arrived at the Eternal Palace the day I left along with many others celebrating outside today. Your Royal Guard Commander saw that Lambere's message of your arrival here was delayed long enough for many of your loyal aristos to join you, along with most of the Royal Guard. You need to thank Aristo Marshon for bringing the royal crown."

"It was necessary to sneak these items past the notice of the Regent, my uncle Gilchrist?"

"I am sorry, Your Highness."

"No need. I didn't recognize my attackers, but they taunted me as the would-be king. Did they find Emory?"

"Emory is at Hearthron, wounded, but alive."

"He betrayed me, didn't he?" He looked at Norbert. "I had plenty of time to think while I lay in bed. Many things have become clear. No one could have known where we were headed unless they were informed. Someone tampered with my saddle's girth. Did my uncle kill my family?"

"I have no proof of that. I know he has tied himself to the Aristo of Yonger, whom I suspect works for King Clement. Yonger handfasted your cousin."

"So he tried to kill Em and Tate so his son might inherit? He is a traitor."

"I believe so, but I have only circumstantial proof."

"Earl Rikon," Warrick drew a breath. "I know in the past my conduct and duty have not inspired confidence, but you've always shown great loyalty to my father. I would exceedingly appreciate you becoming my King's Marshal."

A start showed how his request had surprised the earl, but he responded without hesitation. "I will gladly accept your appointment, Your Highness."

~ * ~

Drew watched Warrick's coronation ceremony with half his attention. His mind kept drifting to the ceremony of the previous day. He, Vesper, Selwyn, and Aristo Aurelias stood in the Lambere family stall, positions exclusively close to the altar. Another negotiated incident in an endless round of situations between Duke, aristos, and clans. It had been determined that Drew would stand with Vesper in her father's stall. Clan Cader took position as extended family down the side aisle. Aristos and clan chiefs took front standing before the altar followed by the clergy accompanying the Bishop, followed by others as the Bishop and Norbert dictated. Even positions in the balconies had been conferred by authorization.

It was a new world for Drew, and an uncomfortable one. For the Earl Rikon he held a fascinated respect. His gift for organization stopped many incipient arguments, and the man's loyalty to his king could not be doubted. Clansmen always respected loyalty.

A side-glance showed Vesper enthralled with the ceremony. She sensed his regard, smiled, and tucked her hand in the crook of his arm that held his ceremonial staff. Her attention briefly fell on the staff brought with his clothes from Vere, then returned to the Bishop's long service given in solemn and reverent tones. Drew's body seemed to lighten with pleasure and expand with contentment. He placed his hand over hers.

Warrick knelt throughout, frozen in his supplicant posture. Though awesome in its significance, Drew suspected the ceremony lacked in the usual majesty of such occasions. He looked at the back of his new king's head. Warrick's hair glowed in multicolor light from the sun pouring through the stained-glass windows. The jeweled crown glinted when lowered to his head.

He speculated about his new king. Even in Vere rumor brought reports of this young man's wildness, his pranks, and negligence. What he witnessed showed a very different person. Warrick seemed somber, detached, and often inattentive. Much of that could be attributed to his recent wounds and the terrible loss that resulted in his crowning today. Drew wondered if he could overcome his guilt to focus on the guardianship of trust the crown embodied.

Warrick rose and turned to accept the accolades of those present. Afterward the aristos approached by rank and swore fealty to their new king. Then each of the clan chiefs knelt and swore.

Yesterday the Earl of Rikon had detained Drew and declared he must swear too, but Drew had declined. "I am neither Aristo nor clan chief. Each aegis swears to protect their Province and has no court function. Traditionally, they have not been welcomed there."

"You speak as if your duty were abolished. I tell you that both you and Aegis Aldous remain of extreme importance to Kaereya in its present crisis."

"No one believes anymore. Few even think of Aegises as more than a folktale."

A coarse sound had erupted from Aristo Norbert that Drew took for a laugh. "Then you should hear the screams and petitions for the Aegis of Easure."

Drew had felt surprised, then shrugged. "That family died long ago."

"I know. Those of Wessure, too. It seems the northern and southern provinces protected theirs better."

"Fewer aristos hold power in those provinces, and both Vere and Kennetsure value their traditions and take pride in them." He snorted softly. "Their stubborn pride probably saved them, us. Me."

"Your presence would be a good gesture. Believe me, most of the aristos here are praying for the return of the aegises but do as you must." The gaunt, harsh-looking man switched subjects. "Once Warrick is crowned, his first act will be to knight you and your cousin Selwyn."

"What?"

"You saved his life. I know it goes against clan custom, but this you must do."

Now he waited to be called before the new king. Warrick gave a short speech and then Drew and Selwyn were ushered before Warrick. This ceremony, while feeling strange and undeserved, gave Drew a sense of gratification. Selwyn, he saw, was nearly overcome with the honor. It startled Drew. Selwyn was always so restrained, even in anger.

The ceremony ended, and the food planned for Drew's wedding feast now served for the coronation. His stomach growled as he took his place next to Vesper, and she giggled hearing his body's discomfort.

"We even have places of honor at the banquet planned for us," she said, eyes sparkling in unseen laughter.

"I don't care if we eat with the horses as long as you sit next to me. I am tired of all this pomp."

"Not overcome?

"No. It seems so artificial, not at all of the land."

"I can't believe that we are here as witnesses. Who would have ever thought it?"

"Will you regret going back to Montoren?" His throat tightened. Montoren had little to offer compared to this manse in Lambere.

"Certainly not! This is fine for a new experience, exciting and heady. At heart, though, I am content with my position. Montoren is peaceful and beautiful. Besides, the garden needs my attention."

"Was Alfred at the Coronation?"

Her eyes slid away from his and her face reddened in embarrassment. "Yes. He sat atop the screen behind us. He must have had a spectacular view from there."

"And you've had no dreams or visions?"

"Yes I have, but I don't know what they mean. One persists though. Drew, you must give your stave to Warrick."

"Give my stave..." His lips closed, clipping off his next words. Vesper looked at him with eyes that reminded him of clear mountain water running over moss-covered river rocks. Such action would be a sacrilege to the clan. He considered Vesper's serious expression then glanced away.

She had accepted him believing he had nothing, knowing nothing about him, expecting only hard work and little advantage. What she had given him was honesty and time. He had given her a love tainted with secrets and a Clan's dislike. Now she knew herself a duke's daughter, able to have anything she desired. He had no bride gift. Kuff didn't count. He knew she thought of the horse as his, and always would. He bit his lower lip. Even if his clan shunned him, this one sacrifice he would make as a gift to her. "All right." His voice sounded gruff and ill-pleased, not at all what he wished to convey.

"At the banquet, with the gifts of the earth upon the table. That's what I see."

"Let me think on that."

~ * ~

He felt awkward and conspicuous, but Vesper bespoke Selwyn and the next thing he knew, the Earl of Rikon told him he could speak before the blessing. He felt a nagging irritation with his beloved.

"And do you have words for me to say, too?"

"You are the Aegis. The words will come to you." She had accepted it so easily like she expected it. Even when she made him uneasy and angry, he could do nothing but please her.

So he stood before the food-laden table, before Warrick and the loyal aristos of his Court. They stared at him with curiosity and expectation etched on their faces. "Your Highness," he said, and stopped to gaze at the floor, baffled at what to say. Soft murmuring started. His gaze rose to meet Warrick's.

"Your Highness, I cannot swear fealty to you for I was given in fealty to Vere generations ago. My family has honored their oath to King Ewald III. Instead of an oath, I give you my clan stave to represent my family's continuing oath to Vere, to the protection of the land, and to the protection of Kaereya."

Warrick rose with both hands extended and accepted the stave like it was a treasure beyond reckoning rather than carved Vere hardwood with a simple pewter cap.

He bowed to his king in deep respect, saying, "King Warrick, may Kaereya prosper under your rule." He backed away from Warrick and returned to Vesper amid a chorus of cheers. He looked about him. Even Clan Chief Terril and all clansmen pounded their staves on the marble floor, the drumming echoed through the high vaults overhead. He swore then and there, to believe Vesper's visions, even when they involved unthinkable actions or even the unseen Alfred.

~ * ~

"How does your gift work?" the Earl of Rikon asked. Selwyn, the clan chiefs, aristos, Aurelias, and King Warrick listened. For several hours the group had poured over the problems of repelling the Pertelonese and retaking Hawk Island.

"It's hard to explain, but I know how the land feels. When something is wrong or out of place, it feels like clothing that has twisted funny or become too tight. Sometimes, I can feel the animals that live on it, feel their fright at intruders. It worked better when I had many cousins and my parents around. When so many of my family died, it became more difficult. Now different clans help. We have formed a watch of the borders."

"What do you do?"

"Most often, I urge the land to action. Use it against intruders. Vere's landscape is easy. Landslides develop from moving a single rock. Swollen streams cause fierce floods. When that doesn't work, facing an army of armored clansmen usually does. The great Vere Rift keeps such incursions to a minimum."

"Have there been many incursions into Vere?" Warrick asked.

"Once or twice a year, thieves mostly. My grandfather repulsed Cygnese efforts. Every so often a Sunderlune city tries.

"Can you do this in Easure?"

"No." Clan Chief Terril answered. He stood foursquare with his arms folded on his chest. "Through all the years, no Aegis has done such a thing. They get land sick out of their own provinces. The last time Drew left Vere, he was carried back, too ill to stand. We feared for his life. It's how we knew he had the gift."

"Drew is here in Wessure with no ill effects," Aurelias said.

"Your pardon, but it's the girl. Got him fair distracted."

"Is that true?" Warrick asked, disappointment lacing his voice.

Drew hesitated. "It's different than before."

"What is different?" Selwyn asked.

"This land, I can feel it. As a child part of my illness was an inability to feel the land. It was like losing my sight or hearing. Now, the taste of Wessure lingers on my tongue, its texture and its fragile nature. I don't know how to use it, not like Vere. It is too different. Of Easure, I am not sure I can do anything to be of help."

"Your presence will be enough. The people scream for their Aegis," Norbert said.

"I am not their Aegis."

"It will not matter."

Eighteen

Ottillie watched the way the tribesmen assented to Aldous's every wish, containing her excitement. Even Leander accepted his Aegis's desire to travel without a blink. They were to take camels in a direct line through the desert to Gotte City.

When she asked him about his forbearance, Leander told her, "He never asks for much. For him to ask to leave Kennetsure means the endeavor at hand is very historic. It is up to the rest of us to lessen the danger for him."

"This is more important than fighting Pertelon invaders?"

The Zekarac Knight's eyes followed the activity in the courtyard. "More news came. Warrick has been crowned at Aristo Aurelias' seat at Lambere. Quillon reports the Vere clansmen and their Aegis are there.

"That means they must plan on fighting. But I thought an Aegis could not leave his Province."

"Only if willing to endure land sickness. One of the animals carries desert soil. The Aegis have strong bonds with their land, but not unbreakable."

"But won't the people panic if they know he leaves Kennetsure?"

"No, Lady Ottillie. They already realize when he is gone, Kennetsure will never have another Aegis. They grieve already but are willing to give Aldous all the freedom he desires."

Ottillie stared at him, always surprised at the Kennetsurean's even temper. To take two septuagenarians on an arduous journey, and though an invading army was no small task and required some fortitude.

Leela laughed at her expression. "It has been many years since we've traveled, Ottillie, but I haven't forgotten how. Don't worry, I've insisted they take the route through the Great Salt Marsh because you hate boat travel."

Leander's lips quivered in a suppressed grin.

"Although," Leela said in disgust, "there is enough water there, that it nearly makes no difference. No, no, don't bury that in a pack, I don't want to have to dig for it later."

Leela's white head wove between the working men as she helped them re-pack things properly. It often took two or three attempts to get one camel packed. When departure finally came, nine camels stretched out along the trail from the lead animal.

Each day of the return journey Ottillie worried they would run into Pertelon troops, wondered how Leander planned to avoid the invading troops, and agonized over Eldin. The Royal Guardsman had ridden directly into the oncoming forces. She prayed he brought warning soon enough, and that the Holy One preserved him. She rode next to Leander with Leela and Aldous safely surrounded by tribesmen.

"You worry overmuch, Lady Ottillie."

"You find nothing to worry about?"

"Not for a while. Even then, we shall prevail. You forget we ride with the Aegis of Kennetsure."

"What about the river ferry?"

"We will cross the Southern Thou safely." He gave her a grin that did not lessen her anxiety.

Ten leagues from Gotte City, Leander said, "A storm approaches, put on your talma."

"We have company," she said, pointing.

"I see them. Do as I say."

Alarmed, but unwilling to show it, she wrapped the long cape with its fitted head cap around her. They continued until a handful of Pertelon's cavalry stopped them.

"State your business," the uniformed leader said.

"We are a trade caravan making for Gotte City."

"You must submit to a search before you go further." He needed to curb his horse, skittish in the gusts of wind, to stay in place. The other riders also had trouble with their animals.

"That would not be in either of our best interests, Captain." As Leander spoke a blast of sand whirled about them like stinging whips.

"Are you threatening us, desert scum?" The officer's horse pranced in place and worked at his bit under the man's tight control. Ottillie saw the white of fear circling the creature's eyes.

Leander laughed. "No indeed, Captain. The Lady Doane does that." He spread a hand behind him. "A storm out of the southern desert comes."

Feeling the wind, Ottillie looked in the direction Leander indicated. Behind them a brown cloud rose, hiding the horizon. It rose to lofty heights, rapidly covering the sun. In the sudden overcast sky, the wind-carried sand that bit her skin and eyes. The Pertelonese were not prepared, and the officer, after giving Leander a fright-lined look promising future retribution, turned his horse and galloped off with a few shouts from his following squad.

"They cannot outrun the storm," Leander said. He indicated she move her camel forward and took the reins from her.

Ottillie flipped the hood over her head and arranged the face netting, tucked it into the front collar, and pulled the last layer down over her eyes and nose. Then the storm hit with savage fury, battering her body with fierce blows. Her camel moved forward, and through the thin fabric, she could see the hind end of the animal leading hers. Her eyes blinked and watered from the sting of the sand. With agonizing slowness, the trip continued through the wail of the wind, although the storm's full strength never hit them.

The intensity of the storm lessened as they reached the outskirts of Gotte City. Although the sand and wind still gusted about, it no longer bore the stinging load of grit. She pulled down the cloth covering her eyes and felt the sand slide away from the folds of her mouth scarf. Taking a deep breath of air through her grit-lined mouth and nose, she looked about her. No cavalry rode near them.

"Horses do not withstand desert storms well," Leander said, noticing her searching gaze.

Inside the city, she realized he took them to what must be a prearranged location. As her camel passed through doors, Ottillie found Leander had brought them to shelter. As he helped her dismount her camel, drifts of sand fell from her talma.

"Welcome to the Aegis's magic," he said and strode away.

She removed the hood and shook more sand from her hair and clothes, still trying to blink her eyes free of irritants. The Aegis Aldous looked exhausted despite his triumph. He smiled at Ottillie. They were all in a huge warehouse. Leander gave orders. Men led the camels away, and she could hear the neighing of horses in the background.

"How do we get out of the city and onto the ferry?" Ottillie asked Leander who watched his Aegis. Like all his tribesmen he wore an expression of concern.

"We don't. Pertelon troops think they hold the city and have guards at the bridge. We cannot expose Aldous to such danger."

"We go back, then?"

Leander finally looked at her, an irrepressible amusement expressed in his eyes. "Of course not. We will take the tunnel."

"Tunnel?"

"Yes. A remnant from before the Cataclysm. We gain access from this building. We will rest here for this night. At full dark tomorrow night, we continue our journey. So I beg you to rest now."

With a motion of his hand a woman approached, she bowed her head, smiled, and took Ottillie's talma, and bid her follow. She led Ottillie to a small bedroom. Ottillie blinked continuously, cleansing her eyes. She thanked the woman as she wiped the moist grime from her face. "May I wash first?"

"Certainly, Lady Ottillie. We are honored to have you stay with us."

"Who is we?"

"Another of the Aegis's Doane tribes living here in Gotte City. We are gratified and honored to provide service."

"But the Aegis did not protect you from an invasion."

"The Aegis Aldous is very old and the loss of both Seward and Ward Aegises has weakened the Great Chloe's spell. Plus, Aldous is a gentle person. He did not wish to send tribesmen against a much greater force. Instead, he sent a warning and helped us prepare. Sometimes the strongest defense is the least resistance. Pertelon only thinks she has invaded Kennetsure, as her troops found out today during the storm." She looked at Ottillie. "Many troopers lost their way and never returned. May the Holy One keep their souls. The Lady Doane is a harsh mistress."

Ottillie returned her look. "Only those who know the land should try to claim it."

"Come, Lady Ottillie, we have a washroom, although I would have preferred to take you to the baths in my house, it is too dangerous for you to get there through the city. There are Pertelon troops in our streets."

The washroom was adequate. Wrapped in the long, thin drying robes common in Kennetsure, Ottillie eased into her pallet with a contented sigh and slept.

~ * ~

They all carried torches and led horses except Leela, who walked with a hand on a tribesman's arm. Aldous followed Ottillie carrying a torch. Ottillie found the sand filled-bottom of the tunnel easy enough to walk, although her steps often took her through ankle-deep water. The tunnel sides curved, proving the growth hanging from the roof hid a spherical form. The dark bands of roots that lined the fissured walls of the tunnel undulated as the wet surfaces alternately reflected and absorbed the light of the torches marching past the ancient material. A remnant of the Cataclysm Leander had told her.

Sounds of running water mingled with the sounds of water falling drop by drop. The sounds scared Ottillie. Fright laced her blood, made her believe those noises, so loud and persistent, must be a prelude to a deluge of drowning water. Water to claim her as it had her mother.

"Lady Ottillie, move ahead, why have you stopped?" Someone shouted from behind. Leander stopped and looked back at her, but Ottillie couldn't take another step. A hand took hers.

"It is all right, Ottillie. I won't let it cave in. It is just dark and wet." Aldous soft voice spoke near her ear.

"That night." Her voice broke and she bit her lip.

"Yes. Just like that night, and you survived. Come, I have your hand."

A deep breath shook her. "Thank you, Aegis Aldous, but I will do this on my own."

"There is no need." He kept hold of her hand and walked.

Leander had turned and moved forward. She tightened her grip on Aldous's hand, grit her teeth, and focused her sight on the back of Leander's head as he led them into the cold dark.

It took forever. Her boots squelched in years of accumulated muck and the cold water deadened her toes. The wet edges of her trews clung to her legs. It all added to her terrorized discomfort. She would scream soon, and bit the sides of her cheeks, afraid to make any noise. Even the taste of blood didn't ease her jaw's tight grip.

She tripped on her next step and caught herself before she fell. Her horse threw its head back saving her balance. Her next step also hit the ground before she expected. It took a moment to realize she walked up an incline.

"See? We are on the ramp. Soon we will be out of here." Aldous's words filled her with hope.

Relief poured through Ottillie. Optimism buoyed her flagging spirits. Before long she saw light ahead and thanked the Holy One for seeing her through the tunnel. Aldous let go of her hand with one soft pat. As she walked the steep incline to safe land, embarrassment flooded her. Once on firm ground in the warm daylight, she stepped quickly to pull her horse forward and out of the way of others escaping the chilly depths. With a deep breath, she sank to the spongy tall grass. When she opened her eyes, she looked around her. Although she could hear the Thou River not far away, it was out of sight behind the huge trees and shrubs of Slip Island.

"Feel better?" Leela asked.

"Yes. You heard?"

"It's uncomfortable for most of us used to the openness of the Doane. Get dry clothes and come warm yourself by the fire. It is always so much colder here. Dampness, you know."

Someone had pulled logs and rocks around the fires, as more than one had been lit. Ottillie sat on a log and started removing her boots. She smelled the coffee before Leander offered her a cup.

"Be careful, it's hot." He sat on a rock opposite her and smiled his gracious smile. His deep eyes laughed at her. "See? It was easy. We are safe here. Tribesmen watch, as do the inhabitants of the Great Salt Marsh. Rumors spread about this fierce and strange marshland, its hidden traps of swallowing sand and carnivorous plants. Even Pertelonese fear this side of the river. Now we can have fun. You will enjoy the hunting here."

"Is Aldous all right? Not land sick?"

"Aldous feels the twinges of the journey but Leela has sewn packets filled with desert soil and filled his pockets. He does fine. Leela says something in the spell has changed that eases his leaving Kennetsure."

~ * ~

Leaving the ninth war council in as many days, Warrick stopped Drew with a touch on his sleeve. "Clansman Montoren, may I speak with you?" Warrick had watched the serious young man for several days. He envied the Aegis, so little older than himself, envied him his wife and the loyalty given him. Yet, he saw too, the constraints put on him that he accepted with tolerance and occasional anger, but mostly humor. The same restraints Warrick had rebelled against so hard and shucked so easily. Montoren had lost his family, too, and now carried the burden of his birth. Before leaving Hawk Island he would have laughed at Drew Montoren, laughed at the concept of an aegis. Now he hoped the stories true. Unsure of what he wanted, Warrick only knew he needed to talk.

Those with the Aegis stopped, as did Warrick's entourage of guards and courtiers.

"In private?" Warrick asked. At Drew's nod, the clansmen melted away. "In my room?" Warrick's Royal Guardsmen followed them, stationing themselves outside the door. With a hand, Warrick indicated two chairs set in a window enclosure. He watched the clansman sit in uneasy caution. Warrick settled himself, unsure how to start. Without volition, words came. "You lost your parents."

"Yes, several years ago."

"Norbert says it was probably part of the same conspiracy that killed my parents."

"The Earl of Rikon?"

"Yes." He bit his lip, unsure. "He thinks a hidden army has been slowly destroying Kaereya for decades."

Drew Montoren seemed to know what he wanted to hear. "For a long time, I felt their death was my fault."

"You did? Why? How did they die?"

"My father took my mother on a trip to west Vere. I stayed at Montoren, studying. The aegises of the North and South have always kept close ties. A shipment of gifts from the south had just arrived. Aldous, the Aegis of the South, had sent me materials to study and I was anxious to start. When my parents did not arrive at one of the clan strongholds, clansmen went searching for them. They were found at the bottom of a ravine with their escort, taken by a landslide, but I already knew by then."

"How? Wasn't your father an Aegis?"

"No. My Grandfather was the previous Aegis, but I should have known. I knew it wasn't natural. Felt it when it happened, knew something was wrong. I felt them die."

Warrick watched tears roll down the cheeks of the Aegis's still face. "I was wild with rage and grief. The clans helped me find those responsible. I destroyed them, not thinking, I killed them before I found out why."

"You must have been very young."

"Old enough to use common sense. The attack seemed so senseless. Terril and the other clan chiefs took the men for robbers."

"At least you brought your family justice. How could it have been your fault?"

"I had not taken up my responsibilities. My Grandfather still lived, although very old. My father's death, I'm sure, hastened his own. I did not watch and listen to the land. If I had, I would have sensed the presence of those who did not belong. So you see, unlike you, it truly was my fault."

"If I had not run away to get out of handfasting someone I didn't wish to..."

"You would probably be dead. The attack was well planned. In fact, I'm surprised they carried it through when you went missing."

"Norbert said I was to be the scapegoat, blamed for the horrible events, then show up dead myself, unable to contest the lie. Whoever planned it did not plan well enough to guess Norbert would remain loyal to me, or at least to my father, or that Aurelias would give me his staunch support. I made many dislike me with stupid pranks and universal disrespect. Even if my family's death can't be laid on me, the death of my cousin can."

"He died protecting his king. He knew by then what you were, so it became his duty. As king, you must prepare yourself to see many supporters die. It is not necessarily for you, but for what you represent."

"As the clans do for you?"

"Yes."

"Was it hard?"

"To accept the limitations such commitment puts on you? To never be able to do something without involving many others? I have done so twice. Once to Handfast Vesper, the next to bring my horses here. You see the results."

"To be watched and treated like some precious jewel or helpless child?"

"It is always hard. I suspect it will remain hard to the end of my life. At least Vesper does not do it. To her, I am just Drew."

"You are lucky in your choice. I think I may have ruined my chances with the one I now want." He swiped his hand across his trews and changed the subject. "What do you think of our plans to retake Hawk Island and Anatole Island?"

"We know Orveka's walls held against the Pertelonese, stopped them from taking the Little Steps to Hawk Island, so there is hope there, but I think Norbert puts too much emphasis on the general population rising to the flag of an aegis. As to Hawk Island, we don't know yet if the Regent will uphold your rule."

"More aristos arrive daily to pledge their faith to me, but not a word from my uncle." Warrick looked out the window at the troops practicing in the surrounding fields. "They come because of Norbert and Aurelias' reputations... and the rumors of your presence. If the Earl of Rikon is right and the remaining aristos fall into line and swear fealty, I think we have a chance. I think Aurelias and Norbert know more of this than I."

"To send merchant shippers to plug the end of the South Thou River was inspired. The merchants know their livelihoods are challenged if Pertelon takes the ocean ports and will therefore be diligent in protecting the ports. It will save you men and ships needed elsewhere. I know Aldous will make the enemy's trip through Kennetsure and the Southern Thou difficult."

Warrick glanced at the other man. "You don't seem pleased with your long-earned but new-found fame."

His Aegis gave a mocking smile. "Mostly, I've had to keep my existence secret. To bear a banner is a new experience. Now I am to carry two. My new father-in-law has seamstresses making them as we speak. They even make one as if I were the Seward Aegis for when the army enters Easure."

~ * ~

Vesper woke with a start. Drew was already gone. In a panic that the army might have already left, she hurriedly dressed. Last night Drew and her father had finally agreed on something. She would be left behind in the care of Quillon and with her bodyguard, Kissre. Memory of her visions quickened her steps down the hall and staircase.

She was halfway through the main hall when she saw the servants still carried baggage to the wagons. Time, she had time, they had not left. Slowing her rushing feet, she swept her hair into neatness, flipping the loose strands behind her shoulders and arranged her clothing to neatness. Dizziness overcame her and she stopped.

She stood in a room full of threads hanging from an unseen ceiling, as though she walked through a series of giant looms. A breeze blew through them, tangling some and lightly shifting others like grass in wind. Each thread made a distinct noise, a note that added to a harmonious melody. She could not see through the threads and there was no clear way through or out. She heard Drew calling her, needing her. "Which one?" she asked. A woman sat there, her hands and body moving as she twisted threads onto a spindle.

"All are true, only one is true. Choose."

Vesper touched a shiny filament. A muddied and road-worn rider entered the hall at Lambere. Coming down the stairs in a fine chemise and surgown, Vesper took his message. As she broke the seal blood wept from the wax. The few droplets coalesced into a trickle that became a stream flooding.

"Lady Vesper," a voice broke through her stupor. "Lady Vesper, are you all right?" It was Kissre addressing her. "You stopped so suddenly and looked so terrified." The woman apologized for touching her, then her look turned to one of temper-ridden patience.

Embarrassment flooded Vesper's cheeks as she realized she stared at her bodyguard. The woman's face hardened into implacable lines.

"I... Yes, I'm fine. I just suddenly realized why they are going. The thought of losing a husband as well as so newfound a father, took my breath away. That is all." Lies. Truth, but presented as lies to hide her secret. In her haste Vesper had been unaware of the guard's presence.

The vision was so strong, so vivid. She must travel with Drew. She must. She would not stay here to receive news of his death. At the door she walked across the portico to look over the stone balustrade at the bustling courtyard below her. The men had not mounted yet. As she turned, the servants exited the lower arch entryways with steaming cups. At the bottom of the steps she took a tray from one of the servants and walked first to Selwyn, offering good wishes and safety, then she gave her father one of the cups. The duke had already mounted. "Good journey, Father, I pray you every success."

"Thank you, daughter."

Vesper looked up in surprise at the choked emotion she heard in his voice and added, "May the Holy One protect you. I would welcome seeing you very soon." Dizziness gripped her and she put a hand on his knee. With a sigh, she smiled. She saw him, far in the future, an old man with children around him. Then the vision changed, and he was just a lonely old man.

"What do you see?"

"That you will live a long life."

"You did not look happy about it."

She gave him a faint smile. "The future is uncertain, and I don't have the knack for true prediction."

"And I could be happy or unhappy?"

"Our lives are entangling in so many ways. Please take care of yourself. Promise me to take care of Drew?"

He nodded. "To know you safe here will relieve both of our minds."

She smiled and took the last cup to Drew. Everyone was mounted now. Tears sprang into her eyes. "I should be going with you. I know I should. Please let me come."

"Not this time. I won't endanger you in Easure's doings. Wish me well."

"As you, I am already part of it." She smiled. "Good journey, Drew." She watched him take a sip of the stirrup cup. "Come back to me..." She gasped and dropped the tray to hang onto his stirrup and knee. The world whirled around her.

"Don't cry, Vesper, please don't cry."

"Don't dismount, boy, it's bad luck. She's only unhappy." Clan Chief Terril spoke, his hand waving at the woman guard Aurelias put in charge of his daughter. "Here, you," he indicated Kissre with a hand. "Take the Lady away."

Vesper clung to Drew's leg in the center of her own maelstrom. She felt Kissre's hand on her wrist, gently disengaging her clasp.

~ * ~

Several leagues down the road, as the column reached the split in the road, Norbert looked at Aurelias who rode next to him. "Did you believe her?" He stopped his horse while a wagon on the northern road turned their way traveling west. The driver was ordered to pull off the road to allow the cavalcade to progress.

"I don't know. Her mother never divined."

"I hope she is not wrong."

"What are you talking of?" Warrick asked from where he rode before them. He held his horse until theirs moved beside his.

"Your majesty did not hear?" Norbert asked. His mount sidestepped as Aurelias' horse turned before his and started to take the northern fork in the road.

"No, I did not hear. Of whom do you speak?"

"The Aegis's wife, she prophesied as we left," Norbert said, urging his mount forward.

"Vesper? What did she say?"

"She told her husband," Norbert said, "that as he crossed Kaereya, he would become the land."

Aurelias broke in. "My daughter is a seer, as was her mother."

Norbert looked at his friend who only stared straight ahead. "She will survive, Raymond, you need not worry. She is deeper based and better balanced than Lorelei ever was."

"There was nothing wrong with Lorelei," Aurelias said, frowning at Norbert.

"I didn't say there was. But Vesper has inherited your level head, and I fear, from what you've said, your stubbornness. Even you must admit Lorelei was a flighty will-o'-the-whisp."

Aurelias didn't answer except for a disgruntled huff.

"Is it true? Have you asked him? Have you asked Drew?" Warrick asked. "Indeed, my mother told me an ancient story about an Aegis of Kaereya to come."

Norbert turned to look at Warrick and noted even Raymond turned in surprise at the king's intimate use of Drew's name. Another glance showed Warrick holding up, but the King's Marshal decided they would need to rest soon.

"He said he could feel Wessure," Warrick said. "He is riding with Selwyn and the clan chiefs, is he not? Have him join me and we shall find out."

"I doubt he can tell you anything, Sire, until we enter Easure."

"He should be riding with me anyway. Ask him to come forward."

~ * ~

Half the day after the men's leaving, Vesper spent brooding in her room constantly interrupted by servants inquiring for her needs. She had only one, and they could not fulfill it. By late afternoon, she started planning. Two days passed before she found an opportunity to initiate her plan. Luckily, her father's people expected her to act like a proper duke's daughter, not a hoyden in Eudora's well-ingrained disguise.

Kissre took her job seriously as did the man Quillon. She held a niggling grudge against him for his actions in Norost's market. At her recognition, he had apologized. Neither he nor Kissre let Vesper out of sight until they felt assured that she had accepted staying. Of the two, Kissre was the most intimidating. While slightly older than herself, taller, and when not frowning, attractive, Vesper had never seen so disciplined and militant-looking a woman.

Her father's housekeeper chose the next day to show her around the manor. Vesper supposed, with Duke Aurelias and all his company gone, there was now time for the tour. She also suspected Quillon ordered the staff to keep her occupied, but she learned a great deal about her father's house and asked many questions. Alfred joined them, pensive in his close inspection of the buildings and grounds. She asked to see all the outbuildings, the kitchens, the stables, barns, and sheds. Only Alfred, frowning in curiosity, noticed her thefts, and of course, he said nothing.

The next day, just before sunrise she rose and put on the old blue riding clothes she wore from Vere, and a pair of boots found in the stable's tack room, worn and a little large but wearable. She arranged her clothing the closest she could to Wessure fashion. Inside a heavy, felt shawl she tied journey necessities. At the last moment she added a small silver candlestick, a few inconsequential bangles, all found in her room, and a flint strike stolen from the kitchen. She dropped it out the window and hoped its thud went unnoticed. She tied a rope borrowed from the stables in the previous day's thefts around her waist. After threading the rope through the legs of her room's massive armoire, she lowered herself out her window. Once on the ground she pulled the rope free and hid it behind the shrubs.

With the old shawl wrapped around her head and shoulders, her chemise pockets filled with food, she quietly slipped away in the disorder of those coming and leaving the manor for their day's work. Finding Alfred following her caused no surprise.

She walked for leagues refusing offers of rides in passing wagons. Near noon she came to a fork in the road. She headed down the southern fork toward Easure. When finally too tired to walk, she stopped for the night under a tree some distance from the road. In the dark she rummaged in pockets for packets of cheese and bread, then wrapped in the shawl, settled for the night.

Waking to the creak of a passing wagon, Vesper took a moment to comprehend her surroundings. She groaned as she stretched and tried to rise. After the previous day's walk, her feet hurt. Pained her enough she didn't think she could go much further. Luck was with her. A tinker passed her, stopped to ask her of her needs and where she was going. "My mother is grave ill, and I must journey several days down the road to take care of her."

"Climb up then, a companion and talk will make the journey shorter."

She rode with him for the day. For the next few days, offers of rides came easily. After the first time, the lie came easier and she often embellished on it. Each time she uttered her lie, she felt Alfred's eyes drill a hole between her shoulders. It was only by chance she saw the driver of her last ride talking to what she recognized as a King's Constable, showing the officer her bracelet and her small bag of trading goods. How had he found them? He thought her a thief! A servant girl who had stolen from her mistress. Appalled, Vesper opened her mouth to protest, but quickly snapped it shut.

They would stop her, and she could not allow that. As afraid of being caught as any thief, she backed away. Scooting between two buildings, she passed a small service yard lined with laundry, animal pens, and a slop pit, and escaped toward a nearby wood. Gaining that protective shelter, she ran in frenzied panic; ran until her lungs felt near to bursting. She stopped, her chest pounding, wondering which way to go when the ground beneath her feet crumbled and fell away.

~ * ~

The change crept into Drew's awareness so gradually he hardly noticed it, overcome with worry over Vesper. Only Selwyn's grab on Kuff's bridal had kept him from returning after hearing the message Quillon sent. He had tried to sense her, scouring the land, but it was too large, too unfamiliar; still, he concentrated. Then the strangeness took over, pulling him out of himself, out of the recognizable world. He thought he called for Selwyn before all reality dissolved, but it was too late if he had. Water pushed his falling body, caught him in strong currents and eddying whirlpools from which he could not escape, filled his screaming mouth with suffocating liquid and his ears with a pounding pressure. He sank through thick weeds, slime, and muddy sediment. His weighted body cut through the gossamer layers of rock like a honed knife.

An eternity later he hit a hard edge of insufferable heat and felt himself melt over its scalding surface. He writhed at the agonizing pain, at the heavy weight crushing him. His body dissolved, destroying sinew and thought until only an immense, incredibly fine jelly remained, a translucent, pliable extract of Drew.

Curiously, as he thought he would vanish, he felt himself rise like a cloud blown by the wind, distorted by drafts, lighter than air. Up through granite, shale, and sandstone, through all that made up the land of Kaereya and beyond it. He became only a mere point of existence but absorbed all.

His senses took over. He felt the textures of the soil over the breadth of his awareness, smelled the odors of the earth, tasted its range of sweet, savory, bitter, and salty zests, saw its spectrum of shimmering colors, heard the vibrations of movement as a majestic song. Air caught and lifted him. Higher and higher he rose until the world's surface lay far below him. Faint and feathery clouds floated through him bringing soft gusts of cold, sweet scents.

Spectacular below him in blue, green, and brown beneath swirls of white frosting, lay his home. Awe choked him. While he watched, mesmerized by the sight, his body and mind calmed, seeming to accept his unnatural position. Only the steady rhythm of his heartbeat disturbed the quiet. Slowly that beat conquered sensation. It dominated his awareness.

He felt his body reshape, regain its weight and shape. Fear followed. "No, no, not now." With his plummet, he screamed.

"Drew! Drew!" Selwyn's voice yelled in his ear. "He is coming round."

"Land sickness?"

Drew tried to remember that voice.

"Not like any I've seen!" That was Selwyn, upset.

The more anxious Selwyn became the louder he got. Drew smiled within his daze, accepting his return to reality. For a few minutes other voices droned like an angry buzz in the back of his mind.

"Stop yelling," he managed at last. With his remaining strength, he opened his eyes. Selwyn's face filled his vision. As his cousin moved back, another came into view. Recognition. The Duke of Aurelias. His father-in-law. Vesper. "Has she been found?" he asked.

With the negative answer, he told them, "Let me sleep. I'm tired." His eyelids dropped.

"You've slept for near the whole day. Don't fall back asleep."

"Not sleeping. Visiting."

"What did he say? Visiting? Do you think he hallucinates?"

"I don't know."

"Visiting the land. Different. Scary. Glad to be..." Drew took a soft breath and awareness faded.

By the next morning he felt better, embarrassed at holding up the king's army for so long, but remained unwilling to articulate his experience to anyone. The overwhelming sense of the land remained and kept extending his perception. A new pain struck him with sudden violence. Vesper. With all he felt, he was too distant to feel her. Alone and no one knew where with only a woman guard tracking her. He had seen a reflection of his anguish in Aurelias' face. Duty kept them both from turning back. "Quillon is right," Aurelias had said last night when Drew finally awoke and asked after her. "It is safer for Vesper with only one rider following her."

"Where are we?" His hands held a silver cup bearing a ducal crest. The hot cider was laced with clan aqua vitae. He crouched before a morning fire. The warmth felt good, the spirits poured heat into his gut. Coming from his tent, he had found Selwyn arguing with Aurelias' servants about packing the camp and saddling their mounts. Selwyn broke off and offered him the drink.

"We crossed into the Step Islands of Easure just before you took ill." He looked around at the tall reeds and water grasses surrounding the sporadic placement of tents with distaste. "They tell me this place is called Left-Together Island. Will you be able to ride today?" He placed Drew's saddle on Kuff's broad back not really needing to be answered.

"Yes. I must go and apologize to King Warwick. He did not need to stop the army on my behalf."

Selwyn continued saddling Kuff.

"I could saddle my horse."

Selwyn snorted. "I'm lucky to be allowed to saddle our horses. Warrick has been to your tent as often as Aurelias. He wants to believe Vesper's prediction has come true, half believes you suffer land sickness, which means it won't, or worse that you're going to die of some illness before saving his kingdom."

"And Aurelias?"

An amused smile cracked Selwyn's tired face. "He's afraid he might have to tell his daughter he allowed her husband to die, and in between worries about finding her."

"I'm not dying, but do wish I'd let Vesper come, even as much as I've no wish for her to see me like this."

"What is like this?" Selwyn's attention seemed riveted on checking bridle straps, girths, and buckles.

"I'm not sure. It happened. The adjustment is difficult."

"Not land sickness?"

Drew gave a weak chuckle. "Yes, land sickness, but sickness of overmuch rather than lack. I don't want this, it is too much, too overpowering."

"How much do you feel?"

He read the hidden, contained look in Selwyn's face from old. It was unfair. The one burden he longed to share and couldn't, was what another craved so much. "Too much, too far. It frightens me."

"Can you use it?"

"In time, perhaps. Right now, I can barely live with it."

~ * ~

The steep embankment dropped to a shallow river. Sliding, she could not stop her plummet into the water. Gasping as her head broke the surface, Vesper found her feet could touch the bottom. In sodden chagrin she waded to the river's edge where Alfred lay, crumpled in a laughing heap. It was the first time she had heard his voice since she was ten.

Standing in the shallow water, begrimed and bedraggled, she didn't step on the shore. The gravel-lined edges of the small stream would hide her footprints and the thick shrubs lining the shore would be impossible to walk. She followed the river until assured of her escape. With cold-stiff fingers she gathered kindling and wood and started a fire with the flint striker found in her pocket. Wrapped only in her shawl she hung her clothes on sticks near the fire to dry while she cast dire looks at Alfred, who became inflicted with laughter whenever he looked at her.

After another day, she conceded she was thoroughly lost. Appealing to Alfred brought no help. He only shrugged and looked as lost as herself. The days were warmer, but the landscape was far too different to be the right direction. It didn't matter. Communities existed by all rivers. Sooner or later she would come to one and get back on the right road. A day later the river broadened, and its current slowed in a vast expanse of grassy hummocks, willows, and a wild tangle of growth.

Twice her foot sank deep into the sandy muck and she pulled and crawled her way to firmer footing, terrified of becoming ensnared. More often, birds rose from close by in startling motion and noisy splashes.

"I am not afraid, I am not afraid," she muttered.

She came upon strange trees, their limbs growing downward into the water like huge stilts forming a living labyrinth of entangled trunks. Their tops hung in stringy entwined tendrils that looked more like roots than leafy branches. Insects swarmed about her head in irritating droves and others bit her unseen, her slap always too late. Humidity brought physical misery and the undrinkable salty water tantalized her parched throat. Fear gripped her then, and not only for herself. Visions showed the shield shattering. Drew needed her.

~ * ~

Chloe's Story

"Lady, you cannot keep on this way. All this traveling. Not even I can keep up and I'm thirty years younger!"

"I've sent a message to an old friend. Timing right now is important, Melissa, I want the Holy One's blessing. In a few days it is the third day of Sixth Month. With our year date, this is a holy convergence. A spell that needs the help of coincidence is a chancy thing, but Talent attracts Talent, and maybe with the Holy One's intercession this spell can be lured in the right direction."

Chloe was tired but refused to bow to her fatigue. "We've spent a year traveling, I will not give up yet, my bones are too old for a repeat performance."

Melissa sniffed. She was pregnant again from one of several indiscretions along the journey, and not well with it. "A bit of soil and blood in a box. I'm glad I haven't paid much attention to your lessons."

"It might work. The Aegises were willing to help. A secondary spell, a compelling, can be placed. Hope, Melissa, is sometimes a stubborn thing."

"Not more stubborn than you, Lady."

Their carriage stopped and a man uniformed in the Bishop's livery opened the door. He extended an arm to Chloe to help her. Once on the cobbled ground, she asked, "Please help my friend, she has been ill."

The man's eyes skittered from the stomach leading from the carriage to Melissa's middle-aged, but still comely face. His face remained impassive at Melissa's speculative grin and fluttering eyes.

Chloe sighed. A hand grabbed her arm, turning her.

"Aristo Chloe. It is good to see you." The Bishop's arms gave her a warm embrace of welcome.

"Just Chloe, please. It shall be hard to call you Bishop, now. You've always been Monsignor Otto to me." She sighed. "So many years have passed. Let me look at you." He was as gray as herself, and somewhat stooped in age. "Who would have guessed we would have lived so long?"

"The Holy One must still have need of us. I am interested to hear what brings you back to Cliff City."

"The hope that you would help me." He led her up the steps as they walked. She had not been in Aron Cathedral in years. It took longer for her eyes to adjust to the darkness of the interior. Looking around she saw it had not changed. "So beautiful," she whispered. The drone of voices and noises filtered through the vast expanse of the interior. The fragrance of incense lingered.

"I have rooms in a building off the west transept. It is faster to reach it through the cathedral. Tea waits for us."

Once in his rooms she settled into a chair, glad there was no one else involved. "Very nice rooms, too. I didn't know the clergy lived so lavish." He poured her a fine bowl of tea and she inhaled the brew's fragrance with satisfied pleasure.

He laughed. "The Holy One doesn't require I live like an ascetic, Lady Chloe, and little belongs to me. How is Charm Island?"

"Not quite so grand but comfortable enough. More than I expected, but the Holy One blessed my life there with much bounty." She saw a plate next to the pitcher of cider the Bishop preferred.

"Almond cakes! I haven't had any since leaving Charm Island."

"You have everything you need there?"

"My home is the veritable fertile plain. There are wonderful almond trees there. Anything we don't have is gifted. Of late, many Doane nomads have started journeying to my island. It is most disconcerting, but I am too old to put forth the effort needed to end it."

"But not too old for this last journey? You said in your last letter you had visited the four keeps."

"It has taken the better part of a year, but my mission is nearly finished."

"With this visit?"

Chloe gave him a sheepish smile. "Otto, I need your help to correct my mistake, and I fear church policy might prevent you from giving it."

"What do you need?"

"In old-fashioned terms, I need to cast a spell."

The Bishop sat back in his seat and stared at her. "Tell me."

"I have had a vision, how far in the future I don't know. It is only one of several. The only one to offer hope for the future." She told him of the vision, then her idea of how to compel the vision.

"It involves the present Aegises?"

"In a way. What I saw was the chance for one with their Talent to see all of Kaereya. I want to help make it happen."

"Lady Chloe..."

"It is possible! It is how I tied the Aegises to their provinces. A vector carried the needed change throughout their bodies. I developed it from something I learned while in Cygna."

"This will create the protection needed?"

"Only if circumstances are right, if someone with the bloodline touches the soil and with the Holy One's help, they somehow find it. It is a poor attempt, but it is all I could think to do."

"To complete your spell protecting Kaereya from war? That is a great goal, Chloe, but most likely impossible. And what you have described sounds very much like prohibited learning."

"I don't think so, I only used my mind Talent as the Cygnese call it, and natural substances like blood."

He sighed. "Since the last war, the cultivation of faith has diminished. People act more interested with the pleasures of the flesh rather than preserving the soul. I don't expect that to change."

"You're right. It is most likely impossible. Much is left to circumstance. This won't change anyone but those capable of sensing the land and those upon it. Hopefully, to help maintain peace, but who knows what the future might bring? The Aegis drawn will not be able to see into the hearts of those in charge of Kaereya, but he will sense the land of the whole country, perhaps even the essence of the people living upon it."

"Long before the Cataclysmic Centuries God visited us with a message of peace. Humankind has not always remembered the message."

Chloe snorted, then frowned. "Humankind has rarely followed any of his paths." At Bishop Otto's offended look, she added, "I am as guilty of sin as the next person. Age and isolation have removed my diffidence, but I did not mean to offend you."

"No," he said accepting her implied apology. "What you say is true. So you want to bury some soil in the sanctuary?"

"I want to feel like I fulfilled my promise to Ewald."

"I thought you already had. You set the Aegis Spell, didn't you?"

"The spell stands, but the Aegises are hardly remembered. The country remains imperiled. Strife can strike from within as well as without.'

"Strife," he said, "is the natural condition. Your spell doesn't give insight into or the means needed to change the hearts of anyone. How do you plan to change that?"

"Visions tell me of possibilities. Is it unholy that I might know what the future holds? That sometimes I see the different strands of likelihood? It has happened so little. I must try, Otto. I must." Chloe bit her lip. "This spell needs your blessing."

He looked at her in quiet study for an overlong moment. "Since your plan doesn't violate any religious tenet, I see no reason to refuse you."

Chloe rested all the next day, although actual sleep eluded her. At twilight, she and Melissa went to the Cathedral and waited until the monks finished their Nocturn. Their combined voices raised in prayer sent her into another short dream-vision. A fear-ridden world full of agitation and darkness and with a premonition of death. She gasped back into reality.

"Lady?" Melissa whispered. "Are you ill?"

"No, I'm fine, as much as I may be. I've been soul searching and questioning my motives. I think I want to go back to our room, Melissa."

"Too late, Lady, the Bishop is here."

The Bishop appeared before they could stand, indicating they should follow him in silence. He took them to a room to wait. Not much later he led them into the sanctuary. Without a word Melissa handed him two small, plain lead caskets, each with a star impressed on the lid.

At his expression, she said, "You can look inside. It is nothing profane. Only soil from the four provinces drenched in the blood of the four Aegises and the vector already spoken of."

Bishop Otto opened the box and looked at the fine as powder dried soil it contained. "How?" He looked very perplexed.

"It acts like an illness. The spell will live harmlessly in those boxes almost forever, until and unless the contents touch someone susceptible to the spell."

"How will they find them? And how do you control when they are found?"

"That is the Holy One's part of this spell," Chloe said. "It can happen. I've seen it. One man surrounded by the symbols of the four provinces. I only try to ensure it happens. Believe it will happen."

"Belief is a strong tool," the Bishop said and took the boxes to place them on the altar.

Chloe found it unnerving to listen to the mass performed in the empty cathedral. Most candles were already gutted. Those few alight, burned low, left at the altar from the last service. The Bishop presided alone. She and Melissa kneeled a short distance from the altar. Melissa had the foresight to bring pads to kneel on. Chloe was glad, not thinking of such needs, and knowing she could not have knelt so long without one.

The service ended. Bishop Otto handed Chloe one of the boxes. "You will find a place for the box?" she asked. "It must be hidden to stay intact for the future."

"It is already opened and waiting." He spread his hand and they saw. At the heart of the great Cathedral's transept, a block of stone had been pried from the floor and a small opening dug.

Alarm spread through Chloe. "You didn't dig this?"

"Hardly," he said. "I have monks who never ask questions." The women watched as he placed the casket he held at elbow's depth beneath the floor. Together the three of them pushed the soil back into the hole and moved the stone into place.

"I have listed this spot as taken and holy. No one can be buried here. The site will not be disturbed."

Chloe regarded the Bishop's face and knew he skittered a dangerous path for a Bishop. He understood her concern.

"I too, have had dreams, Sorceress Chloe. Sometimes, we can only rely on faith."

He gave Melissa a lantern and took one himself. "You have more work to do tonight, I know someone who wants to help you."

Chloe opened her mouth to protest but decided he was right and already this had spread beyond her control. She had to believe in her mission. He walked them all the way to the Eternal Palace, through the main gates and checkpoints without question. In the dark corridors of King's Hall, a woman stepped out of the shadows.

Shocked, Chloe stopped, nudged Melissa, and then curtseyed. "Queen Sophia." It was all for naught. This woman would not help her.

With a wave of her hand commanding silence, the old Queen mother approached. She nodded acknowledgment, then indicated they should follow. A short walk took them into the throne room.

Queen Sophia turned and whispered. "At this candlemark those night creatures of the court are preparing to leave for their rooms." Her eyes searched Chloe's face. "Sorceress Chloe, you look surprised to see me here. I know you do this for him. That is why I am helping you. We both loved him. You are the only one who would believe I knew you were coming and why. It has given me new hope."

Chloe felt tears threaten. They came much easier with age. Thankfully, the relative darkness of the room hid her anxious discomposure. "Your Highness, these many years I have regretted what happened, but the truth is, I had little say. When the king demands, his subjects obey. You know that. But I do beg your pardon for the injury I caused you."

The Queen gave a sad smile. "Do you think you were the only one? You at least tried to keep a semblance of secrecy, and I knew you were shamed by it. It was a humiliation, I expect, for both of us. Others have not treated me with as much courtesy or respect. In the end, I decided it made a difference. Your service to Kaereya, and to my Ewald, did more good than you ever committed evil, and I forgave you. You also did not linger in court once he dropped you, and you not only left the court but also the country. If I had considered your position, not poisoned other minds to you, and kept you at court, perhaps you could have saved the next king, my son Ewald." Her lips twisted in a bitter smile, and she took the small casket from Chloe's hands and smiled. "Do your magic, Lady."

"The magic is already in the box, Your Highness. I only wish time to meditate, and perhaps see the outcome of this casting."

There, in the presence of Melissa, Bishop Otto, and Queen Sophia, Chloe performed her last spell holding the box. They thought her creating magic, while she summoned a vision. What she said escaped her conscious mind, for something came over her tired being during her unawareness. What was left of her perception saw a vision perhaps, but somehow different. She saw many men sit here. King after king, each surrounded by Royal Guardsmen, aristos, intrigue, and trouble.

Vaguely she heard herself talking as if controlled by another's mind, "In the darkness of time, when chaos rules, let four in one complete the spell of five..." The room changed, and she felt not those near her, but other minds that hovered near, just out of reason's range. Other emotions and purposes dwelt there, including wickedness and evil. She sensed it. The malignancy swallowed the air and soiled it, wrapped around her body without touching it, undermining and subverting all. The sound of her chanting voice brought her back to her surroundings.

Finished, she sank to the floor.

"Chloe, are you all right?" Bishop Otto asked, propping her up against his knee.

"Yes, fine. I need to rest, just for a moment."

Queen Sophia drew a flask from a hidden pocket. "Here, sip this."

Chloe sputtered at the distilled drink and noted Melissa's expression of humor and appreciation.

"A practical Queen. I wished I'd served you when I was at court," her life's friend said.

A definite snort erupted from the old Queen. "No, you do not, you chose the right mentor. Age puts many things in perspective, even for a queen."

"What did you see?" Melissa asked Chloe. "Were we successful?"

"I pray so. I hope so. The box will be found. How far into the future, I cannot tell, only that our grandchildren and theirs shall not live to see it happen." She started crying.

"The box?" the Queen asked, picking it up from where it lay next to Chloe's hand. She looked at the five-pointed star engraved in the lid. "Five, the pivotal number of understanding, knowledge and truth. First number of time. How fitting."

"Also the number of hell, ignorance, bigotry, insanity, foolishness, concealment, secretiveness, and even impulsiveness," Chloe said. "Nothing is certain, is it?"

The Queen's eyes stared at her. "Bishop Otto said it held a talisman to protect the king?"

"To protect Kaereya. It must be hidden," Melissa said as Chloe was still too shaken to speak much sense.

"I have just the spot,"

Melissa followed the old Queen. "Here?" Chloe heard her say.

"Yes. The throne is going to be rebuilt soon, the new throne will encase this in stone. No one will ever know it is here."

The Bishop stayed with Chloe and listened to the other women.

Then he whispered to Chloe, "What did you see?"

"How do you know I've seen anything?"

"I saw it in your face."

"I saw mankind. There will be no king, and no Aegis left." She looked at her old friend. "Pray for this casting, even though I know such are often held unholy. There is much evil in this world."

Nineteen

Hunger and thirst drove her, but she continued to follow the flow of water. A stream seemed to carve through the swampy area. In the morning she licked the collected dew off the broad leaves of plants living between the tree roots. Constantly wet from the waist down, she rested on low tree trunks to dry, but it didn't help much. She now realized where she must be.

She looked at disgruntled Alfred. "Somehow we have wandered into the Great Salt Marsh, it can't be anything else. This is much farther south than the Stepping Islands." He glared at her.

The only consolation was Alfred found the going as hard as she did and with none of his kind around to help. Twice, in a sudden flashing twist of movement, jaws reached for the diminutive Alfred. Only his quick agility saved him. Each time, Vesper swallowed at her vulnerability and watched where she put each foot. She kept to the gravel-lined shallows outside the tree groves, where the footing was easier. High, dry grassy hummocks gave resting space. Still, occasionally, the stream flowed through one of the tangled groves of strange trees. Once her hand, touching a branch for balance, felt it slither away from her fingers. She screamed.

A short while later she heard something large moving behind her. Keeping as quiet as she could, she moved with careful stealth. No matter which way she went, the sound followed. Alfred looked as worried as she knew she felt. Stupid, so stupid. How could she not plan her route, know the way before she started? So shortsighted. She'd die here, and Drew would never know her whereabouts.

Her foot caught and twisted, tripping her. She plunged into the waist-deep water face first, in an ungainly plummet. Vesper tried turning to right herself, to get her face above water. The boot held her foot fast, locking it at an ungainly angle in the twisted roots. She thrashed in the water, unable to pull herself upright, and too deep to keep her head above water. Ominously, she heard another loud splash nearby.

Fear drove her underwater to tug at her foot. She came up gasping for air, hands flailing, and tried again. The wet laces of her boot were cinched tight. She yanked on her leg, bracing against the branch roots pulling on her foot. Burning lungs drove her to the surface. Twisting she went under and jerked again. Useless. Surfacing, she stared into huge, sharp-toothed jaws. A scream tore from her throat and she gagged, salty water filling her mouth. She went under a last time blinded by a flash of sunlight.

Her arms flailed in a final effort to ward off the danger. No jaws pierced her, and air hunger propelled her upward.

Her face broke the surface, and her eyes opened upon a drab-green snout next to her head. A sword hilt emerged from its crown, held by a hand and wrist etched in fine blue lines. A booted foot shoved the carcass aside, pulling the blade free of the creature with a dreadful sucking spurt. Hands followed her leg down beneath the water. In short order her foot was free, and Vesper grasped at her rescuer and nearby branches to pull herself upright.

Recognition came immediately; Kissre's frown intimidated more than usual. Wet blond-brown hair clung to her head. The strands drooped along her cheeks in lines as long as her frown. Clearly her bodyguard was in a massive rage as she jammed a long knife blade into the sheath at her waist. Sun glinted on the gold piercing her brow and ears, adding a primitive savagery to the incendiary temper. She spewed vitriolic denunciations at Vesper.

Recognition of some of the words pierced Vesper's recovering senses. Blushing furiously at the vulgarities, she judged it probably better she didn't understand all Kissre said. Alfred sat on a branch next to her grinning in idiotic pleasure.

"You are right. I've been vastly stupid. The last few days have proved that very clearly." Vesper's voice tore from her in gasping bursts. She stared beyond Alfred's branch. A great buckskin horse stood there, wet, bedraggled, lost-looking, and so incongruous Vesper giggled.

A sigh escaped her censuring rescuer. "It has also been no small endeavor to bring Bother into this morass," Kissre said, her voice still harrowing, but lower and less harsh.

Vesper giggled again, then vomited salty water. She choked, wiped her mouth, and gasped. "Having only dragged myself here, I can imagine. He looks as unhappy as I feel. How did you find me?" She hung on the branch humiliated and exhausted in equal portions.

"I've been tracking you since it was discovered you had fled."

"Tracking? How?" Vesper said, diverted. "I left no trail."

Kissre gave an offensive laugh-snort as she gathered her horse's reins. "Can you walk?"

"Yes, I think so."

Alfred jumped into the saddle as the buckskin passed, causing the horse to raise his head with a soft grunt and glance back. Snorting, the animal shook his great head and followed Kissre. The woman motioned Vesper toward a large grass hummock a short distance away. It turned into an island of dryness. How she had missed it Vesper couldn't fathom.

She collapsed on the rough grass, closed her eyes, and slowly caught her breath. The hot sun brought some warmth to her chilled body. In the stillness Vesper heard the huge horse chomp the meager remains of last season's grass seed heads a short distance away.

Kissre plopped down next to her and pulled off her boots. She emptied the water they contained and swore. In the silence that extended between them the idle splashes and sounds of birds seemed louder. The marsh had a distinctive smell, not fetid, but a mixture of sodden earth, decay, and salt tang.

Opening her eyes, she looked at her bodyguard. The woman half reclined, propped on her muscular arms. She gazed straight ahead. A guard's vest topped her trews, and Vesper noted the blue tattoo circling her right wrist and hand rose high unto her arm nearly to the shoulder. She looked more comfortable than Vesper felt in her sodden, sleeved jacket and divided riding skirt.

"I was beginning to believe I'd die here." She said at last.

Kissre didn't look at her, didn't move. "No chance. Your father gave you into my keeping. My life would have been forfeit if I'd found you dead. Now I've only lost my position." Her head turned and she glared at Vesper. "It was a cushy one, too. Get out of those clothes. We'll need to dry out before moving on." She rose and went to her horse.

"Why should you lose your job? You found me." Vesper grabbed the blanket thrown at her and rose to remove her wet things.

"You should never have been able to leave the manor. If I'd known you a thief, I would have kept closer watch. My own fault, I should have slept in your room."

"I'm sorry. I didn't mean to cause anyone trouble, but I need to be with Drew." Even as she spoke shadow visions formed around him. Another change came. It involved Kissre.

Kissre's frown returned. "I've already suffered a dressing-down from Quillon. You must return to the manor. He has men out hunting for you. If he had anyone capable of the manor's defense, he would be tracking you."

"How come you found me, then? And why if you aren't employed anymore?"

Kissre gave her a flat look. "I'm a better tracker. You were my duty. My reputation is at stake."

"I will not go back." Wrapping a blanket around her nakedness, she gave Kissre a defiant look. "I will escape again and again until you give up and leave me. You must sleep sometime."

Kissre looked at her and swore. "I don't want to have to tie you."

"You will have to." She changed tactics. "Kissre, please, I am married to Drew, he is my husband. My father's desires don't enter into this. I can't tell you how, but I believe that I must go to him as strongly as I believe the broken moon and sun cross the sky. If I am there, he will be safe."

"But not if you remain at your father's manor, as requested?"

"Then Drew will die."

Whatever Kissre read in Vesper's face caused her own to firm. She swore and turned away. "You know this how?" She looked over her shoulder.

"I see it, in dreams, but I know them true."

Kissre turned away and stared out over the marsh. Eventually, she removed her scabbard and threw it to the ground. "Can I trust you to remain here? I need to find some dry wood for a fire."

Vesper felt her face redden. "I haven't stolen or lied so much since a child. I am sorry. I promise to remain."

Making a rude sound Kissre headed down the length of the island. Vesper watched the woman's strong gliding stride out of sight. More visions replayed one on top of another and Vesper found herself gasping, faced with a terrible quandary. If she listened to her foresight, she had to make a death choice. She wanted desperately to save Drew, but at what cost? Kissre's life? Trade one for the other? Yes, yes, part of her shouted. Another part quietly remarked, 'she saved your life'. Her senses turned inward to examine her problem. After reflection, she decided she must go to Drew, and Kissre had to come with her, even if it damned her soul.

A short while later she heard Kissre returning. The guard's arms were loaded with kindling and dead branches. Silence stretched. Vesper watched as Kissre made a fire. Two more trips for wood and Kissre still hadn't spoken, but she wore an abstracted look.

"I will speak to my father. He won't let you go."

Kissre made a sour sound and swore her disbelief.

"If he does, Drew will hire you. He is always practicing arms, so he must need men-at-arms. How did you track me? I thought myself very clever in covering my escape." It was clear Kissre didn't credit her offer, barely believed her intelligent.

"I followed your boots. They belonged to one of the stable lads, and he felt most abused by their theft. There is a crack in the sole. When you hitched a ride, I started asking at each home, hamlet, and village. When you ran, I followed your tracks again. I have your bag of treasures." She gave Vesper a disgusted look. "You left a trail of tracks, broken branches, fabric scraps, and flattened grass. It was easy enough, just slow. How did you cross the Northern Thou and how did you know the King traveled that way? If you knew that, then why did you come south? I thought you meant to follow the Aegis."

"I did follow Drew. At my father's manor, I overheard the plans for the army to cross the Northern Thou and travel through Wessure in the hope to attract more men to fight the Pertelonese. I had hitched a ride with several traveling wagon drivers, one who crossed the river at the raft access, and then I followed the road and it led here."

"You hitched rides with complete strangers? Are you daft?' Kissre huffed in dismissal. "You should have taken the northern fork." The unspoken 'idiot' followed with an audible sigh.

"Should have is a little late, now. The southern fork looked like it went east." Vesper exposed her temper in her tart tones. "It was my first experience at arranging travel. I made a few mistakes. I thought the road heading south and east the most logical. Do you know how to get out of here?"

"Not exactly, but I'm sure we're just a day or so west of Teeg. You were at least smart enough to follow the main waterways." Kissre rose and removed a canteen from her saddle. She took a sip, looked at Vesper, and offered her some.

Taking the canteen in shaking hands she drank deeply until Kissre pulled it away. "Easy, we'll need it. Have you eaten?"

Vesper shook her head, desperately wanting more water. Kissre ignored her and waded into the water. She pulled the carcass from the water and carved it up. In short order she had chunks of meat spiked over their small campfire. Then she set stakes to hang Vesper's clothes. Chewing the strange meat, Vesper found it tasted heavenly and sucked the juices freed by her biting teeth.

"Are you taking me back?" After her question, she endured a nerve-racking silence.

"No."

"Why?"

A rough, brittle sound burst from Kissre. "Because I'm a dolt." She looked at Vesper. "Civic duty. I've already lost my position. Can't lose it twice. And because I believe you."

"Why?"

"I have a sister who knows things no one can know. I've heard the legends about the Aegises. If there is magic remaining in this land, you could very well have it. That's all." Her look didn't encourage Vesper to ask questions that might jeopardize her victory.

They camped on the dry ground. Vesper slept, rousing once to find Kissre still up, keeping watch. The next day Kissre delayed their start while she took her turn sleeping. The day heated rapidly, and the spring sun beat down in uncomfortable strength on Vesper's tender skin. Her conscience burned with it, too, but Drew's safety was at stake.

After she was sure Kissre slept, she checked a strange contraption the woman had made. A square of fabric was placed over what Vesper knew must be a hole. The pile of dirt dug from it sat to the side. Each corner of the square was held by a rock and several smaller stones weighed down the middle of the cloth. She wondered at it, but Kissre had not explained her purpose. While Kissre slept Vesper spent time removing unnecessary padding and stiffening from her jacket. Its looser fit felt more comfortable. The hot sun burned her arms and face, and she watched Kissre's surprisingly fair skin also turn red.

It was very hot by the time Kissre rose. First thing, she checked out the fabric-covered hole. From it she pulled a water flask, offering Vesper some. "A sun still. Not enough to quench the day's thirst, but enough to keep us alive. We could not go far without it." From another still that Vesper hadn't noticed, Kissre pulled a second flask and offered her horse the contents.

Vesper gave Alfred some while Kissre attended Bother. He remained silent, but Vesper knew from his doting look he approved of Kissre. Strangely, Kissre stepped around Alfred when he stood directly in front of her like she knew him there but ignored his presence. Alfred smiled and gave Vesper an evil look. It unsettled her.

They set out the way Kissre had come, the guard led with her sword drawn. With each step she tested the bottom beneath the waters before moving. A precaution that relieved Vesper's fears after her watery encounter. Vesper followed close behind. Bother waded in the rear, pulling each huge foot out of the water, and holding it aloft before reluctantly re-submerging it. He seemed very bewildered... if it were possible to judge a horse's expression. Vesper gave Alfred one dirty-look for his dry, comfy ride atop the horse before ignoring him.

Kissre found another dry hillock in the late afternoon just before dusk. They were all hot, tired, and wet. This island was surrounded by a grove of the unnatural tree. Travel had been as hard as all the other days, although Kissre found easier ways. Her guard ordered Vesper to remain while she disappeared to search for dry wood. Guilt assailed Vesper. Bother, his wheaten coat stained with mud and green slime, munched on dry grass, sending a baleful stare in her direction. Her own stomach growled.

Swishing grass sounds alerted Vesper of Kissre's approach. Once she had fed the fire, Kissre unsaddled Bother and rubbed his coat clean, checked his feet, and spent a long time talking to him in low words Vesper couldn't hear. That Kissre worried about her precious horse irritated Vesper, until the ungracious thought reminded her of

Drew and his Kuff. None of this was Kissre's fault, and her most valuable belonging had been put at risk on Vesper's behalf. More guilt smote Vesper. She planned to put Kissre's very existence at risk.

Once Kissre had set water to boil for tea, Vesper could stand it no longer. "I must tell you something. It will be safer for you to take me to the nearest town and go your way..."

She hesitated as Kissre laid down her sword. The guard had been cleaning it but started preparing tea. Kissre didn't look up from her task. "You've seen me in one of your dream-visions?" Her short blonde hair fluttered in the soft breeze, tangling into waves of light and dark hair. The air picked up some of the dried tea leaves Kissre poured from her hand into the water.

"Yes."

"My death?"

"Yes." Her hands had curled into tight fists and she consciously released them.

"Don't put too much alarm on it," she said, shrugging. "All mercenaries face that risk. It is nothing new."

"But—"

Kissre talked over her interruption. "If you think you can save your husband from fate's hand, then I believe I can save myself in the same way. They say forewarned is forearmed."

~ * ~

Snorting and heavy hooves thumping the ground startled Vesper awake. Bother squealed in alarm. Vesper looked for Kissre, but she was gone. Alfred stood balancing on the alert horse's withers, grasping strands of black mane. Vesper rose and searched the darkness for danger.

An angry porcine squeal filled the air. A second shriek made her search for Kissre's sword, but the scabbard was empty. Kissre was out there. Bother, his head high and nostrils flaring, stared into the dark. Vesper searched in the direction he looked. Further down the island a burning glow swung. Briefly the flames erupting from the branch's end shot sparks that illuminated Kissre's face. In that flash, Vesper saw the glowing eyes and shadowed shape of a very large fen boar.

It was clear the animal refused Kissre's attempt to drive it off. The two danced back and forth, the boar attempting to circle Kissre and avoid the swing of the burning branch. Kissre stepped away from its lunges and the twisting head. She aggressively pursued its retreats. Their match lasted a long time before the boar turned and ran back into the grove. Kissre stood for a moment, then started back toward the camp.

Vesper screamed warning as the black shadow emerged from the side, moving fast. Kissre turned and her sword came up just in time to meet the creature's charge. The force dropped them both to the ground. Vesper heard both swine and human screams and watched the struggling pair roll down the incline and into the river's edge. Splashing sounds proved the confrontation continued.

The pig emerged and ran. In its desperation it gave no notice of direction. With uncanny accuracy Bother's hind hooves marked the creature. With a solid thump it flew in a wide aerial arc. Vesper would have laughed at Alfred's tight clutch on Bother's neck if she hadn't been running to Kissre.

Dripping wet, her guard staggered back up the bank. "You're all right? Where is it?"

"Bother kicked it." She pointed in the direction and tried to help Kissre.

She shook off Vesper's hands and walked in the direction the pig had flown. Vesper followed ignoring the orders to stay behind. The creature lay dead, ugly, and coarse looking. "I did not want to kill it," Kissre said, nearly weeping.

"Before he was kicked, he seemed to be running all right."

Kissre sighed. "No, see where I stabbed it? It would have died soon."

"You're wounded. Did a tusk gore you?"

"I don't know. Felt something when I fell."

"Come back to the camp. Let me look in the fire's light."

Although there were angry scratches on her leathers and down one arm, most of the blood came from a branch thrust completely through the loose skin and muscle of Kissre's left shoulder. Vesper inspected the wound and ticked in upset.

"Damn trees," Kissre said. "Their branches lie under the water, over the water, and pop up through the land."

"I have nothing to help ease the pain, but this must come out. Your blood should cleanse the wound."

Kissre looked at the wound and nodded her assent. She added a warning. "If anything happens to me, you must take Bother, but do not saddle him. Ride him bareback, leave the saddle. He is trained not to allow anyone to ride him saddled but me."

"Nothing will happen to you." The emerging ends of wood were too short to grasp. With an apprehensive look at Kissre, she warned, "This will hurt." She took Kissre's knife, cleaned it, and pushed on one end of the stick, shoving it through the wound. Kissre made no sound but passed out before the operation was over. Once Vesper had enough to grasp, she pulled the short, broken branch out. Before throwing it away she noticed the clear liquid seeping from its end and tested the liquid with a finger touch to the tongue.

"Water. Drinkable water," she said to Alfred and laughed.

She let Kissre's wounds bleed freely before stopping them with a heated blade. After, she gently washed them with the marsh saltwater. Kissre roused, but Vesper told her to sleep, and surprisingly, she did. While Kissre slept, Vesper skinned part of the boar and cut the best pieces of meat. It was too heavy to drag the carcass to the water's edge. Other swamp denizens would come to scavenge, creating a dangerous situation. She hunted until she found Kissre's sword at the water's edge. Returning to camp she cleaned and dried it while she kept watch. Within a short time the sounds of feasting assailed her ears, but all the animals stayed out of sight, away from the fire.

Dawn's light breached the night's darkness none too soon.

Kissre woke before true light. She stared at the skewered meat drying by the fire, then said, "A most unusual Aristo daughter."

Vesper laughed. "You know the least of it. Have some water." She lifted a branch hacked from a grove tree and poured the liquid between Kissre's dry lips. Kissre looked suspicious, then sipped. Done, she laughed. "Freshwater all around, if you know where to look. I suppose you used my sword?" At Vesper's nod, she made an exasperated sound but voiced no complaint. With the water Kissre seemed to recover. She forced herself up and saddled Bother.

"You must mount Bother if we are to travel today," Vesper said.

"I can walk."

They argued. Kissre won. Vesper fretted over the seeping wound but Kissre ignored her. By night infection had set in. Not only the puncture wounds but the scratch marks were red and puffy. In the morning, with Kissre nearly senseless, Vesper saddled Bother.

Somehow the great horse found her no threat and allowed her to saddle him. Actually, Alfred stood at his head holding the bridal, helping more than Vesper had ever known him to do. Vesper bullied and pushed Kissre into the seat, ignoring all protests. Once in the saddle, Kissre fell forward over Bother's neck. "Keep her in the saddle," Vesper told Alfred as he clambered up behind her. He nodded.

Taking the sword in hand, she found it heavier than it looked. With an upward look at Kissre and Alfred, she patted Bother's nose, took the reins, and started their day's journey.

The sun was falling into the late afternoon sky. Vesper stopped for a minute and straightened. Her shoulders ached from carrying the sword's weight all day. After a long moment of stillness, Bother nudged her in the middle of the back and Vesper turned to him. She rubbed his forehead and murmured a few soothing words of encouragement.

"I really am most sorry you have to put up with me and apologize again for being the cause of your presence in this swamp," she told the horse softly. "Please hold still so I can check Kissre again."

She had no fear of him, for although bigger than Shally, he was just as gentle. Twice she had slipped right beneath his legs and he had taken care not to step on her even though water splashed his face and eyes. Still, she kept up a gentle murmur of words to soothe him. She felt Kissre's face. The woman's green eyes slowly opened.

"How long?"

"It is late afternoon. I'm looking for a place to set up camp."

Kissre only nodded, although she did sit more erect in the saddle.

Bother's sides expanded and Vesper heard his inhalation. He neighed once and started moving, pulling the reins from Vesper's hand. She tried to catch up with him, but the animal kept two steps ahead of her. With a small hop, he jumped onto a raised hillock. Thanks to Alfred's assistance Kissre stayed in the saddle. Vesper caught Bother's tail as his rear passed her and used his momentum to help pull herself up the bank.

In the middle of the island, last year's grass bent over in small knolls, but Vesper could see green shoots starting up between the brown shafts. Bother kept moving, outpacing Vesper. She dropped the sword and chased the horse, but he came to an abrupt halt and started taking long drafts of water from a small pool.

Vesper tasted the water. It was fresh and cool, a small spring in the heart of the marsh. She drank a handful of water, then went to help Kissre down.

"Loosen the girth," Kissre said, but she leaned over too far for Alfred to hold her and fell into Vesper's arms. They both landed with a soft crunch in the dry grass.

Once free of Kissre's weight, Bother moved off to nip at the new grass growth. Vesper made sure of Kissre's comfort, then with Alfred's help, freed Bother of his saddle. She pulled off his bridle and rubbed him with a knot of grass to get the marsh weeds off him. "Damn, one day and you've ruined his training."

Vesper returned to Kissre when she spoke and looked at the wound. The sound of animals rushing through the water and thumping over the ground alarmed them both. Bother's head rose in alert, and even Alfred stood, looking around.

"Where's my sword?"

Vesper ran and searched in frantic haste for the lost weapon. With a glint of late-afternoon sun on steel, she found the sword and dragged it back to Kissre, who swore at the misuse of her blade. She grabbed Vesper's arm and hauled her to the ground.

"Stay down and stay quiet," she hissed. "Might be Pertelonese soldiers."

Vesper nodded at the order. The sound of far-off voices and the sound of movement through the marsh frightened her. Kissre used the sword to help prop herself to a squatting position. The thumping sound of branches breaking and of hooves clopping forewarned that they were in the path of something approaching in desperate haste. Vesper froze and Kissre fell over her, covering her own head with her arms. Peeping up through the grass, Vesper saw the fleeing forms of several marsh deer as they jumped over where they lay.

Bother snorted and screamed a defiant squeal at something coming behind the deer. He rose on his haunches and flayed the air with his forefeet, then shook his head and pawed the ground.

Kissre rolled with a grimace to her knees and lumbered to her feet, both hands grasping her sword's hilt. She stood there several minutes. Vesper heard a hail, then the sword dropped and Kissre sank to her knees. "It is all right Vesper. A group of Kennetsurean hunters led by a Knight of the Zekarac Order." Her guard passed out.

Vesper took the sword and rose from the grass to stand next to her companion. Several men with arrow-knocked bows approached.

Thinking every moment her last, Vesper quietly waited.

"Lorelei?"

The feminine voice naming her mother startled Vesper.

"It is impossible. I'm seeing ghosts," the voice, definitely a woman's, continued.

Then Vesper recognized the man accompanying the strange woman and answered in deep relief.

"No. I am Vesper, her daughter. This is my friend Kissre. She is very ill. Is that you, Sir Leander? Can you help us?"

His woman companion turned to Leander. "As strange as it seems, finding her here, she must be the daughter of Raymond Aurelias, Duke of Lambere." She hurried toward Vesper, giving her a bewildered look, then knelt to look at Kissre.

"No, Lady Ottillie. I have met her before, she is the wife of Drew Montoren, the Vere Aegis." Leander gave a sign of greeting to Vesper.

Kissre, coming out of her swoon, pulled her head away from the hand checking her.

"Don't like help?" Ottillie asked Kissre. She touched the face below her again and looked at Vesper. "She is feverish." Lifting the edge of Kissre's shirt she looked at the festered wounds and grimaced. She looked at Vesper. "Leela knows all about healing, she will help your Kissre. Help me get her up."

Leander helped Ottillie until Kissre was supported between them. Kissre looked at Vesper, then Leander.

"My horse. Don't let anyone try to ride him. He is safe now. Just don't ride him."

Leander answered Kissre with calm words. "No one, mistress, will ride your horse. You are safe now, as is your horse and your charge."

It was like the reassurance released her. Vesper watched Kissre slump between the two, too weary herself to offer help.

Leander's men appeared from all around to circle them. Leander organized the return. One Kennetsurean lifted Kissre and carried her off. Others gathered equipment and led Bother away.

It was a relief, and Vesper sobbed, nearly too exhausted to stand. Ottillie kindly supported her, wrapping her arms around Vesper in the first comfort she had felt in days.

"Camp is not far. You can make it. Come."

Once in camp an ancient, small woman, introduced as Leela, tended Kissre. Vesper sank into a slump next to her offering advice and telling how the wound occurred. Leela worked cleaning Kissre's injury under Vesper's vigilant eye. Leander approached with questions he put to Vesper. She answered unaware how disjointed a ramble her story, interspersed with her own questions to Leela about her medicines and treatment, sounded.

Finally she turned to Leander in exasperation as he repeated questions. "It is very simple. I became lost trying to follow my husband because he left me behind. Knowing he will need me, I disregarded his wishes, my father's wishes, and caused Kissre great harm. My father ordered her to guard me. She tracked me into the marsh. This stupidity is all my doing." She turned away from him and gave her attention to Leela and Kissre.

The old lady gave Ottillie an amused glance before returning her attention to Kissre. She involved Vesper in a long rambling monolog about comparative treatments.

~ * ~

Ottillie watched even after Leander left with an exasperated, "Seer," and a shrug. Several times she noted Leela's surprised look of shrewd appraisal as she talked with Vesper.

Leander returned. "We need to send a bird to Quillon. He will want to know his charge safe."

Aldous came up and stood next to Ottillie. "How did you enjoy your hunt in the Great Salt Marsh?"

"My hunts seem to take on a life of their own. There is no telling what might occur during one. I'm thinking of giving up the sport."

Aldous turned his attention to Vesper as she rose to her feet, Leela telling the girl she was satisfied with Kissre's current condition.

"Lady Vesper?"

The girl nearly swooned.

Ottillie grabbed her arm. "Are you ill?"

Vesper smiled. "No, just very tired." Her eyes returned to Aldous. "You must be Aldous, the Aegis of Kennetsure."

A broad smile crossed Aldous's face. "How is Drew?"

Ottillie saw the pleasure drain from the girl's face. "He travels with King Warrick and the army to help secure the east."

"But his power is seated in the north!" Ottillie said.

Water lined Vesper's eyes. "No longer. I saw his shadow spread over all of Kaereya," she looked at Aldous, "even Kennetsure."

"Ahh, a seer at last! Leander said so, but we hardly dared believe it. No wonder I feel comfortable here," Aldous said. "Lady Vesper, it is my pleasure to meet you. We are traveling to join Drew, so you may safely accompany us. How is your guardswoman?"

"Kissre will be fine," Leela said.

They all turned to look down at the woman just as Kissre's eyes opened.

The guard's eyes moved to Vesper. "Is this the death you foretold? You're not very good at it, are you?"

"Lie still," Leela cautioned with a hand against Kissre's shoulder. "You are among friends." Leela's eyes moved to Vesper. "You delivered your charge to just the right place, Kissre. Vesper can take classes with Ottillie. Now I have two students of magic."

Ottillie clearly read Vesper's bewildered expression. Leela must have also, for she offered comfort. "It is true, Vesper. I have a few Talents myself and can sense yours, know how to train it. You will see, it doesn't have to control you."

Three days later Ottillie rode next to Kissre beside the wagon. Ostensibly to watch Kissre should she falter riding so soon. The mercenary intrigued Ottillie. As she practiced her new Talent, she found Kissre particularly impenetrable, which offered an instant challenge. Besides, she was curious about what made an attractive woman seek work as a mercenary?

Kissre had looked down her nose and huffed, "Less dangerous than prostitution," to her ill-bred question.

Despite Kissre's obvious irritation and monosyllabic responses, Ottillie chatted. She smiled to herself. Court offered harder nuts to crack than Kissre. Plus, Kissre's wound hampered her defenses. With an abandon that would have shocked other aristos, Ottillie bared herself to Kissre, her position, her birth rank, her problems, and worries, while asking innocently intrusive questions. Kissre didn't respond with the same openness but was probably unaware of what she gave away. Family problems, Ottillie decided.

When they arrived at the tail of King Warrick's army, she saw a sardonic smile cross Kissre's face as she observed the crowd gathering for their arrival. Looking, Ottillie identified her father, his friend Raymond Aurelias, and Warrick among the assembled aristos. King Warrick, now. "Which one is the Vere Aegis?" she asked Kissre.

"The blond just to Aurelias' left."

"Which one? There are two." Both were similar, Kennetsurean heritage evident in features, but translated into a light northern look.

"The taller one is the Aegis's cousin."

Just her size, Ottillie grinned with a quickly made insight.

"Ahh-ha," Kissre said. "Something besides a female mercenary for entertainment?"

Exposed, Ottillie faced Kissre's observant stare. "I beg you to accept my apology. You do interest me. I only wished to become friends."

"Mercenaries don't make friends."

Perceptive and blunt. Ottillie smiled back at the scowling visage. "I am not a mercenary."

"I am."

"Then it must be a one-sided friendship. Everyone will consider it another of my eccentricities."

Kissre tried to level her with a look, but it failed to faze Ottillie, and she smiled back. She turned to watch the blond giant.

Abandoning a lost battle, Kissre said, "The cousin's name is Selwyn. Good luck. Clansmen are a reclusive bunch."

Ottillie side-glanced at the diversionary tidbit. "What makes you so interested in this reunion and so suddenly generous with information?" She thought Kissre wouldn't answer.

"Vested interest."

"That sounds premeditated."

"It is. Vesper's actions cost me this position."

"Honor required you to retrieve her?" Receiving no answer, she turned her interest to the waiting men. Her father walked forward to greet her. Ottillie bent down to place a kiss on his cheek. "Hello, Father. I see my news was not needed."

"I am happy to see you safe, Ottillie."

She smiled and dismounted, then hugged her father. Looking she saw Leander already dismounted. Kissre slowly lowered herself from her horse and loosened the girth before taking the reins and standing with an inscrutable expression. An unpleasant expectation assailed Ottillie, and she turned to look at Vesper, surprised at feeling the girl's dread. Vesper stood staring with defiant trepidation at her husband and father. Leela descended from the wagon, followed by Aldous. A beaming smile broke from Leela and Ottillie felt her elation.

The young Aegis walked up to his wife, raised her hand, and kissed it. Ottillie heard Vesper's soft plea, "I am sorry, Drew, but I could not remain behind."

"We will talk of this later, in privacy."

A charming smile crossed Vesper's face. "Oh, grief, Drew. Everyone here is aware we shall have a dreadful row. In the meantime, I am very pleased to see you." She threw her arms around her husband and hugged him. "Yell at me if you must, but I won't go back. I am needed here. You need me."

"Kissre, I would speak with you."

Ottillie turned to the irate voice of her father's friend, Raymond Aurelias. She had not noticed his approach except for the eruption of gruff voice, but it was clear Kissre had.

"Your Grace," the guardswoman said.

"No, you won't," Vesper said, leaving Drew and moving to Kissre's side. "Kissre did nothing but her duty, and I will not have her dismissed or reprimanded for my fault."

Ottillie laughed at both Kissre and her employer's identical expressions of outrage at Vesper's intrusion.

"This is no affair of yours," Aurelias said in what he must have thought a civil voice. "I hired her! She was ordered to protect you and failed in that duty."

Aurelias' angry tone surprised Ottillie. Generally a composed and genial man, she had never heard him raise his voice. She looked at her father who viewed the situation with as much interest as herself.

"She saved my life! She followed her orders even knowing Quillon had already dismissed her. If you cast her off, I shall hire her!"

"With what?" Aurelias shouted.

"I will ask Drew to hire her. She would be an asset to his clan. If he won't, I will pay her myself from the dower lands you gave me! I expect it is enough to keep Kissre's hire! Then I can give her duties such as I see fit! None of this is her fault, and she should not have to pay for my lies and deceit. Further, if we must argue in public, I tell you now, I will follow neither your orders nor Drew's if I know them to be wrong."

Ottillie had to bite her lip to prevent another unseemly laugh. It was true. aristos, clansmen, and Kennetsurean tribesmen all listened to this public spat. Aurelias looked about to explode. Any number of aristos had to be amused at the display. Wherever Vesper had come from, she was nothing like Aurelias' two meek wives. Matter of fact, she was unlike any Aristo lady. What surprised Ottillie was the young Aegis's response. He walked to his wife's side.

"If hiring Kissre will make you safer," Drew said to Vesper, "then, you're hired." He turned to Kissre and extended his hand to the mercenary in the clan's peace greeting.

From Kissre she felt nothing. Ottillie couldn't feel Kissre like she could nearly everyone else there, but the woman usually stood stone still. She puzzled over it and decided Kissre's training demanded her constraint until orders unleashed her. A soldier would need such discipline. Kissre took the extended hand knowing clan custom, but said, "Thank you Aegis Vere, but it would be improper—"

"You cannot hire her because she is still under contract with me," Aurelias said, his exasperation clear.

"I hate to break up this family reunion, but I need to reclaim my throne. If you don't think a war council is required to settle this matter, perhaps you can join me in one to settle my affairs?" Warrick smiled. "You must be Aldous, Aegis Kennetsure?" He graciously greeted both Aldous and Leela, spending several moments in conversation. Turning, he gave a few orders and aristos ran to his bidding.

When the surrounding audience vanished, Warrick looked at Vesper. "And I thought I set the standard for rebellious behavior. I have nothing on you, Lady Vesper."

Vesper blushed and started an apology, but Warrick only picked up Vesper's hand and kissed it, just as Drew had. He smiled a wicked smile at Drew and walked away with Vesper's arm linked in his. "Come, no apology, I cannot be angry with the woman, or the men, who saved my life. Not this soon anyway. Before my council meets, let me offer you refreshments. I want to hear why you felt you needed to come to a war. My Aegises can sit in and listen. It should be most entertaining."

Ottillie watched as her father, Aurelias, the two Aegises, and other aristos followed the king. "Well!" she said moving to stand next to Kissre. "It looks like you are still employed, Kissre, but I'm not sure by whom."

"You, Lady Ottillie, have a perverse sense of humor."

"Not humor. Honesty. You will come to appreciate me," Ottillie amended, "it is a trait sorely absent at Court. I look forward to our friendship, Kissre."

"I don't. You will plague me, I'm sure."

"Yes, but right now you're only unsatisfied with Drew's encounter with Vesper. You are a bloodthirsty creature, but your wishes are doomed to dreams. The Aegis Vere is love-crazed for his wife. He will rant and threaten, wearing his ire out on that meek-looking fluff, while she will endure with the iron will she has displayed over and over these past few days. He has already lost."

Kissre snorted. "I know. I only hoped to view a few rips and rents before his defeat."

"And you her guardsman. Tsk, tsk."

A broad grin crossed Kissre's face. The first humor Ottillie had seen. "Yes, but for her, I had to near carry Bother through that miserable damn swamp. Neither of us has recovered yet."

Ottillie inspected the expanse of spotlessly groomed horsehide. The horse had earned great favor among the Kennetsurean men who had cared for the animal during Kissre's recovery. "Only now do I fully understand your wish for vengeance. But then, you brought her here rather than to Quillon."

"You know Quillon?"

"No. Leander told me of him."

Kissre shrugged. "She is a witch on a mission. May the Holy One show her the right way but keep her out of mine."

"She predicted your death."

"A common expectation among all soldiers. Why don't you go make eyes at your clansman prey?"

"A put-down, and to a Lady, too. Kissre you improve on acquaintance." Smirking, she walked away. A little later she came in for her own chastisement.

"I am no more pleased to see you in an army camp planning war than Drew or Raymond to see Vesper." Her father told her later as they sat sharing dinner in his tent.

"What is happening?"

"It doesn't look as if we'll have trouble getting the Eternal Palace back. Duke Hearthron has sent messages of peace and fealty to his dearest nephew. It says little more. I had hoped he would not, but wishes are cheap, and I think Warrick realizes his duplicity."

She ignored her father's complaint. "Have you heard from Eldin?"

"Pertelon controls the Southern Thou as far as Gotte City. Most of our eastern garrisons are either under siege or already lost. We used Raymond's merchant mariners to block final access to the ocean. That is Clement's drive, of course. Control of a sea route, control of commerce."

Ottillie kept her worry at her father's switch in topic to herself. Her father had his full share. "And Warrick?"

"Much changed. His grief and guilt over his family seem to consume him." He told her the story he learned from Aurelias.

"He likes flirting with his Aegis Drew's wife."

"You noticed? He has developed a strange friendship, almost a dependency, on Drew. He still likes to tweak him. I suppose a remnant of his old nature."

"I have some interesting stories to tell you." She told him of Chloe's second spell for an Aegis to combine the four provinces.

"You think legend is at work here? The Easure and Wessure Aegises are dead."

"Since finding Vesper, Aldous and Leela do, too. The rumor already spreads among their Kennetsurean retinue. And they have close ties with the Clans. The whole army will hear the story before tomorrow's dawn. You don't look happy about it."

"Prophecy has a way of going askew when you least expect it. In the meantime, it might buy Warrick goodwill. The banners of the Aegises have already produced results."

"I thought you said the Wessure and Easure Aegises dead? Their signets fly outside," she asked, raising a brow of skepticism.

"Raymond had the banners made for all the provinces, and it is true Drew feels the land here, but he doesn't claim to be the Easure Aegis. Matter of fact, he hates the deception. He says there is not much he can really do."

"Vesper says that in a vision she saw a shadow of the Vere unicorn spread across Kaereya."

"Let us hope it is true or enough believe it to make it come true. Men arrive daily from all over Kaereya to join Warrick's army. In every hamlet we enter, people cheer the Aegis as much as the king."

"How does Warrick accept that?"

"In some twisted way, he enjoys it because it so obviously discomfits Drew. Besides, Drew rides next to him, so it's hard to tell who is acclaimed. My sources say the people believe Warrick went in search of Aegis at his father's order."

"Nudged to belief by your sources? It might assuage Warrick's guilt that the people cheer for the Aegises and not him. I shall have to study Warrick. What of Eldin?"

"He is at court, working for the Regent."

Ottillie swallowed her surprise. "For Gilchrist? How? He was to ride the Southern Thou's eastern circuit and notify the garrisons."

"Gilchrist's orders, as Regent, outranked mine, particularly when I was dismissed. He ordered Eldin to bring his daughter from Yonger's estate back to the Eternal Palace."

"The garrisons were never warned?"

"No."

"How did Gilchrist know?" She changed her question. "Did he conspire...? Is Eldin involved in betrayal?"

"I have no proof." What he didn't say made more import on Ottillie.

"It is hard to believe." She fell silent after her comment, wondering if she had misjudged Eldin. "I won't believe it until I hear it from his lips. Tell me about the cousin."

"The cousin?" Her father looked bewildered, then thunderstruck. "Selwyn? Warrick knighted him. And Drew. He has protected Drew these many years. A loyal man. Why?"

"I have two surprises for you."

"Just tell me Ottillie, I want no games."

She smiled at her father's dry tones, rose, and stretched. "The first is that I think I am husband hunting. Wish me luck."

Her admission shocked her father but didn't daunt him. "And?"

"Leela tells me I am a witch." With a smile she kissed her father and left.

~ * ~

Chloe's Story

Melissa joined Chloe next to the sailing ship's railing, her late pregnancy weighing on her. Her erstwhile apprentice still appeared a little green.

"Are you feeling better?"

"Yes."

Chloe smiled at Melissa's curtness, so unusual. "Fresh air will help, and we will be there shortly. That is Dream Island. We shall be home soon."

Melissa took a few deep breaths and her color improved. "It smells better up here. Not as putrid." They stood in silence a few moments looking at the now calm waters. "The sea motion makes me sick. I swear this is my last pregnancy. What ails you, Lady?"

She should have known Melissa would read her as easily as she did her. "I have failed. I don't know how to tell everyone, or express how very sorry I am." She looked back across the waters, feeling the tears on her cheeks.

A rude noise answered her. "Sorry, Lady? Why? Every person in Kaereya knows you set a great spell. We are in no position to judge the results. Leave that to the Holy One."

"Without belief the spell won't work. Few in the King's Court believe, Melissa. The Aegises are forgotten. The new king has no heed for me or them. Sophia's Ewald asked me to protect Kaereya from strife. I have failed him, and now fail her."

"The common people believe. They're the ones who count, not the hoity-toity court."

"The Aegises are already nothing but toddler tales."

"The spell is not true, then?"

"The first spell will endure, but I have had visions. The families will die out. The second will break before fruition, one box's contents discarded. The Aegises will protect the borders, but I fear the inner turmoil of our future." Her eyes focused on a single black form flying from Dream Island. "A single crow. An ill omen."

Melissa huffed. "Nonsense. You did your very best for a very ungrateful man."

"A king cannot be grateful, only political. My life has been full of mistakes, and I was warned good acts cannot negate evil ones. I fear my unworthiness has offended the Holy One. My best just wasn't good enough."

Melissa made a repudiating hoot. "Lady, what you can't choose, can't be laid at your door. Don't let a priest's ranting about evils upset you. They all condemn sins of the flesh, but I still enjoy them. Look at the church, too. They are not faultless and don't necessarily speak for the Holy One."

"Melissa, have you had any visions?"

"You know I ignore them."

"You have not been a very good apprentice," Chloe admitted.

"No. I am sorry, Lady." Melissa ignored Chloe's chiding.

She knew Melissa felt better when she began looking at the crewmen, and finally made eyes at the Captain.

"But a good friend. You need not have come into exile with me."

"Like I would have wanted to stay in Court waiting on a nasty bunch of harridans? You were the best thing to ever come into my life, Lady."

"You lie. You have had a vision."

"Dreams. We all dream, and few give the truth. I saw a falling knife."

"A dagger and a shield tumbling endlessly?"

"Yes. The shield hit the ground, then splintered into pieces on the rocks."

It was Chloe's vision, too. Melissa placed her warm hand over her icy one where it gripped the railing.

"Lady, do not trouble yourself so. Let the future take care of itself. We took care of our present. Those in the future must take care of theirs."

Twenty

Warrick lay on a travel bed in the ducal tent of Aristo Aurelias. It now served as his royal tent. His continued weakness forced early stops for night's camp that angered him. He cursed his weakness as another sign of his failure.

His uncle's betrayal and Emory's betrayal preyed on his mind. Could they have conspired to murder his entire family? Their family? To gain the throne for Emory or for Uncle Theodulf? Tate could not have known, else would he have died defending Warrick? They could not have meant for Tate to die. That was the crux of his dilemma. How could he take revenge on Tate's father and brother?

Norbert suspected Aristo Yonger, but only inconclusive evidence supported his Marshal's suspicion. What was he to do? Warrick rolled to the bed's side and sat up, sinking his head into his hands. He heard Norbert's voice outside his tent, and he bade him enter.

"Good news, Your Majesty. A courier arrived with a message from Regent Theodulf."

"Why had he not sent it when he heard I was alive?" Warrick picked up the envelope and studied the Regent's crest embedded in the wax.

"I cannot tell you Duke Hearthron's thoughts, Sire."

"I was hoping they would force a confrontation. That I would have a chance to bring arms against my family's killers."

"The identity of those individuals is not confirmed, yet."

"I might never get to take retribution, may I?" Warrick looked around his tent, but his vision was inward rather than on his surroundings.

"You kept the crown, Sire, that might be the best revenge possible."

"But I will have to live with constant suspicion of everyone around me?" Warrick looked away. "Maybe that is proper—a just punishment." He broke the wax seal and began to read.

"No, Sire. You did not cause your family's death."

"It feels like I did."

"We reach Alaric Island tomorrow. Aristo Marshon also sent me a message that the other half of the army has reached the Rock Road outside of the bridge to Hawk Island. The northern route is sealed and protected."

Warrick swore and looked at his uncle's message. "My uncle says he and the court wait to greet us and will meet us at Low Bridge on Hawk Island's western side. He must have judged the futility of his position and decided on a new plot. I shall be watching." *Watching, but doing what?*

"I will assist you, Your Highness, in all your endeavors. A widespread belief claims your left court on a secret mission to find and bring the Aegis Vere to Hawk Island."

Warrick smiled, not misunderstanding the first part of the message. "Thank you, Norbert, for everything." If Norbert took care of his uncle, was he to blame? Would guilt scourge him? Would Tate haunt him? He sat straight, seeing Tate's face in death, accepting his cousin's perpetual possession. A flash of insight showed him his revenge, and how Norbert would act. He would not, could not, harm Tate's family. Did that preclude blocking all advanment at court?

As Norbert took his leave, Warrick turned to him. "My father was a good judge of character. I promise to try and earn the loyalty you gave him, and me."

~ * ~

As the only Ladies traveling with the army, Vesper rode behind Drew and between Ottillie and Selwyn. Often during the trip, Vesper had felt like a rose between two thorns. It was apparent Ottillie felt an interest in Selwyn.

At the end of the day, Ottillie muttered to Vesper, "He is as contained as wine in an untapped keg."

Vesper laughed knowing Ottillie saw herself tapping the keg. A glance showed Kissre's sardonic eyes also watched as Ottillie courted Selwyn.

Ottillie had tripped the night before on gear strewn where Selwyn worked. The premeditated fall brought Selwyn's laughter and a hand that pulled Ottillie upright in one heave. The stratagem might have worked. Unfortunately, several courtiers, too late to help the 'Lady' to her feet, inquired anxiously about her wellbeing. Selwyn's expression had closed, dooming Ottillie's designs.

A restrained smile covered Kissre's face, showing she had heard Ottillie's remark. Vesper gave the guard a grin as she turned away to help Leela order the camp. Ottillie came with her.

"A fine time to pick for a romance," Leela said as she scooted out of the way of the Kennetsurean men setting her tent. Vesper watched as most of the Kennetsureans accompanying Aldous meekly followed Leela's orders. She saw it was what they would do without the old woman's supervision anyway.

"Not much of a romance," Ottillie said with a sad sigh.

"More of a shameless hunt," Leela said.

Vesper giggled. "I've heard of Ottillie's hunting prowess."

Leela tsked and checked the progress of the fire and dinner's preparation. "The country is invaded, murder and mayhem circulate the countryside, and magic has been left in hands like yours."

"And Vesper's, not to mention those of the Aegises Drew and Aldous. And yours."

Leela took a taste of the pot's contents and ordered more salt. Taking another sample, she nodded at the cook, satisfied.

Ottillie continued, "Besides, it is as good a time as any. I am a realist. You have to take what is offered when it is offered or go without."

"I don't sense your future lying in Vere."

"My future lies wherever I want it. I am tied by no duty to any province, and I don't plan to live off my father forever."

"Are you sure?" Leela asked.

"My father would love my remaining with him, but it is time for me to establish my own place. Past time."

"I meant being tied to duty." Leela walked away to order how her packs were unloaded and where to place her necessities in her tent. Both Vesper and Ottillie trailed her, Vesper picking up various small items pulled from the packs and carrying them to Leela's tent.

"Have you sensed something?" Ottillie asked, suddenly curious.

"I'm no seer. You'd have to ask Vesper."

The sun caught Leela as she turned to Vesper, the evening rays displaying her age, but her eyes were sharp and clear. Vesper saw Leela, but another woman, too. The vision disoriented her.

"What do you see?" Leela demanded.

"I don't see anything," Vesper answered, and blushed as both Leela and Ottillie gave her disbelieving looks.

Leela turned to Ottillie. "But I do know this. You have only come into your gifts and have no idea about what to do with them. I don't believe you will find answers in Vere."

~ * ~

His uncle, the Duke of Hearthron, and the remaining court waited as the king and his army crossed Low Bridge to Hawk Island. Warrick accepted the warm and flattering greeting with equanimity.

Speaking kindly to his uncle, Warrick accepted Gilchrist's surrender as Regent, graciously thanked him for his efforts on Kaereya's behalf, and offered sincere condolences on the death of his son Tate. Warrick also stated his pleasure that his cousin Emory recovered from his wounds at the Hearthron estates. Warrick made sure his face and eyes gave nothing away.

Of course, the news of the new king's arrival had seeped into the city. It became apparent on the remaining ride through Cliff City to the Eternal Palace that the people were overjoyed to see him and believed him responsible for the Aegises presence. The crowds cheered him but bellowed approval to his Aegises.

He smiled at Drew's discomfort but enjoyed his Aegises' recognition. How many generations had their families quietly and unobtrusively served Kaereya? Served his father and grandfather?

The aristos merged into Warrick's cavalcade as he headed for the Eternal Palace, but his army marched onward toward the Tiny Step Islands leading to Orveka City on Anatole.

He refused to use his father's rooms and asked to visit Aron Cathedral while all else was settled. The whole court followed him there, the Bishop insisting on a special mass. His guilt and pain overwhelmed him as he ran a hand over the temporary markers covering the stone vaults. With his hand against the vault, he silently asked forgiveness and pledged to his father to serve Kaereya.

In the days that followed, Warrick hid his more tortured thoughts. Only slowly, as plans began for the retaking of Anatole Island, did the difference in his Court become apparent. He cast those expecting the old Warrick into confusion, watched his uncle blink as he used the royal pluralism, and let all discover King Warrick accepted flattering praise with equanimity. Dressing himself in sober comportment and mourning, he ignored entreaties for games or sport while work remained.

He focused himself on the needs of Kaereya and how to expel the invaders and kept track of everyone's comings and goings. Even with old friends he was reticent. None understood his preference for the young Aegis and the councilors who had traveled to Hawk Island with him. No court appointment was made without Norbert's recommendation, and no activity was conducted without Norbert and the two Aegises in attendance. He knew Drew ambivalent about his position, but right now he needed Drew. Drew was his pattern, Norbert his mentor, and Aldous fast became a trusted advisor.

~ * ~

Summoned to the king's Audience Chamber, Ottillie dressed with special care. She had no illusions. If Warrick desired her presence, he wanted something from her. Although she had traveled to Hawk Island with the king, Warrick seldom spoke to her other than that required by courtesy, and she had in truth expected no more.

As she approached the Audience Chamber, a Royal Guard opened one of the doors. The room was dark, the deep wood paneling absorbing most of the light entering the room. Small clerestory windows circled the room, each segment consisting of four small square panes arranged in a cross pattern. Warrick did not stand on the dais where the light concentrated, but at the side of the room with some of his courtiers. With her second step she dropped into a deep curtsey and heard Warrick order everyone else out. The door closed behind her with an audible snick, but Warrick remained silent for a moment, observing her.

"Lady Ottillie, your father and the Sorceress Leela told me you have a rare Talent." Warrick's statement did not surprise her as much as learning Leela had talked with Warrick.

"She told me you know the heart of a person's words." Warrick moved, pacing around her.

"Your majesty..." Ottillie remained in her curtsey, shocked and trying to compose herself. "I have a meager gift that sometimes allows me to know how another feels at a particular moment, but Sire, it is a new thing, untrained, and fallible."

He stopped before the end of her short speech. Stepping before her, he offered a hand to help her rise. She placed her hand in his and allowed him to assist her. She stood a half-head taller than the king. Prince Warrick had always stood apart from her, not caring for the size comparison.

Today, King Warrick disregarded the difference. He looked different. Of course, he wore royal accouterments, but it was more than that, even in his mourning. He looked stronger, more formidable, but somehow more compassionate. She sensed the darkness of his desires, and the turmoil and uncertainty writhing inside him.

"Even that might help me. I ask your assistance."

"Your Majesty, I will help you in any manner, but again, I must caution you that what I perceive is often open to interpretation. Leela teaches me, but I find it difficult and hard to believe myself. Further, my position at court makes me leery of my gift becoming common knowledge."

"Lady Ottillie, I know you have reason to doubt me, but I have the highest regard for your father, and also have no wish to expose you to the cruel vagaries of those at court. I know my summoning you to my presence will cause gossip. For that, I apologize."

"Do not think on it, Sire. Only those for whom I have no regard will say aught." She already knew what he wanted. Revenge, retribution, knowledge of those guilty. Forgiveness.

"I will do my best to help find those who killed your family. But for your sake as well as mine, let me relay what I might learn to my father."

The shrewd cunning that entered Warrick's eyes told her he understood. "I've also learned you are somewhat a scholar of the Sorceress Chloe and her spells. Is it true she set a second spell for an Aegis of all Kaereya?"

"Yes, Sire, but later she wrote that the spell would fail."

"Why?"

"I don't know. She only said she foresaw it. I don't know how she expected a box of dirt to do anything, anyhow."

"A box of dirt?"

"Soil. From the four provinces." The king's discomfiture drew her curiosity. He actually fidgeted, something she knew foreign to Warrick.

"A box like this?" He retrieved a small box from the mantle above the room's fireplace.

"Lady Chloe's spell box!"

Ottillie's astonishment made her forget deference. Quick steps took her to inspect the box with her gaze. "Is it truly one?" She looked at him with expectation.

He looked at the small lead box in his palm. "I don't know."

"I've read about them. Her journals are in Egan." Words poured out of her in a rush as her fingers roamed over the embossed top. "At least most of them. Where did you find it? In the throne or in the cathedral?"

"There are two?" His voice stumbled, and seeming almost against his will he asked, "Do you know what they were they for?"

"It was the keeping of her second spell." At his blank look, she explained. "She saw the first spell wouldn't do what she promised, and she tried to protect Kaereya from within with a second spell. She foresaw that it would fail. Does it still contain the soil?"

"No. It is empty." Her observant eyes asked the question he evaded. "You may pick it up."

"They found it when the Throne Room was refurbished?"

Warrick didn't let his gaze waver. "I stole it from the throne soon after the stone was removed."

She held the box, staring at it.

"Even then doubt beset me, but I was angry. I took it with me when I left. The contents must have emptied while in my bags. Aurelias' servants cleaned my gear."

"It would have looked like dirt. Luckily, the spell didn't seem to be needed. Drew had the power to become the Aegis Kaereya without it."

"Was that its purpose?"

Her head nodded while she inspected the box. "A most undistinguished-looking vessel. I'm not sure how it was to work. The soil was from the four provinces, soaked with the blood of the first Aegises. Somehow, she expected it to call to one of the Aegis. Touching the contents would engage the spell."

She turned at the odd sound leaving his throat. He covered his face with his hands. She saw them wetted with the moisture escaping his eyes.

"Sire, do you want me to summon help?"

"No! No. Thank you." He lowered his hands. "After my family's death, I thought it some sacred talisman to preserve the monarch. I thought I had assisted in the murder of my family."

Ottillie smiled. "No, Sire. But there is another box buried in the floor beneath the transept in Aron Cathedral. It was placed to attract anyone with Aegis potential. Somehow, they would know it was there. Chloe seemed to think the contents were destined to be uncovered, used to produce the new Aegis Kaereya. You can split the contents between the two boxes if you like. Perhaps deposit this one back in the new throne? That is, if it makes you feel better?"

He looked at her open face, lacking either condemnation or the desire for favor so many faces showed him. "I think you are right, Lady Ottillie. Something safeguarded and safeguarding the throne for so many years, should be restored where it belongs. Even the thought makes me feel better." He hesitated. "After I was attacked while traveling to Lambere, Drew, Selwyn, and Vesper rescued me. Brought me and my possessions to Lambere. Do you think it possible Drew touched the soil then?"

Ottillie felt surprise. "If so, you engendered the spell."

~ * ~

Norbert stood behind Warrick as his uncle, the Duke of Hearthron, faced his nephew. Warrick had just appointed Aristo Aurelias, Duke of Lambere, as Supreme Commander of the King's Army.

His uncle's indignation was clear, but Warrick displayed no pleasure in it. It had not been part of his petty plan for comeuppance. This was the business of Kaereya, and he had done what he thought right. It was that simple. His uncle was untrustworthy.

Gilchrist had frowned when Warrick first made the appointment, then stepped forward from Warrick's left. "Nephew, with all this sudden responsibility thrust upon you, and taking the advice of unfamiliar councilors, I'm sure you have not considered a Wessure leader might not inspire Easure troops?"

It amazed Warrick that Gilchrist still didn't understand the magnitude of addressing him informally before the assembled aristos. He thought his nephew as malleable as before his father's death. Warrick remained inscrutable. *He would learn.*

"Aristo Gilchrist. Uncle. You have served Kaereya well, but Aurelias has the experience here, and the Aegises will offer him excellent advice. We have placed our confidence in them."

"You do not trust me, nephew?" Gilchrist asked.

Warrick refrained from smiling at his uncle's pathetic tone. "Aristo Gilchrist, you have been burdened too long with our responsibilities. This is our duty, now, and we must prove to our people we can do so without your esteemed guidance or they will never respect us."

"Your Highness, Aristo Gilchrist's support will be most appreciated on Anatole Island," Aurelias said.

His uncle stiffened and looked at his rival. "There has been no call for troops."

"There is now," Warrick said. "All seats must send their manorial service of men, equipped and ready to fight. I know, Uncle, that you will want to lead your contingent of men."

Aristo Yonger rose in agitation. "But my lands are already under the control of the Pertelon!" He spread his hands in supplication. "King Warrick, I cannot fulfill my obligation."

"You are not expected to, Aristo Yonger."

Warrick cursed himself. Whatever his look, it alarmed Aristo Yonger.

~ * ~

"You are the Duke of Lambere's daughter?" a slow voice asked. Ottillie turned with Vesper to face Lady Agino. The lady wore high court style; her surgown's hem crawling behind her like an undulating slug. Her daughters stood with her, and Ottillie wished to slap away the smirks on their faces and in their minds. The oldest held her mother's arm, supporting her.

"Your Grace..." Ottillie stressed Vesper's title, feeling the Lady Agino's condescension. "...Lady Montoren, may I introduce Lady Agino." She pasted on her smile as she made the introductions in her haughtiest manner. "Aristo Agino's lady wife."

She watched Lady Agino stiffen at her tone, felt the lady's affront and also her sudden sense of caution. Whatever unwise words she was about to utter changed. Patronizing innuendo might be acceptable to an inferior Aristo's daughter, but not to the daughter of the ranking Aristo of Wessure.

"Then the bloodline is confirmed?" the Aristo's lady asked, scorn oozing from her pores. Her eyes fastened on Vesper. Some small movement drew her gaze to Kissre, who stood behind Vesper. Lady Agino gave the guard an unfazed frown.

Ottillie watched Kissre from the corner of her eye. The guard did nothing except maintain the Lady's stare. It was enough. Lady Agino blinked, took hold of the hand supporting her elbow and took a backward step.

"My father," Vesper said, "searched me out. I was lost to him when my mother and twin brother were murdered."

Ottillie's smile deepened as Vesper's voice hinted that she suspected Lady Agino of the crime. Her protégé learned quickly.

"Well." Lady Agino straightened. Her daughter's hand fell away. "I am sure he is delighted, even if you come married to a clansman."

"His Grace is most pleased, as is King Warrick, with the family's tie to the Clan Cader, and to the Aegis Kaereya," Ottillie informed all, including those eavesdropping on the conversation. "I'm sure you've heard, Her Grace and her husband the Aegis, saved the king's life."

"Yes. I do believe that rumor has made the rounds. It is true? It must be a whole new way of life for you."

"Some changes must be borne with no matter how difficult. My father's love eases the transition," Vesper said at her most demure.

"And you, Lady Ottillie, are to be congratulated. I heard from Aristo Yonger you traveled to Egan to find the Kennetsure Aegis."

"I set out for Zankiri, but to study only," Ottillie drawled.

"But such a successful adventure. Such jaunts cannot make you more marriageable unless you plan to marry a nomad?" Lady Agino hid her smirk in a smile. "But then, maybe Warrick will find you someone for your service to the crown."

"That, of course, is always a possibility, Lady Agino," Ottillie answered. The lady's tone suggested Ottillie serviced Warrick on a public street. "The king seems most pleased with those who remained loyal to him through these last difficult months. Do you wish me to mention your interest to him? Maybe he can help you with your daughters? We all know how uncivilized a place court can be, and how difficult it is to arrange a well-bred bonding for Handfasting. Have you just come from the gardens? How are they today?"

As Aristo Agino was well known for having breached the stream without reaching either shore, and Warrick had noticed the Aristo's lack of timely fealty, the Lady Agino's overripe color blanched. "The sun is reaching its zenith and it is turning too hot and sunny for the complexion." The lady fanned herself looking quite ill.

"We'll leave you then, to find some shade." Ottillie smiled. They took several paces away from Lady Agino in silence before she exploded in ire. "That brass-plated Aristo harpy." She kicked a plant and watched the petals of the blossoms shatter and fall to the ground. She added a few curses for good measure. "I hate court. Always have."

"Did her stab about Warrick cut the wrong way?" Vesper asked.

"A defense I learned long ago. At court everyone has something they wish forgotten. Right now, no one who remained at court wants to be mentioned to Warrick." Ottillie shook off her discomfort.

"It worked quite well."

In two more steps, both she and Vesper burst into smothered laughter. They were halfway down the walk lining the shrub parterre before they regained proper decorum.

"This is an ugly place," Vesper said as they entered the high terrace gardens. She had regained her usual quiet manner.

The royal gardens bloomed in the lush excess of early summer. "How can you say so?" Ottillie asked surveying the landscape. "The gardens are judged the best in all of Kaereya."

"Not the garden, the people. I am very glad I met you first, Ottillie, or I would not have a very good opinion of anyone at court."

"Don't mind Lady Agino. She is excessively proud and nosy into the bargain. Besides, you outrank her. There are good people here. You could gain entry to the highest circles at court if you chose."

"What about you?"

"I am not welcome there, nor do I aspire to those circles. I would not mind, Vesper, it is only natural."

Vesper turned on her with a mental broadcast of asperity. Sometimes Ottillie found her new Talent worked too well. "Natural for whom, Ottillie? You expect that I should turn my back on you when you are the only one who shows me courtesy without condescension, or worse, impertinent questions? When your conversation doesn't drip poisonous venom and your advice has saved me from embarrassing blunders that might have harmed Drew? Besides, do you think me deaf? I've heard the slurs floating around about you, me, and Kissre."

Ottillie cast a glance at Kissre and smiled. In fact, Kissre's impenetrable expression fared better at court than Vesper's openness. She wished she had been privy to Aurelias' meeting with Kissre, but Kissre had a gift for keeping her mouth firmly closed under the severest provocation. Her own experience with the mercenary-guard proved that.

Kissre's exotic appearance produced ripples of varying emotion through the more prurient and more prudish segments of the Court. Sensing the lascivious urges and witnessing the scandalized gazes offered amusement and provided another reason to accompany Vesper. With an inner laugh, Ottillie speculated that Kissre spent her off duty warding off a surfeit of unwanted advances.

"You think I don't know they call us the bastard, the orphan, and the barbarian?" Vesper had continued unaware of Ottillie's wandering attention.

Ottillie laughed. Those were the least of the slurs. She chose one of the more innocuous she had heard. "How about the cow, the doe, and the dog? Or the giantess, the elf, and the ogre?"

Vesper laughed, then sobered. "There are worse. The whore, the fraud, and the freak. They are terrible."

"You notice none with courage enough to say it to your face," Kissre spoke for the first time.

"Are you a freak, Kissre?" Ottillie asked, provocation thick in her tone.

"Are you a whore, Lady Ottillie?"

"Kissre! Of course she isn't!" Vesper said.

Ottillie gaped, then burst into laughter drowning out Vesper's defense. "It's all right Vesper, and a good thing we cannot be overheard here. I've been goading Kissre for days trying to find a sore spot. I know." She waved an apologetic hand at Vesper. "I've shocked you. It is a very perverse habit, but I think in Kissre, I've met my match. At least I finally wrung a response from her." She turned to Kissre. "I apologize. In that ducal uniform you look quite… attractive and in a most unmilitary way. Do you wish to wager that the next court fashion shall have a military motif?" She continued without an answer, "I shall have to remember you can defend yourself with words as well as weapons. A cautionary note. By the way, how many hecklers have you had to fend off?"

Kissre scowled at her, understanding her when Vesper did not.

"The army commandeers leave tomorrow." Vesper's statement stopped Ottillie's laughter, and she took Vesper's hand in a warm clasp. "I know."

"Most of the army have already gone, but Drew goes now. He will feel better away from these unpleasant people." Contained tears made her friend's eyes bright.

"Don't cry, Vesper. It brings out the blood lust of the nastier denizens of Court. Luckily, they are not all beastly, Vesper. Selwyn goes, too. He will protect Drew." She cast a look at Kissre. "And at a guess, you might have to get along with only my wicked company."

"No! Kissre, not you, too?" Vesper said.

"It is my profession." Kissre glared at Ottillie, then sighed. "But no. I stay to guard you. Your father doesn't trust anyone at court, and after the duke talked to him, neither does your husband."

Vesper turned to her guard. "You seek to convince him otherwise?" When Kissre said nothing, Vesper gazed at her with a curious look. "I will reinforce my father's good sense. You will be safer here."

"I don't need your protection," Kissre replied, almost in malicious intent that shocked Ottillie. "No matter what your vision ordains."

Vesper looked miserable. "There are so many influences at play…"

"Whatever your vision, it is my fate, not yours to interfere with."

Vesper burst into tears, and Ottillie held her and patted her back until she quieted and hiccupped and said, "I thought you might have an interest there."

She had caught her indiscreet comment before Ottillie realized she had made one.

"He is no easy conquest," Vesper added.

"All the better. So few of my size offer competition." She sighed. "But he gives little away, and I can only occasionally feel surface emotion on him, then usually irritation. Tell me, do you think there is interest?"

Vesper threaded an arm through hers as she wiped her eyes. "I suppose your provoking humor allowed you to survive in this hornet's nest. Selwyn would want to do things in a proper form. If he senses your interest…"

"He would have to be insensate not to," Ottillie said glumly. "Although, I have not felt any response."

"If he senses your interest, he will want to court you in proper form. Especially with you being a Lady."

"Proper form? Lady? You think he expects me to parade myself at a Handfasting? What an idiot!"

"You are a Lady. He is only newly knighted, and a clansman, not an Aristo."

"An Aristo lady who is known for not acting the lady's part. Has he no sense?"

"The beloved daughter of one of the most influential men at court," Vesper said.

"Damn." Ottillie considered her options. Time was short. "I will have to take a direct approach, I suppose."

"That should not prove difficult." Kissre's voice floated forward.

"And she bites, too," Ottillie said with all the practiced hauteur available to her.

Kissre actually grinned. Then she sobered. "Lady Agino mentioned she heard from Aristo Yonger that you went to seek the Aegis Kennetsure in Egan. How did he know? I believe I heard you mention to Lady Montoren your journey was secret? And who besides you and Warrick would know what transpired between you?"

"Nothing transpired between us," Ottillie said. "The whole court only speculates."

"Of course, the whole court knows you visited his audience chambers at his request. Many did. There should be no hint of suspicion."

It suddenly occurred to Ottillie how much Kissre heard. "What are you suggesting?"

"That maybe someone needs to investigate who knows so much about you, who might learn what service Warrick requested in a private audience."

"Everyone at court keeps track of Warrick."

"Even before the royal murders?"

"You know something," Vesper said.

"Just an observation. If not for my service to Lady Montoren and the interest she generates, I would be ignored here. Servants and guards are invisible to those they serve."

"And?" Ottillie asked.

"Tell your father to look for someone intimate with Warrick, known and accepted by the royal family, yet able to travel through the Eternal Palace or Hawk City unobserved."

~ * ~

Thanks to information supplied by Vesper, Ottillie knew where to locate her quarry. Her source proved accurate. Selwyn worked grooming horses in a barn on the edge of the palace's lower southern pasture. Numerous caves in the steep cliffs had been carved and enhanced to provide stabling. She still wore Court dress, perhaps a mistake at the wary look she received. He wore clan riding clothes. The brush he held stopped its motion over the horse's rump.

"Lady Ottillie."

"Clansman Selwyn." She didn't quite know how to go on.

"What can I do for you?"

Ottillie laughed at her sudden feeling of inadequacy. "That depends on how you feel." She exhaled. "To hell with coyness. I'm a witch, a bastard, brash, brazen, and too old to wait for Handfasting. I'll have you if you have a mind to have me." The one person who she needed to fathom emotionally, she couldn't. Too composed. He didn't answer. That spoke volumes, as did his silence.

She pasted a smile on her face. "I see. You dislike me or have no interest, and don't wish to offend my father. You need not worry. This was only my notion." She turned and walked back down the barn's aisle. *Mishandled!* The most important conversation of her life and her words were like a street woman's. For the first time in ages, Ottillie felt like crying, but that could wait until she reached her room.

A hand grabbed her shoulder and twirled her around suddenly. Hard lips pressed down on hers. Ottillie felt herself lifted. Lifted! It was delightful and she threw an arm around Selwyn's neck.

"I'm a surly, moody, bad-tempered clansman with a despised heritage among aristos, and I'm told a sad, prankish type of humor. I've been praying I read the signs right and wondering how to approach you. Vesper said you would entrap me, but I was too dense to understand."

"She told you?"

His hand fingered a strand of red hair fallen from its appointed place. "Long before I ever saw you. A blazing red fire would take me. That's what she prophesied. I didn't tell anyone because I thought she meant I'd die. She won't even remember doing so. Since seeing you it has taken on a whole new meaning. You would choose the night before I leave to spring your trap."

"A night lasts a long time if you let it."

"Not long enough, I'm sure. Let me put this horse away, my Aristo Lady."

"And then?"

He picked her up and twirled her around in a circle. "Tonight is as good as a Handfasting, but next year's ceremony, we go through the formalities, even if already bound."

She laughed and threw her arms around his neck.

~ * ~

The trip had been unusual for a Vere-bred man. The intrusion of water on his senses in every step of his journey through the Little Steps insured that. What didn't enter his mind through his gift, touched him physically.

The air, unlike the crystal purity of his Vere home, felt heavy with humidity. New scents, a synthesis of floral sweetness and rancid decay, and the constant screech of soaring coastal birds bound the shoreline in a distinct presence. The sun seemed more intense. Its light flickered on the water creating a luminescence far different from the skies of Vere. Small trees, twisted under the ceaseless push of prevailing winds, vied with strong but pliable grasses. The small islands, caught within the incredible Thou River and Haral Lake vistas, held power over his senses.

The horses' slow climb up the cliffs of Anatole into the walled recesses of Orvika left another. The city, huge and hulking as any trapped creature within its cage, stretched his tense senses. Noisy accolades as the army moved through fermenting streets revealed the citizens' strained emotions and disbelief of the situation in which they found themselves. It was a relief exiting through the city gate on the opposite side of the city. The unaccustomed acclaim twisted Drew into a tight plait.

The camp lay outside the city walls on rolling hills above the plains of the lower, eastern side of the island. Soldiers rose as he passed and their expectations at the sight of him made fear eat through him like maggots on a carcass. Shortly his father-in-law called a war council at a site overlooking the enemy. After another steep climb to the heights above the city, Drew saw the bivouac of the Pertelon Army.

"The enemy makes no move. They just sit there," Aristo Agino said.

Aurelias lowered his sight glass. He turned to the Royal Guard Commander. "Your men did well to hold them to the low ground.

"We had the advantage. Besides, they have what they want—a stranglehold on the eastern side. From there they can protect their ships as they sail to the southern waters. At this point defense is easier. They wait on us," the commander answered.

The Kennetsurean Leander stood next to Aurelias' horse, still looking through his sight glasses.

Drew reined Kuff to stand next to Aurelias' mount. Selwyn and Clan Chief Terril pulled up next to him. "To attack?" Drew asked looking out over the low eastern end of Anatole Island. The Pertelonese looked like mere specks across a long sloping expanse checkered in pasture and crops.

"Yes. You think you can help?" Aurelias answered.

"Impossible," Agino said.

Drew frowned. He didn't expect deference, and his father-in-law seldom gave it, but the Aristo Agino's abruptness made him feel foolish. "They are well entrenched."

"We have the better ground," Aurelias said. "But their defenses look formidable."

One of Aurelias' captains spoke. "With their ships they can circle behind us and take the Tiny Steps. That would cut us from our supply lines and Hawk Island."

"They won't. Warrick has placed mariners in the islands. They fight pirates on the high seas, so have experience. The enemy's only safe route is following their coastline along Haral Lake to the South Thou," Aurelias said.

"High seas and rough water might deter them," Drew said, feeling how he might push here and there to accomplish that.

"Good." Unlike others, Aurelias didn't question Drew's talent or doubt his ability.

"Something is troubling you," Drew said.

"The grass between our lines is thick and high, a good hiding spot for..."

"Clansman can prevent that," Clan Chief Terril said.

"Have you ever been in a real battle?" Agino asked Drew.

"No. A few border skirmishes. His Grace is the one with real battle experience."

Aurelias huffed a single snorted laugh. "Not enough. Each one is different from what you expect."

"What about the Protectors?" another captain asked. "Aren't the Protectors supposed to make sure all countries follow rules of engagement?"

"So the tales say," Gilchrist said.

Drew noticed the man's tone and the discreet exchange of looks passed among those standing behind the duke.

"Many believe," Aurelias said. "Others think them just stories." He passed his glass to Gilchrist who had held out his hand. "I've heard King Clement is one who doesn't believe. Don't expect him to hold to any rules."

"It is true," Leander said. "Pertelon tried to invade Kennetsure's eastern border some years ago. For the most part, Clement's army fights in a conventional way, but if things don't go his way, he has other means of winning."

"Prohibited weapons?" Drew asked.

"Yes," Leander said. "Canons. He used them in the south."

Drew listened to the surprise surfacing around him but remained silent a moment. "Are you sure?" he asked, at last as he raised the glass to view. "I see nothing."

"Can your magic stop them?" Aristo Agino asked, alarm entering his disdain.

"I don't know."

"Can you not sense these weapons? I thought that's what your magic did?"

"He is not this land's Aegis," Clan Chief Terril said, over loud.

"We must find out, for I fear we will have to take the battle to them and their canons, if they have them," Aurelias said. "How do we attack them?"

Several aristos offered plans. Aurelias did not dismiss them out-of-hand, aware of the sensitive natures and elevated pride of the men involved.

"A daylight frontal attack would fail," Leander said. Aurelias turned to the Zekarac Knight whose statement was hooted by several.

"All battles are fought in daylight," Aristo Yonger said.

The Kennetsurean remained calm. "Mostly," he said, nodding at the Aristo. "But if they have cannon, they sight their weapons better in daylight. There is more than one way to advance including harassing their flanks. That might create enough of a diversion to allow a direct frontal approach."

"A coward's way!" the same Aristo shouted back.

"Prohibited weapons only you claim they have," another said. "Aristo Aurelias, I will gladly lead a charge against the enemy."

Aurelias remained silent a moment. "Aegis Montoren, do you have any suggestions?" Several masked sniggers ran through the gathered aristos. Aurelias noted the stiffening postures of the clan chiefs present.

"About prohibited weapons? No. But the Clans and I will reconnoiter the enemy's positions. I agree a frontal attack will be very difficult, and Sir Leander's flank assaults might spur them to bring the battle to us."

"We must attack. They will not come to us. I can see it will take someone with a backbone to push these intruders out," Agino said. The aristos seemed aligned with their spokesman.

From there the argument ensued, but Drew had bumped Leander's arm and he said no more. He saw Aurelias sigh and knew there was only one way to settle the issue. A war could not be waged on unsupported suppositions.

Drew noted Gilchrist's satisfied expression and saw Aurelias' covert glance at the Aristo. He sensed the animosity between them. Aurelias turned his attention to Leander. "You've fought Pertelon?"

"Yes, Your Grace. They will use their weapons if they get close enough."

"How did you stop them?" Aurelias asked Leander.

"Sand. The Aegis Aldous uses it to great effect."

"If they use them, then both the Holy One and the Protectors shall take our side and Pertelon will be defeated," another Aristo said.

"Just in case they don't," Aurelias said, "I suggest both the expected frontal assault with unexpected flank assaults, at night and by stealth. The tall grass will hide many men placed at night for a first-light attack."

Twenty-one

"What have you heard?" Gilchrist asked. He lounged in a camp chair twirling the ale in his tankard and watching the motion. Aristo Yonger had been treating him with a lack of diffidence and a nervousness agitation. Both aroused his suspicion. The Aristo entered holding a missive received from Pertelon's King Clement. It arrived in a message pouch from a Hawk Island courier, a reminder Yonger had a hidden network of instruments. A network Yonger kept strictly to himself. "Are the cannons in place?" He knew the answer. Clansmen and Kennetsureans had already reported the placement of three cannons.

"Not enough." Yonger grimaced. "But the ships are off the eastern coast. It doesn't matter yet. They must lure Aurelias' army into firing range."

"In the meantime, any attack will be safe enough to participate in."

Gilchrist watched Yonger lay the message down on the small table and fill a tankard for himself. The Aristo downed the contents in several swallows and quickly poured a refill. He looked around Gilchrist's tent in loathing.

"Disgusting place."

"A war camp? Really, Yonger, it should be second nature for a land-grabber like you." He briefly wondered how his daughter felt about this craven man, not that she had a choice, or that it mattered.

"There are easier ways than having armies face off. Safer ways."

"Have you told them to Clement?" He laughed at the hate-filled look Yonger aimed at him. "Does your informant trust you implicitly, or does he even know of your motives? I've heard an undercurrent of suspicion about you." He laughed again. "I've even been warned to distance myself from you."

"Who?" Yonger demanded while straightening and slamming down his tankard.

"Agino. No one to worry about. Does your information tell you when the cannons will land? Do you know?"

"The sea on the eastern end of the island has been too rough to land the canon." He smote his hand with his other fist. "That damn Drew Montoren's work I'm sure. I have been ordered to kill him."

"Our efforts would be easier without him," Gilchrist agreed.

"Clement ran into witches in Cygna. That's why he tried to wipe out any magic vestiges in Kaereya."

"His agents just missed Drew Montoren? A large oversight. Killing him in a camp under heavy guard might prove difficult," Gilchrist said. "Although, I must admit, the effect on morale would be devastating."

Yonger snorted and moved to look out the tent's open flap, his hand grasping one of the supports. "He will be dealt with, never fear. I won't let that youngster destroy my future... or you."

"Aristo!" Gilchrist feigned surprised dismay. "What do you mean? I've supported all your goals." He rose to refill his tankard.

"While keeping your own hands unsullied," Yonger answered looking over his shoulder. "It's time, Duke Hearthron, to dirty your hands." He returned his gaze to the men working outside the tent.

"What do you suggest? I ask my troops to turn on the Aegis? Don't be ridiculous. They are loyal men. Those I left on at my estates are even more loyal. They have reason to be."

"You are so smug in yourself! You have no idea of how Clement works. Others like you are out there, working as he directs. There is another agent at court, you know. Clement didn't put all his confidence in you."

"No, but none were so well placed, I'm sure. I expect he didn't put his total faith in you either. You should place your trust in me. Especially when we both know King Clement will sacrifice us in the blink of an eye." He smiled as he saw the affirmation of the truth in Yonger's face as it turned to him from the camp view. "Your men are supposedly behind enemy lines, but you get regular reports. Have them take the Aegis out in honest combat. Neither you nor I can be held responsible."

"But if it is discovered my men…"

"Have them dress as common soldiers. Who knows what flotsam might attack the Aegis's banner?"

"And if it is discovered?" Yonger moved toward him.

"They have been behind enemy lines. Obviously coerced into this heinous deed. You couldn't have had contact with them, could you?"

Yonger looked at him. "No. I suppose I couldn't have, could I? Especially if no one survives." His eyes fell on the folded message next to the pitcher.

Gilchrist picked up the paper and held it over the time candle. "Don't want to leave this around, do you?"

"Indeed not."

Gilchrist smiled as Yonger watched it burn. Dropping the last edge to the rug-lined floor, he stomped it out with his boot. Yonger bowed and left the tent.

"Indeed not," Gilchrist said to his back, his fingers running along the edge of paper under his vest. "You will pay for Tate's death, betrayer." After a few minutes of thought, he sought out Aristo Agino.

~ * ~

Vesper watched Leela pour the tea, made after a careful ritual, into three beautiful cups. Her butter-colored Kennetsurean tunic flowed into ever-changing soft folds with her movements and the breeze coming in the open window. The summer air scent permeated the air and Vesper sighed in pleasure. Alfred lounged on the windowsill, watching gulls swoop outside the tower room allocated the seeress.

"You have done very well with today's lesson, Ottillie," Leela said to Vesper's fellow student. "Your sense of another's emotions is far more accurate. You read both Vesper and me very well." Light from the window highlighted the old sorceress' white hair as she handed Ottillie one of her precious cups. "Although I could wish you had a better teacher. Kissre, come join us. You are a distraction and have stood by the door long enough."

Vesper turned her head to look at her guard. Kissre stood in a relaxed but alert stance, looking a little bored. Turning back to Leela, Vesper caught Ottillie's harassing smile aimed at the guard. Kissre ignored her redheaded tormentor.

"I am on duty, Lady Leela," Kissre said.

Leela laughed. "Vesper?" Her new teacher held a cup toward her, that Vesper gingerly took, still afraid she might inadvertently crush the fragile-looking material.

"My ordering or pleading will do no good, Leela," Vesper said. "My father gave her orders, and I'm afraid only he can change them."

"Then, Kissre," Ottillie said, twisting her head to look at her. "You must stand on the other side of the door. You can guard Vesper as well from outside as in."

Kissre obeyed. Ottillie grinned. And Vesper realized Kissre would probably find more amusement on the other side of the door.

"So duty-bound," Leela said, tsking in exasperation. She took her cup and breathed the vapors coming off the hot brew.

"And impenetrable," Ottillie added. "Although the bullies at court give her wide berth now."

Leela took a sip from her cup and relaxed. "Much better. A cup of tea on duty would not injure her reputation. Why is that?"

"They taunted her for days and got away with it. Play acted sword fights with her, mocking her. She didn't react. One of them made the mistake of accidentally pushing me into Vesper," Ottillie said.

"And?"

Vesper smiled. "They all found themselves on the ground. It happened very fast and with great force. She stepped over them and motioned us away." She took a sip of tea, pursing her mouth into a prim line that both conveyed mockery and innocence.

"You look like you've swallowed a whale whole," Ottillie laughed at her. She took up the story. "When the young aristos' took their complaints to Warrick, he asked Kissre to show him what she had done. She did. When they were on the floor again, he congratulated her," Ottillie finished with a grin.

Her friend recounted the event with admiration but had teased Kissre over it. The continual goading irritated Vesper, perhaps because of her own guilt over Kissre's future. She looked into her cup, avoiding expression. Kissre's temper had to be tried by the constant barrage of friend and foe, and she had led her to this place to save Drew. At least she was safe here, not at the front, but guilt still made Vesper's moments uncomfortable.

She was glad her guard had left the room, though. It was unnerving having Kissre watch as they worked through Leela's lessons. Having Alfred's presence was enough to deal with, although he seemed to find it entertaining since he always showed up for the lessons. The rest of the time he abandoned Vesper.

"You are very hard on Kissre," Leela said to Ottillie as if she read Vesper's disquiet.

"It is a game."

"One Kissre knows you are playing?"

Ottillie laughed. "Since she is winning, I am sure she does!"

"Are you using her for entertainment, Ottillie?" Vesper asked.

Ottillie acted injured. "No! I like Kissre." She sighed in failure. "I've tried to sense her but can't. It goads my curiosity."

Vesper read the frustrated furrow on Ottillie's brow clearer than her words.

"Not even Kissre has a sense of Kissre, I'm afraid," Leela said, sipping from her cup. "And what does your guard think of your refashioning?" She inspected Vesper's new raiment. "Very elegant. I detect Ottillie's attention to detail. But the lines and color combinations differ from Ottillie's usual choices."

"Ottillie has been of great service in guiding me in matters of dress and manners. I have thoroughly enjoyed myself, but never realized I needed so many clothes. Kissre would not presume to comment, but she finds my fittings tedious."

"Vesper is as conservative and tight-fisted as her father."

"What did you expect, Ottillie?" Leela inquired, waving a hand at her raiment. "How many can wear... what are those colors?"

"Butterscotch, lemon, and wine."

"Yes. A veritable feast. Well, it is lucky I am the teacher here, and not the student. I don't know if I have Vesper's restraint."

"How many students have you had?" Vesper asked thinking it time to intervene. Both Leela and Ottillie loved verbal sparring.

Ottillie grinned at her. "Turning the subject?"

"You've been horrible. First to Kissre, which is like kicking a chained animal. She is, you know, very dedicated and loyal."

"And well paid?"

"Then you start on Leela."

"Excuse me, but Leela started on me. And don't worry about Kissre. I don't unsettle her at all. Matter of fact, I think she quite enjoys watching me make a fool of myself." Ottillie quibbled but she followed Vesper's lead. "Well, Leela, how many?"

Leela looked abashed. "You are my first. Kennetsure, let alone all of Kaereya, hasn't been awash in likely students. To get two at once is quite remarkable."

Both she and Ottillie started at their teacher's admission. "Then where did you learn?"

"Do you mean to tell us you don't know what you're talking about?" Ottillie said drowning out her words.

Leela chose to answer Vesper's question. "A long time ago there was a seeress among the Doane nomads that come to Egan. On each trip to Egan she would teach me a little, then leave. The next year she would return and teach me more. She told me she couldn't stand staying in one place too long. She was a healer also, although far more capable than I. She could actually mend an injury with her mind, see an illness within the body. It was most remarkable."

"What happened to her?" Vesper asked.

"She left and the tribe disappeared into the Doane. It happens. She always told me it was my duty to teach those I found."

"Who taught her?"

"Another witch." She sighed and smiled at Ottillie. "That's how it is done in Kaereya. I also read Chloe's journals. After reading about Cygna, I dreamed of going there to learn. Only there can you find teachers in these arts."

"Cygna doesn't welcome strangers," Ottillie said.

Leela sighed. "Not anymore. Some traders enter. Ages ago a few Cygnese scholars visited us, but not Talents, and not in the last hundred years or so."

"You remember?" Ottillie asked in a provocative tone.

Leela straightened and glared at Ottillie. "Egan keeps excellent records."

Vesper giggled and changed the subject again. "Ottillie said King Warrick wants to dig up the church."

"What's this?" Leela asked, instantly engaged. "Have you convinced him to search for the old spell?

Ottillie explained Warrick's predicament. "He said he would talk to the Bishop."

"I should like to participate if Warrick would permit, and I'm sure Vesper might be inspired by the surroundings."

"Thank you for my part of the self-invitation, but I have enough problems with inspiration and have no wish to seek out more."

Leela waved a dismissing hand, her tunic floating about her arm. "You are gaining better control and understanding of your visions. You should welcome them."

"I will ask," Ottillie said.

"Well," Leela said, putting down her cup. "I think it is your turn. Don't look so apprehensive. Ottillie and I are here, and we can help you interpret your visions. Relax as I taught you and let it happen."

Vesper shifted uncomfortably. "It is so confusing. They come one upon another now."

"Anyone or anything dead?" Ottillie asked.

Vesper glared at Ottillie. "I still see the falling knife and the shield. They tumble through the air endlessly, then the shield shatters on rocks."

"Falling knives have traditionally foretold dangerous strangers."

"Seer symbols?" Ottillie asked.

"No, common superstition," Leela answered. "It seems as good a guide as any. The shield with the Vere Aegis symbol must be Drew."

"But it shatters! What does that mean?" Vesper said, moving in her anxiety. "When I had visions before, it was as though another's eyes, but now more often in symbols I don't understand."

"Through another's eyes for definite probabilities, symbols for abstract possibilities."

"You're making that up," Vesper accused.

Leela shrugged. "It is the best I can do under the circumstances."

"A shattered shield might mean danger, or that Drew is injured," Ottillie said.

"Or that the spell is broken," Leela said, "or changed. The Vere shield shatters and spreads pieces on the land of Kaereya. It fits what has happened."

"Then why do I still see it?"

"Do you see Drew injured or bleeding?"

"Sometimes."

"And?"

"Sometimes I see Kissre. Sometimes I see a dragon. Grief, Leela, I see dragons, unicorns, and Fair Folk. I see all kinds of unexplainable things! How am I to make sense of it?"

"Well," Leela interrupted. "The dragon usually represents the Easure Aegis and that is not Kissre. The Easure Aegis has been dead many years. There are no heirs left," Leela said and sighed. "Looking back, it is possible Clement had a hand in that, too." She remained silent overlong. Ottillie looked at the old woman in concern before Leela spoke again. "Now that I've had a moment to reflect, my guess is that the symbols represent some distant future, and the other visions regarding incidents happening closer to the present. Go ahead and see if you can encourage a vision."

Leela's guessing didn't reassure Vesper. She reluctantly put her cup down, found a comfortable position, closed her eyes, and took a series of deep breaths. Nothing happened except Ottillie exhaled, and Vesper looked at her.

"Sorry, I was holding my breath."

Leela looked at Ottillie in disgust before encouraging Vesper. "Think back, Vesper, to when you've had visions. When did they occur?"

"When I was tired or gazed at the fire overlong." Vesper opened her eyes. "And when I looked in the mirror in my bedroom."

"Visualize the mirror in your mind. What does it look like?"

"A round of blue glass that reflects things slightly different from how they really are." This time she didn't close her eyes, but she felt her mind drift away in a dreamy way. Everything became unfocused.

"What do you see?" Leela asked.

"Berneta is making bread. I can smell the kitchen at Montoren. She is giving a little boy warm bread. I don't know the child."

"Try again. Look at the mirror." Vesper reformed the mirror in her mind, felt its image form, felt her own gasp of surprise.

She was back in the chamber of hanging threads. Each string scintillated with iridescent color and sound, but all seemed white. The old woman was gone, a younger woman sat at a loom, beating the weft from the hanging strands into the warp. It was herself. Her double smiled at Vesper as she passed the shuttlecock through the threads. "Choose one," she said. Vesper did not return her smile and twirled once to look about her. She reached out and touched one of the singing threads. The room changed.

"What do see, Vesper?" It was Leela's voice, demanding.

"A room. Dark wainscoting, four small windows form a cross, but no furniture. Warrick is there, alone."

"How do you know it is Warrick?" Leela asked.

"I see him. He holds a box."

Ottillie gasped recognizing the room. "You've seen..."

"Quiet!" Leela said.

Vesper opened her eyes in shock, her body jerking in startled movement. "The knife. I saw it again. Tumbling over and over."

"It's the dangerous stranger. Look back Vesper, and see what Warrick sees, feel what he feels," Ottillie demanded.

Vesper closed her eyes and swayed in a hypnotic motion. It took a moment, but the vision remained. "He is sad. Always sad. He is opening the box." She screamed in agony, and felt arms around her, reassuring her. The door banged and she heard Kissre enter. Time passed, or at least she thought it did. Vesper looked at the three women in the room staring at her.

"What happened?" Leela asked.

"Someone stabbed him. Stabbed Warrick, in the back. Someone he trusts."

~ * ~

"Ride next to me," Aurelias ordered as he passed Drew and Selwyn. Their gray horses stepped into line with his as they went to inspect the change in the battle lines. Aurelias knew the three horses presented an impressive sight to the assembled army, knew brave displays often encourage the common soldiers. This one was tied to the magic Drew represented. His Wessureans called the horses and clansmen 'North Vere'. The accent had been misheard as 'Novere' by the rest of the army. He was afraid Drew was stuck with the name for his horses.

On his left the Duke of Hearthron rode, assuming his right to that position. Fifteen aristos, messengers, and his squire fell in behind them, including Aristo Yonger, whose lands were invaded. He had a discreet watch kept on the two men. Yonger rode in safety behind Aurelias, disseminating criticism of the plan and predictions of defeat with every utterance. Aurelias fumed but tried to remain positive at his presence. Gilchrist delegated his arms captain to lead his men.

After several skirmish attacks by the Pertelon Army, the enemy had been slowly pushed back day by day, and Aurelias held Drew by his side.

"The Pertelon lines have moved back a half league," Aurelias said when they reached the bluff overlooking the armies. "Do you know if they've been supplied?" he asked Drew.

"Scouts reported two ships offshore that have not unloaded," Drew said.

The land gently sloped eastward toward the river lake where the Pertelon Army entrenched.

"They've retreated less than three leagues," Yonger said, "It is still eight leagues to their main camp. There is no way to prevail over such a distance. It is impossible."

"The clansmen have worked in closer. They will add some protection as the foot soldiers advance," Drew said.

Aurelias watched his son-in-law, the younger man's anger at being held behind the advancing line evident. Although better trained for battle than many of the soldiers on the field, Drew was considered too valuable, and he chaffed at the restrictions placed on him. Each night a combined force of clansmen and Kennetsurean tribesmen worked behind enemy lines, scouting, harassing the soldiers. So far it had been a battle of slow attrition.

The cost of whatever land tricks his son-in-law performed showed. This land was too new feeling for him, and he still learned it, his cousin reported. His fatigue contributed to his short temper but Aurelias noticed he was given little leeway by his clansmen.

In the hills surrounding them, guardsmen and clansmen hunted for stragglers, for potential assassins left behind. As the enemy's foothold on Anatole Island shrank, Aurelias had concerns the Pertelonese commander toyed with him, felt he was allowing his army to walk into a trap.

Shouting and the movement of men to the left drew Aurelias' attention. A small platoon of men broke through the woods and with bows already knocked. It took precious seconds to realize they were not Kaereyan soldiers. Several knelt while the rest charged his group. Pulling his blade, Aurelias shouted to protect the Aegis and wheeled his mount in unison with most of the aristos. Royal Guardsman and his personal troops charged the attackers. They quashed the futile attack quickly and he was surprised at the lassitude he felt after the brief encounter.

He turned to see if Drew was all right, but everyone's alarmed face looked at him. Looking down, he felt surprised to see the arrow emerging from his hauberk, then he fell into darkness.

~ * ~

Ottillie wished to avoid company knowing how disturbed she looked. She needed to tell her father Vesper's vision and was in somewhat of a hurry, so ducked down the stairs to the tunnels. Must, sour decay and pollution offended her nose. Carefully she raised her skirt hem and watched her step. Grimacing, she ran through the filth. Slippers were not meant for such a foul place.

She happily opened the door out of the tunnel. Before starting up the staircase she stopped to wipe her slippers clean on some gunnysacks stacked by the door. She stilled, sensing two people nearby, on the stair landing one flight above her. One mind repelled her with its slimy falseness. The second's emotional identification was new to her but not the voice. It took little time to place it, even in the low pitch of their words. Recognition brought a wish to have never come this way. Eldin spoke.

She had known Eldin still with the Royal Guard, but she had not sought him out. And it was clear—those she eavesdropped on sought to hide their presence.

The unknown voice rose slightly with an ultimatum. "Do this or lose all you seek to gain. The Pertelon army will succeed in any case. Without Warrick it will end all the quicker."

"There is the Aegis. He will rally the Kaereyan Army. Pertelon won't easily win."

"That is already taken care of. The spirit of the Kaereyan army will crumble and break with the loss of this so-called Aegis. Pertelon has superior power and will win in any event, but it is quicker this way. You chose your side, now you must prove your worth. Clement doesn't reward cowardice." The talking ceased with one set of footsteps stomping upstairs.

With dismay Ottillie heard a second set come down the staircase. It was useless to step back into the tunnels, as she would be seen anyway. She waited. It was not the stranger she sensed coming down the stairs, but Eldin. At his first sight of her he stopped.

"I didn't expect to encounter you here," she said.

"How much did you hear, Ottillie?" Eldin spoke in a low, desperate whisper. She sensed her answer didn't matter.

"Why, Eldin? You were beginning to improve your status. Why treason?" She whispered.

"Improve my status!" His face contorted into a dangerous mask of malice, but the vehemence in his voice never raised its level. In a quick, agile movement, he pulled a knife from his belt sheath and took two steps to twist her arm behind her back.

Even taller than Eldin, a strong woman and forewarned, she couldn't move. The Royal Guards had taught him how to fight, how to kill, and Eldin's slight form hid exceptional strength. His blade dug against the flesh under her chin. She felt a liquid trickle down her neck and held her breath, waiting. Fear temporarily overwhelmed her. She squeezed her eyes shut with a strong sense of loss. Perspiration broke on her forehead and prickled under her arms as she waited.

Against the pressure of the blade, she spoke. "They've asked you to kill Warrick. Don't do it, Eldin. You cannot."

The knife just as suddenly left her throat. "By the Holy One, Ottillie, I cannot kill you." He stepped back. He laughed. "This is a farcical situation. You could squash me by falling over."

She opened her eyes and looked at Eldin. He appeared more like the man she remembered, but despair framed the humor in his eyes.

"I am tall, not fat," she said, brushing down her skirts and pulling out a kerchief to dab her neck. The cloth came back bloodied, but already the minor wound sealed. "And you had the sharper weapon."

"For that, I am truly sorry."

"It is the slightest scratch. Why? I have worried so about you. Was your need that strong? You deceived me, deceived my father. You never warned the garrisons."

He turned his head from her. "Call for help, Ottillie. Let's get this over. I only acted how everyone expected me to act." He spoke in his normal voice.

"Not everyone. Many saw the good man you were. Whom do you act for, Eldin?"

"You don't think I act for myself? You think me incapable of a well-planned deception that has already cost several aristos their precious holdings?"

"Please?"

He didn't answer her plea. "Hate, Ottillie. It twists you out of shape. May you never know its bite. Then, how could you with such a loving and powerful father?"

"Excuses?" She stood looking at him, unable to stop her pity response.

When she said no more, he sighed and repeated, "Call the guards."

It was an instantaneous response. Stepping from the entrance to the tunnels, she walked slowly to the staircase. "Go, Eldin, if you can't tell me the conspirator, just go! For the sake of our friendship, for what I know you have endured, get out of Kaereya."

"That makes you a conspirator, Ottillie. I won't sacrifice you to save myself."

"I'm not asking you to. As for conspiracy, I know what will happen to you, and I don't think I could bear it. I have made no oath to anyone. You know I will go directly to my father. You cannot reach Warrick before he puts even more Guardsmen about the king. My faith in the Aegises and in Kaereya's internal strength allows me to do this. I will confess my sins and live with them."

Eldin again approached her in a few long strides. His hand stretched toward her and touched her cheek. "I would not have killed Warrick for him, Ottillie, but the king will die." He leaned in and kissed her on the cheek. She withdrew from him, but his hand caught hers and curled her fingers over the paper he placed in her palm.

His quick smile faded, and he withdrew a step from her. "You won't find the other conspirator with that, Ottillie. I don't know who he is. We meet in dark places and he is always hooded, never shows his face. I give you this in return for what you are doing for me, and I swear to you I had nothing to do with the old king's death, nor any of his family, nor anyone else's family." He stepped back from her and looked away. "A letter also came to me in Gotte City. One I didn't tell you about. I was promised a manorial position in the newly established monarchy. It's all I've dreamed of for a very long time. Respectability. It means everything. There are those in the Eternal Palace who would never give it, no matter how often I earned it." His lips twisted in anger that he slowly controlled as he turned to look at her. "Forgive me, but I will find it in Pertelon."

"You won't, Eldin, not until you find it in yourself. I won't see you again. Knowing you would not harm the king will assuage my conscience some small bit." She reached up and pulled a gold chain free from over her head. "Here. You will need money. Sell this."

He took her offering and looked at it, then pulled a chain free from his neck. "You will want this back."

"No. Keep it. You will need it."

A laugh broke from him. His eyes truly sparkled now. "Your Easure dragon has not brought me good luck."

"You live, and I'm setting you free for the sake of our past friendship, that is indeed luck."

Eldin laughed, a sour sound lacking all joy. "I will miss you." He had opened the door before he looked at her again. "If I had position to offer, I would have asked for you, even if you do tower over me."

Ottillie bit her lip in sadness. "I would have accepted with or without. Goodbye, Eldin." She had shocked him. It was clear in his eyes.

"Come with me. You are of a state of birth that will forever hold you back here. Together we could do much to improve ourselves."

"I cannot. Just be glad I hold our friendship higher than my father's duty to bring you to mortal justice, but I will never think of you again." Whatever Eldin saw in her face, caused hope to leave his eyes. The door closed behind him.

Holding her chin steady, Ottillie began to slowly climb the stairs, taking care there was no one lingering about them. Halfway up a notion struck her, and she started running. Foolish, stupid girl, she damned herself. The conspirator, whomever it might be, might enlist more than one assassin. Eldin was but one tool, and he knew more than he said.

She flung the door of her father's apartment open. Thank the Holy One he was there. "The king is in danger, and they plan to kill the Aegises, too."

Her father looked up from where he sat talking to Corbin Napier. Both looked shocked and rose. She closed the door and explained what Eldin had told her. "Do something! Protect Warrick! By the Holy One, how can I tell Vesper this?"

Her father wrote a note and told Corbin to hand it to Warrick with the message only the king should read. "Make sure he is never left alone!"

Corbin nodded and left the room, quick for his large size.

"Tell me exactly what happened." Her father closed the door behind Corbin. "What happened to your neck?" He roared in outrage, noticing the cut. "Who did this to you?"

"It is nothing, listen." She waved away his concern, her voice sharp. "You must send a messenger to Aurelias, to Drew. He must be warned." She told the past candlemark's events to her father.

He called a page and gave orders. "Get Kissre Pierce, you know of whom I speak?" The boy nodded and raced away. By the time the mercenary arrived, he had written out a message and sealed it. Vesper followed Kissre as the guard entered the room. "Take this to Aurelias with all haste, place it in his hands only! I will personally guarantee the safety of your charge."

"No," Vesper said. "She cannot." Ottillie felt Vesper's turmoil, her hope and despair, guilt and shame wrapped in one package.

"She must. Kissre I can trust with this message. I need all the others I trust to protect the king."

"Why, Vesper?" Ottillie asked.

Vesper ignored her and turned to Kissre, putting a hand on her sleeve. "I am most sorry, I have lied to you, manipulated you into coming here to serve my purposes."

"Is this about my dying, again?"

"Yes."

"Then why try and stop me now?"

"Because I cannot trade your life for Drew's life. I thought I could when I first convinced you to come, but it is wrong."

"What have you seen?" Ottillie asked.

"Until Kissre found me in the Great Salt Marsh, I had been assailed with the vision of Drew's death." She raised her eyes to Kissre. "After you saved me, I had another vision. I saw a dragon slain. What I didn't tell you was, with that vision, the other changed, and Drew lived."

Kissre laughed. "Because of this?" She held up her marked hand. "I told you then that all mercenaries face that risk. It is nothing new, and I am trained and used to protecting myself."

"But the vision hasn't changed, even with you here and not with Drew."

The appeal failed. Ottillie felt no emotion, saw no reaction. The blue-traced hand took the extended envelope from the King's Marshal. Without flourish Kissre left the room. Vesper started crying and Ottillie wrapped an arm around her.

"You know your visions only predict, and any circumstance can make them change. She is at least forewarned."

Her father wasted no time at that moment castigating her but put her through an intense interrogation. Rebuke came later, followed by forgiveness and understanding. Except shame and fear didn't depart as easily as Eldin escaped. Her actions could have grave consequences. A traitor remained free to act.

Although the Royal Guards hunted the tunnels, hunted Cliff City, and Hawk Island, they did not find Eldin. Half sorry, half glad, Ottillie knew whatever happened, she had to live with the consequences of her actions. She had sacrificed one friend for another. Drew's safety for Eldin's undeserved safety. Her possible relationship with Selwyn for a poor reflection of friendship. How would Selwyn feel when he learned she put Drew at risk? She prayed the Holy One to give Kissre's horse wings.

~ * ~

Drew listened to the land. This ground was as old and enduring as Vere. Erosion-rounded granite peaks rose out of the deep river and formed many of the islands. The moon pulled the water in a familiar age-old cycle he had experienced in Wessure. Here, it would have different effects, flooding, and high tides. In the moonlight he saw the beaches and the high cliffs lining them settled with waterfowl and hawks. Along the vast expanse of shoreline, waves shattered in the mouths of caves and subterranean chambers, swamps and quagmires filled quiet backwaters. A glimmer of light on the eastern horizon showed the night's reign nearly ended. He hated the dawn's impending arrival.

By Gilchrist's order, tomorrow, on the long stretch of slope below him, Kaereyan men would face the Pertelonese, perhaps for the last time. Time was short. As ranking Aristo, Gilchrist took charge of the army until Warrick appointed someone new. The new commander had decided on decisive action, declaring they "had wasted too much time worrying about prohibited weapons that never appeared."

His father-in-law lived, but according to the healer, badly wounded.

He immersed himself in Easure, from the hill borders of Vere to the endless southern sand wastes of Kennetsure. Intuitive awareness came to him with clarity and surety, but with no accompanying revelation on how to use it.

A pounding distraction interrupted him. Even from here, he heard and felt the powerful hooves of a single horse approaching at speed. A messenger. It pulled him back to reality.

On the slope below him, Drew saw a great horse, pale in the moonlight, rush the slope to where the Kennetsure Army camped. He recognized Kissre's Bother. Fear flicked his apprehensions like saltwater on a bloody wound and brought him to his feet. Selwyn stood next to him, placing a tight grip on his shoulder. Aurelias' mercenary pulled her sweat-lathered horse to halt before camp aides holding lanterns. Starting down from his own precipice, he agonized at what news she brought.

Before he and Selwyn arrived in camp, Kissre strode toward them, leading her horse. Drew noticed the wet sides of the animal before he saw the rider's exhaustion.

"They would not let me see Aurelias," Kissre said, then explained her presence. "The Earl of Rickon sent me with a message for the Duke of Aurelias. I will not give it to another Aristo." Looking at his face she said, "Vesper is fine. She is staying with Norbert and his daughter. He swore he would protect her. Ottillie found a traitor at court."

Drew asked, "Did Aristo Gilchrist demand to see the message as it came from the King's Marshall?"

"Ottillie?" Selwyn asked at the same time. "Found a traitor? Is she unharmed?"

Kissre's head swung to Selwyn in unison with his. "Yes—to all. I had specific orders on delivery of the message."

Selwyn reddened in irritation, then huffed, "Why come to us?"

"As His Grace's son-in-law, I felt I could ask you to intervene with Aristo Gilchrist so I might complete my charge. It is very important, and is between my employer and his close friend, Aristo Norbert, Earl of Rikon, and not for any else."

Selwyn and the clansmen behind him came closer as she spoke, all aware of the slight given the king's uncle. Drew looked at the very foreign-looking woman, yet with the familiar blonde-brown hair, face, and body structure of some of the eastern Vere clans. The clansmen present recognized her as their own, saying for all her gold jewelry and the tattoo, her linage was apparent. Her looks augmented the trust her words already secured. She continued after the brief silence.

"I cannot give the message to you, but I know the contents. There is a plan afoot to kill Warrick. Another to kill both Aegises, in particular, you." She looked at him. "The Aristo Agino told me His Grace is wounded but no more. Is it so bad no one can see him?"

Drew ran a hand along Bother's sweaty chest, checking the big buckskin. "He needs to cool down." At his signal, a Clansman took the reins and led Bother away with orders to 'walk him cool', while

Drew watched with a pensive expression. "I did not think Aurelias so badly injured he could not speak. We will check." Drew headed to Aurelias' tent.

Kissre fell in step next to him, ignoring her rancor at being told how to care for her horse. Selwyn and some other clansmen followed. Before they reached the tent Aristo Agino intercepted them.

"I've already refused this person entry. The Duke of Aurelias is resting."

"As family, I presume I can visit him."

"He is asleep."

"He sleeps overlong don't you think? I want to speak with the healer."

"His Grace, the Duke of Hearthron sent his own healer to treat the Duke of Lambere. He has returned to Hearthron's camp to help the wounded there."

Ignoring Agino, Drew entered the tent. Aurelias lay on his camp bed in something deeper than ordinary sleep. A light sheet covered his naked body and bandages crisscrossed his chest. "How long has he been this way?" he asked Aurelias' squire, who kept watch from a nearby stool.

"He's been this way since the healer left. The man said he would sleep while exhausted from the wound."

"Did he say how long he would sleep?" Drew asked and bent over Aurelias.

"The healer said maybe days," Agino said, having followed them into the tent. "He left a mild draft to help with the pain."

"Campaign Commanders do not take drafts to help ease pain," Kissre said with no deference at all. She picked up the flagon and smelled it. In placing it back on the table she knocked it over. The contents spilled onto the rug lining the tent floor.

Agino shouted in dismay and gave her a demeaning, indignant look. "Clumsy bitch! You have no say in this whatsoever!"

She took two steps toward the Aristo. Agino backed to the tent flap. "If you have harmed my employer, it very much becomes my say and your regret." Her hand fell to her sword hilt. Agino left.

"Kissre?"

She turned back at his voice. "I know enough healing, Aegis Montoren, to know you don't give someone what was in that flagon, not if you want them to wake."

"I'm sorry, sir," the squire, Thomai, said. "There was naught I could do when they sent His Grace Gilchrist's healer to help. I didn't know what to do, except watch for treachery."

Kissre gave him a disgusted look. "That flagon contained more than a mild draft. You could have gone to the Aegis or sent someone if you were worried about leaving him alone. You have failed in this service to your master. Quillon will be informed," Kissre told the young man.

The threat worked and the squire looked ready to burst into tears but nodded his head. Drew listened but ignored the situation to give his attention to Aurelias. Kissre joined him, quickly taking off the bandages.

"I think His Grace may have suffered from too much skill," she said at his look.

"I doubt Aristo Gilchrist will send his healer again."

"I have some small knowledge of wounds—mostly from experience. Perhaps we can find a better treatment," Kissre answered. She looked at the chest wound. "This is not so bad. It did not hit a vital area. His gear must have kept it from going too deep. It is clean and not seeping."

She turned to Thomai. "Get the Zekarac Knight, Leander. Tell him to bring a pitcher of coffee. Ask him also to find another healer."

A few candlemarks later they sat before a campfire outside Aurelias' tent and waited for the duke to wake. The clan chiefs and Leander sat with them. Kissre asked after the strategy of the campaign.

"Have they done night attacks?" Kissre asked.

Selwyn huffed in disgust. "Yes, but they have been discontinued. Aristo's influence on Gilchrist. They thought them useless."

"Do you see opportunities?"

"Not many," Terril answered.

"I cannot manage the land," Drew answered.

"Someone betrayed you to the Pertelonese," Kissre said.

"My presence has been no secret."

"You are a target now."

"We will keep watch, Lady," Selwyn said from where he squatted before the fire.

"No Lady, no title. Just Kissre."

Before long Gilchrist also arrived with a coterie of adherents, including an agitated but vindicated-looking Aristo Agino.

"What is this? A war council without me?"

Kissre rose and spoke before anyone else could move. "Aristo Aurelias' son merely informs me of His Grace's health and how I can be of assistance."

"Why have you ignored the healer's advice for our Commander?" Gilchrist asked.

"Because the man didn't seem to know much about battle wounds. My personal guard acted out of common sense and her vast battle experience."

Drew looked behind him. Aurelias stood, wrapped in a sheet, and braced between his squire and a Kennetsurean healer, haggard-looking but awake. Those before the fire rose in respect and Aurelias motioned them down.

"I am, of course, glad to see the army's Commander restored to his senses," Gilchrist said, "even if not fully recovered. It is important, Raymond, that I lead the attack tomorrow."

~ * ~

Clan Chief Terril rode up and spoke as he reached Drew standing on the hill's crest. "The aristos are forming for their frontal attack. We have been ordered to work from this protected hilltop. They think to hold us from the battle." He spit, just missing Kissre who stood beside him. She sidestepped his expectorate.

Drew gazed out over the land with his eyes squinting against the bright light.

Kissre swore and everyone's attention turned to where she looked through her sight glass. Taking the glass, he saw what caused

Kissre's profanity. Across the long expanse of land, teams of horses and men drew long cylinders into position.

"What do you see?" Clan Chief Terril asked. The charge horns blew and the Kaereyan army moved forward. Drew handed his Chief the glass.

Kissre swung to a clansman, "Run to Gilchrist. Tell him to sound retreat, by the Aegis's order! Hurry!"

The man glanced to Drew and Terril before he turned and rushed away. They watched from their vantage point, but Drew knew the clansman could not travel fast enough to stop the assault.

"That Aristo will not retreat," Terril said. "Too power hungry for common sense."

The army moved forward in predictable patterns and those on the hill watched, helpless to intervene. The cylinders exploded with a roar of sound and flashes of yellow light and smoke. On the field, grass and bodies hurtled into the air. Drew felt it like a wound to himself as barrage after barrage hit the soldiers below, many untrained and drawn by his presence to this deadly undertaking. There was nothing he could do to help.

The charge halted in chaos as the retreat horn belatedly gave sound. Disoriented and confused, half the men retreated in the wrong direction. Drew sensed the madness around him and used it. Ground birds hiding in the grass suddenly flew up under the feet of the fleeing men. Startled, the frightened men fell to the ground to avoid another aerial assault. Disturbed by the bombardment, thousands of resident field rats raced toward the canon. They arrived and flooded three, four, even five thick, over the feet and legs of the cannoneers and the Pertelon soldiers settled behind them.

"Parlor tricks," Drew muttered. "That's all I can offer."

"It stopped those going in the wrong direction," Selwyn said and motioned toward the men who now struggled back toward their own line.

"Diversion. They wanted a diversion. Why?" Kissre's voice floated to him, soft and puzzled.

"You call this a diversion?" Terril asked, his voice rising with his incredulity and anger.

"They only confused the army, drew attention to this one action. Their horse and foot have not followed up on a successful bombardment." She looked at Drew with clear surety. "You are the prize on this field." Her words were matched with action as she pulled her sword from its scabbard and rose to search the surrounding terrain. In reaction, Drew heard other blades, Clansmen's, emerging from scabbards, and pulled his own.

"There," he said, "The ground is disturbed over there in the wood flanking the field." He buried his guilt at allowing the horrible scene he'd witness impede his oath of protection. They all heard them now. Drew made sure every rock rolled from beneath their feet, every wind-fallen branch cracked under their weight, that their every step gave away their presence. Drew rushed forward screaming Clan Cader's battle cry, Kissre kept pace at his side. Selwyn and the clan paced around him. They did not stop as men emerged from the wood's edge but rushed to meet the enemy.

One foe raised a fist filled with a tube aimed right at Drew. Kissre screamed a warning and grabbed his buckler arm and flung her weight into him, pushing him aside as she flung herself over him. She acted so fast it befuddled reason. Drew saw the small tube fire with a sharp crack even as Kissre moved. He felt it hit her, felt her body jerk at the sudden invasion, felt the projectile hit his chain mail with stinging intensity. Kissre sagged in his arms and he lowered her to the ground. All around him clansman screamed and hurtled past him. Already a red stain spread over her right shoulder. He cursed and placed a hand over the flowing wound trying to stop the seepage. The clash of steel weapons entered his awareness.

"Go," Kissre whispered, her eyes flicking open. "They are after you. Get to safety."

He rose and joined the men fighting. He focused his anger and let his practiced reflexes carry him into the engagement. He killed a man and hardly realized it until his opponent fell. He looked for others, but the clanging stopped as quickly as it had started.

In the stillness that followed he realized the battle over. His clansmen prevailed, surrounding him in protection. Selwyn and Terril searched the enemies' bodies. "They only had one of those things," Selwyn said and swore. "By the Holy One, where is the Protector? Are you injured?"

Drew didn't listen. He moved back to Kissre. Her eyes opened but focused over his shoulder. "Vesper knew," she said. Drew sensed Selwyn standing over him. "Told me I'd die. Get the Aegis to safety. They hunt him."

"Shut up. Vesper's visions are often vague and inaccurate," Drew said. He cut open the jack she wore and looked at the blood oozing from a circular wound. "Save your strength. Take her to the healer."

Selwyn motioned to two clansmen. They nodded; one lifted her and with the other guarding, retreated. He nodded at Drew's shoulder. "You need a healer, too." Drew looked down and looked at the bent links. "No, I don't bleed. It's Kissre's blood." He showed Selwyn his bloodied hands.

A lethal rage filled him. So much loss of life, he would not let it continue. He looked at Kissre's blood, feeling his calling, feeling his promise, his family's promise for endless generations.

Closing his eyes, he clenched his red-stained fist. His mind delved into the land around him, never having felt so driven. His searching mind wove over and under the land until he found the perfect weapon.

Beneath his feet he felt the rock tremble. With uncanny insight he allowed water to crash upon weakened joints, accelerating erosion. In expanded awareness, he felt the essence of those around him, those both alive and dead on the field. He felt Aurelias and his coterie of officers ordering a retreat, and Gilchrist still directing his men to fight. He even felt the enemy and spared them a moment's guilt and pity.

With a rumbling and shaking both heard and felt, all living things froze in place, seeking escape and safety. The noise increased, and with a sinking sensation of power and authority, Drew pulled the land out from under the Pertelon encampment.

~ * ~

At the surprise sound of the retreat horn, Gilchrist exploded in anger at his lieutenant, told his officer to stop the fool blowing the order and reform the troops. In the sky, birds swirled in agitated flocks. He waited.

Beneath his feet the ground vibrated, but not from the report of canons. The eyes of the berated officer widened in shock. A deep silence fell all around them. Gilchrist looked down, but there was nothing to see. Everything remained the same as before except for the perceptible quiet. Even the clanging of weapons on armor and the screams of men fell still as battle stopped. The air seemed heavy with the premonition of disaster. He shook his head.

"Why did you call retreat?" Yonger asked riding up. "Now is the time to hold firm to our cause."

"I didn't. Move!" Gilchrist yelled at the lieutenant.

Beside him, Aurelias appeared, dressed, and mounted, but not armed.

"I gave the order. Retreat, gather the wounded, get them off this land, get the mounted out there to help," he ordered the men surrounding Gilchrist.

"We are in the middle of an advance, and their weapons are still pointed at the battlefield!" Gilchrist said.

"Now!" Aurelias screamed as the men hesitated. He spurred his own mount forward. Ahead of him the line wavered. He heard the battle horn sound retreat once more. Several Royal Guardsmen rode with him. At his order, they leaped from their mounts and started checking bodies. Several wounded were unceremoniously pitched over saddles. "Get them off the field. Move, move," he shouted to his retreating army. Other officers took up the refrain as the ground's shaking increased in intensity. Able-footed soldiers began running in a terrorized frenzy. He slowly dismounted and ordered two wounded soldiers placed onto his horse.

As his horse was led away, his squire rode up to jerk his horse to stop next to Aurelias. "Your Grace, you must get to safety," the boy shouted. He jumped down and held his horse for Aurelias to mount. "The field is clearing, Your Grace, please, you must leave."

Aurelias, seeing the boy's terrified face, looked around him. It was true; the men were evacuating the field. The horse screamed as the ground perceptibly fell from beneath their feet.

"Please, Your Grace, please, Your Grace." The squire continued his plea as they both staggered to stay standing.

Aurelias grabbed the reins and mounted the skittish horse with the boy's help. He held his hand down to him. "Come."

"I can't mount with..." The ground heaved again and Aurelias leaned forward and grabbed the boy's arm and swung him around behind him, feeling the strain on his wound. He spurred the horse away from the shaking ground. The scrawny animal stumbled and scrambled across the heaving land.

Behind him Aurelias heard the Pertelon Army scream as if with one voice. Once back on the rocky high ground, the tired animal fell into a walk. Men gathered there, and Aurelias realized here the ground remained firm. He turned and looked behind him. Dust clouds rose, obscuring the view, but not the distraught screaming. From the promontory, Aurelias saw the enemy trapped, and shuddered hearing the rush of water.

~ * ~

As the caves beneath the land collapsed, the southern end of Anatole Island sank like a fallen crust; debris rose in swirling clouds heavenward. Drew turned to watch the last of his handiwork and heard the screams of thousands of men reverberate within his mind. Waves of crashing water, boiling in their sudden passage, submerged the site. Slowly what had been land became a whirling eddy of angry water, just another jagged shore of the lake formed by the Thou River.

Drew sank to the ground, as devastated as the land by his destruction.

Twenty-two

"Warrick sends a message recalling us to his presence," Aurelias said as he entered Drew's tent. "We will take the wounded with us. Half the army will remain here under one of the aristos I trust. Will you be able to travel?"

Drew glanced at his father-in-law. "Yes. I'm not injured or ill. I don't know what happened, I just felt so... exhausted. How is Kissre?"

"Kissre will live to fight again. After what you did, I'm not surprised you feel so. What you accomplished... well, it is nothing short of miraculous."

"Nothing short of murderous. I am sorry I failed you. I should have found a more peaceful solution before so many lost their lives, but never before have I been able to do such a thing."

"Don't drown in guilt, Drew. War is a vicious business. Remember it was Pertelon who invaded Kaereya. You did nothing more than what every Aegis has sworn to do. It was an edifying demonstration to King Clement about Kaereya's Aegises." Aurelias snorted. "And one to our aristos."

"Captured Pertelon soldiers and probably many Kaereyans think the Protector acted."

"Several stories circulate, but every Kaereyan on the battlefield knows what happened. Enough saw you."

Aurelias left. Drew knew what the duke said was true, but never had he killed so many. It weighed heavy on him, and the reverence with which his clan, the other clansmen, the Kennetsurean nomads, and the general soldiers treated him was torturous. Even Selwyn seemed to treat him with a deference that hurt.

He realized his actions had changed his life forever. Maybe when he was away from this place things would return to normal. Vesper, he wanted her and half-feared she would also change, hoped she did not hear what he had done. He rose from where he sat on his bunk and left his tent.

The acts of Kennetsurean obeisance and the nods given to clan chiefs followed him. He entered the infirmary tent and walked down the long line of cots. A healer stepped from Kissre as he approached.

Kissre gave him a grin that looked ghastly on her pale face.

"You look as bad as I feel," she said.

He laughed. "You've been wounded twice on behalf of my family."

"The wages of my profession. It is expected, so don't think on it. I am well paid for this."

"Not enough. I do and will. I owe you my life."

Kissre shrugged his statement away. She at least treated him as any man, nothing more.

"The wounded travel with us back to the Hawk Island and the Eternal Palace. I will have a wagon made available for you. The Clansmen will offer you protection on the trip back."

"Thank you, Aegis Montoren, but I have already told the healer I will ride Bother back, and I will ride behind His Grace, Aristo Aurelias, as is my duty."

He looked at her knowing her strength barely enough to stand, but also knew when to capitulate. "If you insist, but only if you call me Drew. Since I ride next to the duke and the clansmen will blend with his footmen, it is a moot point." He nodded and left. At his word, the clansmen would make sure Kissre's journey was eased in every manner. The benefits of his new position obliquely occurred to him with some satisfaction.

~ * ~

Gilchrist made sure he was among the first to enter the tent for Aurelias' meeting. He cast a fleeting glance at the Aegis and his clan leaders and stood next to them offering a picture of solidarity. Other aristos and officers trailed in and waited. The heat of day lingered, making the wait uncomfortable. It took several minutes for everyone to arrive. Aristo Yonger was one of the last to enter.

Aurelias wasted no time. "Many of you know what the Aegis accomplished."

"Can you prove it wasn't the Protector?" Aristo Agino asked, "After all, Pertelon used prohibited weapons."

Gilchrist heard a few yeas backing Agino's statement but remained quiet himself.

"What you don't know," Aurelias continued, unperturbed and patently ignoring Agino, "is we have a traitor among us. The Aegis was attacked during the confusion of the last battle. Someone among us worked against the Aegis, against you, against King Warrick, and against Kaereya." His eyes marked each man in the tent. Most looked back unflinching. "We found this on one of the bodies." He pulled out a wrinkled piece of paper. "Aristo Yonger, it is addressed to you with the message to kill Drew Montoren."

Gilchrist contained his smile at Yonger's expression of shock.

"No! I never... a lie! A lie, I say. All my men are behind enemy lines, I could not contact them, even if I desired!"

"You could if you were working with Pertelon," Aristo Agino said. "You have any number of servants here who could carry your orders. Did you kill King Frederick, too, betrayer?"

"No! I did not! I would never leave such a message, I burn them..." As his words registered, Yonger twirled. His gaze fell on Gilchrist, but before anything left his lips, a knife found his neck. The blood spurted and sputtered. "Blood for blood," Aristo Agino said. "I claim this traitor's life by my ancient right of blood-tie to the Royal family."

An argument broke out over Agino's right, which he defended with absolute certainty.

Gilchrist looked at Aurelias's anger-suffused face. It was too comical, but he maintained his act of dismay. The manipulation of a few fools like Agino, ordering one dispensable man to carry a verbal message and join Yonger's forces, insured all fingers pointed in the right direction. Before his stooge left his presence, Gilchrist had planted the purloined, all-important piece of evidence into the man's pocket. There was nothing left to tie him to any of this. Then he incited Agino with how he would have killed the murderer of his dear wife's cousins, reminding the Aristo of his own blood tie. Even if someone held suspicion, it proved nothing.

~ * ~

To Aurelias it seemed the entire population of Cliff City turned out to watch the army's return. Only the aristos and their senior officers joined his column winding its slow way up the road to the Eternal Palace, and they displayed their heraldic banners and pageantry in colorful disorder. The remaining army, the common soldiers, encamped at the crossing to Hawk Island. That so many of them returned spoke of Drew's achievement on the battlefield.

Aurelias soaked up some grim self-satisfaction. Despite the army's losses, Drew had helped him grab an uncertain victory. That it cost the Aegis was obvious. A glance showed him Drew's withdrawn, nearly oblivious state.

The street was lined with people waving paper dragons and whirligigs in bright colors. Larger kites and other airy festoons lined the streets. He hoped Drew didn't know it the symbol of the Easure Aegis, but expected he probably did, as nearly as many paper and fabric icons of the other Aegises—unicorns, sphinx, and mermaids—fluttered in the light breeze. The burden placed on his son-in-law seemed to grow beyond comprehension. He decided it was up to him to help ease this burden and ensure his daughter's well-being.

As they entered the Palace grounds, he found it as gaily decorated as Cliff City. Aristos stood in their court best. Lines of Royal Guardsmen held their lances in salute, from the gates outside the outer parade ground to the inner courtyards. They finally halted before the king and his court. Grooms ran among the mounted, grabbing horses. Aurelias briefly glanced to where Kissre sat atop Bother and smiled as one of his men beat a clansman to the mercenary's aide, loosening the girth as warned before helping her dismount.

He watched briefly while she was helped down and grunted at her sheer perverse stubbornness. Aggravating beyond reason, he would not let her leave his employment, not now. She had proved her worth and loyalty time after time, and now he owed her beyond mere pay.

The first cause of his debt stood next to Warrick looking very much the lady and with a likeness to her mother that pierced his heart, but only briefly. His good friend, the Earl of Rikon, stood on Warrick's other side with his fiery-haired daughter Ottillie. Another good friend to his Vesper, and probably the source of Vesper's impeccable deportment. He snorted. One hoyden teaching another. It amazed him how the prospect of the future looked brighter, more interesting, more joyful.

His eyes took in Aldous and Leela, as vigorous as people half their age, of other court notables and acquaintances, some friends, some competitors, some enemies. For the first time in years, he felt a certain optimistic sense of peace. Yes, the war would go on, and Kaereya could not expect Drew to extend himself in such a way except in the most extenuating circumstances, but now hope existed where it had not. Pertelon had received a potent warning.

He waited for Drew to walk up to him after dismounting and for the others to assemble, but before he could greet his young king, Warrick stepped forward. Disregarding his position and status, he took Aurelias' hand in the peace greeting and gave him a word of thanks before moving to Drew and every other man present, giving the same greeting.

As the king moved down the line of surprised aristos, Vesper approached. She curtseyed to her father, rose, and kissed his cheek. Aurelias held her close for a moment. She smiled as she stepped back, then moved to Drew. Her eyes filled with concern and love, although she followed the same courtly steps. Drew, however, placed his hands on her shoulders stared into her eyes with an expression that made Aurelias frown, then relax in acceptance.

With a total disregard of Aristo etiquette, Drew pulled his wife into a warm embrace, locked in his arms about her, and devoured her with a kiss. Applause broke out among those viewing the unseemly spectacle.

"They are very young," Leela sighed as she greeted Aurelias. "And need each other. It is a very touching sight in a place where love is all too rare. The court shall not soon forget. I hear Kissre has injured herself again. She seems accident-prone. Do you want me to care for her?"

Aurelias laughed. "If you can."

"I know her prickly nature, but there are methods that work with even the most disinclined patients. I've heard you need healing too, which can be arranged while we exchange talk of the war front and what has happened here."

It became clear Aldous felt no compunction at interrupting the two lovers. He grabbed Drew's hand, then hugged him, garbling about honor restored at long last. Aurelias lost the thread of conversation as he greeted Wilhelm Norbert and Ottillie.

"We have much to speak of," Norbert said.

"I was afraid of that."

Long, tiring candlemarks passed before he settled into one of Norbert's comfortable chairs with a flagon of wine. Leela, Aldous, and Ottillie joined them. At her father's request, Ottillie told of Eldin's betrayal.

"Your message nearly came too late, but Kissre and Drew managed to salvage the situation. Kissre by saving Drew's life, and I expect you heard what Drew did. It is a scary thing to know one person capable of such destruction." He then told of the perfidy practiced against himself and his suspicions of actions against Yonger. "I can prove nothing against Gilchrist."

Ottillie smiled, drawn from her sober attention to his story. "I knew Kissre's worth. You must make sure she cannot return to her nomadic ways."

"Already taken care of," he said. "Even if I hadn't made her sign a long-term contract with renewal options on my end only, I assure you neither Drew nor Vesper would let her go easily. In the meantime, we know Eldin could not have acted alone. You did not recognize the person with whom he spoke?"

"No, his voice was too low. I know I did not like the feel of his mind. I've felt most here at court and none felt like it."

"Is it possible to disguise a mind?"

Ottillie sighed. "Yes. Leela says so and tells me I am too inexperienced to detect it."

"You will be pleased with Vesper," Norbert said. "It seems her visions were needed here at court and Warrick takes them most seriously. She was very upset the day of the battle. Told Warrick the murderer who killed his family betrayed Kaereya, betrayed him. Luckily, she now has warnings of coming attacks and we try to keep her out of public situations whenever she feels a vision coming."

"She can predict their coming?"

"Yes. It is very eerie to watch," Ottillie said. "Nearly as eerie as feeling another's emotions." She took a long drink from her cup.

"What? This witch thing not as you expected?" Aurelias asked.

Ottillie looked at him with a seriousness he seldom associated with Norbert's daughter. "Not at all. I feel for Vesper. She told Warrick the waters would destroy the army."

Norbert sighed, adding, "Unfortunately, she didn't know which army."

Aurelias momentarily contemplated Warrick's reaction to the prediction. Then sighed. The future was seldom clear and straightforward. "Feel for the people of Kaereya who must become accustomed to magic in Kaereya," Aurelias said.

~ * ~

At Ottillie's connivance they entered the cathedral with Warrick. It was long into the dark hours, past when even the latest revelers retired. Vesper found the atmosphere disquieting and would have welcomed Drew's warm arm around her shoulders rather than Alfred's detached presence. Her hands clutched a shovel. Ottillie carried a pry bar, while Warrick stood holding another shovel. Leela held a lantern so they could see.

"Quiet, ladies," Warrick whispered, admonishing them for some low whispers.

"You received the Bishop's permission?" Vesper asked.

"Yes, the Bishop knows, but he didn't want anyone else to know, and didn't want to participate."

"This is it," Ottillie said.

"How do you know?" Warrick asked.

"The journal said in the center floor block underneath the transept. This is it." She matched her actions to her words and tried to work the edges of the stone up with her fingers.

"That's useless," Warrick said and knelt. He placed the shovel to the side and used his belt knife to dig at the edges.

Ottillie tried again and the stone budged, but it was hard work. Vesper helped Warrick, putting her shovel's edge under the stone while he put hands on its reluctant edges and pulled it free. The three younger people dug in turns, none of them very adept.

"You must reach it soon," Leela said, "they could not have buried it too deep."

Vesper stopped and wiped her brow, noticed Alfred's attention drawn away. He stepped into the darkness. "It had better be soon," she said.

"Very soon," Ottillie added. She scooped another shovelful onto the pile by the hole's edge.

"King Warrick, who would believe you participated in such clandestine and base employment?"

They all turned to the voice. Only a dark shadowed figure and a glint of reflection from the lantern light on steel disturbed the quiet shadows of the church.

"Wen?" Warrick asked, identifying the voice, his own filled with concern.

"Yes, Wen." The shape emerged into meager light, exposing the king's servant. His face became defined by deep shadows, then his figure. The betrayer was dressed in rough travelers' garb. Three more shadowed faces lined up behind him.

Wen raised a sword and pointed it at Warrick's heart. Warrick threatened with his shovel. The blade came to within feet of Warrick's chest but remained out of range of the shovel's swing.

"You always were a stupid boy, too confiding in your friends, in me. Too negligent, too indulgent, never seeing what was below your nose—you are not fit to rule. I do your subjects a favor."

"By murder?" Leela asked. "That's treason."

"I will be safely out of reach by the time they find your bodies, my duty completed. Ending this dynasty will bring a better rule, a more capable king," the servant said. "My apologies, ladies, for the necessity of your demise with your monarch, but Clement will be glad to know three witches went with the late king of Kaereya."

Vesper raised her shovel, taking a step forward. "You will not take him without a fight."

"Vesper, no!" Ottillie shouted, even as Warrick put out a hand to stop her.

Wen's sword flicked. Vesper shrieked and dropped the shovel; her hand flew up to cover the sliced fabric of her arm. Blood seeped between her fingers.

Warrick swung the shovel even as Wen stepped forward. The traitor's step faltered. As Wen tried to recover his footing, he stumbled, and his sword arm dropped.

Flickers broke the shadows with an accompanying thud as arrows struck flesh. Shocked surprise turned Wen's head as he fell. Warrick's shovel arced harmless above his head. With a quick move, Warrick's boot hit Wen's jaw and the servant lay still, an arrow piercing his chest. Wen groaned, blood trickling from his mouth. Other groans showed arrows had struck the men behind Wen. Vesper found her legs too weak to hold her. Before she sank to the floor, Ottillie's arm supported her and helped ease her down.

Shouting voices erupted and echoed around the sanctuary. Before she knew it, Drew knelt next to her, bow in hand. Others moved behind him, including Selwyn who rushed to Ottillie. Drew dropped his bow and inspected her wound. His face told her he was too angry to speak.

"It is the smallest of scratches," she whispered, which was about all she could achieve.

Two Royal Guardsmen hauled Wen to his feet and then dragged him from the church. Others hauled the bodies of his henchmen away. Royal Guardsmen circled their small group and took defensive postures. Alfred emerged from the shadows looking very smug. Vesper smiled at him. She had seen his foot trip Warrick's servant.

Leela looked at the wound with Drew. "Not the smallest, but not a dangerous one either. I need bandaging." She looked at Ottillie.

Drew threw the skirt of Vesper's surgown aside and ripped a section off her chemise. "Another chemise?" she asked with a weak smile. Drew scowled at her.

Ottillie tore hers as well and formed it into a pad she handed to Leela.

"You are sure she will be all right?" Warrick asked, also kneeling on the marble church floor to watch while Leela wrapped her arm.

"I will be fine," Vesper assured him. "Finish your business here."

"You're going to your bed," Drew said starting to lift her.

"No, we aren't done yet. I want to see this." At his stubborn look, she added, "Please?"

Drew turned to Ottillie. "Did you organize this?" he asked. "It was far too dangerous for any of you."

"It was a communal effort," Warrick said. "But done at my instigation."

"Not at all," Leela said. "We all played our parts."

"You knew you would be attacked?" Norbert asked Warrick in a cold voice as he joined his daughter and Selwyn. "We were almost too late." He turned an angry visage on Ottillie.

"No! Do you think I would put them in danger?" Warrick asked, frowning.

"No, he didn't know," Ottillie said, her hand on her father's sleeve.

"We knew you would never agree, Sire," Vesper said.

"We inveigled him here," Leela said, looking slightly abashed. "It was the only way to expose the traitor. Kissre gave us an oblique hint. We made the plan when Vesper foretold someone planned to kill Warrick, and Ottillie finally realized where she felt the traitor's presence. With sufficient dropped hints, we thought he would show up." She sighed. "I could wish Kissre healthy. She would not have botched the proceedings." She looked at the small hole in the church floor. "Probably digs better, too."

"You agreed to this lunacy?" Drew roared at Vesper. "You endangered yourself and the king?"

Vesper felt weak but placed a placating hand on his sleeve. "It turned out all right."

"I left a note for my father," Ottillie said in weak defense.

"Stop! No squabbling." Warrick said. He turned and bowed deeply to the three women. "I would have risked much more to catch such a traitor in our midst. Is he the guilty one?"

"Of your family's death?" Leela asked. "If he lives long enough, questioning should prove that one way or another, but I predict so, both Ottillie and I felt him. Do you still wish to find the box?"

"Now more than ever," Warrick said. He picked up the shovel, but Selwyn took it from his hands.

"With your permission, Sire." Selwyn placed his foot on the shovel's back and pushed it into the soil. Another guardsman picked up a shovel and helped. They moved vast clumps of the dry soil.

"Help me up," Vesper demanded. "I want to see." Drew helped her to her feet, his arm secured around her waist. They all watched.

"Careful," Leela advised. "It was no more than elbow's depth."

Selwyn gently prodded the hole's bottom until it hit something with a distinct metallic thump. With bare hands he dug around the soil and emerged with the box. He rose and handed it to Warrick.

Warrick took the offering, his fingers rubbing caked soil off its exterior. "The star," he sighed, and looked around him. "It matches the other." He handed the box to Ottillie and pulled its mate from a sack by the hole.

"Let me hold the empty one, Sire," Ottillie said. "You divide the contents."

Warrick nodded and they exchanged boxes. He lifted the small latch hinge and raised the lid. Necks strained to look inside the box, but it was only bone-dry dust. Ottillie opened the box she held. Warrick slowly divided the dust. It rose in small puffs between the boxes as he poured. The puffs caught and swirled in the drafts of the church and seemed to take on a life of their own.

Abruptly Warrick pulled back and sneezed. His hands shook with the force and dust jumped from the edges of the box. Ottillie moved her box to catch it.

Warrick closed and latched the second box. With infinite care he replaced it in its hollow in the cathedral's floor. "Cover it."

There was more soil left when the hole was filled, Selwyn stomped on it while Leela swept the excess soil in the hole. The stone was replaced but it was a little higher than the others.

"It will settle," the Royal Guardsman said, putting his weight against it.

"Here, Sire," Ottillie said, handing Warrick the still open box in her palm. Once he held it, she brushed the dust in her palm into the box.

Warrick closed and latched the lid. His eyes rose to Ottillie's. "Thank you. Thank all of you for what you have done for me, more importantly, for Kaereya."

Vesper watched as Ottillie continued to rub her hands, a strange expression on her face. "Ottillie?" she asked.

"It feels funny. I feel strange." Both Ottillie and Drew gasped in unison.

Her father grabbed her. "What is wrong?"

"She feels the land, and I feel her through it," Drew said. "It isn't possible."

"Egan," Ottillie said, closing her eyes, "It's like I'm there, I can smell the air, feel the heat."

~ * ~

"Well, you have certainly turned events." The craggy voice broke Vesper's musings and she stopped in her tracks. Her hard-sought privacy in the king's garden already disturbed, she looked around her.

No one stood there. Her glance lowered.

"You spoke to me!"

Alfred stood garbed in shiny green and orange leaves and hollyhock flowers taken from the king's garden. "I heard you! I know I did. Where have you been? I haven't seen you in a fortnight."

Alfred didn't speak but extended his hand. She reached out and felt him place something in her palm.

"Why? What is this?" She looked at his somber face. "You spoke to me can't you say something more?" She sighed and a few tears of frustration welled over her lower lids. "You're leaving me, staying here, aren't you?"

At his smile, she instinctively smiled back. "And this?" She closed her eyes and suddenly saw Fair Folk all around the palace grounds. Opening her eyes, she saw only Alfred. "It's an invitation," she said in resignation. "Where do I take it?"

Alfred put his hands on his hips with a stern frown.

Vesper laughed despite her forlornness. "To the garden at Montoren Farm. I shall place it on the stone bench. Will your friends understand?"

At his broad smile, she sighed. "All right, they will. Will there be no more Fair Folk at Montoren, no more unicorns?"

Alfred gave her a disgusted look and waved her away before he turned and disappeared into the shrubbery. With a hard swallow, Vesper looked at the simple acorn in her hand, and closing her fingers protectively around it, raised her hand to cover her mouth and stop the small gasps of threatened tears. She blamed her easy tears on her pregnancy, not on the realization she was finally grown-up or for the loss of anything.

~ * ~

"There is no true magic?" Warrick stood in his audience room alone with his Aegis Kaeraya and his wife.

Drew thought about Warrick's question. "Magic is all around us, but you have to believe in it. It is no substitute for dealing with reality. Even those with Talent must live as everyone else."

"And Lady Ottillie? Will she return to Kennetsure with Aldous and Leela? I need her here."

"Let her go. It would be too cruel to keep her here now. She needs Aldous to teach her about the desert. Leela says it is an unexpected, but very welcome development, and all from Kennetsure are euphoric. It is a relief to know the Aegis line there will continue."

"Ottillie is related? I thought it had to go through a direct line?"

"She might be, perhaps through her mother. Leela doesn't know but says Chloe's spell might have worked on anyone with Talent. She didn't expect it to produce a specific Aegis."

"Can Easure and Wessure regain an Aegis?"

"Anything is possible."

"We all breathed that dust. Do you think it will affect any of us?"

"How do you feel?"

"Different, but I don't feel land." At Drew's look, Warrick added, "People. I sense them, maybe." He sighed. "It could be my imagination."

"Or experience?"

Warrick grinned. "So many changes. It is all hard to comprehend."

"Vesper says you should not seal the box in the new throne. If the soil confirms an Aegis, you must keep it to hand."

"So Norbert and others have advised me." Warrick laughed, his lips twisting into a frown. "My King's Marshal will forgive me for everything but Ottillie, I think. You are taking Vesper to Vere?"

"Yes. I want my son born there."

Warrick smiled. "Congratulations. When?"

"Thank you, Sire. Perhaps a few months after the next handfasting."

"So you made your year."

Drew smiled. "There was no doubt of that, and many more to come."

"Then you cannot return to court for Handfasting."

Drew looked up. "Perhaps. You have plans?"

"Yes. I rely on your desecration. Princess Pia has agreed to come back. It is all arranged. She has already accepted my ring, but it is good to follow accepted public rituals. You must come then, for First Day."

"We would be honored."

Warrick laughed. "No, you won't. You may not complain, but you'll lament every time you leave your beloved plateau. You must get used to it. It will give us time to plan how to get Pertelonese soldiers out of the rest of Kaereya. Clement will try again, but Norbert says we have some breathing space. Thanks to you."

Drew couldn't help the small sigh that escaped him. "I'm getting used to feeling all of Kaereya, Sire. Vesper has told me we will have to journey to each Province. It is a daunting vision."

"Maybe we should make it together. Once we have thrown Pertelon out. The monarchy has been too long riveted in Easure. If you wouldn't mind, I'd like to speak with your Lady wife privately?"

Drew nearly refused, but with one glance at Vesper, he bowed and left the room.

"Who is he?"

"Sire?"

"The small man you smiled at, the one who tripped Wen in the chapel?"

"You see him? No one else ever has, except maybe Kissre, but she never said so."

"The woman among your father's men? Is he Fair Folk? I keep waiting for others to say something, but they don't seem to see him."

"I believe he is. Alfred has been with me since early childhood." Vesper bit her lip and smiled. "He is staying here."

"I know. He moved into my closet. He is quite at home sleeping on the Robes of State and lacks any regal respect."

"Well, if you wish him to remain forever quiet, tell him he isn't really there."

"Thank you for the warning, but he hasn't spoken yet. I welcome him. I think I might need my own special magic."

~ * ~

Ottillie found Selwyn helping the clansmen prepare for their journey home. She had not seen him since the night in Aron Cathedral. Now, she sensed his knowledge of her presence. Only after he finished his task did his gaze come to her. Then it moved to the Kennetsureans following her a discreet distance away.

"We have to talk." To make herself approachable she had worn a simple russet surgown only a few shades darker than her hair, embellished only with a simple braid. His glance showed the failure of her effort. "I did not plan this."

He turned to watch the horses being strapped with baggage. "I know you did not. What is there to say? You must go to Kennetsure, and I must go to Vere. I know all about Aegis responsibility."

"Why must you go to Vere?"

"It is my home." His bleakness hit her like a stone.

"And you love it more than any other place or thing?" She felt his upset and realized he thought she would set him aside.

Selwyn turned to her. "I have always stood by Drew. It is my duty."

"You don't wish to take up another duty with someone who desires you? Someone who loves you and wants to make a family with you?"

"He is my only family. How could I forsake him now? Especially now, when he most needs my help?"

"And I must leave my only family here in Easure. Drew has all the Clans to protect him. He has Vesper. He has everyone at Montoren, people he has known all his life. He has the protection of Aurelias' men-at-arms, and the protection of the Royal Guards Warrick will send with him. Can I not request this one person from him?"

"It will be very difficult, but of course you can. Especially for this service." They both turned at Drew's voice. He walked up to them. "If it is your desire to go with Ottillie, go. I would rather see you happy than accept your sacrifice."

"It is dishonorable."

Drew laughed at him. "No, it is not. You will have a harder duty. Getting back into Kennetsure will be difficult. Ottillie and Aldous, even Leander will need your support. And just think, your son might be Aegis."

"Or our daughter," Ottillie inserted. "Come with me, Selwyn. Be my husband. But only if you want me as I want you."

~ * ~

Even after the summer's actions, Drew found the cavalcade tedious. He seemed the only one to find it so. The clansmen in the Duke of Lambere's entourage seemed to revel in the deference accorded them. He missed Selwyn more than he expected. Not even Clan Cader's protection brought the certain assurance of his cousin's company.

"You will see him again," Vesper said. "Ottillie will not end his love for you."

"It is an adjustment," Drew answered. "He has always been by my side."

"Your country always surprises me with its majestic views," Aurelias said from where he rode on Vesper's other side.

"Enjoy the views. My home is not a ducal residence, not at all what you are accustomed to."

Aurelias gave him a leveling look. "I have campaigned in very rough circumstances, and as you know, I can live in a tent if necessary. You will have to build to your new status."

Drew clamped his lips tight shut.

"Don't turn clansman on me. You know it true, no matter how your family has kept their secret these past generations."

"You two sort this out," Vesper said. "I am going to check on Kissre." She turned her horse and rode back on the side of the road.

"I do not plan to rebuild the keep. What I have is enough."

"Don't be obstinate. Your existence is exposed now, and the Aegis of Kaereya cannot live in too modest a home. You will have people seeking you out, not the least of whom will be the king. Will you show him to a tent? You will also want accommodations in Cliff City. Inevitably Warrick will call you to court. He will provide you rooms in the Eternal Palace, but if you value privacy, you must have your own residence within the city." Aurelias continued, unveiling his plans for them. "You could, of course, use mine."

"You must talk to Vesper about that. Whatever she wishes is my desire. Right now, I am more concerned about Vesper than about building."

"Her safety is my objective, also." Aurelias remained quiet a moment. "I thank you for allowing me to come. This opportunity to see my grandson born means much to me. I know you could have refused."

Drew sighed inaudibly. "You are Vesper's father and have done nothing but acted for her good and safety. You deserve to be with your daughter at this time. Besides, as fathers-in-law go, you aren't too bad, just aristo, and stubborn."

Aurelias looked affronted. "Well, you should speak!"

"If you must plan buildings, plan the rebuilding of Ward and Seward Keeps, for I have no bent in that direction." He saw the task light Aurelias' eyes and wondered what nightmare he had unleashed.

"I will help with Montoren, also. Visiting will give me insight into the needs and possibilities of the place."

~ * ~

Freda burst into the kitchen spouting words so fast Eudora was forced to calm her before understanding came. Changing her apron and straightening her headdress, Eudora went to the mayor's reception hall. The mayor and his wife along with Brandt and Alvina looked nervous as they stepped onto the porch to greet the duke and his entourage. The front doors stood open, and Eudora could see the tumult outside. Two of the standards among the milling horses struck Eudora with disbelief. One with the ivory, rampant unicorn of Vere against a midnight-blue background drifted over all present. The banners of the Duke of Lambere filled her with fear. Clansmen dismounted and held their horses in groups, while a young man helped an elegant lady dismount.

The lady and her escort followed the Duke of Lambere toward the Mayor's greeting party. They were halfway to the door before Eudora recognized Vesper. Schooling herself to calmness, she retired to the kitchen and waited.

~ * ~

Mayor Kellsie warmly greeted Aristo Aurelias, the Duke of Lambere. It was such an unlooked-for honor. Drew smiled as he listened to the fawning compliments and inquiries. Little attention was paid to him or Vesper after a brief dismissing glance.

"I'm traveling to Montoren Farm," Aurelias said. "King Warrick gave me some business to conduct with you and it luckily gives my daughter a chance to visit her foster mother."

"Montoren Farm? But..." The mayor's next words faltered as he looked at the clansmen talking in groups around the manse plaza. Mayor Kellsie's eyes wandered to the couple beside the duke.

It was clear recognition came slow.

"Vesper?" Alvina clearly doubted her perception. A gasp burst from the Mayor's wife.

All eyes were drawn to his elegant wife. Drew looked at her, too. Ottillie's influence made Vesper look dramatically different from the last time she had been in Norost. Although not in court dress, her apparel proclaimed quality.

"Hello, Alvina. You look well. How lucky we are to find you at home with your parents."

"Brandt and I live here. Brandt has been appointed Deputy Mayor." Her childhood playmate basked in her pleasure of Brandt's position.

Brandt stepped forward and took Vesper's hand, placing a kiss on its back. Drew managed to contain his temper at the look Vesper received.

"Vesper, it is good to see you. We have missed you, have we not, Alvina?" Brandt said.

A boot stepped on Drew's foot, drawing his incensed attention to Aurelias and away from Brandt's expression. Aurelias stepped to his daughter and took her hand from Brandt.

"Her Grace, Lady Montoren, now." He held her hand as he moved to present her to Mayor Kellsie. "You know my daughter, Vesper, and her husband, the Aegis Kaereya."

"Aegis Kaereya?" Mayor Kellsie said.

"Your daughter?" Alvina said over her father's words.

"Surely the news has reached Norost of a Vere man's fame? Yes, Drew Montoren. Perhaps, though, we should discuss this business in your chambers?"

"We heard of an Aegis saving Kaereya, yes, but not by name."

Drew hid his smile. The Mayor looked unhappily surprised, but responded pleasantly, inviting them into the manse.

Vesper smiled at her father. "I should like to talk with Eudora while you men talk business."

"We will talk with Eudora together," Aurelias said. "You and Drew are part of the business at hand."

Drew watched Vesper's lips tighten at her father's decision. It made it impossible for her to politely refuse. Alvina and her mother escaped into the residence.

"He is right," Drew said in a voice only Vesper could hear. "You know Eudora has done nothing wrong, so trust her and trust your father." He raised her hand and kissed her fingers relishing the look she gave him. Throughout the meeting, he sympathized as she tried to contain her anxious fidgets.

Aurelias explained Warrick's desire that Norost's tax revenues be sent to the Aegis. He also gave the Mayor edicts establishing Montoren's boundaries and manorial rights. Drew gave the Mayor credit, he handled himself well given the changes coming to Norost.

"Now, Mayor Kellsie, if we might speak with Mistress Eudora?"

"Do you wish privacy?"

"As she is your employee, I would request that you stay." At Aurelias' request, Vesper's eyes turned to Drew. They waited in silence while Brandt left. Shortly the Kennetsurean woman entered in her usual serene manner. Vesper moved to rise, but Aurelias' hand detained her. "Vesper, you will not speak until this matter is cleared up. Do you understand?"

"In all ways but birth, she is my mother. I will greet her so." Vesper stared at her father, and he removed his hand. Vesper went to Eudora with a smile, a kiss, and a hug in greeting. Eudora said nothing but smiled at Vesper and returned her hug, although her eyes looked haunted. When Vesper returned to her seat, Drew took her hand. Aurelias indicated a chair to Eudora.

Before Aristo Aurelias could ask, Eudora spoke. "You wish to know how Vesper came into my keeping."

"I wish to know if you murdered my wife or conspired with others to do so," Aurelias said in a quiet voice underlined by command.

Eudora gazed at him with calm-filled eyes. "I did not murder Lady Lorelei. I thought, Your Grace, much the same of you."

"You thought I murdered my wife? How? I was nowhere near her!" Aurelias' face contorted into a shocked, angry gargoyle form.

"She ran away from you, seemed very frightened. I thought it possible you had hired someone to rid you of a mad wife." Eudora took a deep breath. "The Lady's prophecy has finally come true. She said you would find the girl."

"Eudora," Vesper said, earning a reprimanding look from her father. "Please tell me—tell us—what happened."

Eudora didn't immediately respond to the request. She looked at the Duke of Lambere. "I did not kill Lady Lorelei. It would mean I had also murdered my sister, Lady Lorelei's maid."

"I am aware of the connection. Quillon recognized you. What happened?" Aurelias asked.

Eudora's soft brown eyes turned to Vesper. "I was a midwife in service in Mal Colum in Wessure. Part of Kennetsurean practice is to take service outside our province. It is a part religious, part philosophical, custom. My service was nearly at an end, and I looked forward to going home. Then my sister Sesa brought Lady Lorelei to me. The Lady was ill and in labor. At first, I thought her only traveling, perhaps to join you, as she had a trunk with her. There were no outriders, though, and Sesa needed my help to unload the trunk. Later I thought perhaps she and Sesa together had loaded it into the small cart they traveled in.

"The Lady's flight had brought on early birthing, and through much of it, she talked in rambling, nonsensical speech, neither listening nor reacting to Sesa or me. It was apparent, though, that she was terrified. She spoke of murders and plots. She spoke of you, Your Grace, of danger and having to escape."

"It wasn't from me," Aurelias said, frowning.

"I didn't realize until later, after the birth, that the Lady was a seer. I had never encountered one before, but I had read about them. At one point during her labor, she insisted we move to another location. It was horrible, but she wouldn't relax enough for the birth to proceed. So Sesa and I took her to a small house that I knew empty. She settled down and got on with her business. The boy was born first. Then Vesper. She fed the babies and seemed lucid and happy. Then closed her eyes and said Raymond would find the boy right away, but not the girl. Not for a long time. I assured her that she and the babies were safe. I took Vesper to bathe and dress. She just smiled as she gave her to me and told me to protect her. Then she asked Sesa to help her write a letter. I took Vesper and bathed her." Tears tumbled down the woman's cheeks and Drew had to hold Vesper from jumping up and going to her.

Eudora took a deep breath and wiped her face with the palms of her hands. "I spilled bathwater on the blanket I meant to wrap around Vesper. I took her back to Lorelei, but she was asleep. Sesa held your son." She closed her eyes. "I can still hear her humming to him. He was fussing and Vesper asleep, so Sesa said to put her in the travel bag." Her eyes opened. "There was no other bed. She would bathe the boy while I went to get more blankets. I was gone such a short time! When I got back, I found Sesa lying on the floor. When I lifted her, when... she was dead."

Eudora's hands brushed her cheeks once more. Vesper broke from Drew's grip and went to Eudora. She knelt by the chair and took one of Eudora's hands while wiping Eudora's face with her other. Eudora cupped Vesper's face with her free hand.

Drew looked at Aurelias. His father-in-law sat like granite looking at Eudora.

Clearing her throat, Eudora turned her face from Vesper and looked at Aurelias. "Someone had knifed her in the back. I ran into the other room and saw Lorelei and the baby lay on the bed, both dead. After that, things are a little muddled. I don't know how much time passed, but I heard whimpering.

"Vesper still lay in the travel bag. I wrapped the blankets around her, picked up the bag and left, and went to a friend to ask her to store Lady Lorelei's trunk in my house for me. I left Mal Colin that very night, and left Wessure. I walked for days. The letter addressed to you was in the bag, but I was afraid to send it. By the time I rationalized Lady Lorelei wouldn't write you a letter if afraid of you, I'd already fallen in love with Vesper and couldn't chance any harm coming to her.

"Who else but you would have tracked Lady Lorelei down? It didn't make sense. So I hung onto the letter. As long as I kept the secret, I knew Vesper safe, no one else knew she existed. Whoever killed Lorelei didn't realize she had birthed twins."

"Why did you send it then?" Aurelias asked.

"I didn't. It was in the trunk with all Vesper's belongings, her mother's possessions, and mine, here in my room. One day, while putting things away, I noticed the contents didn't look right. Someone had searched through the trunk. The only thing missing was the letter to you. That was years ago. I apologize for suspecting you of such a terrible crime."

Aurelias sighed. "I give you mine also. I believe your story. I've learned hunters stalked my family. You have saved my one living child. It seems I owe you a debt of gratitude."

Suddenly, Mayor Kellsie rose and opened the door calling for his servant Freda. When she arrived, he told her to fetch her mistress.

"The mistress has taken to her bed, sir. Said she was feeling ill."

"Tell her to dress and come immediately." Suddenly he excused himself and left the room.

While they waited, Drew spoke to Eudora. "I would like to request you to come and make your home with us at Montoren Farm. Become part of Clan Cader."

"That is generous of you, but I don't know... I long to see Kennetsure."

"You must come," Vesper said. "You are my family. You belong."

"Well, you will want to see Vesper's baby, anyway," Aurelias said and laughed at the pleasure in Eudora's eyes. "That's what I plan. That will give you time to decide what you want to do. You are certainly welcome to leave this employment. The Holy One knows your service has certainly earned any reward you choose." Aurelias went to the window and watched the milling crowd. "I wonder if Ottillie's Lady Chloe knew how her last spell worked, if she knew how exalted the Aegis would become. Your heirs will hold your position and mine." He laughed at Drew's look, but at that moment Mayor Kellsie returned with his weeping wife.

Winifred Kellsie looked about the room and sank into a curtsey to Aurelias. "Your Grace."

"There is some confusion about a letter sent to me, Madame Kellsie. Do you know anything about it?"

Winifred's fear-filled eyes went to her husband. "I sent it. I thought my husband having an affair with my housekeeper. I was angry, disgusted at her sanctimonious demeanor while acting a wanton. My husband refused to let her go when I asked, said I imagined things. So I searched her room for proof and came across a letter addressed to you. The only reason for her to have the letter, the only logical one, was to bleed money from you. I thought her daughter your by-blow."

"If you read it, surely you realized the truth," Eudora said shocked.

"I did not break the seal." Winifred's voice showed her contempt. "Then it would have been a worthless thing, possibly tampered with. I did not expect Aristo Aurelias to come so soon. When he arrived, I knew it was to punish you, but then Vesper was Handfasted by a mere clansman. Punishment enough."

"Why did you hold it for so long?" Aurelias asked, shocked.

"I held the letter for years trying to decide what to do. Finally, I sent it knowing it would cause trouble for Eudora, whatever message it contained, and would most likely proclaim Vesper the bastard everyone believed."

Aurelias rose from his seat shouting, "My daughter is no bastard!"

Winifred Kellsie cringed and shrank into her chair.

"Well, you best look for a new housekeeper, for Eudora will travel with us," Drew said. "Eudora, certainly your service here was wasted."

"For new servants," Vesper said. "As part of my family, surely Freda and Marwyn should also come."

"My service was always to the Lady Lorelei and to Vesper. I only stayed so Vesper would know where to find me.

~ * ~

Chloe's story

Chloe closed her journal. This would be her last entry. Shortly, if one believed the priests, the Holy One would take her, and she would see Dustyn again. She supposed she would have to pay for her sins first, but devoutly looked forward to their reunion. For the last three nights she had seen him in visions. Only this afternoon, or was it this morning? He asked her to join him for tea. Dustyn who had never tasted tea. She sighed. Her mind played tricks on her. Her memory worked overtime churning out scenes from her life. Everything seemed so real, like it had happened yesterday.

She had outlived her time; all her friends were dead, except Melissa, who tearfully waited with her for her to take her last journey. She had not expected such devotion. She left everything to her daughter and her friend. It was all written out as she wished.

Everything was taken care of except for her final breath. She wished it over.

Through the years she had learned to live with her failure. She had started in obscurity, contributed little, and would end in anonymity, forgotten by those who had known her, those who weren't already dead.

Magic died with her. Melissa never having gained control of her gift. It was gone now, decayed in disuse. Chloe thought Melissa just as happy about its loss.

Melissa entered the room, smiling at her mentor. When she didn't speak, Chloe noticed her youthfulness, the Aristo clothing. Taking another look, she saw it wasn't Melissa at all, but a pretty girl, dark-haired, like her daughter. They weren't in her bedroom on Charm Island, but somewhere else, a forest. She could smell the pines and inhaled deeply. It brought back memories of Cygna. A horse stood nearby, gray with pale mane and tail and black legs. Chloe smiled, admiring the animal. As it turned his head toward her, Chloe saw for one instant the spiral of a single horn, and in a second glance, it was gone. The girl ran a hand down the horse's long face and smiled. She started to walk away, and Chloe stretched out a hand.

"Wait..."

The girl turned with another smile and reached out to put something in her hand. Chloe looked down. A common, scaly, brown acorn sat in her palm. She looked up, but both the girl and the horse were gone, dissipated in the mist of illusion. She blinked and saw her bedroom walls.

Melissa entered the room with a tray of herbal tea and Chloe's dinner. "Have you had a good day? It is beautiful out. Sunny, but the sky is full of mares' tails." She looked at Chloe and set the useless tray down.

She squeezed her lips together, as eye-stinging tears fell to her cheeks. A hand placed over the staring eyes closed them. The body was already cooling, the flesh ashen.

She noticed the faint smile on Chloe's lips. She picked up the journal from where it had fallen on the floor and held it to her chest. The book fell open to the last page.

A seer comes, the spell...

It was scrawled, unfinished, in Chloe's spidery age-hampered hand. At long last Melissa placed the book down and looked at Chloe. "He should have let you live your life without obligation, but you would never let me tell you that, would you? I promise, Lady, they will know of your great spells. All of them."

Picking up the cold hand, she realized the fingers were curled over the palm. She lovingly straightened the fingers to fold the hands over the stilled chest. Surprise caught her when something dropped from the hand. Looking at the floor, she picked up the object.

An acorn. Where had that come from? She sighed. Probably one of the grandchildren. They were forever bringing Chloe things. She turned back to Chloe. Looking at the faint smile, it must have brought her brief happiness.

She slipped the acorn into her pocket and left to get her daughters to help her, her mind making lists of all needing done. Bliss must be told. Should she dress Chloe in red Kennetsurean dress, her gray Cygnese wedding dress, or in her Kaereyan court robes? Her journals, she supposed, should go to Egan. Yes, the Aegis would keep them safe.

Halfway to the door she stopped and dug the acorn out of her pocket. A gift was a gift, and this was her last. Returning, she placed the acorn back in her friend's palm and curled Chloe's fingers around it. Then she left to find Bliss.

Meet Rhobin Lee Courtright

Born and raised in Michigan, Rhobin spent one year in Colorado and twenty years in Missouri raising her family and working as a business writer. She now lives back in Michigan on twenty acres of forest near the small village of Luther. Always interested in science, history, nature, and art, her overactive imagination led her to speculate on life beyond Earth, and the 'what-ifs' of changes to humanity that soon turned into fantasy and science fiction novels. She writes about writing and her quirks of mind on her blog at www. rhobincourtright.com

Other Works From The Pen Of Rhobin Lee Courtright

Aegis Series:

Magic Aegis - Centuries ago, the witch Chloe cast the Aegises spell, binding four men and their descendants to protect Kaereya. Now, when needed most, magic is lost.

Change - Her mother demanded two things of Tyna...that she never expose her true nature and that she never enter Cygna, the land of witches. Now, her mother is dead, and her sister has abandoned her.

Acceptance - Responsibility and duty drove mercenary Kissre to find her estranged sister in Cygna, the land of witches.

Legend's Cipher - What Bertok had not related when the bishop gave him this mission was his most buried secret—he possessed an unnatural ability.

Black Angel Series:

Rogue's Rules - Traitor, mutineer, deserter—slanderous words fixed to Ensign Jezlynn Chambers' name.

Loser's Game - Jezlynn has plied the pirates' trade but won't let anyone use the signature of the Black Angel to hide their crimes.

Devil's Due - Command ordered Jezlynn into the Space Service Corp, yet it is one thing to think you can accomplish a goal, another to achieve it.

Angels Thread - Just when Jezlynn believes she has overcome her past it returns to haunt her

Home World Series:

Home World Aginfeld - On technically advanced but feudal Aginfeld, Alix Risseu is held for theft...the sentence is death. Only Alix is innocent.

Nanite Warrior - Hearing herself claimed as wife, Xandra gave a weak laugh. "Bad luck just won't end, but this time, I'm sure yours is worse than mine, husband."

Dragoons' Journey - Brigit has moved constantly for years, now a message offers her freedom on Aginfeld, a place her enemy, the Colonial Pact, desperately wants.

Home World Reax - Maera escaped the future planned for her on Reax, so what could make her return? Learning of her home planet's devastation.

The Carolingians:

Constantine's Legacy - Leonard must learn to be the Frankish warrior his father Radulf, the Dux Provinciae, demands. His difficult training is nothing compared to the dangerous deceptions he discovers.

Letter to Our Readers

Enjoy this book?

You can make a difference

As an independent publisher, Wings ePress, Inc. does not have the financial clout of the large New York Publishers. We can't afford large magazine spreads or subway posters to tell people about our quality books.

But, we do have something much more effective and powerful than ads. We have a large base of loyal readers.

Honest Reviews help bring the attention of new readers to our books.

If you enjoyed this book, we would appreciate it if you would spend a few minutes posting a review on the site where you purchased this book or on the Wings ePress, Inc. webpages at: https://wingsepress. com/

Visit Our Website

For The Full Inventory
Of Quality Books:

Wings ePress, Inc.
https://wingsepress.com/

Quality trade paperbacks and downloads
in multiple formats,
in genres ranging from light romantic comedy
to general fiction and horror.
Wings has something for every reader's taste.
Visit the website, then bookmark it.
We add new titles each month!

Wings ePress Inc.
3000 N. Rock Road
Newton, KS 67114